# The Empire
# of Night

# The Empire of Night

*A Christopher Marlowe Cobb Thriller*

# Robert Olen Butler

The Mysterious Press
an imprint of Grove/Atlantic, Inc.
*New York*

*Published simultaneously in Canada*
*Printed in the United States of America*

FIRST EDITION

ISBN 978-0-8021-2323-7
eISBN 978-0-8021-9189-2

The Mysterious Press
an imprint of Grove/Atlantic, Inc.
154 West 14th Street
New York, NY 10011

Distributed by Publishers Group West

www.groveatlantic.com

14 15 16 17    10 9 8 7 6 5 4 3 2 1

For Kelly
who hears every word

# 1

I know a stage-door Johnny when I see one, and I know a tough guy. This was no Johnny. I had my reasons not to look at the facade of the Duke of York's and perhaps that's how I came to notice him down the alleyway on the south side of the theater. The midsummer's late sunlight was almost gone and the play-going crowd was hubbubbing at the front doors, and here was this lurker in the shadows, around the corner, on the way to where only the company of actors was supposed to go. He'd crammed a bouncer's body into a three-piece serge and his trilby hat was pulled down and tipped forward.

I gave off pretty much the same impression, I realized, but I wouldn't want to see somebody like me down this alley either. He was turned sideways and looking in my direction, probably thinking similar thoughts.

There was nothing to do about it. Sniffing around on the sly for my government while still trying to more or less sniff the same way for my newspaper had made me excessively suspicious of my fellow man. I would have been a busy guy indeed if I'd tried to deal with every mug who put me on edge.

The trilby and I stared at each other for a long moment, and then he broke the gaze and slid away down the alley, fading into the shadows. I shrugged him off and figured it was time to go to my seat. Which meant I had to face the wired sign thrusting out over the Duke of York's portico. In my coat pocket was a ticket for the front row of the stalls, so I had to deal with this.

I turned.

The theater event of the decade, for a limited run only, was ringed in electric lights: ISABEL COBB IS HAMLET.

My fifty-six-year-old mother.

When this ticket showed up on a bellhop tray at my hotel without a note, it took me by surprise. As close as I'd been to the theater all my life, I'd been unaware that the theatrical event of the decade was about to happen in London, much less that it involved my mother. I hadn't heard from or about her for fifteen months. A couple of years ago she retired from the legitimate theater, refusing to carry on in a profession that no longer let her pretend she was a twenty-year-old beauty. She was still pretty much a beauty. But she wasn't Juliet anymore. Or even Kate in *Shrew*, which an audience in Memphis finally, infamously, made clear enough to her, summer before last.

There would be no older-woman roles for her, by god. She would rather leave it all behind. But here was a clever way around that problem. She was playing the most famous man in the history of the stage. A young man, even.

Under the portico now, I found myself on the edge of a gaggle of shirtwaisted women, talking low among themselves, a few with a bit of purple, green, and white ribbon pinned near the heart. Suffragettes, their focus shifted by the war. Instead of marching and chaining themselves to railings, they were starting to drive trams and buses and work in factories. Some of these women near me even gave off a whiff of sulfur from a munitions plant, their hands and faces beginning to turn faintly yellow from the chemicals.

As we pressed together through the doors and into the foyer, my mother's name floated ardently out of these voices. Their new exemplar. She was to be a man. To be and not to be, of course. But tonight a man.

I sat on the right end of the first row, very near to her as she came downstage, alone and soliloquizing, wishing that her too too sallied flesh would melt, thaw, and resolve itself into dew. I was trying hard

2

to relinquish myself to the illusion of the stage, trying to forget who, in life, this was before me.

To my surprise, this was not difficult. Isabel Cobb was indeed a man. She was a small and slim Prince Hamlet, her hair cut shoulder length and died dark blond and worn loose and wavy, as a young man of the time might, being hatless in distracted grief, and though my mind knew how tightly my mother was wrapped inside her black doublet and though I recognized her voice, which was always low and a little husky even as a woman, and though I recognized those vast, dark eyes as the maternal origin of my own, she convinced me.

And I wondered: did she convince herself? Perhaps. I heard no tang of irony in her voice as she, being a man, a son, railed against a mother's hasty sexuality. And though this Hamlet before me was believably his own man, he and his qualms reminded me of my mother. Not that I shared the prince's vehemence. But as he rolled the word "frailty" in his mouth like an overripe grape and then named it "woman," stirring the suffragettes in the crowd to a titter, I stopped seeing the play. I lifted my eyes from Hamlet's indictment of his mother and looked up, far up into the fly galleries—uniquely visible to the residents of the front row—and to the catwalk there, its pin rail wrapped with thick hemp ropes. The catwalk was empty and my mind lifted much farther than the flies: I stood outside a room at the Gilsey House in New York. Though it could have been a room in any of a hundred hotels or boarding-houses around the corner from a hundred theaters in a hundred cities on the headliner circuit, where one of the great stars of the American stage and her son lived while she worked. The star was my mother, and she was my father too, my Gertrude and King Hamlet both, though my actual father was no king, was not even a ghost, was an unknown to me, to this very day. But what son needed a father with a mother who could convincingly become anyone?

This flash of memory, me standing in the hushed and carpeted hallway of New York's Gilsey House, could have been any from a multitude of memories of my childhood or adolescence in any of those other hotels, but in the front row of the Duke of York's it was the Gilsey and I'd just turned thirteen and my cheek was still damp from her kiss and she expected me, as always, to understand that she was about to shut the door in my face and send me away—it had been thus for as long as I could remember—I was much younger than this when I'd first been cooingly sent away from her door—and at the Gilsey House her leading man had pitched in, had given me a wink and a nod and a *Good lad*, and her play—what was it? a Clyde Fitch, perhaps—had run a tryout month in Boston where I'd been bid a similar affectionate adieu in the hallway outside a room in the Hotel Touraine with a different leading man, and I liked this Boston guy okay, and I thought he and I would have this understanding for as long as the play ran, which everyone hoped would be at least a year in New York. But the producer canned him before the play left Beantown, and this guy at the Gilsey was a new wink and a new nod. My mother always seemed to have a hasty hankering for her leading men. And I always seemed to be seeing them off together at a hotel door and then turning and walking away. Having quickly learned not to linger, not to listen.

All this ran quickly and hotly and stupidly in me from the front row of the Duke of York's, so it took me a moment to realize what I was looking at. The guy from the alley was on the catwalk. Once I focused on him, I could picture the last few moments. He'd eased out slow to a place at the rail. And now he squared around to look down to the stage where Hamlet was finishing his soliloquy, bidding his heart to break, and this guy had a real intense interest in this Hamlet, who was my mother.

I had a real intense interest in *him*. I concentrated on his face as he watched Hamlet greet Ophelia with feigned madness. I wanted to read his eyes, but they were a little too far away, and I wasn't looking straight into them. But the stillness of him, the casual privilege of his pose, made them seem hard, as insolently hard as his stare from the alleyway. Shakespeare and Isabel Cobb faded into a buzz in my head as I focused on this man and on my instinct that he was up to no good.

And then he turned his attention to me, casually, as if he'd known I was there all long.

We had a second extended face-off.

I was right about his eyes. They seemed dead, these eyes. As dead as a bullet casing.

He returned his gaze to my mother.

I was tempted to slip from my seat—right that moment, with Hamlet tormenting the girl he loved—and go through the stage access door into the wings and find my way up to the flies.

And then do what?

*Cool off now,* I told myself. For weeks I'd been sitting in a London hotel room preparing for the next assignment. Necessarily so. But I'd been idle for too long. This guy reminded me what my body had been trained for and primed for. Which, however, certainly *hadn't* been to cause a public ruckus over some lug because I didn't like his looks or his sneaking around.

I lowered my face. I concentrated on Hamlet advising his girl to be off to a nunnery and then making a flourish of an exit. A few moments later, with Ophelia still boohooing about her boyfriend's madness, I looked up once more into the flies.

He was gone.

I let it go.

At the first intermission, after Hamlet vowed to catch the conscience of the king, I went out of the theater and down to the side alley and smoked a cigarette there, watching the shadows, waiting for a tough guy in a trilby. Nothing doing.

Back in the theater, through to the next curtain, I kept a frequent but fleeting eye on the flies. No sign of him, and now Hamlet was swearing that his thoughts be bloody or be nothing worth. At the beginning of the act I'd have embraced that recommendation. As the curtain came down for the second intermission, I'd finally been able to drift in the other direction. So I went out and smoked another Fatima and kept my back to the suffragette chatter nearby on the sidewalk and thought about how my mother was indeed Hamlet, as it said rimmed in electric light above my head, and she was a good one, neatly balancing the classic introspective inaction with the strength to kill.

Inside the theater once more, she held my undivided attention through to the prince's last words—*the rest is silence*—and in the script there is but a single word of stage direction: *Dies.* For most actors who have taken on Hamlet, the rest is *not* silence. The rattling or sighing or moaning or gasping are considered by the usual tribe of actors to be the sweet dessert to a long night of emoting. I feared for my mother now, in spite of the surprising subtlety of her performance so far, feared for her excesses. And she surprised me once more by dying with simply an exquisite lifting of the face to the spotlight and a closing of the eyes and, thereby, an ineffably rendered release of spirit.

I admired her performance, but I did not like to witness this, in much the same way as I did not like her closing a hotel room door upon me. I felt she had left me forever. And with her death upon my mind—for it was hers as well as Hamlet's that I was thrumming to—I lifted my own face once more, to the flies.

And there he was. He was watching once again at the railing, and as my mother played at death he leaned toward her and his jacket gaped briefly and showed a holstered pistol on his left side. I wished ardently that I was carrying my own.

From the early days of my reporting career I got close to a fair number of criminals. Tough guys, all of them. Tempered-steel tough. But I'd heard a number of them talk about their mothers, think about their mothers, and inevitably these tough guys turned into simpering idiots of a variety of sorts, from weak to reckless.

So it was that even as I wished I had my own pistol with me I was grateful I didn't. I felt trigger-itchy at that moment and it was possible my hand would have drawn my Mauser and would have pushed the safety button and would have waited for the slightest movement of this lug's right hand toward his pistol, with the wrong kind of look on his face, and I would have shot him. Maybe not aiming to kill. Maybe just to disable that right arm.

Without this option, however, I clearly understood that shooting him would have been the wrong thing to do. At least till his pistol was out and coming to bear on her. And then I would have simply killed him.

# 2

As it was, he didn't do anything but watch for the last few moments of the play. Then the curtain fell, and when it rose and the calls began, he was gone for good.

The audience clapped loudly and the rest of the cast came and bowed and lined up on the sides and they joined the applause as my mother appeared. She bounded downstage center and the women in shirtwaists and suffragette ribbons all stood up and cried, "Bravo! Bravo!" and my mother bowed deeply to them as a man and then she straightened and flounced her hair and she curtsied as a woman. The suffragettes cried, "Brava! Brava!"

All the while, the rest of the viewers were applauding loudly, some of them rising to their feet as well. As did I. My mother did not look my way.

A boy brought roses from the wings.

I'd seen bigger ovations for my mother, but the few actresses who'd done Hamlet before had been pilloried in the press and heckled from the cheap seats. I hadn't read her reviews, but I heard not a single rude sound from this audience, and that seemed a triumph to me.

I lingered to let the crowd murmur its way out of the auditorium after Mother had finally stopped taking bows and the house lights had come on. Then I crossed before the front row. But instead of going left, up the aisle to the exit doors, I went to the right, up the steps and through the stage access door and into the wings with its smells

THE EMPIRE OF NIGHT

of greasepaint and sweat and dust burning on the electric stage lights. The actors had all vanished, and squaring around before me was a lanky man in shirt sleeves and bow tie. The stage manager, I assumed.

I was ready to explain myself to him, why I felt privileged to go through an unauthorized door and head straight to the dressing rooms, but he immediately said, "Mr. Cobb."

"Yes," I said.

"Would you like to see your mother?"

"I would."

"This way." He turned on his heel to lead me toward a door at the back wall.

I stepped up quickly to walk beside him.

"There was a man with a gun up on your fly floor," I said. "Are you surprised?"

He stopped. He turned to me.

"A gun?" he said.

"Inside his coat."

"Yes," he said. "I'm surprised."

"Do you know who he might have been?" I asked.

The stage manager hesitated at this. He was thinking in ways that I could not clearly interpret. Then he said, "Not if he was in my flies."

"And if he hadn't gotten that far?"

"Your mother has fans."

This was no fan.

He turned and moved on. "Please follow me," he said.

Something was odd here, but I didn't push the point.

As we passed through the doorway at the back of the stage wings, I said, "How did you know me?"

"Your mother has a picture of you in her dressing room."

This didn't surprise me.

I followed him along a short passageway and we cut back at the next turning and entered an enclosed staircase.

Her dressing room was on the second floor. The door was ajar and emitting female laughter.

The stage manager knocked and the laughter faded.

"Prithee show thyself," my mother called out, using the lowest Hamlet register of her voice.

More female laughter.

The stage manager leaned his head past the edge of the door to look in. "Your son," he said.

I did not hear her reply, if she made one. Perhaps she gestured. The stage manager pulled back at once and opened the door and I stepped in.

She sat with her back to her makeup mirror, still in her costume of trunk hose and doublet, the doublet unbuttoned, however, showing a finely embroidered lace blouse beneath, straight from a Mayfair shop no doubt, her own private joke throughout the night's portrayal of Hamlet, a secret assertion of her modern womanhood. She was flanked by four suffragettes, two on each side, their uniform dark skirts and white shirtwaists making them look like a ladies string quartet about to go off to play in a palm court at a local hotel.

I stopped a single pace into the room, my hat in my hand. My mother rose. Quite formally, even solemnly. Then she took a step forward and opened her arms. "My darling Kit," she said.

I came to her and we hugged and she smelled of greasepaint and mothball camphor and she felt all bones and sinew inside her man's clothes.

"Isn't he handsome, my dears?" she said.

The women simply made little muttering sounds in response, ready for the vote but not for boldly voicing the sort of sentiments my mother was challenging them to have.

I focused on her suffragettes, as my mother resisted my incipient withdrawal from her arms, assessing them as she would have them assess me.

They were varying degrees of young—Mother had brought only the more impressionable acolytes into her closest circle—but three of them did not hold my eye even for a moment. One, though, had a strong-jawed, wide-mouthed sort of farm girl prettiness, the kind of girl you'd enjoy trying, briefly, to pry away from her horse.

Mother was letting go of me now, pushing me back to arm's length but keeping her hands on my shoulders. "Where have you been for the past year?"

Where *she* had been was a more interesting question, but I politely did not ask it in front of the young women for whom she was still performing.

"Ah yes," she said, as if just remembering. "I read your stories lately. What a fine writer you are. I taught him to write by making him read a thousand books in countless star dressing rooms on three continents." The "him" was the only indication she'd suddenly started to talk directly to the other women, as her eyes kept fixed tightly on mine, shining that light of hers on me, making me a willing part of her present performance.

She said, elaborating on her perusal of my stories, "But Constantinople of all places," she said. "All those poor people suffering under the Ottomans. A terrible business. Why would you ever go out there? I thought you were the great chronicler of bullets and cannon shells and men in battle dress, my darling."

I did not have a chance to reply.

"And your ordeal on the high seas," she said, the light changing in her eyes, giving off more heat and less illumination. "Did you get my telegram?"

"No."

"Well, I didn't know where to send it."

*Then you already knew I didn't get it.* But I didn't say this.

"He was on the *Lusitania*," she said.

The suffragettes clucked softly in sympathy.

"Closer to three thousand," I said.

Her eyes narrowed. "Utter non sequitur, my darling," she said.

"The number of books you had me read. I figured it out not long ago."

She brightened.

"In an idle moment," I said. And then, to the others: "She and an ever changing cast of theater people she enlisted taught me everything I knew, before I knew to teach myself." As she had done, I did not look directly at the suffragettes, letting the pronoun suggest I was addressing them.

Mother let go of my shoulders.

She introduced me to the young women, and I smiled at them and shook their hands, their grips still limply disenfranchised, but I did not endeavor to remember any of the names. Even, though it went against my natural inclinations, the name of the pretty one. Immediately after the introductions, my mother ushered them all out of the dressing room, everyone fluttering ardent good-byes and comradely good wishes every step of the way.

Mother closed the door and leaned back against it. "Was I splendid tonight?" she asked.

The question was not rhetorical, though I knew she knew the answer. "You were," I said.

"Yes I was," she said.

"Does all of London realize it?" I asked.

"Much of London."

Some of the critics surely sneered at any woman playing the role. But she seemed content, so I did not ask.

"Poor Bernhardt," she said.

Sarah Bernhardt played Hamlet in London in '99 to vicious reviews. Mother was inviting the comparison. "You did better?" I asked.

"Yes," she said. "But I was referring to her leg. They cut it off only a few weeks ago and she gave it to a university."

From Isabel Cobb's Hamlet in London to Sarah Bernhardt's losing a leg, service to my government had put me behind in my reading.

"Gangrene," my mother said.

"So you're doing better than the Divine Sarah in legs as well," I said.

Mother lifted her face to the ceiling in a loud bark of a laugh. But when her face came back down, she grabbed a chaw of my cheek between her thumb and forefinger and gave it a squeeze and shake to match the laugh. "I feel bad for her," she said.

I have a pretty high threshold of pain, but like those Chicago thugs going soft about their mothers, I felt the same at thirty-one years old about Isabel Cobb's uninhibited mother-cheek-pinch as I did at ten: it hurt like hell.

She finally let go, and she sat down in the chair where she'd been presiding over her suffragettes. I sat in the chair at the idle makeup station next to her. Edged into the frame of her mirror was my formal portrait in a cabinet card, a thing she'd insisted I do for her six years ago upon hearing that the *Post-Express* was sending me off to Nicaragua on my first war assignment.

She caught me looking at it.

"I carry you with me everywhere," she said.

I turned to her.

In spite of her being made up as a man—a melancholy man, no less—and being an age that tormented her always for what she no longer was, my mother was still beautiful, her face, in impact, all dark eyes and wide mouth, both restlessly shaping and reshaping in attentiveness to whoever was before her.

It had long pleased me to be able to make her eyes and mouth abruptly freeze. Like now. "Can you think why a tough guy with a gun would be stalking you?" I said.

But I had her for only the briefest of moments. Then, with a tilt of the head, her eyes veiled themselves like a cat showing its trust, and her mouth made a dismissive moue. "Not at all," she said.

She sounded sincere. But she was arguably the greatest living actress of the American stage. She could sound however she liked. What I needed to figure out: had the oddness of the question itself been enough to make her pause for that brief moment or had it revealed she was now lying?

I had good reason to suspect the latter.

Last year she got involved in some undercover detective work in New Orleans while she was trying to make an escape from the theater.

"Are you still in bed with Pinkerton?" I said.

"What do you take me for?" she said. "Old man Pinkerton's been dead for thirty years."

She winked.

"Okay, Mother," I said. "I usually let you get away with ending a serious conversational topic with an ambiguous theatrical gesture. Not this time. Does the wink mean you're not sleeping with a dead man but if he were alive it would be a different matter, or does it mean you're not sleeping with a dead man but you may still be working for his detective agency?"

This stopped her face once again.

She squared around to me, leaned forward, straightened her back, and pressed her hands onto her knees. A manly gesture. A man with more backbone than Hamlet. But I recognized it from a lifetime with this woman as a no-nonsense Isabel Cobb gesture. She said, "Listen to me, my darling. Consider my ego. Did you think I would be happy to play that role for long? Going after two-bit hoodlums for a corporation of private dicks?"

I kept my own face still. I wasn't going to let her get away with the ambiguity of a rhetorical question.

She knew. She smiled a that's-my-boy smile. "It was beneath me," she said. "I am not now nor will I ever again work for the Pinkertons or any other detective agency."

She held my eyes steadily with hers.

Okay.

"Okay," I said.

She didn't move.

"That leaves the man with the pistol in his coat," I said. "He was in the flies above you."

She didn't flinch. Her face was placid, but she said, "That's unsettling."

How to read my mother? That had been a daily challenge for much of my life. It probably made me the hell of a good newspaper reporter that I was. Right now I believed what she was saying about the detective work; her reasoning acknowledged who she was behind the mask. This quiet in her also felt real. I supposed. But she was perfectly capable of playing, from her actor's book of tricks, *Placid and Calm*. Playing the untrue thing was her life. If the calm were true, wouldn't she be squeezing every flinch and flutter from a fictitious endangerment?

She said, "Maybe the theater put on some security. A woman playing a man provokes a lot of people on both sides."

"Your stage manager said he didn't know who he was."

She nodded faintly. Then she shrugged. "We do only a matinee tomorrow and the run ends Thursday night."

There wasn't much left to say about this. It worried me. But this was my mother I was dealing with.

I let her change the subject. "Do you tour on from here?" I asked.

"Yes."

A few moments of silence clock-ticked away as we looked at each other, as if casually.

"As Hamlet?"

"Yes," she said. "And you? Will you be waiting in London for the German bullets and cannon shells to arrive?"

Another beat of silence and then she smiled. And she winked. She was reminding me that we'd long ago tacitly agreed not to question how we led our lives.

"I'll be touring on," I said.

# 3

I asked nothing more of her. Nor she of me. By the very early hours of the next morning, however, as I lay sleepless in bed in my rooms at the Tavistock Hotel across from Covent Garden Market, I'd become less and less convinced by her performance. Not her Hamlet. That remained swell. In temperament she'd always been something of a man—a tough guy, in fact—trapped in a leading lady body. Indeed, last night she'd played the catching of the murderous uncle at his prayers so fiercely and had so clearly kept that edge in all her character's later delays that she'd utterly transformed Hamlet's Wilsonian vacillation into the overriding desire to kill his uncle only when it was most likely to send him, unrepentant, to Hell. That was Mama. She knew how to draw on her toughness, play it as if that were all there was. Which was why it took me till three in the morning to begin to doubt her nonchalance about the man in the flies with the gun. Something more was going on.

But it wasn't my affair. I was still a war correspondent. There was that. But I was also working for my country's secret service now. Primarily now. She wasn't the reason I was awake. I'd always figured she could take care of herself. And I was my tough-guy mother's son. Which wasn't to say certain things in my new profession didn't get to me. It meant I played the essentials of my character convincingly and I did what I needed to do.

I just might not sleep for long stretches in the night.

I fidgeted mightily around on the bed. I paced about the room, smoking Fatimas. A room I'd occupied for going on ten weeks now. My own issues were about the thirteen months prior to that.

But I was tough guy enough to keep any extended replays of those scenes out of my head. From the battlefields I'd covered I'd learned the attitude I had to hold on to: the man you watched die yesterday doesn't exist today; he fell to yesterday's bullets and you've got today's bullets to deal with. Nevertheless, sometimes it got me to brooding. Only it was in indirect ways.

Like noticing a little girl, maybe nine years old or so, from a working family, passing in James Street with a sad face.

Or a newspaper headline about a film actress—a star—formerly thought rescued but now assumed lost on the *Lusitania*.

Or the arcaded portico along the front of the Tavistock, which felt, in spite of obvious differences, very much like the *portales* of a certain hotel in Vera Cruz.

And making all this worse was the Corona portable on my desk, which I'd paced past a hundred times already tonight and kept my eyes from seeing. This time, however, I stopped. The electric bulb above the desk, wired into the gas-jet fixtures of this sixty-year-old hotel, pissed its yellow light onto a blank sheet of paper in the roller. One more story to write under a phony name.

No. I couldn't think of it as phony. That was the point.

I was Joseph W. Hunter speaking through my Corona now. Joseph William Hunter. Formerly Josef Wilhelm Jäger, which I was keeping quiet about. From Chicago he was publishing widely in the German-language newspapers and the German-American English-language newspapers in the U.S.A. He was a damn good writer, sentence to sentence at least, though he clearly had an agenda. He was a justifier and apologist for the home country.

No. Not *he. I.* I was this guy Hunter. Becoming him, at least. I was still in love with *mein Vaterland* and anxious that my fellow Americans understood why. I was writing about the war as if America was smart to remain out of the fray. As if we were getting the wrong dope about Germany and its goals and its intentions. We had far more in common with the Germans than we did with the Brits.

It turned my stomach but it had to be done. It was quite likely, given recent events, that Christopher Cobb was known to the German Foreign Office as a dangerous man. Journalism was what I knew best as a cover identity and Germany was still courting sympathetic American journalists. Joe Hunter would be useful.

He was in the works even before my mix-up with the Huns this past spring. I'd been creating him ever since I came out of my secret service training in February speaking damn good German, the language training aided by a lifetime of intense and varied private education in the back stages and dressing rooms of the thousand theaters of my childhood and by my mother's gene for mimicry.

I'd lit the electric light with the reasonable intent of making good use of my sleeplessness. I had a story to cook up about a movement among Chicago school administrators who advocated more classes in German in anticipation of a new order in Europe. But I reconsidered. I was Cobb alone tonight. Only Cobb. I reached up and turned the key and extinguished the light.

I moved to the window and opened the heavy blackout drape. It was the newest thing in the room. Since January London faced the nightly possibility of a Zeppelin attack. Since May the attacks had come to city center and were increasing in number and bomb load. The Brits still hadn't figured out how to defend themselves. The airships could climb faster and higher than the Sopwiths and Bleriots of the Royal Flying Corps, and the best the anti-aircraft ground defenses had were Hotchkiss six-pounders whose range was less than half the Zepps' attack altitude. The city was defenseless.

My rooms were at the back of the hotel on the upper floor, the fourth. I looked along the parapets and chimneys of the rooftops stretching north on James Street, all of it barely visible, blacked out, as was the whole city in the overcast night.

And as I watched, the darkness to the west cracked open from ground to clouds with a white searchlight and then with another, the two beams stiffly scanning the ceiling of clouds. I took in a quick breath. These Zeppelins were as vast as ocean liners, piston droning a mile overhead, slowing down almost to a float to aim their bombs, giving off a strange kind of elegance in their dangerousness. They were unlike anything you knew, no matter how much tough stuff you'd seen. They could set off a quick reflex of fear you didn't quite know how to suppress.

I watched the two restless pillars of light searching, searching, and then one abruptly vanished and, moments later, the other. The darkness resumed unmitigated. It had been a false alarm.

In this part of the city the dark was not silent. Though I was high up and facing away to the north, I could hear the muffled bustling at the Covent Garden Market across from the front of the hotel. The market carts and wagons were rumbling in and unloading cabbages and cauliflowers, turnips and tomatoes, broad beans and brussels sprouts to await the greengrocers of London before dawn.

I closed the drape.

I'd been here too long.

I knew too much about this neighborhood.

I was too much like a Londoner, waiting for bombs from the night sky with nothing to do in response but keep the lights off and duck.

I went to the armoire and opened the doors and I felt my way into the bottom of my Gladstone bag. I put my hand to the Luger there, which I'd acquired on a difficult night in Istanbul. I drew it out.

I faced into the darkness of the room and held the pistol as if to fire, holding the grip with the crotch of my thumb pressed into the curve beneath the hammer, the trigger snug in the tip-joint of my forefinger, my hand part of the Luger now, an exact prolongation of its axis. Calming.

And unsettling. I'd been calmed through the other wars by typewriter keys. What had I come to? But this reservation was of the mind. My body, my beating heart were calmed by holding this pistol.

I let the thought go.

I put the Luger back into the bag and I moved to the bed and lay down and slept.

And a knock at the door awoke me. I did not know what time it was. I didn't even know if the sun had risen, the blackout lingering in the be-draped room.

I rose. I moved to the door. There was no peephole in this aging hotel. I turned my ear to the place where a peephole should be.

"Yes?" I said.

"Mr. Cobb?"

I recognized the voice. A bellhop as old as the Tavistock.

I slid the chain lock off its metal groove and opened the door.

"Good morning, Mr. Cobb."

"Good morning, George," I said.

George lifted a long, paper-wrapped parcel with the hook of a clothes hanger protruding from the top. "From a gentleman," he said.

With the door closed and with the blackout drape opened to reveal the light of an advanced morning and with the parcel laid flat on the bed, I tore away the paper and found a tuxedo.

The note pinned to the paper gave an address in Knightsbridge and the present date and a time. No name.

I took in a quick breath, aware how similar the reflex seemed to the anticipation of the Zepps a few hours ago. But with a different feeling altogether. The last time that I'd been sent off on a serious assignment, it began with a tuxedo. My waiting, I figured, was over.

# 4

That night, after the late-coming summer dark, gussied up and still fiddling with my white bow tie in the back of one of the ubiquitous French-made London taxis, I thought about a guy named James Metcalf, my contact from the embassy in May who dispatched me a tux and took me to dinner at the Carlton Hotel to give me a train ticket to Turkey and a license to kill. I expected him to be waiting for me in Knightsbridge.

The taxi drove to the end of Basil Street, just south of Hyde Park, where Basil Mansions stretched a full block long, a continuous row of posh, red-brick, Queen Anne revival mansion flats with half-octagonal, Portland-stone bay windows. The mansions flatironed at the angled intersection of Pavilion Road, and the northernmost door I'd been brought to led into a massive wedge of a very fancy multistoried flat, four floors from basement on up, joined by a circular staircase.

A manservant in tails answered the door and he bowed to me and he said, with lugubrious upper-class overprecision, "Good evening, sir. May I announce you?" Which was just his way of saying, *Who the hell are you?*

I gave him my name. The Cobb one.

"Of course, Mr. Cobb," he said. He had the acceptable list in his head.

"This way, sir," he said, and he led me across the marble foyer and up one circular flight to the second floor, the central feature of which was a large, oak-paneled drawing room. The furniture was all done in the heavy, dark Jacobean style. Oak wainscot chairs mostly hugged the walls; overstuffed, out-of-period wingbacks and a matching couch sat before a walk-in fireplace; and a couple of major, fat-legged trestle tables lined up in the center of the room, one with a side of beef and a guy in chef's whites, the other with drinks and a bartender. But among all this was plenty of stand-around room.

There were a dozen of us, or a few more. All men, all done up in evening wear, arranged in little broods of two or three just out of earshot of each other. I smelled government.

The butler stopped and so did I, just behind his right shoulder. "Lord Buffington will be here momentarily, sir," he said.

Indeed, from near the beef, a large, fleshy man who seemed no less large and fleshy for his perfectly bespoke evening clothes, a man who once might well have been the primary bully among Charterhouse upperclassmen, broke away from his group and moved toward me.

"Mister Christopher Cobb, your lordship," the manservant said, stepping out of the way.

"Cobb," the man said, presenting a large hand and a firm grip that I was lucky to get good enough hold on to return effectively. "I'm Gabriel Buffington."

"Lord Buffington."

He'd given me his casual name, but he nodded to acknowledge that I'd done the right thing in returning his title to him.

And now a man emerged from behind Gabe Buffington. A man I recognized. But it wasn't James Metcalf. It was my other James, the guy who came to Chicago and persuaded my publisher to let him hire me away for the government while remaining ostensibly at work for the *Post-Express*. James Polk Trask. Woodrow Wilson's right-hand secret service man.

Trask appeared around Buffington like a half-back running the ball behind Gabe the Grappler's block.

I sidestepped to take him on. "Trask," I said.

"Cobb," he said.

We shook hands.

"Lord Buffington is our host," Trask said at once, turning his face around to look at the Brit.

Buffington nodded two little smiles, one for each of us.

"Thanks," I said.

Buffington said, "The windows are secured, the food and the drink are plentiful, we have a splendid space belowground. Let the wretched Huns do their worst." Having made this declaration, the lord nodded once more, firmly, for both of us, and he moved off.

Trask watched Buffington. "He's one of the good ones." He turned those blackout-dark, empty-seeming eyes back to me. He waited, as if it was obvious that I was supposed to say something. Since he'd come to recruit me, I'd seen those eyes in other people in his business. *Our* business. I figured he expected me to acquire the knack of putting on these show-nothing eyes, just as I'd acquired the knack for planting an enemy in the ground. A couple of moments of silence had already passed between us since he'd declared Buffington a good one.

I said, "As in 'one of the *few* good ones' or 'stay close to the good ones because the bad ones are very bad.' "

Trask smiled. Very faintly. "Both," he said. "You want a drink?"

"Sure."

"I've taught the Brits to make a Gin Rickey, at least here in Buffington's joint."

It was the only drink invented by a Washington lobbyist. "That may be a violation of our neutrality," I said.

"Too bad," Trask said, and he led me to the drink table and another of Buffington's servants in tails. This one, however, was armed with cocktail shaker, ice shaver, lemon squeezer, long-handled spoons and toddy sticks, a jigger, and a couple of fine, small knives. He used one of the latter to cut us a lime, the halves of which ended up in our two glasses of Beefeater.

Trask took us off to a corner of the room and we sat on a couple of high-backed, carved walnut chairs facing, at right angles, into the room. We were able to watch for anyone approaching, no doubt Trask's intent. We would speak low.

"What's this get-together all about?" I asked.

Trask gave a tiny snort through a whistley sinus. I looked toward him at this commonplace noise he'd made. It didn't go with his eyes. It didn't go with him, this peep of human frailty.

He said, "This is a high-class version of a thing you're starting to find all over London. A blackout club."

"The Zepps," I said.

He nodded. "All you need is a basement and some nervous friends."

"Are these guys nervous?"

"From the air attacks, a few. But mostly from their long neglect of homeland defense and the task of correcting that. They'd all gotten complacent about their island fortress. Their vaunted navy can't do anything about airships. Churchill warned them before he got canned. He foresaw a major air war. I suspect he'll turn out to be correct. Unfortunately, Winnie didn't know crumpets about sea war and land war."

Trask was referring to Gallipoli. Churchill had authored the disaster in the Dardanelles, which wasn't over yet. "I got pretty close to all that," I said.

"Right," Trask said. "Which reminds me. Good work in Istanbul."

I grunted.

Yesterday's bullets.

"That compliment wasn't as incidental as it sounded," Trask said, as if he were a sensitive guy, not wanting to offend. His eyes hadn't moved from me, hadn't flickered through any of this. Not even when he added, "Not incidental at all."

I practiced on my own dead stare.

Trask said, "Sorry to reward you by hitching you to a post in London for so long."

I didn't even grunt at this.

Trask knew how to justify it. He said, "Your Mr. Hunter has been getting some nice response in various places."

"Good for him."

"Now we're trying to do our British friends—the good ones—a special favor."

This declaration was the kind of rhetorical setup Trask liked to execute before taking a sip or a drag of whatever was in his hand. A Rickey in Washington when he sent me off on the *Lusitania*, a Fatima when he asked to enlist me in his covert tribe. And yes, a Rickey again now. I sipped too, waiting.

"They've got a traitor inside somewhere," he said.

"Inside the government?"

"They think so, given what they suspect is getting through to Berlin."

"Will I be involved with this?"

Trask shrugged. He looked off into the room. "We have someone on it at the moment. Looking into a suspect."

He said no more.

I took a pretty good hit on the gin and lime. Old Joe Rickey and his Washington bartender friend had a real inspiration, simple though it was.

"We're still feeling our way along," Trask finally added. "It might be a good time to introduce Mr. Hunter."

"Here?"

"I have a slightly different crowd in mind." He leaned toward me, lowered his voice even further. "Do you know how many of the most powerful men in this country have German blood in their veins? It goes back two hundred years. George the first, King of Great Britain and Ireland, previously Georg Ludwig, Duke of Brunswick-Lüneburg, the only eligible heir of the dead Queen Anne. He didn't even speak English. This was Queen Victoria's great-great-grandfather, mind you, progenitor of three British kings before her. And who did Victoria up and marry? Another Hun, Albert, of Saxe-Coburg and Gotha, who thus named the present royal house. For Christ's sake, the Kaiser himself is Victoria's grandson. There's been a powerful lot of German-blooded begatting over those two hundred years, which has now produced, beneath the Brits' virulently anti-German surface, a small but strategic shit pot of conflicting interests at a very high level."

"Your suspect is one of the begotten?" I said.

Trask nodded. He glanced into the room and back to me. He bent near. "A baronet by the discreetly adjusted surname of Stockman. Given-named after Victoria's German prince. Sir Albert Stockman. He's the great-nephew of Christian Friedrich Stockmar, a German-born physician who became the personal doctor for Prince Leopold of . . . where else? . . . Saxe-Coburg and Gotha. Great-Uncle Chris was sent by Leopold to a marriageable Victoria to vouch for his own nephew Albert. Stockmar vouched well, and after the marriage he stayed on as the young couple's personal adviser. So Victoria took good care of this guy's extended family, including the baronetcy of our Sir Al."

"Why don't the Brits just grab him and interrogate him?"

"It's all suspicion at this point," he said. "And the operative phrase was 'very high level.' Sir Albert was beloved-by-blood by the Great Queen herself, which counts in this country. And though a baronetcy doesn't quite rank the House of Lords, he got himself elected as a member of Parliament. Which, if he's dirty, tells you something about his guile."

From outside, very near, a whistle sounded, shriller, simpler than the bobbies' whistles. An air raid constable. This the Brits were well prepared for. Guys in uniforms with whistles. The conversations instantly stopped in the drawing room. All the faces turned in the direction of the sound—the southern wall and the street beyond.

I looked at Trask. He looked at me. "Here come their cousins in a balloon," I said.

Trask snorted.

I snorted.

But we both rose and moved with all the other white ties and dinner jackets into the circular staircase, going along in a quite orderly fashion, quite calmly, even as the sound of the Hotchkiss six-pounders began to pop pathetically in the distance.

We descended to the ground floor and then we circled on down, into the basement, and we emerged into a large, open space. At one end sat wine in barrels and more wine in bottles in racks, and on half a dozen of the barrels, candles burned in silver candelabra. Against the far wall were more racks, of a different sort, layered with Buffington's guns. In the center of the open space a billiard table was disappearing even now under a white cloth cast over its surface by still another liveried man.

Beyond the vanishing billiard green were three, round dining tables already draped in white and each set with half a dozen dinner places and lit, as well, by candles. Beyond them was an opening to a corridor in deep shadow, leading into the recesses of the basement floor. On one side of the doorway was a piano with a lit stand-up lamp. On the other side was a wall of books, two-shilling editions, books for a man to actually read. For that purpose he had a couple of overstuffed Morris chairs with another stand-up lamp between them, this one dark. The basement—at least on this side of that corridor—was Buffington's guy's retreat.

We all now vaguely drifted in the direction of the set tables until Buffington's voice boomed from behind us. "Gentlemen, the food and the drink will soon follow, and there will be more of both. But first a word."

We stopped drifting. We began to turn toward our host.

He was drawn up to full height, hands behind him, framed against the final swoop of the staircase. He watched us turning to him. He approved. He waited. He encouraged us as we gathered our attention to him by addressing us once more. "Gentlemen." Firmly he said it, though the tone of his voice had mellowed up as well, become comradely, almost affectionate.

When at last he had the full and silent attention of every man before him, he said, one more time, "Gentlemen." This time he rolled the word out as if he were asking us to consider its full meaning. Which no doubt he was, for he went on, "They come now, showing their true and savage selves. They come in the night, sneaking in, dangling beneath gas bags to throw bombs on our homes and schools, on our women and our children. And a few months ago they unleashed poison gas upon our troops at Ypres, violating what civilized men from time immemorial have understood to be fields of honor. This is no longer a war of nation against nation. It is a war of civilization against a new barbarism. We fight to preserve the entire world from a second dark age."

As if, offstage, the sound effects man heard his cue, a bomb thumped distantly and shuddered faintly beneath our feet.

Buffington paused only for a single beat as if to let his point sink in. Before me and to the side I could see most of the men in the room, and I knew I could assume the same of the others: not one of us had flinched. And here in this London home, the bomb's fading vibration in our feet and legs and chest supported Buffington's point.

He said, "Gentlemen, if we fail, this dark age will be longer than the last. Those previous five centuries will seem the winking of an eye compared to this. And the new dark age will be infinitely more terrible. Mankind's vaunted advances of manufacturing and technology can be used for good, but they can just as readily and effectively be used for evil."

One more drub of a bomb, much closer, rattled our knees and stirred the silverware on the tables.

Buffington boomed in response, "Consider *that* the call to roast beef and Yorkshire pudding."

We all certainly were happy to take that attitude, but no one moved. Not even Buffington. We waited for the next one. This moment and the next. The Germans were still working on aerial warfare. So far the raids were widely spaced and had come with one or two airships following a single, ongoing path across the city and flying away. This bomb was very near and from the direction of the earlier, distant blasts; the next would either be farther away along the flight path or it would be right on top of us.

We waited.

"Shall we sit?" Buffington's voice had diminished a little. This was a question now, not a defiant suggestion.

And there was a stroke of sound. More distant. Barely felt in Buffington's cellar.

"Bloody hell," someone said nearby, very low, to himself.

We heard no more until we were sitting with four others at the far table. Trask and I were beside each other and I could look, if I wished, between two steel-gray, slick-maned Brits across from me and down the darkened corridor leading to the rest of the basement floor. We heard one more bomb before the food, like a distant stroke of thunder, someone else's storm.

And then we ate. Our companions introduced themselves but did not declare their work, nor did they ask ours, which made me suspect they were Foreign Office types, secret service no doubt, at least some of them. Their talk was casual but it was bluntly critical about Britain's progress so far in the war. About the disastrous four-week gap between the sea attack and the land attack in Gallipoli, about the severe shortage of artillery shells, about the hasty training of a million new troops, about the U-boat threat and the Zeppelin threat and the sudden vulnerability of sacred British soil after centuries of comfortable insularity.

Trask and I said little.

When the four began to lean toward each other and debate the need to dissolve the government and form a new one, I leaned too, toward Trask, and said, low, "Are all these guys in your line of work?"

Trask nodded. "In varying degrees."

The four men stopped talking abruptly.

I thought at first that they'd overheard us, trained as they perhaps were. But their faces had turned not to us but to a point higher up and beyond Trask's far shoulder.

I looked, and Buffington had arrived and he put his hand on the shoulder of a stout man with a crooked cravat sitting next to Trask. The man needed no word. He nodded and rose and moved off and Buffington sat down.

He said to the other three, "Sorry, gentlemen. Continue."

And they did, with one of them saying Kitchener—who was the secretary of state for war and who all three agreed was responsible for the shortage of artillery shells—had to resign no matter what they did with Asquith.

Buffington drew Trask toward him. I leaned along as well and neither of them made the slightest gesture to suggest I was not invited.

Buffington said, "Stockman's throwing a weekend house party."

"Your man?" Trask said.

Buffington said, "In the vicinity."

Trask nodded. And then he made the tiniest intentional movement of his head, so tiny that I instantly doubted my perception, figured I was an example of how you can overtrain a secret service agent. The movement, I thought, was this very slight turn in my direction—since I'd drawn near, behind Trask's right shoulder—as if it was a subtle gesture to Buffington, reminding him of my presence. "Is she ready?" he said.

What did all that have to do with me?

I sat back in my chair.

My eyes moved across the table and between the two steel-gray heads, who had sat back as well, now that they'd agreed to throw out Asquith and Kitchener and all the rest of them.

I looked into the darkness of the corridor.

And the darkness moved.

That was the first impression, lasting only a brief moment. The darkness shifted, swelled, and then points of light began to clarify into a face, hands, and a piano started playing the instrumental introduction to a song—and I recognized it, the intro to "Keep the Home Fires Burning"—and the face emerging from the shadows of the corridor, heading this way, became clear, and now I recognized it as well, even as I had a sense of movement to my left, Buffington no doubt standing up to address us all. He said, "Gentlemen, in the interests of preserving civilization as we wait out this latest barbarous attack, I give you the great Isabel Cobb."

My mother emerged fully into the room, dressed in black, and she stopped, framed in the doorway, as the men at our table wrenched around, turned their chairs, applauded, and cried out "Hear! Hear!"

The introduction was over and Mother shot the piano player a brief glance as he fumbled a bit with the transition to the verse. I glanced with her, and it was the stout man Buffington had replaced at the table. This was a select and secretive group; Isabel Cobb's accompanist was drawn from one of our own number. He wasn't terrible at this, however, and he found his way into the verse and Mother looked back to us and began to sing.

I heard her voice, but for a few moments, as far as I knew, she could have been singing a soliloquy from *Hamlet*, as I grappled with my surprise at her presence here. And then she was inserting that phony ache into her voice that she was so good at. Phony mostly to my ear, of course; fans loved it. But, indeed, she drew even me in with it now as she sang:

"Let no tears add to their hardships
As the soldiers pass along,
And although your heart is breaking,
Make it sing this cheery song."

The secret service pianist did all right with the transition to the chorus and Mama floated on in, more achy than ever. "Keep the home fires burning, while your hearts are yearning," she sang and she began to work the room, gliding along the tables, singing to each stiff upper lip individually—"Though your lads are far away, they dream of home"—and bringing a tear to each eye and a stirring to each stirrable part—"There's a silver lining, through the dark clouds shining"—and she gave me a little less eye contact than the others and a pat on the shoulder as she slid by. "Turn the dark cloud inside out, till the boys come home."

I watched her as she moved on to Trask.

He lifted his face to her, and a son knows certain things for reasons he can't put his finger on easily. Or the reasons seem minute and insubstantial. But Trask's eyes and my mother's held on each other for one pulse beat, one intake of breath, and I knew there was something between them. This particular son knowing certain things about this particular mother made me think in my usual, weary little way: *lovers*.

Then he nodded, once, very faintly, with those blank eyes of his, and I felt my intuition shift. She was not sleeping with him. She was working for him. *Is she ready?* he'd said. Ready for Sir Albert Stockman's weekend party.

She moved along, singing, "Overseas there came a pleading, help a nation in distress," and Buffington extended his hand and she took it and she sang to him and I had the same first, fleeting hunch about him. She was working for Trask, but she was sleeping with Buffington. And then I felt like the punk kid I once was, standing outside a closed door in a theatrical boarding-house trying to will his mother to live her life in some other way. What way, I couldn't imagine, just some other way.

But in fact I was thirty-one years old and she was fifty-six and we had long ago disentangled ourselves from our shared life. And rightly so. We wrote letters. An occasional telegram. But all of that was strictly private. As public as I had subsequently become and as she had always been, it was not really known—outside of a few of my journalist pals and the close-knit tribe of American theater people—that we were mother and son.

She let go of her host's hand and I let go of the hunch and she moved off to the next table to urge everyone to keep the home fires burning while their hearts were yearning.

I thought of her lying to me in her dressing room. No. She hadn't lied. It was no doubt true that she was not now working nor would she ever work again for a detective agency. But she didn't say anything at all about working for the U.S. secret service. She'd convinced me about the Pinkertons by invoking her ego. Her ego would be thoroughly satisfied playing the role of spy for her country. Just the thing for a great actress who was furious with the theater for not overlooking her advancing age. As a spy she could still be a glamorous leading lady. And her performance had a special edge: her life could depend on it being convincing.

I turned around in my chair, shut out her voice, poked at a roasted potato.

My mother segued from the home fires into an upbeat "Pack Up Your Troubles in Your Old Kit Bag," and then she finished with an even more achy "There's a Long, Long Trail."

The music stopped, the gentlemen cheered, she left, and a rhubarb crumble arrived. In the midst of all this, Buffington rose and followed her up the circular stairway and Trask turned to me as the ramekins landed before us.

"Your mother is working for us," he said.

"I surmised," I said.

And though I felt the irony, given my recent bout of musty hunches, I asked the obvious question. "Is she going after Sir Albert?"

"Yes," Trask said.

And then he added, "So are you."

# 5

The next night Isabel Cobb ended her run in London as Hamlet, Prince of Denmark. She'd swept out of her basement cabaret on the night of the most recent Zeppelin attack on London and it wasn't until Friday morning that I saw her again, when she stepped into a first-class compartment at Victoria Station for the train to Broadstairs in Kent and she sat down across from the American journalist and German apologist Joseph W. Hunter.

Trask had booked the compartment so that she and I would be alone. But she entered playing a stranger, nodding at me and then ignoring me as she settled in, arranging her handbag next to her just so, its corners squared to the edge of the upholstered bench seat. I watched this with a vaguely squirmy sense of recognition. I always did that very thing with the pages of a story as they came out of my typewriter.

She finished with her bag and then smoothed her overskirt, though it hardly needed smoothing. It was a stage gesture. She looked quite summery in a blueberry bolero jacket and straw boater with a matching ribbon and pleated bow.

She turned her face to me now, even as I was thinking how she looked pretty good, and she tightened her forehead as if I were a young man on the mash.

I refused to play along. "We have the compartment to ourselves, Mother," I said, in a tone of *We both know this, so what are all the theatrics for?*

She flared her hands in front of her. "Can't we have a little fun, my darling? Improvisation? How long has it been since we rode a train together? We used to have so much fun."

I shrugged and looked out of the window beside me. A conductor strode past blowing his all-aboard whistle.

"You were always a clever boy," she said. "A talented boy."

We rode enough trains together between theater towns to circle the earth and circle it again. For as long as I could think back, we would play roles together to pass the time. Over the years, I was everyone from a beggar boy running away from an orphanage to a dry goods commercial traveler who was Isabel Cobb's biggest fan and overwhelmed to meet her. She once had hopes I'd follow her into the theater.

The train was moving now, and I turned back to Mother. She was watching out the window. Her face was blank. I knew the look. I'd seen it often, in stage wings just before she would make her first entrance. This blankness was all she would show of the actor's inevitable terror of reinventing herself before a thousand strangers watching from the dark.

This time her audience would be smaller and she would walk among them and things were at stake far beyond entertaining a theater crowd.

I knew to let her be. The outward blankness would last until her entrance cue, and then she would come suddenly alive as if she'd flipped an electric light switch. I glanced at her only briefly and stealthily, but her preparatory state went on and on, through our run across the Thames and through Clapham and Herne Hill, with their old estates turning into middle-class commuter houses, and through our plunge into the dark of the long tunnel beneath the Crystal Palace. Here, the electric lights in the compartment flickered us into total darkness. We clattered through the blackness for a long moment, and when the lights flared back on again, I looked frankly at her and she had closed her eyes.

I believed her fear.

I wanted to reach out and take her hand.

But I knew better.

What would she take as her entrance cue on this day?

The lights blinked off once more and then almost instantly back on and her eyes were open, as if they had been all along and what I'd seen was wrong.

But she was still preparing.

Only when we were above ground and finished with London and into the county of Kent and we were rushing through vast hops gardens, the plants beginning to bloom into gold, ready for the seasonal pickers to come down from the slums of London, only then did she turn her face back to me.

"The curtain goes up," she said.

I nodded.

"What the hell are you doing?" I said.

"What do you mean?"

"This role of yours."

"And you, my son? I was quite surprised to learn about your own specialized acting career."

"You already knew about me the other night."

"Of course." She leaned forward and patted me on the knee. "Aren't we having fun?"

There was nothing to say to that. Of course she was.

I decided to watch the hops for a while.

Trask had briefed me before we parted at Buffington's. I'd been invited to stay the weekend at Stockman House, his family estate high on the chalk cliffs between Broadstairs and Ramsgate. I was following Isabel Cobb, doing a feature story on her for the de facto syndicate of German-leaning American newspapers that were making my reputation. The news hook was the next stop on her tour of *Hamlet*. Berlin. A detail she deliberately withheld from our discussion of her tour in her dressing room. I was to stay alert to—even, at my discretion, seek out—evidence that Sir Albert was indeed actively aiding the German cause. My mother was doing the same.

"This will be an interesting test of your new identity," Trask had said.

I wasn't worried. There had been almost no images of me in the press over these half dozen years of my war correspondent notoriety. I'd insisted on that. My printed words were my public face. There was, however, another issue. I'd said to Trask, "She and I have kept it quiet for more than a decade, but the Germans surely know she's my mother."

He'd simply nodded. We were drinking brandy in the two Morris chairs after everyone else had cleared out of Buffington's basement bunker.

"This is very risky for her," I said.

Trask did a lift of the left shoulder and a tilt of the head in the same direction, both equally minute. A characteristic shrug I'd seen more than once. It usually was meant to stop a line of inquiry. But this time he also said, "She understands the risk. She's made it very clear how disaffected she is with you. I understand she can be very convincing."

I let that sink in. I tried to believe it. I said, "But why recruit *her*? Why take on that extra burden?"

"She was already undercover."

"I know about that."

"So I gather." He smiled, slow and sly. Her Pinkerton work.

"You're not saying she came to you," I said.

He shrugged again. This time it did stop the inquiry. But he added, "It could actually make her more interesting to them."

At that, I should have had a thought about something I'd seen in her dressing room, but I got distracted by her being "interesting" to the Germans.

Trask even followed up on my distraction, though he figured he was simply giving me a more direct answer to my question of *why her*. He said, "She happened to be the best possible person for our Sir Albert. He is her ardent fan."

The hops seemed to have vanished. The field passing was full of cows.

I turned back to Mother.

37

"There *is* something to say to that." This came out of my mouth before I realized I was alluding to a thought of a few moments ago that I'd not given voice to: what was there to say to her "Aren't we having fun."

"Have I missed something?" she said.

"We can't take this as fun," I said. "Of course you knew about me and Trask when I saw you in your dressing room. You knew long before that."

"So?"

"So what the hell were you doing making a show of my being your son? The stage manager knew me on sight. My photo was stuck in your mirror. You did your underappreciated-and-deeply-concerned-but-proudly-loving-mama act with the suffragettes."

"I *am* underappreciated and deeply concerned," she said.

"Trask surely told you these people are dangerous."

"I am proudly loving too," she said.

"Your fate . . ."

"Always that," she said.

"Your fate with the Huns," I said, firmly, "depends on their belief that we are estranged, you and I."

"I know that," she said.

"Then how could you publicly play the opposite?"

"It wasn't public. This man would never in an eon talk with suffragettes or stage managers. And when he came backstage I hid your photo."

I flipped my hands in the air in exasperation.

"So Mr. Hunter," she said, suddenly lighting up in her stage-star way, immediately turning me into this guy. As if that was all it would take to put my concerns to rest. "You and I share some strong sympathies that are, I'm afraid, quickly becoming unpopular in our country."

She engaged my gaze and she was looking at me with veiled but lively eyes and she was smiling a very small, crooked smile. This pose was filed under *Faintly Superior Solicitousness*. She was inviting me to get into character with her now. Like old times on a train on the way to a performance.

"Wrongheadedly so," I said. "This is not the first time our country has had trouble choosing its friends."

For a very brief moment her smile flashed wide: Isabel smiling at her son Kit playing along with her. Then she plunged back into her playlet. "You are so right, Mr. Hunter. So right indeed. But this weekend you will have a chance to write about the greatest actress of the American stage celebrating her triumph as Hamlet in London and then traveling on to play the tragically fated prince in Berlin. I will, by my art, build a bridge between these two warring nations. I take no sides. I love the English but I also embrace our German brethren."

"And do you embrace our host this weekend?" I asked.

There was a stopping in her and then a fluttering out of her part, just a little, in her hands. I tried not to show any pleasure at getting her to briefly lose her performance composure. My sense of our old *game* of this indeed made me feel a sort of pleasure. But for me to have flustered her with that cheap innuendo meant there was some bit of truth in it. And there was no pleasure in that at all.

She recovered quickly. "Mr. Hunter, I never took you for a yellow journalist."

I played at backing off. "I mean, of course, in the same way you would embrace the good people of *Das Deutsche Reich*."

"Well, do forgive me, Mr. Hunter, for misunderstanding you. I am sadly accustomed to young men taking an inappropriate interest in my private life, which is none of their business."

I turned my face to the windows. The cows had given way to apple orchards, the small, green earlies already beginning to appear.

"We need to talk in our actual selves," I said.

"And what are those, exactly?" she said.

I looked at her.

Our eyes connected but didn't hold. She turned her face to the long, even rows of apple trees whisking by. "All right," she said.

"Your man Albert . . ."

"He is not my man," she said.

"Your target Albert."

"Yes?"

"What can you tell me about him?"

"I've said things about America privately to him that make your little pseudonymous odes to the Fatherland sound wishy-washy."

"Wouldn't that make him suspicious?"

"I'm exaggerating." She said this instantly, shrugging.

"Let's talk straight," I said.

"What I said *felt* that extreme," she said. "It's easier for you to write this drivel than it is for me to say it face to face. But I've made myself look as potentially good for the German cause as your J. W. Hunter. And I worked up to it. I know how to play that role with a man. Oh, sir, I've got this little secret that some people would think unsavory but I feel I can trust you."

"Sounds effective." I said this with an edge I didn't want. She didn't either. It was her own fault for putting it in those terms.

We looked at each other and silently called a truce.

She said, "I think he believes me. And he was receptive. You could feel him expanding, glowing. But this was just loose, still rather indirect talk. His receptiveness is nothing like proof."

"There's one thing I worry about," I said.

"What's that, dear?"

"He'll see a resemblance in us."

"I don't think so," she said.

"The eyes," I said.

"No," she said.

"We have the same eyes."

"Nonsense," she said. "You have your father's eyes."

In those rare occasions she'd let herself refer to him, however vaguely—*always* vaguely—she meant it to stop the present conversation. She had never identified my father except that his name was Cobb and he was dead and I'd received from him some good traits and some bad traits. Unspecified. To her credit, she had never once, no matter how angry or frustrated she became with me, never once had she invoked my dead Cobb of a father as being responsible for my behavior. And perhaps a dozen times over the years she'd said that the one thing I got from my father were my looks, which she heartily approved of. Just *my looks.* The eye thing—that they, specifically, were his—this was new. And unwelcome.

I found my next breath hard to take. Impossible to take. And I could hear the clatter of my heart in my ears. Perhaps I had my father's heart as well. Perhaps he'd died of a heart attack. Perhaps I wouldn't have to worry about Sir Albert Stockman looking into my face and seeing my mother and smiling and nodding and later telling his men to kill us both in our sleep. Maybe this clatter was my last.

"You'll be just fine, Mr. Hunter," my mother said, quite low. Not a stage whisper. Not stagey at all. She meant to sincerely encourage me. Encourage us.

I nodded and turned my eyes to the window and saw nothing and then I turned back to her.

"What did Trask say he expected of you?" I asked.

"Whatever I can give him," my mother said. "But at worst, when I get to Berlin, if Albert is what we think he is and he believes my performance, we expect the German secret service will approach me to be useful to them."

And now Trask's declaration struck me as it almost did in Buffington's basement, that this recruitable German agent being the mother of a very effective enemy of Germany made her even more interesting to them.

I was so unaware of cursing in response, I could not even say, exactly, which curse it was that I'd used.

She said, "When a son replies to his mother with the exclamation 'Fuck me,' she is faced with a choice of several interpretations, none of them pleasant."

"I'm sorry, Mother," I said. "Your first 'useful' act for the Germans will be to try to lure me into a trap. You understand that, don't you?"

You could see the same stopping of breath in her that I had felt over my father's eyes. She was silent for one beat and another and then she said, so quietly that I could barely hear it above the clack of the train wheels, "Fuck me."

"That's the right interpretation," I said.

"Mr. Trask surely knows this," she said.

"Of course he does," I said. "And it's what we have signed up for, you and I. You understand that too."

"Yes." Another pause. And she added, "He'll have a plan."

"*We* will have a plan," I said. "We all will."

She nodded.

And we both watched sightlessly for a few moments as the Kentish landscape rolled past.

It was time to get to work. I said, "Have you been to Stockman House?"

"Not yet," she said, squaring her shoulders to me. "But 'house' is British understatement, I'm told. It's a castle. Just not a terribly old one. Built in the middle of the last century by his grandfather."

"Is he all inheritance? Or does he have his own dough?"

"He's got plenty of his own. He's an industrialist, he says. Metals. But if you push him—and I quickly learned not to—it's all milk cans and Oxo tins and dustbins. He's the Industrial Titan of Milk Cans, and he's a bit touchy about it. For some years now, of course, he's a member of Parliament, and that's who he thinks he really is."

"Does he have family?" Though I tried hard to keep a just-trying-to-get-the-facts tone in my voice, even I could hear the fidgety undertone.

She looked at me for a beat, sizing up my intention with that question. Which was, at least in part, to understand the extent of his romantic availability to her.

Does the punk kid you once were ever fully vanish, especially when it comes to your mother, especially when she's the only blood family you ever had? And when that mother keeps casting you in his role, as she'd done ever since we'd boarded this train, and when you and he and she are sharing serious personal risks, his child's issue takes on a new relevance. She had to get close to this man, but not too close.

"A daughter in Scotland," she said. "He's a widower." She paused, waiting for me to openly become the young man with an inappropriate interest in her private life.

I declined. I fed her no cue. She still had the stage.

She said, "His wife died a couple of years ago. An accident."

She paused again. I made a little wide-eyed chin dip to ask for more.

"She fell off a cliff," she said. "He lives on a cliff."

"An accident?"

"Officially."

"Unofficially?"

"I asked our Mr. Trask that very thing." The ham in my mother came suddenly to a sizzle: she paused and let it roll on.

I finally asked. "And?"

"He shrugged."

"Be careful of this Stockman guy," I said.

"I just have to keep charming him. You're the one who'll need to be careful."

"Is this how the boss did it?" I executed Trask's little shoulder lift and head tilt.

She answered with a similar exact replica of Trask's shrug. "*That* way," she said, as if it were different from mine. It wasn't.

I didn't debate the point. I was finished bantering with my mother. We had more important business together. I looked out the window. The apple trees had become cherry trees. Far beyond them a church spire rose against the gray sky in a grove of village roofs.

Mother thought she sensed my mood, though she was a step behind now.

"Just so you know," she said. "Sir Albert's crazy about me."

I kept my eyes on the flash of cherry trees and, flickering among them, baskets and ladders and figures reaching up. The trees were fruiting.

"He'll probably touch my elbow." She paused.

I concentrated on the cherries.

"Or put his hand on the small of my back."

I thought about picking sour cherries one summer day in my childhood. Somewhere in upstate New York. It must have been near a summer theater.

"I will take his arm. Do you understand?"

I turned to her. I nodded. I made myself say, "It's all part of the job."

As soon as I said it, I believed it.

And my mother leaned forward, reached out, took my hand, and squeezed it.

# 6

Albert sent a Silver Ghost to meet us at Broadstairs Station. The liveried driver stood on the platform with feet spread, his hands clasped behind him, as we emerged. He recognized us at once, coming to attention. I almost expected a salute. He took our bags from the porter and handed them off to a man in well-worn blue serge who'd been doing a respectful cringe behind him, and he led us to the Rolls-Royce parked just outside the station door, a landaulette with two leather armchairs and a couple of jump seats in the tonneau, an open driver compartment, and that long, long Rolls hood ending in the marque's nickel and bronze mascot, the Spirit of Ecstasy, a beautiful woman bent toward the onrushing road with her nightie billowing up along her arms like wings.

We drove south down the coast, clearing Broadstairs, and we approached Dumpton Gate, the "gate" being one of the rare, narrow gaps in the otherwise unbroken white chalk cliffs of the Kentish coast. The road had gradually been gathering a loosely intervaled but considerable traffic: dog cart and carriage, Brit-blue Model T and Daimler landaulette, and folks on foot as well, singly and coupled up, buddied up and in families. We followed a dense grove of sweet chestnuts parallel to the cliff line, showing an iron fence flashing within the trees and farther glimpses of go-to-meeting-size tents. Something more than a weekend house party was happening at Stockman House, at least for today. Then the trees ended abruptly and the iron fence emerged and turned toward the sea. So did we, and so did the other travelers on this road.

We all entered a macadamized access road. The fence uprights were taller than a man and spiked at the top. They'd run through the tree line, no doubt all the way from the gap, and also bordered this southern side of Stockman's property, surely to the edge of the cliff. He had a serious security perimeter. And through the fence's transparent blur, beyond the cluster of cream and blue-striped tents set up on the wide, flat green, Stockman House showed itself.

Mother leaned across me to look. For now the place was simply vast—but much wider than tall—and it was black, and this west side of it, away from the sea, gaped open in its center, three long wings around a courtyard.

Mother withdrew, sitting down hard in her seat. My hand lay on the chair arm between us and she immediately put her own hand on mine and squeezed. I looked at her.

"Stage nerves?" I asked.

She stretched out a tight little smile for me.

I turned my hand upward and clasped hers.

As we neared the house, an iron-arched entryway appeared in the fence, with a couple of uniformed local constables pulling the gates open for us. Only for us, for now, as the travelers were simply gathering on the south side of the road, parking their vehicles, waiting to enter the grounds. We slowed and turned in.

The main inner road headed for the courtyard, but the driver shortly angled off into a side road toward the cliff. We entered a driveway circle and went the long way round, to the right, and we stopped, presenting Mother's door to the center of the south face of the house. The driver jumped out and galloped around to open it.

He was a hulk of a man with a thick neck, but he moved quickly and lightly. If he were an American I'd take him for a Wolverine half-back. Since he was a Brit, a rugby footballer. Since he was Stockman's man, though, however he'd acquired his skills, I was willing to bet he was more than a driver. A tough guy. I slipped from my side and stepped clear of the car. I looked at Sir Al's abode.

Sometimes a man's castle is his home. His was well fortified and he was the only family member residing in it, up here high above the Strait of Dover. I glanced that way, at the cloud-begrayed water laid out against the horizon, just beyond which was Calais and the shooting war. If he was a German agent, he was well placed.

The house was Victorian-Elizabethan-Eccentric. Seventy-five years old at most, but it was of quite another era: this wide facade—at least sixty yards, maybe more—was an Elizabethan profusion of glass, two dozen vast window casements transomed and mullioned into hundreds and hundreds of panes on this south face alone.

To my right, at the wing's eastern end, rose a parapeted tower that was more King John than the Virgin Queen. This Gothic tower lifted a full two storeys above the slate roof, its only window a cruciform loophole. And from the top of the tower Stockman House rose higher still. On another two storeys of flagpole flew a whopping Union Jack, nearly as wide as the Silver Ghost was long. Including the cliff on which everything stood, that flag waved a good two hundred feet above the shore. The pole was high enough and big enough that it was even anchored against high winds by four guy wires lashed to the tower parapet. Such an extravagant declaration of Britishness struck me as Stockman wrapping himself in a big flag to hide his treachery.

A striking thing about the house itself—a vaguely intimidating thing—was its stone. Ashlar-worked black flint. An odd contradiction to my eye, this darkly craggy stone, usually found rusticated, made smooth and slick and polished. And even as that thought passed through me, Sir Albert Stockman's polished baritone filled the salty air, booming and yet mellifluous.

I could understand Mother thinking she needed to warn me about her putting her arm in his. Outwardly he was her kind of guy. He was a tall man, taller than me by a couple of inches, bareheaded but wearing an unbuttoned single-breasted day-wear tailcoat with striped trousers and sporting a flash of pink silk in his breast pocket. He had a fine, angular face, chipped and polished from a craggy white stone. He was graying lightly, probably Mother's age but having arrived in his fifties beautifully, in the way she loved, envied, and despised in males. He was a leading man.

I began to move toward the point between them where they were about to meet, him striding to his Isabel Cobb, she taking her own step toward him, and another. They arrived. He caught up both her hands. He bent to her and they bussed on each cheek. I stopped.

They finished bussing and stood back to look at each other. They kept holding hands. I was watching him closely enough to see his eyes not quite leave hers but register me, as I was comfortably within his line of easy peripheral sight and only a few steps away. I tried to portray a respectful deference, slumping a little at the chest, lowering my chin ever so slightly.

"I am so happy you are here," he was saying.

"I am happy to be here," my mother said.

"You'll have time to rest a little," he said. "Today the grounds are open to the good people of Ramsgate and Broadstairs. We will host and feast some of my constituents. You don't mind appearing for them?"

"Of course not, Albert. I am happy to be hostess of Stockman House tonight."

Albert straightened to full height in overplayed joy at this. He bent again, this time toward her hands, one of which he lifted and kissed, somewhat lingeringly.

Mother lowered her face and watched.

Albert rose. "Thank you, my dear," he said. And then he turned his face to me.

"And this must be Mr. Hunter," he said. Warmly. Convincingly so, I had to admit. This was good. I needed to appear useful to a man not only whose heart and history but also whose active, secret allegiance might be to Germany.

"Yes," my mother said, turning to me.

Not "my mother." *Isabel,* I thought. I had to play this role inside my head as well.

Stockman let go of Isabel Cobb and took the three steps to me as she said, "This is Joseph W. Hunter . . ."

He offered me a hand, which I took, prepared for a firm grip. I got one. Luckily I wedged my own hand fully into his and gave him just enough back to let him think I was a substantial enough man but not a rival. Meanwhile, my mother was saying, "Lord Albert Stockman."

He and I were locked in at the eyes. Perhaps it was just the dulled light of the cloudy day but I could have sworn his eyes were almost precisely the shade called *feldgrau,* literally field gray, the color of the German army's fighting uniforms, gray but cut by green, the combination perfect for camouflage in the European countryside.

"Lord Stockman," I said.

"Mr. Hunter," he said. "I am delighted to meet you."

He lifted his chin just a little. I was wrong about his eyes. I stopped indulging my impulse to see him, in every detail, by the light of our suspicions. This wasn't a feature story for the Sunday edition. That newswriter reflex was bad for my present line of work. His eyes weren't *feldgrau.* They were grayer than that.

He said, "I get the newspapers from the United States. We are all very attentive, as you may know, to your country's attitudes. I've read you with great interest."

The locution he used was not uncommon. But he paused, as if to let that soak in. That he'd been reading *me.* Not just my stories. But I got the strong sense he meant more.

"I hope I didn't cause you any offense," I said.

He lowered his chin and gave me a careful look. "Why would you think that?"

"You are English. Perhaps the stories I write are too willing, from an Englishman's point of view, to understand the German side of things."

Stockman gave me a slow, nodding smile. He said, "Perhaps I am trying to understand your President's reluctance to become more involved."

49

I let my Mr. Hunter show his nerves at all this, looking briefly away from Stockman in a deferential shrug. "Just so," I said. "That's my concern on your behalf. If he no longer heard the voice of those Americans who favor Germany, he might be more willing to help you."

I was back to Stockman's eyes and he was focused intently on me, assessing me. He smiled. "Don't worry about that. You are a welcome guest in my home."

"You're too kind," I said.

"Besides, I understand you are doing a story on the estimable Isabel Cobb."

"Indeed," I said.

"You see? I don't hold her appearance in Berlin against her," Stockman said, and he initiated a gentle, socially reassuring laugh. The estimable Isabel Cobb and I joined in.

When the laugh faded into a comfortable silence between us, he said. "I remain interested in your views. We can speak later."

"I look forward to it," I said.

"You are invited for the weekend, of course."

Without giving me even a moment's chance to reply to this, Stockman did an about-face and quickstepped to Isabel. Without a look at me, she tucked her hand into the crook of his offered arm and the two maundered off toward the house. I followed.

# 7

This brief passage toward the castle door surprised me in the claw-scrabble of unease it started up in my chest. We entered the castle through a reception hall with twin suits of armor flanking the door, helmets closed, occupied by a couple more of his tough guys for all I knew. Stockman stopped Isabel and half turned to me and said, "Martin will show you the way." His driver loomed up beside me and extended an arm toward the inner door and swept it to the right. I went where I was told, while my mother and her leading man swept out to the left.

I heard her voice and footfalls fading into stone-echoes behind me, and I realized this was what my unease was all about, my mother and me separating in this place. If Stockman and his boys were what we suspected they were, she could well be in over her head. Alone here, I could be too. I always figured I could handle anything. I wasn't so sure about her.

But it was all very polite. Even Martin was polite, in a silent way. Nonchalant even. If he was a hired tough guy, I had no sense he was under orders to intimidate me or even to keep a special eye on me. He led me along a corridor hung with fox-hunt Aubussons, and ahead was a massive stone staircase, which we were approaching from its great, gray, triangular wedge of a side. As we reached it and began to turn, Martin flipped a forefinger toward an open doorway at the base of the steps. "Billiards," he said. "You can play."

His English—these four words were, I suddenly realized, the first I'd heard of it—was not British in accent, was oddly not accented at all but clipped and precise. I thought: *a carefully trained German.*

We'd made the turn now and the staircase was simply a wall face beside me, but my mind went up these steps. The castle was complex in its layout and I knew I had to simplify what I took in, what I memorized of the layout, or I'd get lost. This staircase seemed worth noting. I reckoned that it ascended within the five-storey parapeted tower.

Martin said, "The stairs lead into the private family wing of the house. I am sorry that guests are invited no farther than the billiards."

His seeming to read my mind was vaguely unsettling, but his treating me like a regular, well-intentioned guest was vaguely reassuring. If I were an ill-intentioned guest his comment would only be an invitation to snoop. As, indeed, I was and it was.

We passed through the Great Hall, its abrupt three-storey lift to a vast hammer-beam roof giving it something of the same heady kick of a big-league church. But Martin was talking again and I focused on him. "That's the library," he said, motioning to a door in the east wall. "The billiards and the books. These are for you to enjoy until we collect you at about five. You may dress casually tonight, as the public will be here for festivities and we will be serving high tea alfresco."

"Are there other guests for the weekend?" I asked.

"A dozen," he said. "Many are here now. You'll have competition."

I assumed he meant at billiards.

At the far end of the Great Hall we entered the arched colonnade of a screens passage and turned left into a staircase. We climbed to the second-floor bachelor corridor of the castle, laid out over the kitchen and pantries.

When we reached my room Martin opened the door and stepped back for me, as if in deference. He even pulled his hat off, showing a spiky crop of wheat-chaff tan hair. He was consciously playing a role. As I passed him, I played my part in his little scene, giving him a nod of gratitude-to-a-servant, but catching and holding for a moment those eyes, which were as opaquely gray as the Strait of Dover.

The room had a narrow set of mullioned windows and was furnished with the simple straight lines of the Arts and Crafts movement: bedstead, wardrobe, hard leather-seated chair, small break-front writing desk.

I sat in the chair and I waited for the cringing man from the station. He and the bags were coming by a separate vehicle. The Rolls was not a touring model and didn't have an elegant way of transporting a great deal of luggage. But I figured Stockman might have arranged that so as to do a quick check of the contents. Certainly enough time was passing.

At last the luggage man arrived, and I took my bags at the doorway and closed him out at once and I laid them—a leather valise and a Gladstone—on the bed. I opened the valise and lifted out books and a toilet case and a notepad. But for this weekend these were mostly just filler to cover the false bottom I was now prying out of the valise.

Stockman's boys might have searched, but they didn't find my Mauser pocket automatic, a rock-hard bantamweight of a pistol with a .32 caliber punch. I pulled it out of the false-bottomed depth of my valise. It was tucked inside a left-hander's leather holster with the flap cut off, so I could wear it in the small of my back and draw it with my right hand.

I laid the holster on the bed, and I freshened up in cold water in my small bathroom and changed my suit from sack to brown mohair, with a fresh shirt and tie.

I slipped the Mauser and its holster onto my belt and centered it in place.

They didn't find my leather pouch of lock-picking tools either. This I put into my inner coat pocket. Or my six-inch tungsten flashlight, which I snugged into my side pocket. Or my Luger, which I left in the comparable false bottom of the Gladstone.

I sat down on the edge of my bed and retied my shoes.

What sounded distantly like a small salon orchestra had arrived, out on the green, and was tuning up.

I was ready to begin.

I wasn't interested in books or billiards. I wanted to look around. I'd carry my notebook and keep only Joseph W. Hunter notes in it, as if the grounds of the castle was local color in the Kent part of my feature story on Isabel Cobb.

I stepped out of my room and closed the door quietly behind me. The corridor was empty. I went along it and down the stairs and emerged in the screens passage. A scullery maid in white uniform and mobcap brushed past me with her face cast down and a quiet "Pardon, sir."

I emerged into the Great Hall.

Though the windows here were limited to the west wall and looked into the courtyard, the place felt bright, for it was faced in white granite. The floor was covered by a single Persian rug large enough to define the foundation of a Sears ready-made bungalow. In its dense weave, hunters on horses leapt and gazelles fled.

A young Queen Victoria—the Stockmar family's benefactress—was on horseback, as well, rendered massively in oils above the white ashlar walk-in fireplace. Beyond her was the doorway into the library. I was sanctioned to go there. Books and billiards. The things I needed to really learn about Stockman were in the unsanctioned places, but it was daylight and Stockman House was preparing to receive the public and Albert's men would be prowling around, so for now I had to interpret what I could from the things I could access. A library was as good a place to start as any.

I set out across the Persian hunting ground, thinking of books. Early in my previous assignment I'd discovered at least a temporary Rosetta stone for one of the Germans' methods of secret communication: a book called *The Nuttall Encyclopaedia of Universal Information*, the placement of whose words were the basis for numbered codes. Not that Al's *Nuttall* would be kept on the library table off the Great Hall. But if they weren't simply tony wallpaper, I was interested in his books.

I approached three Brits in summer tweeds and spats drinking tea and talking low on red-velvet Jacobean chairs before the fireplace.

Middle-aged gents, all of them. Other guests for the weekend, no doubt. One glanced my way as I approached and then back to the discussion, the voices clipping phrases and extending vowels in that toffish, fixed-jawed upper-class British way. The reporter in me thought to slide into their conversation and find out what they know about Albert. But a young American, out of the blue, asking the kinds of questions I'd need to ask to make it worth my while, would only create suspicion. My real work required that I remain mostly unnoticed.

I passed them by and stepped into the library.

The place was chockablock with wainscoted shelves full of books in great, uniform runs of sets, the blues and reds and browns and greens of their spines coordinated carefully into a variegated but orderly panorama. The east wall held a twenty-foot-wide bay window looking out to the strait.

I strolled along Stockman's books, the sets a patchwork of writers and subjects. A dozen volumes of *Illustrated World Geography* running in green into fifteen umber Sam Johnsons into twenty tan Bulwer-Lyttons into a couple dozen French Shakespeares in black and gilt. I stopped here and saw, on the shelf below, another complete Shakespeare, in English, and then next to that a twelve-volume set of the Schlegel and Tieck German translation. *Shakespeares sämtliche dramatische Werke.*

I looked more closely at the Schlegel Shakespeare. They were placed in evenly at the front edge of the shelves. All the books in the library were arranged like this. Not quite flush. There was about a quarter of an inch lip between the edge of the shelf and the spine of the book. And that quarter inch was gray with dust. I pulled one of the Schlegels out. The shelf was instantly wiped clean in a band the width of the volume in my hand. I replaced it.

I continued on, more slowly, looking at the ubiquitous layer of dust. He was not a reader. Not from this library at least. And I also kept an eye out for the German works. There weren't many and they were scattered along. The collected Goethe. Schiller. But Stockman's books were mostly English. Still, if he was trying to make an impression, he didn't mind showing at least some of his Germanic origins. Not that he was reading the English-language books either. Not lately.

I finally reached the wall of stuffed shelves at the far end. I stood with my back to the rest of the room and found twenty-two volumes of a German writer I did not know. Johann Gottfried von Herder. Two of the volumes had been pulled from the shelves recently. By Sir Albert or by an invited guest. I drew one out. The end board was marbled in blue and brown and cream. I opened the cover. The volume was from 1820. *Die Vorwelt*. "The Primeval World."

I lifted my face from the page.

Perhaps he'd made some small sound. Or, if he'd quietly drawn close, perhaps there was some kinesthetic clue, a displacement of air perhaps. Whatever it was, it registered on me so quickly and subtly that I could not trace it. But I knew someone was in the room with me.

I turned.

Stockman was only a few strides away. He stood with his arms folded over his chest, changed from his tailcoat into more relaxed day wear, a three-piece gray linen suit.

I kept the book open in my hand.

Stockman unfolded his arms and moved to me, saying, "I'm happy you're exploring the library, Mr. Hunter."

"It's impressive," I said.

He stopped just a bit beyond arm's length away.

He glanced at the volume in my hand. "Do you read German, Mr. Hunter?"

"Pretty well," I said. "Do you, Sir Albert?"

"I do," he said. "How are you with the Fraktur?"

Fraktur was the broken-angled, heavy black letter typeface Germany had used for nearly four hundred years. His identifying it only by its esoteric name in the question struck me as part of what was likely to be a subtle, ongoing test of my Germanic credentials.

"I should read it more often," I said. "I do all right, but it still strikes my eye oddly."

He smiled. "Of course. Were your parents born in their homeland?"

"Yes. They came to the United States when I was very young."

"My family background is German as well," Stockman said. "As is the case with a great many Englishmen."

"Your present royal family . . ." I began, hesitating only for a fraction of a second.

He finished my sentence. "Is Saxe-Coburg and Gotha."

He looked at me for a moment. Though it was very brief, I felt certain it was filled with a serious, subtle, rapid assessment of me. He made a decision and said, "Some might say that a royal family by any other name would be a different royal family."

"Would not smell as sweet," I said, bringing his sly joke closer to the Shakespeare quote and to the political point we were quietly deciding to share.

He laughed out loud, a bright, sharp bark of a laugh.

He flipped his chin at the book in my hand. "Do you know von Herder?"

"I don't."

He smiled. He nodded to the shelf behind me. "May I?"

I stepped aside. He moved forward and removed a volume of von Herder and searched its pages for a moment. He found the passage he wanted and handed the book to me, taking *Die Vorwelt* from me. "Beginning of the second paragraph on the right-hand page," he said.

I read it. Another little test. I struggled with the wildly angled letters of the Fraktur and then with the German itself. He watched patiently. But he did not let me off the hook. A few moments along he said, "Apropos of our recent observations."

Then I had it. Though it probably took less than a minute, it felt like a very long time. But I knew that for the circumstances, I'd done this fast. I lifted my face from the page and smiled at him. Just in case he was open to the suspicion, I let him think for a moment that I'd overstated even my modest declaration of proficiency in German and I was about to confess. It would be all the more impressive when he realized I was, indeed, far better than I'd claimed.

"Shall I translate?" I asked.

57

"Please," he said.

"The heart of it," I said.

"I'd be interested in your selection."

I let go of the literal enough to make it read smoothly in English and I went to the heart of the message: "The English are Germans, and even in recent times the Germans have showed the way for the English in the most important matters."

Stockman slowly unfurled a small, one-sided smile. I could easily read approval into it. For a clever boy passing a tricky test.

He said, "Can I have your assurance that my personal views and sympathies will be strictly omitted from any story you write?"

Though the context was almost mellow in tone, I'd never heard the word "strictly" spoken with such bite. It leaped from the sentence as if he'd flashed a pistol and threatened to use it. Perhaps he had.

"Of course," I said. "I understand the delicacy of your position. I often feel it myself."

I sounded convincing.

He made one more brief, evaluative pause.

I'd passed another test.

"I have a few minutes," he said. "Perhaps the only ones for the rest of this day. Would you like to sit for a time?"

"Of course," I said.

He led me across the room and into a cluster of modern overstuffed reading chairs before the bay window. Beyond were a hundred yards of dense, manicured grass. Very simple. No garden. A fieldstone path to a waist-high stone fence. I wondered if that was where Lady Stockman went over.

Beyond the fence lay the wide stretch of the Strait of Dover, its surface gray starting to mitigate, becoming the vague blue of slate now, as the clouds were beginning to break.

Stockman pointed to one of the wingback reading chairs. I sat.

He didn't. "Brandy all right?" Stockman asked.

"Of course," I said. "Thanks."

He went to a drinks table beneath the apron of the far right segment of the bay window. That part was a casement, I could see. And
the baronet himself poured us snifters and carried them over. He sat
in the companion chair—the two were at a slight angle toward each
other—and he handed me a snifter.

"A fine Armagnac," he said. "I prefer it." Meaning, I presumed, to
the more popular Cognac.

"To Armagnac," I said, lifting the snifter in a toast.

We touched glasses.

The brandy was a deep red sunset on the tongue and a noonday
sun going down.

"You do understand German quite well," Stockman said.

"We spoke it in the family," I said. "I had sense enough to keep it
up afterwards."

He said, "You understand, of course, that I am thoroughly British."

"I understand," I said.

"But I find that compatible with a regard for Germany and a regret
over this animosity that has sprung up between us."

"The English are Germans," I said.

"Just so."

"Strictly speaking," I said, "the United States is not yet allied to one
side or the other, but I feel the same tension at home."

"I do love my country," he said.

He had turned his face to the window. No eye contact. He allowed
the ambiguity but would not overtly share it: which country was that?

As frank as he'd become with me, it sounded as if this was as far
as he would go. He might well have decided I was no threat and,
indeed, a friend of Germany. The declaration of his Britishness and
the rhetoric suggesting a compatible Germany and the wrongness of
the war were undoubtedly risky for a Brit, given the anti-German
war fervor felt by most of his countrymen. But this was no doubt a
position quietly kept by a number of other Englishmen, who nevertheless remained loyal by the light of a democracy's highest belief in

the freedom of thought. He didn't have to be an active German agent to be talking like this.

He intended to show me no more.

I thought: *He has just run an automobile-size Union Jack up a castle-roof flagpole.*

Which led me to gently prod him. "That enormous flag above us," I said, "flying over a British castle on the way to the mouth of the Thames. Isn't it a sharp stick in the eye of a Zeppelin commander, daring him to drop his first bomb here?"

"Their realm is the night," he said. I knew the answer, of course, that the flag was invisible when the Zeppelins typically came. But it was the hint of a hush, the tinge of a tremor in his voice over this subject that I'd wanted to evoke and listen to. Just for starters. And all of that was clearly there in his voice. A good actor would kill to render that vocal nuance at will.

"They are impressive, aren't they," I said.

"They are the future," Stockman said.

I said, "The Londoners stiffen their upper lips and elevate their bravado, but I think the Zepps unsettle them."

"Terrify them." Stockman inflated the verb I'd deliberately diminished. Intensely so.

"The airship war is getting stronger," I said.

He drained the rest of his Armagnac.

He was saying no more.

I thought to press on. To probe his feelings about the poison gas attack at the Second Battle of Ypres, about the lesson felt in London and Washington and Paris and Berlin from that battle: the Allies still weren't ready to effectively fight a war. And it wasn't just about the gas. Or a shortage of artillery shells. Kitchener was struggling to properly train his million promised troops. The Anglo-French army had no near prospects of breaking the German line. Germany was growing fearless. And the Zepps would soon rule the night.

I wanted to work Stockman up, now that he was comfortable with me. But my credentials with him were too fresh. I risked undoing them if he sensed I was baiting him.

He stood up, moved away. The bottles rattled at the drink table. "Would you like a refill?" he asked.

"No, thanks," I said.

He returned with a renewed snifter and sat.

He drank. He said, "What do you know about Isabel Cobb?"

I hid in a sip of my brandy. I could easily have seen this as ominous. I'd tried to finesse him into showing me signs of his allegiance to Germany in a weapons-and-havoc way. He could well be doing likewise, looking for a conspiratorial connection between me and this woman he was wooing.

"What sort of thing?" I said.

"I'm interested in her background. You're writing about her. Something I might not know."

It was one of the Kaiser's own precious Prussians who formulated "the best defense is a good offense." So I said, "Since you read American newspapers, you may have seen a Cobb byline. Christopher Cobb. It's not well known, but that's Isabel's son. They broke off contact more than a decade ago, as I understand it."

I watched Stockman's face. It didn't register much of anything. Old news, maybe. "I've heard about him," he said. Nothing more. No follow-up question. He was simply waiting for something he *didn't* know.

Okay, I thought. Maybe it actually was my mother he was assessing now. As a potential spy. Or a potential lover.

"I didn't realize this till recently," I said. "She sings."

"She's singing tonight," Stockman said.

"Sorry. I haven't been working the story for very long."

Stockman stirred in his seat. Sipped. Looked out to the late afternoon sky, which was brightening.

He did indeed want to know about her men, I thought.

I drained my Armagnac. I wished I had another. I'd slug it down quick. But for what we needed to accomplish, my mother and I, Stockman had to stay interested, and this opportunity would not last.

I lowered my voice. "Man to man?" I said.

"Yes," he said, keeping his eyes out the bay window.

"From what I can gather she has no . . . affiliations."

He turned his eyes to me. Me, who had become his mother's pimp. In service to their country.

His look was man to man. He was grateful for the news.

Then he glanced away, toward the library door, responding to a cue that I had missed.

I looked too.

Martin was standing there, changed from his chauffeur livery into a two-piece gray suit.

"I'm afraid it's time to attend to my beloved constituents," Stockman said.

He rose. I began to rise as well, but he stopped me with the flash of his right palm. "Enjoy the books," he said.

I sat back down.

"Help yourself to the brandy," he said, and he turned abruptly and strode across the library floor. He reached the door and paused, speaking a few words to Martin, whose eyes slid briefly to mine as he listened.

Either I'd passed all my tests, as I'd thought, and he was telling his tough guy I was okay, or I was dead wrong and he was issuing a warning. Or a nasty instruction.

But as Stockman pushed past, Martin lingered for one small moment and looked to me, seeing that I'd been watching, and he gave me a slight nod. I nodded back.

I figured I might be all right for the time being.

Then Martin vanished and I was alone in the library.

I stayed where I was. A thing had lingered in my head, from the words unspoken. The matter of the unprepared Brits. Night before last I'd sat in a reading chair next to Trask's in Buffington's bomb shelter and we'd gotten around to our own unpreparedness. The United States had a hundred thousand troops and about that number of National Guardsmen. The Germans alone had two million in uniform, well trained. And Wilson was still twisted around trying to find his backbone, even with a hundred and twenty-eight dead Americans on the *Lusitania*. He'd issued no call to arms, instead offering tardy, mealy-mouthed, diplomatic pipsqueaking.

After we'd fallen for a time into a brandy-begot, brooding silence, Trask had leaned to me and said, "He won't do this on his own, you know."

He meant Wilson. I nodded.

"These machines are getting better," he said.

He meant the Zeppelins. I nodded.

"All of them."

Airplanes too. The tanks. The artillery.

"The nasty stuff as well," he said.

The gas.

"I know what you mean," I said.

"We are important," he said. "You and I, and Buffington's boys too. They understand. That's why we're helping out, you and I."

I thought I knew what he meant. But I leaned closer. "Explain that," I said.

"Easy," he said. "*We* are driving the . . . what? The cart?"

"The cart," I said.

"No," he said. "Too humble. The train."

"The train," I said.

"No," he said. "That's got a track heading in a certain direction already. I wish that were so."

"The bus?"

"Sure," Trask said. "The bus. A sixty-horsepower bus and we know the route. You see?"

I did. "The *secret service* is driving," I said.

"Yes," he said. "The secret service. We'll find out the real stuff about who's our friends and who's our enemies and we'll make it so clear that even Woodrow Damn Wilson will have to do what's right."

I sat back in my chair. My glass was empty. I understood.

I rose now from the reading chair in the library of Stockman House and moved toward the drink table. But when I arrived, I put the empty glass next to the bottle of Armagnac. I looked to the library door. It was empty. I was alone. I put my hand on the latch of the casement and I turned it. But I left the window closed. My mother was singing tonight. Everyone would be watching, including her would-be lover. I now had a quiet way back into the house.

# 8

The salon orchestra began to play. "Songe d'Automne," a sad little waltz.

Did Stockman arrange this song deliberately, having his covert joke on us all?

Surely not. Only those of us in first class knew what had been on the musical program in the grand dining room on the *Lusitania*'s last voyage. I'd heard the song myself. I'd heard it again in Istanbul. This time I froze at the library window. It was a popular tune for these little strings-and-piano salon orchestras. But the song had found me twice since the torpedo, and that felt a little excessive, as if it were a Siren singing from the bottom of the North Atlantic, wanting to take another crack at me.

I stepped away from the window.

The Stockman House event was starting. I needed to be visible. I hoped to catch Isabel Cobb for some reportage. And perhaps some private words in a cloaking crowd of constituents.

I crossed the library and entered the Great Hall. The Brits by the fireplace had vanished. At the far end I passed through an arched doorway beneath a music gallery and into the courtyard entrance hall. The yard itself lay before me, shadowed from the reemergent sunlight, and I recognized Martin, even from the rear, even wearing a gray trilby. He was standing just outside. I'd get a better reading on my status shortly.

I straightened in a reflex of stage nerves. I wanted to feel the reassurance of the Mauser lying solidly against the small of my back. It was there. I certainly did not want to use it tonight.

I stepped through the door.

Beyond Martin was another tough guy, watching the far end of the courtyard. He was also in a gray suit and trilby. A serge suit just like Martin's. They were in uniform, these two. Stockman's little army. Martin heard me, turned to me.

He nodded again.

I figured a guy like Martin wouldn't make the show of another nod to a guy he was supposed to be keeping a suspicious eye on. He'd be playing it close.

"It's clearing up," I said.

Martin grunted. But it was a grunt of agreement.

I moved on by him and across the fieldstone courtyard and onto the verge of the castle's wide, western green. It held three of the big, blue-and-white, open-sided canvas tents that the Brits called marquees. The nearest was off to the right, next to the service wing of the castle, and it bustled with bodies setting up the high-tea food service for the public. The marquee directly ahead of me, due west, about a hundred yards away, was the source of the waltz, the salon musicians dimly visible at the far end, on an elevated platform. To the left was the third tent, set with folding chairs, and flowing past it was the vanguard of the public, now unleashed upon the grounds, some peeling off to sit, some moving on toward the music, others veering away to prime places on the grass and beginning to spread blankets.

I was glad for the hubbub. Martin and all the other Gray Suits would be the watchers tonight, stationed out here, keeping an eye on the unsorted public wandering the grounds. They'd have their hands full. Stockman would be working his constituents, with Isabel Cobb on his arm. I needed to be patient. And careful. But I figured I'd have a chance to look around inside. For only a limited amount of time, however. I needed to think this out. To make a plan.

Something moved at the right periphery of my sight.

I looked.

The other Gray Suit had stepped up even with me, a few yards away. He had a boxer's battered-and-mended nose and close-cropped dark hair.

He did not look my way. He was watching the flow of townspeople.

I strolled into the green.

I tried to reason things through. If Sir Albert spent much time at Stockman House—and it seemed that he did—the confirmation of his connection to the Germans was somewhere in the castle. The most likely place was wherever he did his personal work. An office. I kept moving toward the music marquee.

But I was mostly thinking about the house behind me.

"Songe d'Automne" dipped and rose and dipped again, to a finish.

I was nearing the tent. The elevated musicians were silhouetted against the now sunlit distant tree line.

Men in seersucker and women in percale were flowing into the chairs set before the music.

The ensemble struck up "Maple Leaf Rag," the song's brothel-born syncopations sounding odd with all the inappropriate strings. But the smattering of gathering crowd applauded in recognition.

I stopped and turned to look back at the house.

My eyes instantly were drawn to the flapping of the British flag up its high pole on the Gothic tower. The wind was brisk. The sun was shining.

All of this registered on me as stage whiskers and greasepaint, this elaborately fortified flag and the high-society orchestra putting on music hall airs. Stockman was trying hard to be English, and a man of the people, no less.

Where was his office? Not on the kitchen and bachelor side of the castle, surely. Perhaps over the library. But more likely in the south wing, the family quarters. It was formalized as private. Visitors knew never to wander there. And he no longer had any family residing with him. I'd go there first, when I had the chance.

I turned away from the house but wished, as well, to distance myself from the music. I walked north, toward the cliff edge along the gate, passing the marquee next to the service wing. The black-and-white-liveried kitchen staff was laying out food on a long row of folding tables. At the end of it, three men in blue serge were setting up another row at a right angle. Two of these boys were heading toward a stack of collapsed tables a few yards outside the tent while the third was unfolding the legs of the next table in the new line.

I realized these guys were dressed not only like each other but also like the baggage handler who met us at the station. These were indeed de facto uniforms. The blue suits were the privates in Stockman's army. I thought all this and slowed a step or two as I did and it all happened quickly: as I was about to turn my attention again toward the cliff, the man in the tent popped the last leg of the table into place and looked up.

I stopped.

He turned his face to me.

It was the stage-door lug from the Duke of York's.

# 9

Of course he was Stockman's man.

I broke off our look and kept on toward the cliff.

Stockman had been keeping a watchful eye on this woman he was interested in.

The first flash in me was that this guy was an immediate danger. He knew who I was.

I neared the stone fence at the cliff's edge.

I stopped a few yards short, expecting he might be following me. I didn't want to put the cliff in play if there was a struggle.

I turned.

No one was near.

I looked to the tent. He was blocked from my sight by his two colleagues depositing the next table in front of him. Here were two able-bodied boys carrying one table at a time from a pile fifty feet away. Stockman's privates lacked a certain sharpness and motivation. Which threw an odd light on the lug. This same guy setting up folding tables had been entrusted to slip in quietly backstage, armed, and keep an eye on Isabel Cobb. Had he fallen out of favor?

And it occurred to me: my special fear of him now was based on my having been at the theater in my own persona. But he didn't know that. He didn't know Cobb from Hunter from some other guy who just happened to see a play and give him some dirty looks. Maybe this would be okay.

The other two Blue Suits headed back to the pile of tables. My man was unfolding legs and not looking my way.

Okay.

I turned and moved to the stone fence.

The cliffs separated here at the shore and curved inland, the beach running into a narrow valley. Along the path to my right, out in front of the east wing of the house, the cliffs were high and sheer, heading down to Ramsgate.

I looked over my shoulder. The lug was standing behind a table he'd just set up. He was leaning there, looking out at me.

I turned fully around to him. I thought to take out a cigarette and light it, but the wind had brisked up a bit and I was afraid I'd have trouble with the match, which would, of course, ruin the effect. So I just leaned and stared back. And then I took a page out of Sir Martin the Gray Suit's book of etiquette. I gave the guy a nod.

He returned it.

I had no idea what it all meant.

But I figured I was free to stroll along, which I did, casually, like a house guest out sightseeing, following the curve of the fence and watching the waves on the Strait of Dover. What a swell day. What a swell castle. What a swell host. What a swell guest I was. I wanted to see if there'd likely be any problem sneaking in tonight through the window I'd unlatched.

I looked back. I was out of sight of everyone in the tents. I looked at the castle. This eastern wall held three massive bay windows. The library was behind the central one, directly before me. No doors anywhere on this side the house. No need for a Gray Suit to stand guard. All very reassuring. The flag flapped and drew my eyes up to it high on the tower to my left.

I turned and looked out east toward Belgium, seventy miles away beyond the horizon. Occupied Belgium. Ravaged and brutalized Belgium. Stockman's true countrymen—I was thinking of him definitively this way, guilty now until proven innocent—Stockman's boys in *feldgrau*, were in control over there. If he was working importantly on their behalf, how did they communicate?

The last German agent I'd dealt with, in my recent adventure on the *Lusitania* and beyond, relied on telegrams. That and his *Nuttall* handy one-volume encyclopedia.

The wind gusted up and the flag whopped behind and above me.

I turned one more time and looked at St. George's Cross laid over St. Andrew's Cross in our own red, white, and blue. And I looked at its pole lifting the flag to a point as high above the sea as a Chicago skyscraper. And I looked at those guy wires. And I realized what they'd been reminding me of without it reaching my conscious mind, the kind of thing that would have come to me only if I'd been in the white, metaphorizing heat of writing a story about this place. *The guy wires held the flagpole steady on the tower of Stockman House as if it were the telegraph mast on a great ship.*

Between antenna wires in the guys and wires in the pole, at this height, Stockman had plenty of telegraphic juice to make it to Brussels, if not all the way to Cologne and beyond.

The Union Jack thrashed at me. I knew I was looking at Sir Albert's wireless to Germany.

His office—his real office—had to be below, in the tower.

Now all I had to do was wait until the night came and my mother began to sing.

# 10

At twilight Stockman fed the throngs. By then upwards of five hundred people had been drifting around and lolling around or gathered around listening to the salon orchestra and, in the adjacent tent, to a dialect comic, after watching jugglers and a magician. A two-ring music hall. At the call to high tea they'd all queued into the lug's tent and emerged with substantial enough food on paper plates to make a working-class last meal of the day, which they took to the chairs or the picnic blankets or to the grass or the stone fence. I suspected the area east of the house, before the library, was now populated. I counted on my mother drawing them away when the time came.

As for the house guests—Isabel Cobb and Joseph W. Hunter included—we were gathered and brought to the courtyard and we took our high tea alfresco at temporary tables covered in linen behind a barricade of half a dozen Gray Suits. Pickled salmon and soused mackerel and sliced beef. Boiled eggs and cucumber sandwiches and radishes. Scones and marmalade and sponge cake.

Al and Isabel were side by side at the head of the table nearest the house. I was down the way, at a separate table, surrounded by a London banker, an Edinburgh banker, a Zurich banker, and their wives, who had much to say to each other, not knowing what to make of an American journalist. Which was fine with me. As the daylight waned I waited for a chance to have a few moments with the subject of my story.

I forced the issue as the dozen guests were in the midst of their sponge cake. I knew my mother would not be taking sponge cake. Particularly before performing. I rose, notebook drawn, and I crept toward her table. She was listening to one of the three Brits I'd passed in the Great Hall. He was bloviating about the French trying to run the show on the Western Front. She listened with her elbow on the table, her chin on her fist, declining to play the absolute lady, even in her role as Stockman's hostess. She knew her business. Stockman must have liked her this way. Stockman was also focused on the man, and I crept some more, letting my notebook show in my hand.

I drew near enough and she was bored enough that the movement drew her eyes. I stopped. She turned to Stockman and leaned to him and whispered a few words, in the midst of which he glanced my way. He nodded assent to her—making a pucker-mouthed, veiled-eye show of how *of course* it was all right—and she rose and came to me.

"Mr. Hunter," she said.

"Madam Cobb," I said.

"I'm sorry to have neglected you this evening," she said. "You could use some impressions for your story."

"Just a few," I said. "Before you perform tonight."

We said all this in our best stage whisper. Stockman heard it, though he was looking at the still-rambling speaker.

Isabel took me by the arm and guided me away, out of earshot of both the tables and the line of Gray Suits. We turned our bodies, however, toward Stockman. Nothing to hide.

I would take notes during every word she spoke. Scribble.

I said, "I have a pretty good hunch where to look in the house."

"He's nervous about something," she said. "He and his cohorts."

"About us?"

"I don't know. Maybe. I don't think so. He doesn't try to hide it. The demeanor of it."

"The public?"

"He talks offhandedly about *them*. No. The public's been here before. *This* he doesn't talk about. Not around me."

"Be that as it may . . ." I began.

"Do what you have to do," she said.

She was right about my gist. ". . . Tonight is likely my only chance," I finished.

"Where?"

"The tower."

"Doesn't surprise me."

"You see it?"

"Only the staircase," she said. "I didn't climb it, but I had a chance to look up and down."

"A guard?"

"Not that I saw. I think our man's comfortable in the house."

"Keep the show going tonight for as long as you can," I said.

"You know me when I sing," she said. "Keep applauding, I'll keep encoring."

"Keep encoring even if they don't applaud," I said.

She did a stagey spine stiffening. "You just do your job. I'll do mine," she said.

# 11

Night came without a moon and without stars as well, a high cloud cover sweeping in from the North Sea. The grounds fell dark. Stockman ordered standing torches lit, and he worked the spectators as this went on, sensing a trepidation in each newly lit set of faces and then encouraging them loudly. "These infernal machines will not darken our land!" he cried. He spoke to their fear of the Zeppelins, their hesitation to violate the local blackout. "Let us defy them tonight!" he cried. He repeated this appeal again and again, up close to them, to those who watched each torch flare into defiance. He was the British hero standing up to the Huns. He was with them, palpable in their midst. Whoever was within earshot of one of Stockman's miniature outbursts of patriotic oratory listened, rapt, and then cheered. And the word was circulated, as well, that a special surprise entertainment was imminent in the central marquee. His constituents, who'd dispersed for high tea, began to coalesce into a crowd and move toward the music tent to turn into an audience for Isabel Cobb.

I used this movement of many bodies from all parts of the ground to casually make my own way toward the eastern side of the house, where news of the entertainment had recently arrived. The lawn here was mostly empty now, only a few young couples left, tearing themselves away from the cliff edge to go to the show.

I drifted toward the house and stood for a time in the grass, watching the last of the lovers disappear around the corner. I looked all around now, peering hard into the darkness, seeing no one. And so I was also invisible.

I moved to the casement in the library bay window. I pressed at the sash. It opened. I climbed inside, pulled the sash closed, and stepped at once into the deeper darkness before me.

I stopped. I stood still for a moment to listen. In this room it was quiet enough for the silence to buzz faintly in my ears. My eyes were adjusting. A vague mitigation of the blackness came from outside, from the seepage of starlight through the clouds, from the nearby outglow of torchlight on the other side of the house. I could discern the door to the library. It was closed.

I moved to the door and opened it gently. I looked out. The Great Hall was empty and it was dim, lit only by the glow of the lanterns through the high west windows and by electric light spilling from the kitchen wing through the screens passage. I approached the wall beneath the music gallery, put my back to it, and eased along to the edge of the archway. I peeked into the courtyard entrance hall.

It was empty. The only person in sight had his back to me ten yards or so into the courtyard, beyond the open front doors. One of the Gray Suits. From his stature it could have been Martin.

The crowd outside cheered and clapped and fell silent.

No music yet.

I imagined Stockman making a little speech. He'd probably just mentioned the great Isabel Cobb.

I passed silently and quickly through the hall.

I drew my pistol and my flashlight and started up the wide, stone staircase, making myself take the steps one at a time with a soft, careful stride, holding back my impulse to rush, flashing my light onto each floor at the last moment of approach, pistol ready.

But there were no guards. Not at the second floor, not the third, not the fourth. Each floor was the same: immediately before me a carved oak door with a warded lock, a long corridor to the right along the wing, a blank wall a room's length to my left.

Now I was at the foot of the staircase to the fifth floor—the top of the house proper—and then I reached its landing. If my suspicion was correct about the tower, Stockman's office could very well be at the top of these last few steps, where it could easily wire up to the antenna. If a Gray Suit remained in the house, he'd be here.

I took the turn, and I could see nothing but pitch darkness at the top. I crept up, holding pistol and flashlight at the ready.

Distant now as if it were a memory, I heard another upswell of applause and hurrahing as the salon orchestra struck up the introductory bars of "Keep the Home Fires Burning." Mother was about to sing.

A clock started ticking in my head. I had to be back in the midst of the crowd before she took her last bow.

With the next step and now one more, I was ready for the light and I switched it on and shined it straight in front of me as I rushed the last few steps.

There was no guard.

And this time, no doorway before me either.

I scanned the light to the left.

There was the door, a couple of paces down the way.

This was the room directly beneath the tower. Before I moved to it, I shined the light way off to my right, down the long, empty corridor, and then back very near me, expecting the staircase to continue into the tower.

It did not.

Instead, where the staircase had turned on the floors below, here a stag's head hung on a wall over a vase sitting on a pedestal. There was no staircase going up.

So this door to my left was very likely Stockman's office. Which provided my best chance to learn something useful in this vast house with my limited time.

I moved down the hall and confronted the door. Like the ones below, it was oak. But it was not carved. A new door. A good sign. And it held a modern lock. Pin and tumbler. My favorite.

I holstered my Mauser, put myself before the lock, switched off the flashlight, and took out my packet of tools. A torque wrench and a pick. Though strictly speaking I no longer picked most locks. I raked them. I located the keyhole in the dark and bent to it and I slipped in the wrench, turned it gently to the right, worked the pick in all the way to the rear of the keyway. I levered the inner tip. Up went the back pin. And then I raked carefully but quickly along the other pins, pushing them into their columns. I felt most of them yield on the first pass. It was all feel now. No thinking. All about the fingertips. I delicately increased the wrench pressure and raked again. And the lock yielded. The door opened.

I pushed in, closed the door, put my tools away. The room was large. The footprint of the tower, I figured. The mullioned casement windows faced east and south, mostly filling those two walls, and were dim with the moonless night. I had to be careful about my flashlight.

But I did need it.

I let my eyes adjust, let them prepare to use what little outside glow there was. I could see the form of a massive desk set parallel to the wall that held the door to the room.

I moved to its opposite side, faced it, putting my back to the southern windows. The guards were more likely arrayed in that direction, with the south facade holding a major entrance to the castle. I was standing well away from any possible sight line from the ground. With my body blocking the beam, I switched the flashlight on.

From its top, the desk certainly seemed to be a working desk. Neatly kept, but it was in use. There was an electric table lamp; a crystal ink well with a dip-pen holder; a large, leather-edged desk pad with a blotter surface and the intense hieroglyphs of backward, superimposed, blotted words. In a wire basket sat a dozen pieces of mail addressed to Stockman, some of them by way of the House of Parliament, most of them to Stockman House or simply to his name and Margate. Or Broadstairs. Or Kent. One was stamped but addressed only to Sir Albert Stockman. A hodgepodge of hands, some elegant, some seeming barely literate. There was a comparable, empty basket. One for incoming mail and one for outgoing.

I circled the desk. I sat in the massive, polished oak rotary chair. I shined my light on the desk drawers, opening them one at time. They were filled with everyday things. Pen nibs. A staple fastener. A stash of mailing envelopes, unused. I looked in each, though from the first pull I knew I'd find nothing of importance: the drawers were all unlocked.

I rose. I stood away from the desk.

Of course this wouldn't be easy.

This was the MP's desk. His constituent desk.

His serious stuff could still be hidden elsewhere in the office. He saw this as a secure room, on a secure floor, in a secure house with a private army. I shined my light toward the western wall. Half a dozen four-drawer filing cabinets. Wooden. Clearly also unlocked. He had a file on everybody in his constituency. He had files on his other MPs. Whatever else. And a set of files in there somewhere, perhaps, revealing his unholy ties to Germany but hiding in plain sight. It could take all night to find them.

Applause and cheers wafted faintly into the room from far away.

And the music again. Some damn music hall ditty. Mother would play that one to the hilt.

I turned my light to the wall behind the desk. I'd noted vaguely that it was full of books. My light went to these high shelves, to the top, at the far left, and I began quickly to scan, my hand doing this almost on its own, disappointed from the library downstairs. Codes still in my head, I supposed.

More sets. Sets and sets. Law books here. And then some other sets. Kentish matters no doubt. Sets on agriculture. Sets about hops and cherries and cattle and fish and whatever else.

I was scanning down the center section now, directly behind the desk. Sets. Sets. I needed to look elsewhere.

And then the books abruptly changed.

79

Not sets. Odd volumes, a whole row of them, directly behind and slightly above the desk chair.

I circled the desk again.

I looked at titles.

*The British Almanac and Family Cyclopaedia.*

*Appleton's Annual Cyclopaedia.*

*The Dictionary of English History.*

· *The New International Year Book* for 1913.

I had not seen a set of *The New International Encyclopaedia*. Even if there was one somewhere, its yearbook was separated. These were all books that made finding words easy. They all went from A to Z. Code books for telegraph messages.

My flashlight moved on. Quickly. Past several volumes. I knew what I was looking for. And there it was.

*The Nuttall Encyclopaedia of Universal Information.*

The books were set in here as they were downstairs. And on that quarter of an inch of exposed shelf in front of *Nuttall* was a thin layer of dust.

Since I last knew it to be the book of the week or month or whatever the interval of use was, the Huns had moved on from this *Concise and Comprehensive Dictionary of General Knowledge* edited meticulously by the good Rev. James Wood. It was my first German code book and I felt a little nostalgic for it. How sad for its dusty lip.

I went back and wrote all these titles in my notebook. The German library of telegraphic code books. This was a good night's work in itself.

The second time through, something finally registered on me that I'd rushed past looking specifically for *Nuttall*. An empty space.

After recording all the titles, I returned to it. By the width of one volume, the shelf was wiped clean all the way through the outer lip.

A recent withdrawal.

One code book wasn't here.

And now the obvious thought, delayed by my focus on documents, finally struck me: the wireless set wasn't here either.

Its antenna was directly above me.

I looked up into the dark.

There had to be a room above this office.

The question was how to get there.

And something else struck me at last. I turned my light back to the western wall and the line of filing cabinets. I'd assumed the entrance door to this office was farther east than the entrance doors on lower floors because this room was larger. It wasn't. That wall my white light was drilling into was too close. This room was not a footprint of the tower. It was too small.

I rose. I moved to the end filing cabinet. It was set six inches or so from the wall, as were all these cabinets. I shined my light behind them. Solid wall.

I moved to the door. But before I opened it, I looked back to the western wall. I put the heel of my foot at the edge of the doorjamb and did a yard-stride to the corner. Five paces. About fifteen feet.

I went back to the door. I put my hand to the knob.

I turned stupid. I opened the door and stepped out and immediately before me the shadows had bulked up into the form of a man.

Before I could even twitch I felt the barrel of a pistol press into the dead center of my gut.

Outside, the crowd cheered.

# 12

"This is just to keep you from being stupid," a cigarette-blasted British voice said, pushing a little on the pistol.

"Too late," I said.

"Very well," he said. "From *carrying on* being stupid."

"That's big of you," I said.

"Very slowly upend that light of yours and have a look at me," he said.

I did. The beam came at a sharp angle from below, turning him into a chiaroscuro: a wide, central, corpse-white stripe of a face surrounded by a night-black skull.

It was the lug from the Duke of York's.

"Mr. Catwalk," I said.

"Mr. Front Row," he said.

"You prowl for your boss, I take it," I said.

"And who do you fancy my boss to be?" he said.

"Stockman."

"You are mistaken, Mr. Cobb," he said, his voice pitched down and sounding convincing.

I tried to place this guy in the class system. He sounded, at turns, cultured and working class, never quite either, which meant he was the latter with extended exposure to the former.

It struck me. "You're Buffington's man."

"Lord Buffington," he corrected.

"You're the guy in the vicinity."

"Very near," he said. "Thanks to the baronet's need for a bit of outside assistance."

"At the theater then, you were what?"

"Watching over Isabel Cobb. You and I are on the same side, sir."

"I'd be more inclined to believe you," I said, "if you'd take the pistol off the center of my gut."

"I'm terribly sorry," he said, and the barrel end vanished at once in a twisting of his body and a ruffling of his suit coat.

"You seem to be doing well," he said.

"Did you know about the tower?"

"No sir. I just followed you through the window."

"Bloody hell," I said. "If you don't mind my borrowing a phrase."

"Please," he said.

"Another case of stupid. I wasn't even aware," I said.

"Not at all. I had the advantage of knowing exactly who you are and what you're up to."

"Which I need to resume," I said.

"Of course. But I had to let you know who I am and that I'm at your service."

"And who are you?"

"Sorry," he said. "Jeremy."

"Kit," I said and we shook hands.

"Unless you have a specific task for me," Jeremy said, "I think I'd do better to linger downstairs. If someone is to get caught at this, it should be me. You need to keep your identity intact."

"But no getting caught," I said.

"I'll do my best."

Jeremy half turned to go and then had a thought. He stopped and squared around to me again. "I am obliged to stress, however. If things do get rough, you are to take the opportunity to endeavor a quiet retreat. On no account intervene on my behalf."

I didn't like that thought. If we were on the same team, I was reluctant to duck out on him.

"This is imperative," he said.

I knew I'd be saying the same thing in his place. "All right," I said. And he was gone. As quietly as he'd followed me.

I was left with a tower above me and no staircase to get there.

I returned to the doorway of Stockman's office. I put my heel at the door frame and paced off the five yards. I kept my foot on the spot and took note of where it was: directly across from the left-hand banister.

I paced on, doing the stride I knew to equal about a yard. Seven more to the door of the next room. A little over twenty feet.

I expected this door to give itself away with a pin and tumbler lock. I was wrong. The room had one of the carved oak doors with a simpler warded lock. I drew out my tools. I had half a dozen skeleton keys. On the second try I had the right one. The locking bolt gave way and I opened the door.

I stood beneath the lintel while I shined my flashlight toward this room's left-hand wall, which should have been shared with Stockman's office. Then I leaned back and looked down to the banister opposite that western wall in the office. I didn't need any more measurements. I stepped inside this room, closed the door. The wall before me should have been twenty feet away. It was maybe half that. Against it, left of center, was a massive wardrobe of plain, squared oak built flush to the floor and taller than a man, its only ornamentation being large, beaten-iron hinges and drawer pulls. Of its wide facade—a good twelve feet—the two outer sections were drawers and half-cabinets.

The major center section was a pair of doors. Their small ward lock yielded quickly and I opened them to a thick atmosphere of cedar and moth-balls. Inside, the space was wide enough and tall enough to hang the longest ball gown, but in spite of the smells to protect clothes in storage, it was empty. I had little doubt what was next. The back of the wardrobe was hung with a black cloth.

I stepped in. The cloth split in the middle into a pair of drapes that ran easily open on metal hooks along a heavy curtain rod.

And they revealed the doorway to the tower. This was unconventional castle architecture. Sir Albert's granddad had been either paranoid or up to something covert himself. The door was what I'd expected for the room. It was like the one on Stockman's office, and with the same sort of lock. Made by the same locksmith, I figured, for it felt familiar to my fingertips and the pin tumblers all jumped at my first bidding.

I opened the door inward to blackness. I closed the wardrobe behind me, and I stepped into chilled air smelling of damp stone and of all the spores that grow in the dark. I ran the drapes together and shut the door. I shined my light onto a metal staircase commencing immediately to my left and circling its way upward.

I climbed.

About ten feet I reckoned, and I came to another metal platform. The staircase continued up, to the roof of the tower, no doubt, but I stood before a rough-hewn wooden door. No more picking. This one had no lock. No knob either. Just a latch, which I lifted.

And now I stood in the upper room of the Stockman House tower and searched with my flashlight, keeping it angled low to prevent its being visible from outside, straining my eyes to see into the dim edge of spill from its beam.

On the eastern wall, directly before me, was a single, centered, cruciform loophole, which was used in a functioning castle for safe viewing and medieval sniper fire, the shape to accommodate a cross-bow, not the Christian God.

I knew all four walls had loopholes because I'd seen them from the outside, but only the one in the eastern wall was visible now in full. The west-facing loophole was in the well of the circular staircase. The other two, in this room, were each shuttered by a wooden door on hinges and a hook and eye. The shutter for the eastern loophole was open.

The shutters were probably a Stockman renovation, so he could work up here at night and not show it. The electric lighting was certainly his doing. A stand-up lamp stood in the center of the floor beside a library table big enough to lay out the corpse of even the tall Sir Albert.

The wireless telegraph setup was certainly his doing.

There it was, as expected, a jumble of condensers and transformers, tuning coil and induction coil, ammeter and helix, antenna switch and spark discharger. And at the uncluttered front edge of the table were the two things the jumble served: the transmission key and the head phones.

This was where Sir Albert Stockman transmitted and received coded messages with his bosses in Germany and his underlings wherever they were lurking.

In considering the wireless, the object that had led me here, I'd taken some steps toward it at an angle past the library table. I knew there were other objects of interest on the tabletop, and I turned my beam to them now.

A stack of books on the near end.

That much I'd seen out of the corner of my eye and I expected more. There was a stray volume near the center, but the table was otherwise clear.

I stepped to the wireless table, hoping to find a notebook or a scrap of paper with a message. There was nothing. The key block was even squared up to the edge of the table; the headset's wire was neatly coiled.

I knew Al, understood his ways. I needed to be careful to leave everything precisely as it now was. And this thought made me visualize his next visit here, which reminded me of the clock ticking in my head.

I clenched off the next breath.

I could not hear the orchestra. Had they finished? Had Stockman shut this thing down quick?

But I was, after all, in a flint tower six storeys above and five hundred feet away from that plinky little sextet and that middle-aged voice. Still, all I could hear was the accelerating beat of my heart and the heavy hiss of the silence in Stockman's aerie.

I moved to the northern loophole and opened the wooden shutter. I leaned in, as if to fire an arrow, and turned my ear to the opening.

And yes. The sound of strings faintly drifted this high and slipped in through the slit in the stone. I could not hear her voice, but she was out there singing. At the moment, about how long a way it was to Tipperary.

I closed the shutter, strode to the eastern loophole, and closed its shutter as well. I returned to the table in the center of the room. I switched on the reading lamp, extinguished my flashlight, stuffed it into my pocket, sat on a bent-wood chair.

I put my hand to the stack of books, which also had been squared up to the edge of the table.

I took up each, one by one, thumbed them, looking for marks. All that they yielded were their titles.

*The System of British Weather of the British Islands.*

*The Weather of the British Coasts.*

*The Fourth Report on Wind Structure* published by the Authority of the Meteorological Council.

*Surface Wind Structure Analysis.* This one from His Majesty's Advisory Committee for Aeronautics.

And another big seller from the Brits' meteorological boys: *The Beaufort Scale of Wind-Force, Being a Report of the Director of the Meteorological Office upon an Inquiry into the Relation Between the Estimates of Wind-Force According to Admiral Beaufort's Scale and the Velocities Recorded by Anemometers Belonging to the Office.*

I restacked the books precisely.

And then, the one stray book near the center of the table: *The Britannica Year-Book 1913.* Not stray, really. Simply separate, for it too had been placed with a squared-up kind of precision.

This book I understood at once. It was the present code book for the Germans.

I carefully noted its position, its orientation, and I pulled it before me. Not much larger than a novel, dusky green, twelve hundred onionskin thin pages. I opened it and thumbed for hand notes. No words. But occasionally the first two or three or last two or three letters of a word were underlined in pencil. On page 27, about the Balkan War: *ag* was underlined in *against*; *ste* in *step*; *ity* in *inability*. The Germans' numbered codes—indicating page and line and word—probably had a way to indicate whole words, but they could also spell out words in a pinch or a rush. I tried to fit these underlinings together, forward and backward, just to make sure, but my suspicion was soon confirmed: they were simply highlighted here for quick use.

I put the book back exactly where it had been and, unaware I was even doing it, I stretched out my left leg. I heard a soft clatter onto the floor. I got up, circled the table.

Several pieces of wide, heavy paper, rolled together, were lying on their side near where they'd no doubt been sitting on end, beneath the table. I picked them up, spread them carefully in the light on the tabletop.

They were three contiguous ordnance survey maps, tracking the Thames River from the Isle of Thanet, County Kent, to London.

No marks.

Precious little else here.

I rolled the maps together once more and placed them standing on the floor beneath the table where I reckoned they'd been.

I returned to the chair, set it in its previous place, put my hands on the top of its cane back, and leaned a little against it.

Had I missed something in this room? I looked around. It was bare but for the two tables. I imagined Stockman sitting in this chair alone, shut off from the world, high above the sea, in this circle of pale yellow light, in his wooden chair, reading. These books. Other books that were gone now. Deciphering telegrams from Berlin. Happy in the quiet. Fussily keeping the edges of things straight. Planning. Planning what?

Winds and weather didn't quite add up.

If there was nothing more than this, I could think on these things later. I needed to go. Joe Hunter needed to be protected.

I switched off the stand-up lamp.

I moved to the eastern loophole, unhooked it, opened it, as it was when I arrived.

Though it was still a very small sound, I heard it at once. Coming through the loophole from the east, from out in the strait.

The sound of an engine.

From *over* the strait, I realized.

I could hear the distant drone of gasoline engines. I was willing to bet they were Maybachs, two-hundred horsepower each, attached in fours to Zeppelins. Stockman's bravado at the torch lighting buzzed into my head along with them. He knew they were coming. They knew where he was. He was lighting their way into the mouth of the Thames.

I went out of the tower room, but I did not descend. I went up the inner staircase and emerged through an upright metal door set in a stone enclosure built into the courtyard corner of the parapet. I moved toward the eastern wall, passing beneath my daylong landmark, the massive Union Jack. I looked up as I went by. The flag hung straight down, barely stirring. It was a perfect night for the Zepps. No moon, a high ceiling, the air gone almost still.

I stood at the parapet and looked into the thin gruel of the night. I could hear the orchestra again, distantly, from up here in the open. It was directly behind me, playing "There's a Long, Long Trail." Mother was still working on the wartime standards. She hadn't even begun to encore.

She and the crowd were about to get a fright.

I strained to hear the engines above the music. And there they were. Nearer now. The drone had become a hammering, the piston fire itself almost distinguishable. I strained to see them. And then the stars were moving and then I realized with a quick grab in my throat just how low the Zeppelins were and how near, and they were rushing this way, still only a few dollops of light, perhaps from their undercarriages, but also a vast thickening of the dark above.

Though the Zepps would not drop a bomb on Sir Albert's house, though we were their beacon, their allies, though we were Albert's big show, my hands pressed hard against the stone of the parapet with a terrible realization. These vast flying machines hammering our way, invisible against the dark and carrying a ton of incendiaries, these were the ghosts of future warfare, death from the sky, death that one day could reach to every home, every parlor, every crib, in every nation on the planet. This was mankind's fate pounding its way toward us on a moonless night.

All these things were what my hands knew as they clung futilely to a rock.

And now I felt a quick stirring of the air as a dark mass drew very near, its palpable invisibility pressing against my eyes, and I began to lift my face as it came, no more than a hundred yards above where I stood, and it was quick, it was over the beach and then the cliff and then I was looking up, up, and the air was thrashing, sucking the breath from me, and I was looking directly up as the sky vanished in a grimy dark and then a gondola with lit windows slid over me and the engines combusted in my head and the propellers clacked, and the Zeppelin passed over the castle and passed and passed and passed, as long as a steamship on the Atlantic, and the rear gondola drew its lights over me, and I turned to watch, and the flag was lifting a bit in the currents of the Maybachs, as if the Union Jack were actually thinking of waving for this infernal machine. But it was Stockman's Union Jack, of course.

And the band stopped playing abruptly and there were cries from the green and now another pounding, behind me, and I turned and a second Zeppelin was approaching, slightly to the north, and I could see the lit windows of the commander's gondola as it passed and I could see figures moving there.

Wind structure and the system of British weather and the path to London along the Thames. This was what Sir Albert Stockman was about. These machines. And the second Zepp droned on by and the orchestra started up playing. I recognized the tune. "Nearer, My God, to Thee." The song the newspapers all reported the *Titanic's* salon orchestra played as the ship sank. Courage is an odd thing. In this case, given the actual circumstances, it could seem a foolish thing, a hysterical thing, a cheap imitation, a grimly ironic joke. Except these boys didn't know the circumstances. They were trying to calm a crowd's panic in the face of disaster. It was probably irritating the hell out of Stockman, whose carefully prepared, courageous oratory was being drowned out by some hired musicians stealing his thunder with a hymn.

I needed to rouse myself from all this. The time was right to get downstairs as fast as I could and slip into the crowd during all the uproar.

I crossed the tower, entered the stairwell, circled downward. I caught myself rushing. I couldn't put haste over caution. I slowed as I neared the bottom platform, made my footfalls soft. I stepped back and away as I pulled open the door from the wardrobe. Gently.

I was glad I did.

I heard voices.

I pocketed my flashlight and drew my Mauser.

Muffled still, these voices. Not moving. I drew back one side of the curtain to the inner darkness of the wardrobe. I did not trust the wooden floorboard to take my weight silently. I leaned in as far as I could, turning my ear to listen.

Martin's voice.

Jeremy's voice.

They were both speaking German.

# 13

The button to release the Mauser's safety sat right beneath my thumb. I pushed it.

*Joe Hunter may have to die so that Kit Cobb has a chance to live. I'll shoot my way out.*

The button and the thought happened instantly, simultaneously, before I could make out the German words being spoken.

Then there was a scuffling of feet.

The voices were closer.

Jeremy said, "You and I are on the same side."

He'd said the same thing to me, in English. I tried to decide in which language it sounded true.

Martin didn't seem to be buying it. "Let's look upstairs," he said. "Through the wardrobe. Move."

The words and the tone made it clear he'd disarmed Jeremy and was holding a pistol in his back. If Jeremy was indeed working for the Huns, he was covert enough that Martin hadn't been apprised. But maybe Jeremy was like me. He had this skill. He knew German. I'd tell the same lie if Albert's henchman got the drop on me while I was trying to delay him.

I backed out of the curtain, softly slid it shut, closed the door. I went up. Quietly. Quickly. To the tower room? There was nowhere to hide in there. There was no way to take out Martin when they entered without almost certainly losing Jeremy anyway. And Jeremy said not to intervene. I'd promised not to intervene. Rightly, given his mission and mine. But I wasn't comfortable with that either. Still, the wireless room was a losing hand.

And if Jeremy was telling the truth to Martin about working for the Germans, in the wireless room I'd have to figure that out in some very unpleasant way I could not control.

I went up farther, all the way to the telephone booth–size access enclosure on the roof. I stepped into the space beside the door and listened down the stairway well.

Footsteps on the stairs. No attempt to move quietly.

Martin didn't seem to expect to find a cohort up here.

He wanted to check to see if anything had been disturbed in the wireless room. Signs that Jeremy had been in there.

Footsteps now on the landing below, a door opening, no sound of a door closing, a muffled shuffling of feet receding into the room, a brief murmuring of voices.

I straightened, leaned back against the stone wall.

If Jeremy was truly working for the Huns, he would've done something other than what he did when he'd caught me. He had his pistol in my gut. He sent me on my way. It was his confrontation with Martin that was a problem for him.

I had to assume Jeremy was Buffington's man.

But there was nothing I could do to help downstairs.

He expected that I was escaping right now, with Martin diverted into the wireless room.

I should have been. But that choice had passed.

If the two went back down the steps from there, I could wait for a time and then slip out. I'd have to let Jeremy manage his own fate, as he'd signed up to do, as he'd insisted I let him do.

Martin clearly had the drop on Jeremy.

I realized how little I actually knew of Buffington's operation. Or, of course, Stockman's. Trask probably knew less than he thought, as well. Maybe Stockman had let Jeremy this far into his operation in order to trap him. His fate might already have been sealed.

In which case, Martin could be bringing him to this roof to take care of things. At least to hold him till the crowds went away.

I had no play down the stairs.

I thought of the roof.

I became aware of the wall I was leaning against.

And now voices rose through the stairwell.

"Up we go," Martin said. In English.

Jeremy didn't respond.

I unlatched the door to the roof, the sound masked in the clatter of their footsteps, and I stepped out and closed the door behind me. I circled around to my right and pressed my back against the outer wall of the enclosure. I laid my shooting hand against my chest, the Mauser barrel lying upon my heart.

I waited.

The Zeppelins were barely audible now, flying away up the Thames. The crowd was silent. Stockman was probably orating. I just hoped the music would resume.

Footsteps rasping now onto the stone floor of the enclosure.

I held my breath.

The door latch clacked.

I lifted my Mauser.

Over the past few minutes my eyes had grown accustomed to the dark. I turned my face to the left.

I heard the door open and close.

"Go that way," Martin said. "No quick movements."

And Jeremy appeared, moving off to the right at an angle heading inward onto the roof, toward the flagpole.

Now Martin followed, his right hand lifted into Jeremy's spine. I saw the side of his face from a sharp angle to the rear.

I turned away from the wall and made one quick, soft step forward and another and I pressed the muzzle of my Mauser against Martin's occipital bone.

"No movement at all," I said.

He stopped.

Jeremy did not give him time to figure out the situation. He spun off from the pistol and grabbed Martin's shooting wrist while I pushed the Mauser at the Hun's head just for good measure. Albert's boy wasn't going to do anything stupid, even if he cared about his mission. He was figuring Jeremy and I would have our hands full downstairs. Which we would.

Jeremy had Martin's pistol now and he stepped back in front of him.

I kept my Mauser where it was.

Martin still hadn't gotten a glimpse of me, but I regretted letting him hear my voice. At least I should have spoken German. He probably knew who had the drop on him. I had to assume he did. Which was why I was supposed to have simply slipped away into the night.

Jeremy gave me a look. He shifted the pistol to his left hand, and he drew back his right leg, his body angling that way into a boxer's stance. I knew what was next.

I pulled my pistol away.

And Jeremy threw a hell of an overhand right into Martin's jaw.

The Hun flew back hard and was out cold even before he slammed down in front of the door.

The salon orchestra began to play.

Jeremy and I both briefly turned our faces to it.

"This will make things a little easier for you," he said, lifting his chin toward the music.

"And for you."

"We shall see," he said.

He looked my way again, and I said, "Nice right hand. Were you a pro?"

He nodded a small, slow nod of regret.

"I bet you were good," I said.

"I once went sixteen rounds with Tommy Ryan."

"And?"

"He was prepared to go seventeen."

"Jeremy what?"

"Miller."

"Did you fight in the States?"

"You bet," he said. "For a couple of years. Philly and New York and points west."

This made sense of a little bit of American that sometimes crept into his mix of accents and phrasing and lingo.

"Chicago?" I asked.

"Never made it there."

I liked this guy Miller. He stirred the reporter in me. I wanted to sit him down and talk a while and do a story on an ex-boxer who gave one of the greatest middleweights of all time a run for his money and then turned into a British spy. And I'd have bet good money that his family name was once Müller.

But he and I had other work to do.

"What about our boy Martin here?" I said, nodding toward him.

"How compromised might you presently be with Stockman?" Jeremy said.

"Remains to be seen," I said. "There's a big crowd. He's got his own agenda. If he didn't go looking for me and if I wasn't observed sneaking around, I could have innocently been out of his sight all this time."

Jeremy nodded. He looked down at Martin. "He knows too much about both of us." He stepped nearer to me, and his voice turned as serious as that right hand. "You need to slip back into the crowd now, and then make certain Stockman sees you. After the music ends, stay visible and be patient. I'll divert any possible suspicion from you."

He paused.

He was waiting for my assent. I wondered what his plan might be, particularly for himself after an effective diversion. I thought about trying to help.

He figured that out. "You defied me once, Mr. Cobb. I won't say I was not grateful. But we have to be professional now."

He gave me only the briefest moment of silence to respond before saying, "We have no time for this."

"I understand," I said. I did.

Jeremy tucked his pistol away and moved past me to Martin. He bent and grabbed the Hun by the coat and shirt and lifted the man half off the ground, twisted him around, and flung him down again as if he were a gunnysack of lettuce greens.

I stepped to the door and opened it.

"Mr. Cobb," Jeremy said.

I turned.

"Kit," I said.

"Kit," he said. "I'm grateful."

"As am I," I said.

And I was into the stairwell and circling downward.

# 14

I made it all the way into the Great Hall without seeing anyone. I wouldn't chance crossing the courtyard. I needed to give the appearance that I'd been on the grounds throughout Isabel Cobb's concert. I would trust that Sir Albert had delegated any suspicions to Martin and the boys and was keeping his own attention on his actress and his acting.

I crossed to the library, which remained dark. I slipped in and went to the casement and opened it gently. I looked out. This eastern lawn seemed empty. Jeremy had somehow kept himself hidden here. But he'd had inside information.

I climbed out and pulled the window to.

I strolled now. Casually. I went to the stone wall at the cliff's edge. I followed it north, and the only Gray Suits that gradually became visible were far away, guarding the north entryways to the house. A distant passerby was nothing they would automatically care about.

I followed the curve of the wall past the service wing, past the high-tea tent, and walked toward the music.

The marquee was lit inside by electrical light, the seats packed and the place ringed by standees. Mother had begun her encores. The orchestra was playing a song she could overact to her hammy heart's content. "Some of These Days." It was ridiculous, accompanied by strings and a salon-tempoed piano. Her acting talent was being challenged, no doubt, so as to hide her murderous feelings toward her accompanists.

I could see now, above the heads, the back of the pianist and his upright in front of him. Not Mother, who would be at the center of the stage.

But I began to hear her voice.

Not the words quite yet but her voice, floating out of the tent on a cloying cloud of strings and trying to keep its honky-tonk edge.

The torches were blazing still.

The standees were a welcome sight. The crowd was large and disorganized at the edges. Stockman surely was in the middle of all that. From his limited vantage point he might be willing to believe I'd been around all this time.

My mother's voice clarified now, as she moved into the chorus. She sang, "Some of these days, you'll miss me, honey."

I hesitated in the dark, just outside the torchlight.

"Some of these days, you'll feel so lonely."

I looked along the tent line in both directions. No Gray Suits.

"You're gonna miss my huggin'. You're gonna miss my kissin'."

I moved past the torches now and approached the backs of the standees who were even with the stage.

"You're gonna miss me, honey, when I'm far away."

I peeked between the heads and there, in a front row center folding chair, sat Stockman, his face lifted to Mama.

I didn't even have to shift around to see her. I knew she was singing straight to him.

I backed off, beyond the torches, and I waited for the show to come to a close, not really listening to the music, my mother's voice familiar in the way that a twenty-year-old memory that hadn't come up for about nineteen years would be familiar. Jeremy came and went in my head. He was a pro. He was doing what he knew best to do in the way he wanted to do it. I didn't have to think for him, didn't have to save him. Stockman wanted to come into my head, wanted to rehearse my imminent encounter with him, but if I started scripting myself for Stockman, I'd end up *sounding* scripted, sounding like a liar. I needed to improvise. As if with Mama and me on a train. I stood and waited and now the crowd was applauding and some of the standees were starting to peel off.

I slipped forward, took a standing place at the edge of the tent but a few rows behind Stockman.

Mother was bowing.

I thought: *If they keep applauding, she'll keep singing.*

But Stockman stood up as he clapped. She saw him. She recognized her cue to ring down the curtain. I saw her hands flip down a little. She'd been on the verge of raising them to stop the applause and cue the orchestra and keep on going. But she knew this was Sir Albert's show.

A Blue Serge had appeared at Stockman's side and handed over a bundle of red roses. Stockman headed for the steps up to the platform.

Isabel Cobb rolled her head to project the rolling of her eyes over the applause and she flared her hands, aw-shucksing to beat the band.

Others in the audience were rising too, especially the swells in attendance, seasoned theatergoers accustomed to giving a standing ovation to a famous actress. A small handful of the other folks were starting to slip away, just on the fringes. An outer-edge chair opened up in front of me, still to the rear of where Stockman had been sitting. I stepped forward and slipped in before the chair, as if I'd been there all along.

I applauded.

Stockman presented the roses and the applause surged and Isabel Cobb did her flourishing bow to the crowd, the one with a touch of the forehead and then a rolling hand salute descending as she bent deep.

All this good feeling went on for a while. Then at last the applause waned and Stockman stepped forward, the expert emcee, and just as the clapping stopped he announced in a throbbing tenor projected effortlessly as far as the very back row, "Thank you again, one and all, for coming tonight. Before we part, I ask everyone to rise to your feet so that we might honor our king and our country."

Stockman motioned to the orchestra—this had clearly been arranged beforehand—and they began to play "God Save the King."

As everyone rose, Stockman strode to the front edge of the stage and began to sing loudly, guiding the lyrics to the slightly different, earliest version of the song, from 1745, having his ironic little joke on his constituents, sounding as if he were a rabid British patriot, as if he were restoring the original words to personally address King George V, as if he were singing to this present monarch leading the country in its war with Germany while in fact he was singing to George II, born in Hanover, the second German king of England.

"God save great George our king," he sang and the crowd joined him as one vast voice.

This had not, however, been arranged beforehand with Mother.

"Long live our noble king."

She gave Stockman one small, unveiled glance: *You bastard, whose spotlight do you think you're stealing?*

"God save the king."

The crowd was joining in boisterously now, singing in defiance of the Huns and their gas bags.

"Send him victorious."

The Huns' secret gas bag smiled as he bellowed, even as his voice was absorbed into the crowd's.

"Happy and glorious."

Isabel Cobb was back in character, singing along, smiling all around.

"Long to reign over us."

The orchestra was slowing the tempo. This was the big climax.

The voices filled and stretched at the tent like hydrogen in an airship: "God save the king."

The music stopped, the voices stopped, the place light-switched into silence, and then, one beat later, flared into cheers.

Stockman lifted both his hands high above his head as if the adulation was all for him and then bloomed them outward like a chorus girl as he took a deep bow.

Perhaps no one else could read her as I could. Certainly no one was particularly aware of her at that moment. But Mama gave this guy a look that laid bare her true, undramatized desire: to put her foot in the middle of Sir Albert Stockman's backside and launch him off the platform and into about the fourth row.

# 15

I kept standing where I was as the cheers faded and the applause smattered to a stop and everyone politely took their cue and shuffled away into the night, where they were no doubt watched and herded by suits both gray and blue. I kept standing and applauding, though more slowly now, softly, head angled smilingly to the side to portray the personal accolade of an insider.

Stockman had hastened back to my mother as soon as the crowd began to disperse and was no doubt praising her lavishly. He was no fool. And great actress that she was, she showed no trace of her recent—and surely still lingering—feelings.

She was the first to notice me, turning her face my way and show-ing, to the extent she dared, her get-me-the-hell-away-from-this-man pleasure at my presence. Her turn prompted Stockman to turn.

I lifted the mimed applause to him and nodded in deference. He gave me a noblesse oblige smile that warmed my heart for the mo-ment. This did not strike me as the smile of a man who regarded me with newly formed suspicions.

I was wrong, however, to feel safe quite yet.

Something slithered its way out of him as the three of us walked from the marquee together, heading toward the courtyard and the house, the other weekend guests following loosely behind, the strag-gler constituents floating past us in the dark, bowing in quiet thanks and deference toward their host.

Stockman ignored them all.

He said to me, "I looked for you during our little interruption."

"I'm a reporter," I said. "I heard the engines before most everyone else and I knew what they were and I slipped into the night to see the airships and capture them in words."

"Indeed," he said.

"Don't forget who you're supposed to be writing about," my mother said.

Stockman and I both looked to her.

He chuckled.

I said, "But of course."

I still was not quite sure Stockman accepted my absence. A few minutes earlier I'd prepared for this. At the foot of the stage, Stockman had broken half a dozen steps away to speak to the Gray Suit with the boxer's nose, who'd suddenly appeared. I wondered if they were speaking of Martin, and I worried, for a flash, about Jeremy, but I'd put that aside to have a quick word with my mother. I asked her for a sentence or two from his declamation to the crowd upon the arrival of the Zeppelins.

I played that card now. "I didn't go so far away that I missed your eloquence," I said, and I quoted him. "'We will shake our fists at the sky and we will not run. Our courage will not be shaken.'"

Stockman looked at me. He smiled. "I'm happy you recorded that."

"Naturally," I said.

He was reassured about my attendance, but I recognized the tight-rope he walked in public. It was possible he'd be a little apprehensive about his local attitude being portrayed abroad.

Quickly I added, "Not that I would quote you for my American readers. Your eloquence was to quell a panic, not to legitimize a foreign policy."

"Quite so," he said.

We were approaching torchlight and he and I exchanged a glance that lingered an extra beat, and another, as if we had an understanding.

Beneath my feet the grass abruptly became macadam as we entered the drive in front of the courtyard.

I turned my face to the house.

I'd done what I needed to do. I figured I was square with Sir Albert. Jeremy didn't know that.

The macadam turned to fieldstone and we took our first steps into the courtyard and my gaze was ahead but my attention was on my thoughts, and so it came into my sight simply as movement, quick movement from above, off to the right, a mass plummeting downward and then the heavy thud of it, the thud and cracking, and my mother let out a sharp bark of a scream and I looked now directly at what had fallen and I saw a body hunched into the ground as if it had been trying desperately to dig into the earth but had failed terribly and was resting now, the head twisted sharply away, however, its neck snapped. The body wore a gray suit and was hatless and its hair was spiky and yellow in the electric light. It was Martin, of course.

Martin, Stockman's head tough guy, dead now, but by a hand that was other than mine. That diversion of suspicion was what Jeremy had just given me. Martin was a dead man as soon as he'd seen Jeremy's face and heard my voice.

Stockman turned around at once to the rest of the weekend guests, who'd bunched up close behind. "Stay away," he commanded and then he strode off toward the body.

Two Gray Suits were hustling from the house in his direction.

As Joseph W. Hunter it was better for me to hang back. I was just a guest.

And Isabel Cobb needed me now.

I stepped to her.

Her bundle of roses was lying at her feet.

I put my arm around her shoulders. She was trembling.

"What have we gotten into?" my mother whispered to me.

# 16

For a few moments we just stood like that. Neither Joe Hunter nor I knew what to say to Isabel Cobb.

She trembled on.

Finally I whispered, "It's all just melodrama. You've played this a thousand times."

"Don't be a fool," she said.

She was right.

"Okay," I said. "It's life. But we're acting in it. We can do this."

She nodded.

She lifted her face. But not to me.

I felt a shudder pass through her.

And her trembling stopped, as if the curtain had just risen and she was on.

I followed her gaze.

Stockman was heading this way. He was looking at me as if through rifle sights, me standing with my right shoulder tucked behind her left and my arm enveloping her, pulling her close. I was very lucky that I'd not actually taken her into my arms, even in the chaste way I would have, as any son might have when his mother was suddenly terrified. This tableau was bad enough, as far as Stockman was concerned, as far as his intended woman and this snoopy journalist were concerned.

Mother knew the look. She broke away from me at once, rushed forward to meet Stockman, whose body paused for her, whose arms opened for her, even as his severe gaze remained on me.

She threw herself into his arms with a flurry of words.

"Oh Albert, what's happened to that poor man? Is he dead? And where did you go? It's a good thing Mr. Hunter was nearby. He held me up when I was about to faint. I was swooning away."

She looked back to me from Stockman's chest. "I'm sorry to have frightened you like that, Mr. Hunter. Thank you."

She was a pro. She was convincing.

She laid her head on his chest again. "Can you take me away from this now, Albert?"

His gaze upon me went more or less neutral just before he looked down at Mother. "Of course, my dear."

For good measure, she wobbled suddenly at the knees, threatened to slide from his arms.

Stockman held her closer, held her up. "Be strong," he said. "My people will take care of this. We can go in now."

"Yes," she said. "Please." She pulled away from him just enough to put her arm in his and begin to turn him.

He gave me one more look. Grudging. I'd touched his woman, even if it was innocently. But he seemed ready to overlook this.

I nodded at him.

He did not return the nod, but he looked away as if I were not an issue.

That was good enough.

The two of them moved off toward the door into the house, Mother clinging to Stockman's arm, her head against his shoulder.

A Gray Suit instantly filled the space where they had stood. "Please come with me," he said to all of us weekend guests. "Stay together and follow me quickly."

We complied, and he and another of his cohorts, who met us in the Great Hall, hustled us to the north end of the house and up the stairs, one of them leading us solitary denizens into the bachelor wing and the other taking the couples up to the next floor.

Our hallway was lit with electric bulbs on sconces. The Gray Suit made sure we all went into our rooms and closed the doors, telling us, as we disappeared, to be sure to turn the lock after us.

I did.

I waited in the dark.

I paced.

I waited, and then I softly undid the lock and eased the door open.

I looked out into the still-lit hallway.

"Please," a voice said sternly. "We must insist. It's for your own safety."

I withdrew instantly.

I was stuck.

But it was just as well. My own instincts needed to be reined in now. I had nothing to do but wait until the morning and hope for a few private moments with my mother. And hope that Jeremy Miller had made good use of Martin's gray suit and was rushing safely through the woods or along the shore by now.

I went to my casement window and undid the latch and pushed it open.

I listened. The action was likely to be on the far side of the house.

The clatter of feet. The sound of struggle. These things would never carry as far as this room. Not through a window looking north.

I lay down on the bed.

One thing would carry, however, and about ten minutes later I thought I heard this thing: the pop of small arms fire. Once, twice. Perhaps a pistol or pistols. The sound was very distant. Perhaps Jeremy Miller had just been shot dead. Or he'd just shot his last pursuer dead. Or everyone had been shooting at shadows. Or perhaps an automobile had simply backfired on the road to Ramsgate.

But now there was silence.

And there was nothing to do about it.

I got up. I took off my coat and my pistol and my shoes. I would make no further concession to my confinement.

I thought to turn on the light at the writing desk.

But I did not. The dark was better for now.

I lay back down.

Like Jeremy out there in the night, I started running from my pursuers. Thoughts. I was running in my head from thoughts. Small-caliber ones, which were harder to deal with. The big things to worry about, the fundamental things, seemed easier somehow. That was why I figured I was cut out for the work I'd done over the past six years of my life. At first, I'd dodged bullets and watched men die and I wrote about that. Lately, I'd risked myself in ways that made bullets from a bunker seem reassuringly predictable. I'd learned to kill in service for my country. To kill in unpredictable ways. Dealing with that was simple and it was deep. It was merely how this roughneck planet we all lived on was put together, and so the way to cope was already imprinted in our muscles, was coursing in our veins. But this whole thing about my mother and her men, which was whining after me in my head now: that was all just niggles. Of no consequence to me. Long ago I left off needing to give a damn about how she lived her life. Which was the way it should be for any son and mother. You have to leave, and she has to let go.

So I slept.

And I woke. I didn't know how long had passed or what had awakened me.

I rose and crossed to the window.

Before me was barely differentiated darkness. The dark of a lawn. The deeper dark of the miniature canyon of the Dumpton gap. The dark of the woods beyond.

And a sound.

I closed my eyes and listened.

This sound may have been what drew me: the distant revving of an engine. I leaned out, looked, tried to catch its direction.

To the east, toward another darkness, was the fierce bratting of a runabout engine, moving away now, diminishing. Out there, where I knew the Strait of Dover to be, I could see a cluster of lights. A larger vessel upon the water. And someone rushing toward it.

# 17

Shortly after dawn I tried the hallway and it was empty. I went to the steps, descended into the screens passage, and emerged in the Great Hall. It too was empty. From the courtyard I heard a hammer pounding. Nails into wood.

A Gray Suit, framed in the courtyard doorway, began to turn at my step, and beyond him I caught sight of one of the Blueboys hammering the lid shut on a wooden box about the size of a hotel room writing desk. One more of the same size sat nearby, wrapped at both ends with steel bands. Half a dozen more, the size and shape of steamer trunks, were already done. A little apart were two more of these packing boxes standing upright, each about the size of a three-drawer filing cabinet.

The Gray Suit was the guy with the boxer's nose. He eclipsed the courtyard, putting himself square before me and close enough to try to seem intimidating. I wasn't intimidated, but I was still Joe Hunter the benign guest, so I kept my first impulse to myself.

"Please, sir," he said, straining to be polite when to be so wasn't the sort of order he'd been hired to execute. "Guests are to stop in their rooms or in the dining room until transportation."

"Transportation?"

This guy was looking at me a little more closely now.

"Sorry, sir," he said, working even harder at his politeness mandate. "Plans have changed. You're Mr. Hunter, are you?"

"Yes I am."

"I am to give you this," he said, and he dipped into his inner coat pocket and withdrew an envelope. He handed it to me. "From Sir Albert," he said.

The envelope had my name on it. That is to say, "Joseph Hunter." But I knew the hand. It was my mother's.

"How changed?" I said.

"Sir?"

"The plans," I said.

"Breakfast is served in the breakfast room. The guests will then depart."

"And Madam Cobb? I am in her party."

"She has departed with Sir Albert."

The boat in the night, I assumed.

"Departed?"

"Yes sir."

"Where to?"

I'd reached the limit of Boxernose's authority to speak. "Breakfast is served in the breakfast room," he said.

"Thus the name," I said.

His brow furrowed.

"Thanks," I said, and I turned on my heel and beat it back across the Great Hall and up to my room.

I sat at the desk with the envelope and I opened it.

I unfolded a single sheet of writing paper and there was nothing of Sir Albert here, except, of course, the certainty that he had seen, openly or covertly, every word herein. She wrote:

*Dear Mr. Hunter,*

*Sir Albert and I are very sorry to leave so abruptly. The accidental death of a member of the house staff has cast a pall over our weekend, and Sir Albert has decided to accompany me to Berlin. We would be happy to see you there if you can arrange passage, perhaps through your newspaper. I am anxious that the work we have done on your story will not be wasted and that my true intentions for being in Germany at this time can be accurately represented in the American press. Please wire your arrangements to me care of the Hotel Adlon.*

> *Best regards,*
> *Isabel Cobb*

I folded the letter and replaced it in its envelope and slipped it into my inner coat pocket, doing all this almost fastidiously, aware of the small sounds of it—the creasing of the paper, the ruffle of the mohair. I was gathering myself to think clearly, calmly.

She was safe. For now, at least. She was not implicated. I was invited. Joe Hunter was still viable. For now. Or if the "for now" was as ominous as it might be, and if she wasn't, in fact, safe, and if Joe wasn't either, my actions were clear just the same. I'd go to Berlin.

# 18

The boys in gray made sure we went back to our rooms after breakfast and stayed there. And it wasn't till very late morning that one of the boys in blue knocked on my room door and invited me downstairs, luggage to follow, for my trip to the train station in Broadstairs. I carried the Gladstone myself. It was comfortably weighty, though its only heavyweight secret was my Luger. I'd kept the Mauser in the small of my back. From this point on, that would be my standard practice.

The Blue Serge led me past another of his kind who was to bring my suitcase. He led me out of the house by way of the southern door, as I'd come in, and strode ahead of me toward the Silver Ghost, which sat waiting. He opened the tonneau door. I approached and was about to enter when I had the impulse to look back up to the tower where all the action had been the night before.

The Union Jack was flying.

But the guy wires were gone.

I looked just long enough to make sure I was seeing what I thought I was seeing, and I turned and entered the tonneau without even glancing at the driver.

I sat down in the near seat.

"Your bags will be along presently," he said.

The door clicked closed beside me.

Now I knew what was in at least a couple of those boxes in the courtyard. The whole telegraph setup. The guy wire antennas were gone. The flagpole was no doubt gutted. The wireless itself was carted off somewhere in the night. Along with every other household shred of evidence against Stockman.

They were taking no chances. Even if they'd caught Jeremy and killed him, the guy's disappearance could trigger a search of the house. If nothing came of it, they'd set back up again. Buffington had only one shot at digging into the castle of a member of Parliament.

A short time later my suitcase ended up in the tonneau with me. Nothing and no one else. I seemed to have retained my privileged status even without Isabel Cobb's presence.

At the curb before the front doors of the station, the driver hustled out to open my door and then around to pull my suitcase from the other side of the tonneau. I circled behind him and he offered to find me a porter. I thanked him and declined. I made a bit of a show in presenting him with a crown, a very good tip for the service he'd just done.

He hesitated. Then he took the silver coin.

"Thank you, Captain," he said.

"And where's the Rolls driver from yesterday?" I said, the objective of my silver gambit. "I was expecting to tip *him*."

The driver looked at me a little wide-eyed with uncertainty. He'd been pressed into this job, given the unusual circumstances, and this was way outside of both his job responsibilities and his ad hoc briefing.

"Martin, I think his name is," I said.

"He was the one in the courtyard last night," he said.

"Oh no," I said. "What happened?"

The driver sniffed heavily and held his breath as if he'd just been shivved.

He didn't have the presence of mind simply to walk away. I waited, as if there weren't the least doubt that he'd give me an answer.

"He died," the driver said, still flailing inside.

Without giving him a chance to draw even one more breath, I said, "Did they catch the bloody bastard who did it?"

"Not yet," he said with a ferocity that seemed very personal, that made me wonder what kind of an okay guy our Martin might have been in a bar with his buddies. "But maybe in Ramsgate."

"You got him cornered there?" I said.

"I don't know, Captain," the Blue Suit said, as if I were suddenly a copper trying to squeeze him for a confession. "Thank you for the crown," he said, and he turned and moved off.

Too bad. He probably didn't know much more anyway. But I was left with nothing to allay my fear that Jeremy Miller was dead as a result of protecting me and my phony identity.

It wasn't until well past midday that I reached my room at the Tavistock Hotel. The train ride back through the same Kentish countryside my mother and I had traversed twenty-four hours earlier had filled me, of course, with an even more pressing fear. For her. Miller, indeed, hadn't been protecting my role in this present drama so much as he had hers. I was simply carrying a spear for the leading lady. And she'd been abruptly whisked away by her Othello.

So my bags were unopened on the floor of my room and my hat was still on my head and I was sitting at the desk where I'd been creating Joe Hunter for weeks and I was waiting as the telephone operator connected me to the American embassy.

After I was finally rung through to some inner embassy sanctum, a man said, "Sorry, Mr. Trask isn't here at present."

I left a message for him to contact me as soon as possible.

He hadn't expected me till tomorrow, of course. I went from stuck in a room at the Stockman House to stuck in a room at the Tavistock Hotel.

The only thing that made the next few hours bearable was to lay a pack of cigarettes and an ashtray next to my Portable Number 3 and to turn back into Christopher Cobb and write the lead paragraphs of a king-beat news story about a German spy in the midst of the British Parliament.

I restricted myself to the first three pages, the number I felt confident I could burn in the metal wastebasket without burning the hotel down as well. So those three pages were created slowly, each sentence being refined and rehearsed aloud before entering the Corona and emerging from its platen and then being honed to an Alexander Popeian extreme beneath my Conklin Crescent-Filler.

At last I received a call from the embassy and an appointment on the Waterloo Bridge, and I lit my front-page story with the butt of the last cigarette in my pack and hoped I'd have a shot at it for real someday.

# 19

I stood in the dead center of Waterloo Bridge and leaned on the stone balustrade as the western sky stopped bleeding and started bruising and the lights came on along the Victoria Embankment. Trask suddenly appeared at my side.

"Cigar?" he said, lifting a very good one before me.

"Sure," I said, and we each lit up a ninepence Vuelta Abajo and blew the smoke over the river, which was running about four storeys below us, black from coal tar and Thames mud and the onflow of night.

"I'm sorry I couldn't bring you a chunk of my steak from Simpson's," he said.

"This'll do," I said, taking a second draw. This was some fine stogie, with a heavy body and a taste of plantain and palm, of leather and earth, but with all that gone up together in flames so that you somehow knew all those tastes were there but they made a single new thing.

"I ate dinner tonight with your old friend Metcalf," he said.

I'd had quite a feed with my old friend Metcalf, my embassy contact who sent me off to Istanbul back in May. He took me to Escoffier's eatery at the Carlton Hotel. "Did you understand everything he told you about the food?" I asked.

"I don't care to know that much about a cut of beef," he said.

I didn't tell Trask I listened to every word.

Instead, we shared a nod and we each looked at the end of our cigar at the same moment. Somehow I'd always known to do this, having learned to smoke a cigar like an actor, from actors, but I never knew why it seemed so natural, even necessary. Maybe it was just to punctuate a conversation, which is certainly what it did for Trask and me, at that moment.

"You're back early," he said. Though this was a declaration, he clearly was asking for the story.

You would have thought he'd get a little worked up for that question. Something had to have gone seriously awry for me to be on this bridge with him tonight. But he was languid as cigar smoke. He was a cool customer, my old friend Trask, and in our line of work that was probably good. But I wondered if maybe in this case he already knew the reason.

He waited.

I decided to let him do it his way. I told him about Jeremy and Martin, about Isabel and Stockman, their coziness and their abrupt departure. I told him about the contents of the tower room, the code books and the wind books and the maps. And the wireless. I told him about Stockman's torches and his oratory and then the Zepps.

I'd kept my conclusions and my worries to myself in all this, just stating the facts for him, as starters.

We both seemed silently to understand that the facts part was done with.

We puffed on our Cuban cigars.

The first conclusion to draw from the facts didn't need saying: generally speaking, Stockman was everything Trask and Buffington had suspected.

The next piece of the puzzle begged for conclusions. I handed him my mother's note from this morning.

He slid a few feet away to the spill of electric light from one of the iron standards. He read her message and slid back again.

"The Adlon." He said the name with a sneer in his voice, as if its significance should be clear to me.

"Yes?"

"It's the Kaiser's favorite," Trask said. "Everyone of importance is put there. So the phones are tapped, and the place is crawling with agents."

"I'm worried about her," I said, nodding at the note still in Trask's hand. "That was written before they sailed away. Have you heard anything more from her?"

"Not yet," Trask said. "Even going in through Ostend, they'd still be in transit."

"Does the Adlon suggest anything?"

"If he suspects her, it's the best place to put her. But if he doesn't, it's still best for him."

So I had to live with that worry for a while. Probably for a long while.

I went on to the second one.

"Anything about Jeremy Miller?"

Trask shook his head no. "There's a lot the Brits didn't say, even after we agreed to help, as you no doubt have already gathered."

"I have," I said.

"This is the first I've heard of him," Trask said.

One more fact now. "They won't find anything if they search Stockman's house," I said. "When I left, his boys had clearly dismantled the wireless. They were packing it in boxes at dawn. I'm sure they did the same with anything else incriminating."

Trask grunted.

"The Brits probably don't know this, if Miller's still missing," I said.

"They'd have to assume it either way," Trask said. He looked at the end of his cigar again. It was burning, of course.

Worries were for civilians. I had to move on.

"Stockman seems to be about the Zeppelins," I said.

Trask took this in and then turned around, put his back to the balustrade. He lifted his face to exhale his smoke in the direction of the streetlight.

Only a few moments passed and he took another deep drag.

Trask was a cool customer all right. But I figured he knew how to treat a good cigar. We were smoking these things too quickly. His continuous puffing was a tip-off to his agitation.

And now he seemed ready simply to watch the evening traffic crossing the bridge.

I joined him. I've known a lot of guys like this. The worse things got, the less they said. I gave him a long minute. Then I said, "Don't clam up like the Brits."

He moved his face a little in my direction without giving me his eyes. "I'm just thinking," he said. "You're right about the airships. But this much they say about Stockman. He's smart. He's a *big idea* kind of guy."

Trask was smart too. He was already thinking what I now realized had been nagging at me all along. "Winds and weather and beacons along the Thames," I said.

Now he turned his eyes to me.

"Those aren't big ideas," I said.

Trask smiled. The smile felt personal. It was maybe the first personal gesture I'd ever gotten from him. He knew we understood each other easily.

"Those are matters for a navigator, an airship commander," he said. "At most an operations officer in Düsseldorf or Nordholz or Ghent."

He could have named any of a dozen other Zepp bases.

"It doesn't add up," I said.

"We need to find Joe Hunter a hotel," he said. "So you can answer this." He handed my mother's message back to me.

I put it in my pocket. We both looked at the traffic once more.

A double-decker bus rumbled past.

We didn't have to say it. We needed to drive the bus.

# 20

It wasn't until late the next afternoon that a leather portfolio and a brown paper parcel arrived by way of George, my familiar, aged bellhop. It wasn't until I'd closed the door and placed these things on the bed that it struck me: George was in the employ of one or both of the secret service agencies I was working for. Maybe the hotel management was too.

Indeed, the portfolio that had been entrusted to George's hand from lobby to room door contained all I needed to change hotels and then leave the country as Joseph W. Hunter. A room key at the Faulkner's Hotel in Charing Cross. Tickets and passport for Hunter. A piece of paper with a hotel name and address in Berlin, but a handwritten note at the bottom saying, "Defer to theirs, if offered." Letters of passage and introduction, these the cleverly wrought products of the ongoing irony of America's occupying the German embassy at the Germans' request and with their gratitude. We still officially represented their interests in London after they'd made a hasty departure in July of last year.

One was a letter of introduction on the letterhead of His Excellency Baron von Schwarzenstein, ostensibly by his own hand, granting the bearer official sanction to ask questions. Answers were, no doubt, optional. But at least I wouldn't have to open Joe Hunter's mouth to the force-feed of German propaganda.

And I had an alternate set of papers for a German military identity, a full colonel attached to the *Auswärtiges Amt*, the Foreign Office, including an authorizing letter of introduction over the apparent signature of the foreign minister himself, Gottlieb von Jagow. The colonel could be played as a spy, if need be. I also instantly knew what was in the paper parcel. This man's uniform.

I saw my face on his passport, a picture taken without my close-cropped beard and showing the long, white scar arcing across the center of my left cheek. A perfect replica of a German university fencing scar. A *Schmiss*, the sign of youthful bravery and high breeding. In my case, it was an inadvertent souvenir of my work in Mexico. A useful thing that I despised. In his case, it was a result of aristocratic breeding and education. The name on the passport was Klaus von Wolfinger.

I put those papers back in the portfolio for now. They would soon reside in the false bottom of my Gladstone, along with his clothes. That wasn't me yet, and if that face didn't absolutely have to be mine, I didn't want anything to do with it.

A note on generic American embassy letterhead was written in the same hand that accompanied the Berlin hotel information. Two words: "Good luck." No signature. But no signature meant Trask. No signature was him looking at the end of his cigar.

I was nearly finished packing when the telephone on the desk rang. I answered.

It was the front desk. "A woman to see you, sir."

I went down.

In a corner of the lobby, rising from a red settee framed in two palms, was the pretty-like-a-farm-girl suffragette from my mother's dressing room. She was wearing the dark skirt and white shirtwaist uniform she'd had on the other night, though she'd come with her tricolor suffrage ribbon discreetly omitted from her ensemble and a straw boater with a blue bow on her head.

I moved to her. But it beat me how she knew I was here.

"Mr. Cobb," she said when I'd drawn close.

She offered her hand for a shake.

I took it. I remembered her shake being a meek thing the last time. Now her grip had a little spunk to it, befitting a woman ready to chain herself to an iron fence in Piccadilly Circus so she could vote.

"You've been working on your handshake," I said.

Her cheeks bloomed quickly.

"Now you have to work on suppressing the blush," I said.

We were still shaking and she withdrew her hand quickly at that.

"I don't mean to be critical," I said. "I share my mother's convictions about your cause."

"Good," she said, looking down.

I had to admit to myself, particularly on this late afternoon, that this woman stirred me. I liked a woman trying to be strong. Better still, I liked a woman already strong. Strong even beyond seeking the right to vote. But trying was also attractive to me. I'd been bred into a sympathy for suffragism. How could I not, with a mother who lived her life, always, as if she could be anyone, could do anything.

I put the tip of my finger gently beneath her chin and lifted it.

"I didn't mean to embarrass you," I said.

"It's not just them has to change," she said. "It's us too."

"Neither is easy," I said.

She fixed her eyes on me—they were the color of horse chestnut—and she set her jaw and she smiled a downright comradely smile.

I matched it. Her blush was gone.

And then she abruptly disengaged her eyes and let go of her smile in the flurry of almost having forgotten what she was there for.

She dug into her small brown suede bag and withdrew an envelope. She handed it to me. "From your mother."

The envelope was sealed. It had upon it my full name in her ornate hand: *Christopher Marlowe Cobb*.

"When did you see her?" I asked, too sharply, the tone driven by my surprise and by the reflex assumption that the chronology of delivery was the chronology of composition.

But she stood her ground, this suffragette whose name I'd avoided asking and still did not know. "Thursday night," she said. "At the closing party."

The night before we went to Stockman House.

The lesser mystery resolved itself as well. This was how I'd been found by a virtual stranger. Mother had known all along where I was. It was she who'd sent the play ticket, and now she'd dispatched her suffragette as a courier.

I gentled up my voice. "She must think highly of you," I said.

My sharp tone had braced her. This tone caught her way off guard. She fluttered into the self she was trying so hard to leave behind, and she cast her eyes downward.

"I was honored to help," she said.

"What did she ask you to do?" I struggled to keep her from hearing the sense of urgent business that I felt.

She lifted her face again. I couldn't read her mood now.

I added, "If I might ask."

"She said if I hadn't heard from her by three o'clock on Sunday to come here and wait for you and give you that envelope."

If the weekend had gone as planned, we were to have returned by noon today. And presumably I wouldn't have received this.

My hands went itchy to tear the thing open. I wanted to do that alone. But I found I also wanted to spend a few more minutes with this suffragette, who smelled of something nice but appropriate to the woman she was trying to become. Patchouli and musk and maybe some sweeter things too but only in the background.

"Can I have a few moments with this?" I said.

"Of course," she said.

"But don't go entirely away yet."

She braced up again, as if I'd spoken sharply to her. That sweet, wide mouth moued a little, but it was an ironic moue, an amused moue.

She glided away toward another settee across the lobby.

I tore open my mother's envelope. She wrote:

*My Darling Kit,*
*If you are reading this, things may have gone terribly wrong. I fear you*
*will never see me again. "Accurst be he that first invented war."*

The quotation was from the playwright for whom she named me. Though my present worries for her were, of course, rooted in the very risk she invoked, the fact was that she was very much alive. That she had, however, contrived to speak to me from the grave turned this all into an overplayed Isabel Cobb performance in a second-rate melodrama.

*I am sorry if ever I have wronged you, by things I have done or by things*
*I have failed to do. "Mountains and hills, come, come and fall on me,*
*and hide me from the heavy wrath of God."*

Marlowe again. She was at the edge of the stage in my head, playing to the back row though I was in the front row and able to see the tears, which she was so adept at producing, run through her makeup.

*I have come to this end from love of country. I write this letter from love*
*for you, my son. I have always loved you. Always. From wherever I am*
*now, I love you still.*

The words ran instantly in my head: "The lady doth protest too much, methinks."

And she too turned to the words of the character she'd recently portrayed. His death scene, of course:

*If thou didst ever hold me in thy heart, absent thee from felicity for a*
*while, and in this harsh world draw thy breath in pain, to tell my story.*

Though this too was a quotation from her recent performance, she had removed the quotation marks, had made the words her own, had become, herself, the tragic figure. And since she assumed that my own mortal risks on the same mission had proved to be not as great as hers, I was spared in order to tell the tale of Isabel Cobb's sacrifice for her country.

*I have done my best, which is all anyone can do. The rest is silence.*
   *Your mother*

I folded the letter and placed it in the envelope and then into my coat pocket.

She played Hamlet's death more convincingly than her own, in spite of the liberal quotations from two masters and a little bit of quasi-plagiarism.

I looked across the lobby.

The suffragette was already striding my way.

Perhaps she had thought over our conversation so far and regretted the moments when she seemed a little intimidated, a little weak, a little too traditional in her femininity.

She arrived.

"I saw that you'd finished," she said.

I held up my two empty hands to confirm her impression.

"You didn't wish for me to go away," she said.

"That's right."

She waited for a beat to see if I would carry on from there. I chose not to fill the brief silence, interested in what she would do.

She filled it almost at once. "The skies are clouding up, but not much. It is a Zeppelin night. My friends gather to eat and drink and wait and take shelter. Would you care to share the event with me?"

This all came out in a rush, perhaps even a single breath. Yes, this woman yearned for enfranchisement beyond the vote.

I liked her.

"Yes," I said.

"Good."

She handed me an address on Brook Street, Number 24, just off Hanover Square, written out on a scrap of paper.

"Can you come at eight or thereabouts?" she said.

"Yes."

She did what she'd worked herself up to do and she turned away, as if to stride off.

"One other thing," I said.

She turned back to me.

"Should I know your name?"

Her eyes widened. "You don't know my name?"

"I don't."

She humphed softly. Then she stuck out her hand once more. "Millicent Gibbs."

I took it. She was putting all the muscle she could behind it. "Kit Cobb," I said.

She looked hard into my eyes. "I like you, Kit Cobb," she said. "And you like me. Just don't patronize me."

She let go of the shake, turned on her heel, and strode away.

I figured, in spite of her little lapses, she was doing pretty well with her project. She was right about what had been wrongly creeping into my attitude about her. I liked her even more for tweaking my nose for it.

I beat it back upstairs, finished my packing, and an hour later I'd moved into the Faulkner's on Villiers Street, a modest, four-storey, brick-faced hotel on the Strand side of Charing Cross Station. Its street front split its space with Faulkner's Hosier and Hatter. Just the sort of place for a minor journalist, and no doubt another discreetly government-friendly establishment.

I wouldn't be here long. The tickets put me on the steamer tomorrow night from Folkestone to Vlissingen and then the train onward through neutral Holland to the German border and then to Berlin.

I went out at once and into the Strand and found a telegraph office. I wired Isabel Cobb at the Adlon of my presence at the Faulkner's and my travel arrangements to Berlin. I was vague about my accommodations, saying I planned to stay at a *Residenzpension*, a boarding-house, common in the city.

In fact, Trask had put me into the Hotel Baden, a comparably modest hotel on Unter den Linden, near the Russian embassy and a five-minute walk from the Adlon. I didn't want Stockman to know exactly where I was if I could avoid it.

I wrote at the end: *Am eager to see your performance in Berlin. The play's the thing.*

A covert, needling little joke with my mother. As soon as the telegram was sent, however, I worried that I'd unwisely gotten caught up in whatever it was that always went on between my mother and me and, as a consequence, I'd endangered her. Stockman would surely be monitoring the telegrams to her through the Adlon.

I tried to talk myself out of the worry: he would understand the *deutschfreundlich* reporter's reference to her performance as being about Hamlet, not an American spy; he'd understand the quote as referring to the play being the central feature of her visit to Berlin, not "the thing wherein I'll catch the conscience the King," the King being Lord Albert himself.

But I walked back to the hotel unsettled, eased only by the thought of an enfranchised Miss Gibbs.

# 21

The sun was just vanishing when my taxi slipped along the lilac hedges of Hanover Square and stopped before a flat-roofed, brick town house half the width but just as tall as my hotel. It was a private residence but without apparent servants and without a clear owner, at least on this Sunday night, the door being answered by one of the other women from my mother's dressing room, the one wide enough to be the cellist in that string quartet of suffragettes. She recognized me at once and led me up a single flight to the parlor and I was introduced at the door as Mr. Christopher Cobb to a dozen or so of Millicent's colleagues, about half of whom had also invited men. Most of these guys struck me as dandies, though I didn't look at them very closely, simply registering among them more than one frock coat, apricot tie, waistcoat the color of the Hanover Square hedges in bloom. The women murmured at me sweetly. The men displayed indifference.

Millicent presented herself before me.

"I'm sorry I'm a little late," I said.

"I remember using the phrase 'or thereabout' with the time," she said.

"So you did."

"I will feed you now," she said.

And she led me to a table set for high tea and I grazed a bit. Between the cucumber sandwiches and the dandies in the room I felt as if I'd been cast in an Oscar Wilde play.

Which made me appreciate Millicent Gibbs all the more intensely. She and I drank a pretty good red wine off in the corner. The men kept their distance, and the suffragettes made solitary, hope-I'm-not-intruding pilgrimages over to us to chat briefly, mostly about how they felt nothing short of adoration for my mother.

When the air raid whistle blew in the street, the room upswelled in conversation and bustle like a theater crowd responding to the call to seats at the end of an intermission. "To the basement," a woman's voice cried out, and the group made for the parlor door.

I had no real interest in joining them and merely shifted my weight in our standing position, but Millicent's hand went straight to my forearm to keep me where I was. She had her own plan.

When everyone was out of sight and clattering down the stairs toward the cellar, Millicent took my hand and we left the parlor and approached the staircase. But she and I climbed upward.

Two flights more, in darkness. By my count this was the top floor, but she led me around the banister and toward the back of the house and onto a narrower staircase leading up still farther.

She had not spoken a word. She had not let go of my hand. We reached a small vestibule and she released her hold on me and opened the door.

We stepped out onto the roof.

She closed the door behind us and stood beside me, our arms touching, and she said, "I've been longing to do this. Your mother is intrepid. I know you must be as well."

The warden's whistle was still piping somewhere along the street.

And now the six-pounders began to pop off in futility, out east.

I felt a shudder run through her. My first thought was that she was afraid.

But before I could raise my arm to put around her and before I let the obvious thing back into my head—she couldn't be afraid because she'd deliberately brought us up here—she said, "Come this way," and she took my hand again. The rush in her voice and the firmness of her hand both spoke not of fear but of some sort of dark exhilaration.

We neared the front parapet of the roof and she stopped us. "Here," she said and she knelt, pulling at my hand, bringing me down beside her, and she let go of me and lunged forward. My knees were resting on a soft thing. I put a hand down. A blanket. My eyes were seeing enough now, adjusting in the dark. A searchlight flashed overhead and away. I could see Millicent there, stretched out on her back on the blanket, looking up into the sky.

"Please lie beside me," she said.

I did, placing myself so our bodies touched from shoulder to foot. She did not ease away. Indeed, she gently pressed her shoulder and her hip a little closer. But I sensed this wasn't about sex. Not at the moment, at least.

I was right.

"Do you think they will pass over us?" she said, and she slipped her hand into mine, our fingers intertwining, our bundled hands coming to rest upon our joined hips.

"Do you think they will drop a bomb on us?" I replied.

It was the cue for us to turn our faces and look at each other in the dark, on this open roof, beneath a London sky, on a Zeppelin night.

This we did. And as soon as our eyes met, we laughed.

We turned our faces skyward again and we did not speak. We waited. We listened. The six-pounders soon stopped. I had lately been quite near a Zepp or two on a rooftop. I wasn't looking forward to another. But I was quite happy to be tagging along in Millicent Gibbs's journey to an intrepid self.

We strained to hear the hammer of the Maybachs. I would tell her about these fine engines if she would like. But all we heard were the distant blackout whistlings. A brief spatter of small arms fire. A siren somewhere. And then a long, persistent silence, underscored by the silent scan of a searchlight and another, showing, however, only clouds.

At last the lights stopped and so did the sounds.

She said, "They are elsewhere, I suppose."

"Or perhaps they did not come tonight," I said.

She sighed.

"It makes no difference," I said. "Your courage is the same."

"Thank you," she said. "But I wanted more."

This seemed another cue. Even if she hadn't consciously intended it.

I turned to her on my side.

She looked at me.

I kissed her.

And we began.

She was strong and she did not mind my being strong and somewhere in the midst of the clutch and crash and cling I began to realize something that made me wish the Zepps had come and that they had been enough for her. I pushed the thing from my mind, but when this woman and I were done and lying side by side again and looking at the dark sky above, I could not help but think: Mother carefully chose this woman for me and arranged this very act, her being dead and her having that dark and ironic and utterly tormenting sense of drama that made her the actress and the mother that she was.

I kept my mouth shut.

But Millicent went straight there: "She said I'd like you."

I was ready to bolt.

"And I do," Millicent said.

# 22

I did bolt. Politely. She was not terribly disappointed, being strong. My mother was still very much alive and had miscalculated this whole thing. Or perhaps she hadn't. Perhaps she was even now amused at the thought that her posthumous message had been delivered and had thus set in motion this very sort of playlet for two. She'd relish the irony, given her own two-hander at the Hotel Adlon.

But my playlet had ended its run. I was glad for that, glad to focus now simply on risking my life for my country as a spy in Germany. The irony with *that* being I had to wait to hear from my mother to actually get started.

Word came early the next day. She was happy to receive my telegram and Sir Albert was absolutely insistent that he put me in the Adlon near the two of them. *Still working on my performance*, she said. *Every other night it is in German.*

I vowed never again to engage her in innuendo. But I knew the vow was futile.

I met with Trask one last time, at the A.B.C. café on Duncannon Street just opposite Charing Cross Station. It was a tea and pastry shop mostly (the A.B.C. once having been the Aerated Bread Company) but it was a guy's place, for all that, with severe dark wood tables and chairs, a checker-tiled floor fit for a bar, mirrors on the wall, and a roomful of men.

Trask and I ordered coffee, however, to the faint distaste of the waiter.

We drank, we spoke of its mediocrity as coffee but of its superiority, even still, to yet another cup of tea. At least we were among *men* drinking tea. Trask made this last point; I had not, out of deference to Millicent Gibbs.

Then Trask and I leaned toward each other and lowered our voices to only what was necessary, though the conversational welter at teatime that surrounded us was plenty of ground cover for our conversation. Our business was brief.

"Our English friends will give you some help over there, in case you need it," Trask said.

"You've spoken to them, I take it."

"I have."

He took a folded piece of paper out of his pocket and passed it to me. "This is where and when."

It read: *Thursday night. Nine o'clock. Zum Grau Köter. South of the Stettiner train station on* Borsig-Strasse. *"Too much smoke and noise."*

The place was called the Gray Dog. The "help" would identify himself by speaking of the smoke and noise.

I looked at Trask.

"It's a cabaret," he said.

"One of their people inside Germany?"

"Yes."

"We don't have anyone inside?"

"That would be you."

"How will he know me?"

Trask's hand came low across the table once more.

He put an object in my palm, small but with a little weight. I opened my hand and glanced just before I dropped the thing into a side coat pocket.

A brass *Reichsadler*, the Imperial Eagle, with a blunt-ended pin attached to the back.

"Your boutonnière," he said.

"Any other news from the Brits?" I said.

"Nothing."

"Did you ask?"

"I did." Trask nodded at the piece of paper in my hand.

"You have that in your head now?"

"I do."

He extended his hand and I gave the paper to him. He stuffed it into his inside pocket. "Now," he said. "What was the word?"

I told him the details of the telegram from Isabel, and I asked, "Should I take Stockman up on the offer of the Adlon?"

"You will have no secrets in your room," he said. "The place is an anthill of German spies."

"To refuse him on this . . ."

"You can't," Trask said. "Perhaps it'll be useful for you, as well, as long as you can keep your act going."

"I can do that."

"You need to deal with your extras," Trask said, meaning my weapons, my alternate credentials.

"I told them I'd stay at a boarding-house. Unnamed."

Trask instantly knew what I was driving at. "Good," he said.

"I take it the Baden is safe?"

"Relatively. The clientele is assumed to be of little interest. The German operation along the Unter den Linden is high-level stuff."

"I'll check in at the Baden before the Adlon," I said.

"Tonight I'll send round a tool or two," he said. "The base of a wardrobe is pretty useful. Just in case."

I nodded.

I kept silent for a moment and he shifted needlessly in his seat, as if there was a touchy thing he needed to say but he hadn't figured out how to work it in smoothly.

He said, "Unfortunately we don't presently have an equivalent of Metcalf in Berlin. But if and when you need to leave the country abruptly, make your way to the embassy and invoke my name. They can take care of you."

"All right," I said.

Trask and I looked at each other for a moment. I figured we'd said all that we had to say. But just as I thought to lean back in my chair and finish my coffee, Trask gave me a final thought for my trip. "It's come to this now," he said. "If they think you're a spy and you can't get to our boys at the embassy on your own, they'll assume you're a Brit, take you to Spandau Prison, and shoot you the next morning."

# 23

I left Trask and checked out of the hotel and caught the train from Charing Cross to Folkestone, the night boat to Vlissingen, and a Dutch train to the German frontier. The first test of my Joseph William Hunter credentials came in a wooden customs hall in Bentheim.

My passport was being scrutinized before a Kaiser Wilhelm mustache. The owner of the mustache was an apparent *Bratwurst* and lager fiend of serious proportions, which no doubt was why this infantry captain was in a customs hall and not a trench on the Western Front. He was settled behind a heavy wooden table, and half a dozen times he glanced from the face in his hand to the face standing before him.

He knew I spoke German, from the few words we'd exchanged so far.

I was prepared as a next step to present a fine forgery of a letter of passage and endorsement full of high praise for the bearer, Joseph W. Hunter, from *seine Exzellenz* Baron Alfons Mumm von Schwarzenstein, the Foreign Office minister who manipulated propaganda abroad by manipulating journalists from neutral countries. But before I had the chance, the mustache rose, not a preferred task of the body it was attached to, and the captain moved off and disappeared through a door at the end of the hall.

I did have my Mauser beneath my coat, but with German travelers all around and armed guards on the platform outside, I did not see a good outcome from a breakdown of my credentials.

The captain returned and did not sit. He was breathing heavily. My passport was not visible.

Now he caught his breath.

"Herr Hunter," he said, smiling a little. Kaiser mustaches sometimes made it tough to read a smile. He was being either friendly or sardonic. "I think that has not always been your name," he said in German.

If he had *Cobb* in his head as an alternative, things would shortly get hot. He had not immediately brought anyone back with him, but maybe he was waiting for a couple of boys from the platform to make their way through the crowd.

I played the other alternative. "You are shrewd, Captain," I said in my own best German. "I was born Josef Wilhelm Jäger."

He nodded, keeping that little smile. "I suspected so," he said.

Then he dipped into his breast pocket and removed my passport. He handed it to me. "Welcome home," he said.

After a whispered word from my new German pal, the baggage inspectors gave my suitcase and Gladstone only a perfunctory look and I left the hall and boarded the train to Berlin. I suspected the *Kapitän*'s question about my name was indeed a shrewd guess. Clearer to me was that Joseph W. Hunter was on an approved list in a back room in Bentheim, and that only could have been arranged by Stockman.

Ten hours later, with evening coming on, the train pulled into the Bahnhof Friedrich-Strasse and I stepped out onto the platform, beneath a great, steel-trussed vault of glass, and I heard the sound of men singing. The other platform was loading a regiment of soldiers wrapped in cartridge belts and knapsacks, their rifles slung over their shoulders, their field gray uniforms blending into the twilight. Their voices rang to the high vault above them.

The tune was what struck me first. It was straight from the marquee on Stockman's lawn, straight from his little stage show with Zeppelin accompaniment. These German soldiers were singing a melody that would chill any Brit with national pride: "God Save the King." But the tune had its own words here; it was also used in the unofficial national anthem of the German Empire, *"Heil dir im Siegerkranz."* "Hail to thee in victor's crown."

These boys were deep into the song already as they queued into the train carriages along the platform, heading for the Western Front. *"Heilige Flamme, glüh', Glüh' und erlösche nie,"* they sang. *"Fürs Vaterland!"* "Holy flame glow, glow and extinguish not, for Fatherland."

I strode off down the platform while the boys sang on, dewy-eyed warriors, "standing valiant for one man"—Willie the Second—"gladly fighting and bleeding for throne and empire."

I went down the stairs and out one of the vaulted south doors and into a Benz landaulette taxi. I paid the driver well to do an odd thing: go just a few blocks, let me check one bag into a hotel while he waited with my other bag—I didn't want the Baden people to see me walk in with two bags and then out with one—and then drop me with the second bag at a second hotel less than three hundred yards away.

The Baden had the same profile as the Faulkner's, four storeys and six bays, with its own commercial enterprise sharing the frontage, in this case an international newsstand advertising my Chicago rival, no less, the *Daily News*, above the door.

I left my suitcase in the waiting taxi and checked in with the Gladstone. As soon as I was in the room I opened the bag and took out the contraband in the false bottom. Included now was a branded, compact combination tool, consisting of a handle with four screwdriver blades and a flat-edged metal end to tap a small nail.

The wooden wardrobe Trask recommended I utilize was sitting against the wall. The Baden, the Faulkner's, the Tavistock. I suspected the Anglo-American spy boys had a hand in all these for their own select clientele. But neither could they fully trust the staff. I pried the baseboard loose on the wardrobe with the thinnest of the flat screwdriver blades, put the Luger, its holster and box of shells, and the German officer credentials and his tightly folded uniform inside. I replaced the board and tapped it in securely.

The Mauser stayed in the small of my back. A very bad thing to be caught with, but a necessary thing to perhaps keep from being caught.

The tool went with me. I'd put it into my toilet case. It was an innocent enough object in a room where nothing hidden could be found by using it.

And then I was pulling up to the front of the Adlon, a vast neo-classical box with a mansard roof of green slate. The doorman was uniformed in Prussian blue, the bellhops and page boys in lighter livery of Egyptian blue, one of the latter toting my suitcase behind me with white gloves as the former swept an arm toward the revolving door, where I spun through into the marble and gilt lobby.

My first thought was of Trask's words. The Kaiser's favorite hotel was crawling with agents. Just making my way to registration I noticed some serious candidates. Conversing by one of the sienna marble columns, a couple of guys with the wrong kind of tough-guy faces for their linen suits and patent leather shoes let their eyes slide my way; lounging in one of the settings of brocaded chairs in the reception area, two more broad-shouldered boys done up in tweeds gave me the quick once-over; standing isolated a few paces off the front desk, a close-shaved, hollow-cheeked, lean-and-hungry-looking Johnny wearing a dark gray three-piece and a wing collar openly stared at me. I had to stop looking at the boys who were looking at me so I wouldn't look suspicious to them. Whoever was an agent in this joint was going to do his job and I had to do mine.

I merely spoke my name to the frock-coated boss of the rosewood front desk and he turned instantly to the wall of pigeonholes behind him. This stirred up my wariness again, though their knowing me at once could have been a reassuring sign, suggesting that my coming here at the arrangement of Sir Albert—who surely had the blessing and good wishes of the German Foreign Office—made me a trust-worthy guest.

The frock-coat withdrew my key and an envelope and handed them both to me with a nod of the head. I hoped for something more from my mother. But my name on the outside of the envelope was not in her hand. It was written with a heavy, broad-nibbed stroke. A man's hand. I tucked it away until I was in my room.

Which was on the top floor, the fourth. The floor attendant bowed his way out of the two-room suite and I locked the door and put down my bag. The place was done in Empire style with the furniture in the sitting room all standing on animal paws, from the scroll-armed chair to the divan to the side table to the desk beside the bedroom door.

I stepped into the bedroom, where, fortunately, the mahogany bed, with gold Etruscan helmets on the headboard, had no mammalian touches. For decor I definitely preferred the Baden, which had been done in unpretentious German vernacular.

The drapes were open. I crossed to the glass door, which opened onto a narrow balcony, a wrought-iron balustrade, and the Unter den Linden beyond. *Under the linden* indeed. The street's wide median was thick with linden trees. I angled to my left and gazed upon still more Empire.

The Brandenburg Gate. The Germans' vast sandstone version of the entrance to the Acropolis, its half dozen passage walls fronted with Doric columns and bearing up the bewinged goddess of Victory— *Victoria*, appropriately enough—standing in her chariot, driving four chargers, and hoisting a standard of the Imperial Eagle and the Iron Cross. It was lit with electric light from below, its copper turned victoriously gold but splashed with black shadows. I figured Willie must make a frequent pilgrimage the thousand yards west from his palace at the other end of Unter den Linden to see his own fate writ large up there on the Brandenburg.

Beyond the Gate was the vast linden canopy of the Tiergarten, once the private hunting ground of the prince-electors but now Berlin's centerpiece public park.

I closed the drapes, sat on the side of the bed, and switched on my own, small, night-table splash of electric light. I opened the envelope that had been left for Joe Hunter. It was signed *Sir Albert*. It read: *Dear Mr. Hunter, I will ring you in your rooms in the vicinity of nine this evening. I would be pleased to have a drink with you in the lobby bar.*

At nine o'clock exactly, the phone rang.

# 24

At five minutes past nine I was sitting where Stockman instructed me to sit, arriving there in the way he instructed me to arrive, by speaking his name to the bartender, a clean-shaven elderly man in an Adlon-emblemed dinner jacket and black tie. The man immediately left his post and led me to the end of the room that looked onto Unter den Linden. We turned to the right and went to the farthest corner, beyond the last window. I sat in one of a pair of facing armchairs, my back to the wall. The chairs, like all the drink-and-conversation-facilitating furniture in the place, were dark Spanish leather with cabriole legs and curving crests and arms.

"*Ein Joppenbier, bitte*," I said, ordering a fine, odd German beer made in Danzig, and he nodded and disappeared.

Stockman had arranged for us to be private. This dim, far-corner setup seemed designed for that. At the nearest cluster of chairs and table, before the windows, four young German officers sat huddled close, drinking. Their *feldgrau* was fresh. From that and from the intensity of their drinking and the bloom of their cheeks it was clear they'd not yet seen battle but were soon to be shipped out to the front.

I watched them talking low, laughing a couple of times, but in a subdued way, and then talking again, and now they sat back, first one and then the others, thinking quietly, inwardly, and drinking for a moment as if they were each alone, and now they resumed talking.

A few minutes passed, and then Stockman's towering figure swooped into the bar and headed in my direction. He was dressed in a German-style informal evening suit with silk-faced lapels and a double-breasted waistcoat. I rose to greet him and we shook hands with a nodded hello. He'd arrived before my beer did. As soon as he and I settled onto our chairs—he with his back to the young officers—the bartender showed up, though empty-handed.

"What are you having?" Stockman asked.

"A *Joppenbier*," I said.

He looked at the bartender, and with a soft little nod he held up two fingers. The man vanished instantly.

"You know the beers," he said.

"Some."

"A German will order a *Joppenbier*. Not so often an outsider."

"I am German," I said.

He made exactly the same small, familiar nod he'd just used with the bartender. "Are you not an American as well?" His voice was as gentle as the nod.

"Yes."

"Is that possible?" he said.

I needed a good answer for that and a quick one, to seem sincere, and I tried to think fast. The bartender rescued me by appearing with our beers.

He put two white, lidless steins on the small, polished mahogany table between the chairs. The beers had come very quickly after Stockman's order. Which meant the bartender had deliberately kept mine back until Sir Albert arrived. I was right about the familiarity between them. Not to mention the barman made the delivery himself, even as a couple of black-coated waiters were working the rest of the room. Our Sir Albert was a celebrity here.

Stockman leaned forward and took up his stein as the bartender vanished. I picked up mine as well. Its only decoration was the hotel crest in gilt: the planet earth, upon which sat the Imperial Eagle of the German Empire and below which, in an unfurled banner, were the words *Adlon Oblige*.

He offered his stein across the table and I touched his with mine. We neither of us spoke a toast.

The beer was dark—very dark, nearly black—and it had a pretty stiff kick, and it was heavy in the mouth, almost like syrup.

Stockman put his stein down, as did I.

"So?" he said.

I was unsure enough of my true standing with him that the monosyllable seemed ominous, as if he were trying to bluff me into a confession of something he suspected but could not specify. I'd used that trick myself with some of the stupider Chicago politicians.

I had no choice but to proceed as if everything was just fine between us. "Is it possible to be both American and German?"

"That is my question," he said.

"Can I speak honestly?" I said.

"For as long as we sit in this bar tonight, I would like that to be the rule for us both."

That he would assert this—and with a quickness and vibrancy that seemed utterly sincere—made my breath catch in its ambiguity. Either trust was growing between us or he was laying a trap.

He leaned near. "How much of a journalist are you?"

This didn't sound good. But once more I had no choice.

I said, "I am a journalist whose intention is to properly represent a country, a *Kultur*. What is the measure of such a journalist?"

Stockman considered this for a moment, his eyes intently fixed on mine. He said, "Forgive me for speaking as I am about to. But we are being honest."

"Of course," I said.

"I say this not from a distrust of what you have just declared. But perhaps a concern over what you might include in such a story, no matter how noble its intention." He paused. He let this soak in.

He didn't say he trusted me as Joseph W. Hunter, but I liked his disavowal of distrust. Still, I knew his method. I waited for the threat. I was interested to hear it.

"I am a powerful man," he said. "Here and in England and abroad, even in America. I have associates in all those places. Friends. And they exercise my power on my behalf." He paused to let me work out the implication. I figured his next step was to clarify what offense on my part would engage his friends.

It was clear enough already. I decided it would be a good strategy to anticipate him. "Sir Albert," I said, "I will never publish, never write, never repeat a word you say to me unless doing so is explicitly discussed and agreed upon between us."

"I am glad to hear it," he said.

He sat back. He laid his elbows on the arms of the chair. He intertwined his fingers before him and rubbed first one palm and then the other with the opposite thumb. His hands came to rest.

He seemed satisfied.

"You were going to say," he said. "Honestly."

We'd returned to the question of being both an American and a German.

I had to be very careful now. I'd said the right things so far. I sensed the possibility that I'd won his trust. At least for this evening's conversation. There were things on his mind. He wanted to talk, even still sober, though I had to figure he'd already been drinking this evening. But something about him seemed almost needy. *Careful*, I said to myself. His commitment to Germany and its interests would be fine to hear. But I needed to know his *plans*. I was tempted to try to guide him there directly. Incrementally but directly. But even in this state of mind, even if he'd had a few drinks, he wasn't a dirty alderman ready to brag about his doings. This man was dangerous.

So was I. But I had to be careful.

"I like America," I said. "I grew up there. You cannot help but feel a certain allegiance to the place where you are reared, particularly if it rewards you in many ways. Rewards and even nurtures you."

"Like a benign stepfather," Stockman said.

"Like a benign stepfather," I said. "But there are stronger bonds than those."

"It is not his blood in your veins," he said.

I nodded. He'd leaped in to finish my thought, seemed to want to answer this question himself.

But he said no more. He leaned forward and took up his stein and sat back again. He drank.

I did likewise.

"Eventually you have to choose," I said, to finish the thought.

He took the stein away from his lips. "Do you like this special German beer?" he asked.

"I do," I said.

"Some would say it is too strong in its taste, too thick on the tongue."

Stockman seemed in an odd mood. I wasn't sure if it was just beer he was talking about.

I said, "I don't acknowledge the idea of 'too strong.' It does things the beers of other countries cannot. This is good. No other beer in the world tastes both of the earthiness of malt but also of a sweet something that reminds one of nothing other than a fine port wine."

This made Stockman straighten a little, consult his palate. He smiled. "So it does," he said.

We drank some more.

"Blood is stronger than nurturing," Stockman said, following an associative track in his head that surfaced and submerged and surfaced again.

"Blood is stronger," I said.

"Blood," he said, "does not make itself new with each generation. It is perpetual. It is eternal."

I nodded. He fell silent, working out his thoughts inwardly. I was tempted to again affirm my agreement with him, but I kept my own silence. I didn't want to interrupt his process.

"Civilization is borne onward by a current of blood," he said.

He was speaking German now.

He stopped again. But he did not seem inward. He was watching my eyes, as if waiting for me to comment. Was he testing me?

"The truth you just spoke," I said, also in German. "Is it a quotation from von Herder?"

He smiled.

"Someone else?" I asked.

"My own thoughts," he said.

"Excellent," I said. "I'm sorry I'm not taking any of this down."

"Nor should you," he said. "When I am commenting for the public record, I will tell you."

We were speaking only German now.

"I am eager," I said.

The officers beyond him laughed.

Stockman glanced over his shoulder.

"They go with joy," he said. "Our young men."

He paused. He heard himself. *Unsere jungen Männer*, he'd said. *Our* young men, not *their* young men. As if he had already chosen between his two countries.

So he added now: "That is to say, they *all* go with joy. The young men of both sides."

I nodded. Strictly speaking, his correction remained ambiguous.

He took a long pull on his *Joppenbier*. I could sense his mind freely associating as he did.

He lowered his stein. "Do you know there are three million socialists in the German Empire? The other sixty million Germans detest the beliefs of socialists."

He paused and let me take that in.

I kept quiet.

He said, "No doubt the socialists detest the beliefs of all the rest of us."

This time he did not pause to ambiguate his pronoun.

He said, "So do you know what the socialists are doing, now that the country is at war?" He began to raise his stein, but he immediately lowered his hand again, letting go of the rhetorical question. "You must understand. These are *German* socialists. This is the German Empire we are speaking of. The three million German socialists have joined together with the rest the country. They are sending their sons to fight. Their sons are going to war for Germany. With joy."

Now he took the deferred drink.

The stein came down lightly. Empty. He leaned forward and put it on the table between us. He lifted his face to me without sitting back.

"There are beliefs," he said. "And there are overarching beliefs."

*Glaube* and *Überglaube*. I'd never heard the second word. I figured he'd made it up by piecing two words together. The people of Willie's empire loved to do that, with two words and sometimes with even more. To my mind this was a *Sprachenperle* of German. A pearl of the language. A lollapalooza feature of this *Kultur*.

I realized my stein was empty and I leaned forward and placed it beside his.

He was still suspended over the table.

We were very near each other.

"Blood," I said—*Blut*—to identify the trumping *Überglaube* the German socialists and nonsocialists shared.

"Blood," he said.

"*Blutweltanschauung*," I said. Bloodworldview. I'd expanded Immanuel Kant's famously invented word even further.

Stockman laughed.

He and I pulled away from each other as a waiter arrived and set two full steins of the black, strong Danzig beer on the table and vanished at once, without a word.

The refill had been automatic. They'd been watching and knew what Sir Albert expected.

"You have *Kneiperuhm*," I said. Tavernfame. It was entirely my own word. He laughed again.

We focused for the moment on a long, warming pull of the beer. I'd said the right things so far. I'd made him laugh, and I'd done it by acting German. I could simply keep that up. But it would get me no further. Exploring the *Weltanschauung* of his allegiance to the Germans was way short of what I needed. I needed to know what he was *doing* about it.

At any moment he could reach his limit, either in time or in number of drinks, and call this off. And he could reach a certain point, as drinkers often do, when he would turn from talkative to silent. It was time to push him a little, even at the risk of making him suspicious. It was my work in Chicago for the *Post-Express* to get local prosecutors and lawyers, criminals and politicians, working stiffs and working girls to talk about things they'd rather keep to themselves. A bar and a strong drink were as useful as my notepad and my Conklin. Those and Polonius's good advice, spoken at the Duke of York's just the other night, "By indirections find directions out."

I stuck to German. I said, "I have lately asked myself what I will do if the United States enters the war on the British side."

Stockman lowered his stein. "What did you answer yourself?"

"I would leave the United States," I said.

He nodded.

"I think it is the right answer," I said.

He stopped nodding. He kept his eyes on me but he did not speak.

I could not read him. This could be a sympathetic stare. It could be critical. I doubted the latter, but there were attitudes on a continuum between those two—several of them bearing risks—that would influence what I said next. I was improvising. I was tempted to ask him outright if *he* had now left. If he was in Germany to stay.

Not yet.

"I have no close relatives here," I said.

"That does not matter," he said.

"I have to confess," I said.

I took a bolt of beer. I let him wait for the rest, as he'd done with me a few times already. Then I said, "I was exhilarated by the Zeppelins flying over us on Friday night. I knew where they were going and what they intended to do, but nevertheless . . ."

I stopped again, as if I did not know how to express what I wanted to say. That the bombing of London did not lessen the exhilaration.

Stockman said, "Nevertheless." Not to prompt me to say more but to permit me to leave the thing unsaid. We already understood each other.

But I nudged him. "Do you disapprove?"

"I do not," he said.

"Please don't mistake me," I said. "I admired your speech."

He smiled just a little. "You were very shrewd to understand." And he said in English, quoting my own words, "My speech was 'to quell a panic, not to legitimize a foreign policy.'"

I said, "I find myself thinking about the Zeppelins. How they might end this war quickly."

Stockman leaned back deeper into his chair. His mouth tightened, its line vanishing beneath his mustache.

I thought: *He's withdrawing now, for my mentioning this.* But then the alternative: *He's thinking of his own mission somehow.*

With his mouth still tight, he made one small nod.

And I knew my second thought was right. *My* mission in Germany was entirely about whatever was in his head at that very moment.

I said, "They are beautiful and terrifying but something still seems missing. The English close their curtains and go to the basements and have polite conversation."

Stockman made a short, sharp smile that came and went so quickly that I could consider it only after it was gone.

And now the young German officers cried out as one for another round of beer. Politely. *Vier Biere, bitte.* They laughed at their harmony.

Stockman swung his face toward them, showing his chiseled profile, watching them in his periphery. Or watching me.

I had to back off.

Stockman looked my way again.

He lifted his stein, pausing it before him, pushing it ever so slightly in my direction. He was saying it was time to take a drink and change the subject.

I lifted my own beer in exactly the same way, saying, *Okay.* Saying, *Of course.* And we quaffed.

When our steins were down, Stockman squared his shoulders a little and said, "Madam Cobb is resting from her journey."

He said this in English. On this subject we would speak English.

"She asked that I instruct you to visit her rehearsal at the Lessing Theater tomorrow morning," he said.

I worked hard to understand his suddenly flat tone. Perhaps he was still suspicious of my arm around Isabel Cobb. But if that were truly a serious thing between us, surely this whole conversation would not have gone as it had so far.

He paused. But he had the air of a churning mind. Maybe he had to get a certain number of quaffs in him to stir all that back up.

Then he said, "She had an unsettling moment on Friday."

He was focused on the scene I feared was still working in him, though his lead suggested a different concern from mine.

"She nearly fainted," I said, glad to gently reinforce my excuse for touching her.

"She has died a thousand times on stage," Stockman said, "but she has seen very little of that in real life."

I heard my mother's words in this. She'd been working on him.

"This was particularly difficult," he said.

I nodded. I kept my mouth shut.

Stockman looked me in the eyes. I did not see suspicion. I saw him standing before his constituents, needing to act.

"Martin was a brave man," he said, with an unmistakable tear-stifling tremor in his voice. He paused. It sounded convincing. He was a good actor.

I caught myself. He could be acting, but he could have legitimate feelings. In this present job of mine—in my job as a reporter, as well—I had to stay alert to the complexity of the human mind and heart. You tell yourself that your subject or your enemy is unremittingly bad, and you will fail. More than fail—you'll compromise the value of what you're doing, of who you are.

"Too brave sometimes," Stockman said. There it was again in his voice, the snag at the man's braveness, the breathy slide to finish the sentence.

He looked away. He took a moment.

He didn't have to put on real feelings for me about a hired thug, not in this situation, not in any situation. He wasn't acting.

"He fell from the tower," Stockman said, composing himself with a statement of the obvious.

It was he who had initiated this further explanation of the death to me. That was Stockman the spy. I'd gotten near to his secret self a few moments ago, touching on the Zeppelins, and it prompted him to forestall any suspicion about the other big event from Friday. But he was sorry now he'd brought it up. He really couldn't explain it anyway.

"He'd become careless," he said, with a soft but clear thump of finality.

I could let the silence drag on to put the pressure on him to explain it further. But I knew the answer anyway. I said, "I'm very sorry about your man."

We took another drink. Stockman said, "But it's put Madam Cobb in a state."

"It's good she has her work," I said, finishing the sentence in my head: *nailing you.*

"I suppose," Stockman said.

And the four young German voices that had harmonized to call for a beer, the voices of these newly minted officers about to go to war, took up together once more, singing. "*Heil dir im Siegerkranz, Herrscher des Vaterlands.*" The beginning of the anthem for the German Empire. "Hail to thee in victor's crown, Ruler of the Fatherland."

Stockman did not turn to them. He closed his eyes.

The enlisted men's voices at the train station had rung to the rafters. These officers sang softly, thoughtfully, as if to a child, or to a fiancée. Even the next lines. *Heil, Kaiser, dir.* "Hail, Emperor, to you."

Stockman, of course, had himself sung this very tune on Friday night in the wake of the Zeppelins. "God Save the King." But this time the song's lyrics flowed with pure German blood. His eyes still closed, Stockman began to sing. "*Fühl in des Thrones Glanz . . .*" "Feel the throne's great glow . . ."

Other voices from throughout the bar also began to sing. "*. . . Die hohe Wonne ganz.*" "Fully the highest joy."

Stockman opened his eyes, and he rose from his chair.

I rose too. I was in character. I was Josef Wilhelm Jäger. And yes I sang, my body suddenly prickling into gooseflesh. "*Liebling des Volks zu sein.*" "To be the people's beloved one."

The bar was filled with voices now, rising together in blood and empire. "*Heil, Kaiser, dir!*"

And when we had done, the bar fell into a ringing silence. The silence held for a moment and a moment more and still another moment, and then bodies began to rustle and settle.

Voices resumed, low and murmuring.

A glass clinked from the bar.

Stockman sat down.

I sat down.

My chest was still swelled with the Zeppgas of a Bloodbonding.

I was far from home. The further irony struck me hard now: the precious melody for both Brits and Germans was also the melody for "My Country 'Tis of Thee." Sweet land of liberty, of thee I sing.

As the sole American sitting in a German hotel bar, I came to this thought with no gooseflesh, no urge to sing. I'd already sung tonight. You can call it blood. You can call it nationhood or empire or Fatherland or family. All of it was, at its heart, the terrible, deep, human yearning for an identity. You find it by being part of something larger. Even an impromptu gathering of voices in a bar.

"You must be tired," Stockman said.

"Yes."

"As am I."

We'd sung together. There was no more to say tonight.

We rose.

I reached into my pocket for my wallet and he waved away the gesture.

"Thank you," I said.

I circled the table and he stepped from behind it to face me. We shook hands.

But before I could move away, he put his hand on my arm. He leaned near me. He smelled of *Joppenbier*, as no doubt did I. He said, in German, "They bring only isolated neighborhood disruptions. Commonplace, soon enough."

# 25

I slept and woke and slept and woke again, working Stockman's curtain line over and over in my head. I assumed this had been his response to my leading comment about the Zepp attacks missing something. He'd initially been quite professional and had clammed up. Maybe he and I singing together about the joy of the German Empire had made it personal. The thought that followed his fleeting smile kept working in him, and he finally said a little something. I'd gotten a glimpse at his mission, though it was as fleeting as the smile.

Too fleeting. So the problem with the Zeppelins he'd been studying was that their attacks were too isolated? True enough. Smart enough. But everyone in London knew to fear the day when the attacks were carried out by thirty airships at a time instead of two, when the fires and crumbling buildings would appear all over the city instead of in a few isolated neighborhoods. The Germans simply had to build more of these machines. Which they presumably were gearing up to do.

This was a big idea but an obvious one. I couldn't figure why it would require their secret ally in the British Parliament to come to Berlin. The trip certainly wasn't about being with my mother. Whatever he felt for her, that was a useful ruse. He'd discovered that the British secret service was sniffing around, but his boys scrubbed down the castle overnight just fine. He didn't have to take off in the middle of the night. Indeed, it would have been swell for him if the authorities had stormed in and found him reading a book in the library of a house that didn't hold a single shred of the evidence they sought against him. Perhaps he would have waited another day to depart if Jeremy hadn't shown up, but it had already been planned. He was here for something crucial. This wasn't about building more Zepps faster.

My mind gave out somewhere near dawn.

I woke for good a couple of hours later and headed for the Lessing Theater.

It sat in massive isolation on an odd wedge of land, pressing up against the *Stadtbahn* railway viaduct on one side and looking out onto the River Spree on the other. It resembled a cathedral more than a theater, with twin, flat-topped towers and a central dome. Fronting the building was a portico with four sets of double columns and four more sets above, holding a gabled roof.

I passed through the portico and into the lobby. It was dim and cool inside, for a late morning in August, and I was immediately stopped by a vaguely uniformed old man stationed on a chair. The mention of my name drew an instant nod toward the doors directly ahead of me.

I crossed the lobby floor and went up a short flight of stairs and stood before the center door into the auditorium. My hand hesitated at the handle, as I heard a familiar voice projecting not just to the back row but beyond.

I opened the door very gently and only far enough to slip through and step sideways into the shadow of the aisle behind the last row of the orchestra seats. The house lights were off but failed to shroud the auditorium's golden rococo flourishes on its proscenium and on the facings of the side balconies and loge boxes. The stage was uniformly bright from the electric utility lights. Downstage center was my mother.

She was to-being and not-to-being. A few rows before me, a man with broad shoulders was standing with his head angled backward sharply, as if looking into the dark above. Concentrating. *Herr Regisseur*, no doubt. The director. The estimable Victor Barnowsky, the rival of Max Reinhardt and the creative director of the Lessing, who was personally guiding the acclaimed Isabel Cobb's Shakespearean adventure in Bard-loving Berlin.

My mother was dressed for rehearsal in knickers and a white shirt. She rolled to the end of her soliloquy, and as soon as she heard the fair Ophelia approach, Barnowsky lowered his head and said in good English, but with a heavy German accent, "Sweet prince, may I stop you now, *bitte*?"

My mother gracefully fell from character, moved the few steps to the very edge of the stage, and bowed toward her director. "Of course, *mein Regisseur*," she said.

Barnowsky bowed in return.

A blond actress in shirtwaist and skirt—the fair Ophelia, no doubt—who had appeared upstage, quietly withdrew.

Barnowsky said, "If, please, we may hear this speech in your German. Our German cast will join you tomorrow, but I was hoping to listen just a little. Yes?"

Mother bowed once more, returned to her place, lifted her face, closed her eyes, took a deep breath as she slid back into her Hamlet— her Schlegel-voiced Hamlet—opened her eyes again, and began: "*Sein oder Nichtsein; das ist hier die Frage.*"

Barnowsky watched her for a few lines more and then lifted his face once again to the theatrical heavens, simply to listen.

She was good. The only significant German she knew were the lines in plays. But she could mimic anything. Anyone. Any feeling. Any nuance of any feeling. No matter what the words were. I knew the language well enough now to hear and think and feel in German, and she was very good. And I was struck by this: in the German language, Hamlet's infamous hesitation to kill his murderous uncle was even harder to swallow.

But she would pull off that actor's challenge too, I had no doubt.

She ached and agonized and yearned on until at last she said, "*Still. Die reizende Ophelia. Nymphe, schließ in dein Gebet all meine Sünden ein.*"

She fell silent.

Barnowsky began to clap. Slowly, heavily, and then faster and faster. My mother became my mother and she beamed from the stage. She bowed. She curtsied. She put her hand on her heart.

"Excellent," Barnowsky said. "Now let us have an interval to rest and to eat."

My mother slipped offstage right. Barnowsky moved to the stage-right aisle and started down it. I figured he would surely lead me to her. I stepped through the center entrance to the orchestra and hustled along to follow him. From an opening just this side of the orchestra loge, my mother emerged. She and the director embraced in the way famous directors and famous actresses who were not sleeping together but felt a legitimate warmth for each other during the lifetime of a production typically did.

I slowed. I was watching them in profile, though my mother was turned slightly toward me. She would see me soon enough. I stopped only a few feet away.

The embrace ended.

As Barnowsky was saying, "You are everything in this great adventure that I imagined and still more," her eyes flitted briefly to me and then back to her director.

"As are you, *mein Liebling*," she said.

And now she made a little bit of a show at noticing me.

"Ah, Victor, may I introduce you to my chronicler," she said.

He was turning to me.

"The man I mentioned to you," she said.

I stepped forward, extending my hand to him.

He took it strongly.

Barnowsky had a square face and heavy eyebrows and seemed on the surface to be a roughhouser, reminding me of Ike Bloom's boys from the First Ward. I liked this about him, seeing as he was also one of Gorky's boys and Strindberg's boys and Shakespeare's boys.

"Joseph Hunter," I said.

"I am Victor Barnowsky," he said. "Welcome to the Lessing Theater."

"I don't mean to intrude on your lunch," I said.

"Not at all," he said. "I have matters to attend."

My mother said, "I told Victor you and I needed to catch up. Your deadline approaches."

Barnowsky turned to his Hamlet. He clicked his heels and bowed.

Mother led me in silence back the way she'd come, past the wings staircase and along a corridor to her dressing room.

There were two places at the makeup table and mirror. She sat at one of them and motioned me to an overstuffed chair next to a lacquer dressing screen inlaid with mother-of-pearl cherry trees and geisha girls.

Her first words were abruptly in medias res, either from her flair for the dramatic or from a gathering fright at what we were doing; I could not tell which. "I had no choice," she said. "He woke me and said to pack and we steamed away into the night."

"I got your note that morning," I said.

"Good."

"Are you okay?"

She sat rigidly erect and clapped her hand onto her chest. "Okay? I *wish* my flesh were too too solid to melt and thaw or drown or be shot or however you spies deal with each other."

Flair, not fright.

"You sound okay to me," I said.

"I sound terrified," she said.

"We need to talk straight," I said.

Something seemed to let go in her. Her uprightness in the chair eased abruptly. She looked down. She looked back up. "Of course," she said. "Forgive me for actually enjoying all this."

"Are you?"

"Yes." This came out softly. Almost tenderly. Self-reflectively.

I was afraid I knew why.

Before I could ask about Sir Albert, she slipped into what I took to be another place in her mind: "What happened to that man in the courtyard?"

"The dead man?"

"Of course the dead man."

She had no need to know about Jeremy.

"He fell from the tower," I said.

"How, for heaven's sake?"

For a moment I found myself in the same fix Stockman had been in with me on this subject. How to explain it without explaining it. But of course, invoking *him* was my solution.

"I don't know," I said. "I asked Stockman the same thing and all he'd say was that the man was careless."

She nodded. She looked away from me. Something had come over her I couldn't identify.

I said, "He was a tough guy in Sir Al's employ."

Then it struck me.

I *did* know what was going on in her.

I said, "Did you ask Stockman about it when you were alone?"

Mother looked back to me.

"Yes," she said.

What a life I'd lived with this woman. No wonder we couldn't say anything to each other straight. If it was about anything of importance, I could not hear even a single word from her without trying to read its subtext, hear the persona behind it, figure out if that was really her or somebody she'd simply decided to portray, figure out if there was ever a difference between those two things. *Yes*, she'd just said. And my first reading, my first hearing, my first figuring all told me that she was in love.

Or thought she was.

Or was playing at being.

Or just trying to test me. Or torture me.

Or all of that.

"And?" I said.

"He wept." The tone in her voice was familiar. From her two recent *yes*es. Soft. Not a whisper, but only a few vibrations above one. That tenderness again.

I thrashed about for something to say but nothing was coming to mind.

Then she said, still softly, "Is he an actor, do you suppose?"

Worse yet. She asked this as if she feared it. Her feelings for him were real, not put on out of a sense of drama.

I asked myself the same question. Last night seemed to offer a clear answer. But I was reluctant to admit it.

"Some sort of actor?" she said, pressing the question gently.

I didn't speak.

"I know what you sometimes think of me," she said. "But you said we should talk straight."

I did.

I saw something in her eyes that I'd seen often before about some man or other. But did I really? How do eyes say these things? There seem to be so few variables in eyes. I'd seen this supplicating look, this longing look, this I-need-you-to-believe-me-and-approve look, this I-need-you-to-look-the-other-way look. And in that lifelong, complex, recurring look I also could usually see her own recognition that those feelings I was seeing were, in her heart of hearts, put on. But this look now, in her dressing room at the Lessing Theater in Berlin in a time of war, though it showed all those old familiar things, also showed what seemed to be a new thing.

I would not label it.

Should I talk straight?

"He's acting to his constituents," I said.

"Yes."

"He's acting to Parliament and to his government. He's acting when he says he is loyal to Britain."

"Yes."

She waited for more.

She knew and I knew and she knew I knew that she was asking this in another sense.

Should I talk straight?

"No," I said. "I don't think he's an actor."

Tears filled her eyes.

We sat before each other like this for a long moment.

"One more bad guy," she whispered.

I certainly didn't expect her to leap to this. I didn't remember if I'd ever accused her. Of course I must have. It wasn't just leading men she had a weakness for. It was the bad ones. The drunken ones. The abusive ones. Or so it always had seemed to me.

She tried to shrug. "Of a different sort."

She turned to her mirror. She picked up a makeup towel and dabbed at her eyes.

She looked at me in the mirror.

"I'm an American," she said.

"I know you are."

"I'm a loyal American," she said.

"I know," I said.

She turned around to face me again. "But this isn't America's fight yet," she said. "Is it?"

I didn't say anything to that. Not for the moment.

She was mulling it over.

Then I offered, "That's what you and I are trying to help our country figure out."

That didn't exactly sound straight, even as I said it. Not fully. But it wasn't untrue.

We still didn't know what Stockman was up to, exactly. What he believed about country, about blood, about loyalty: these were just beliefs. He lived in a democracy. Mother and I lived in a democracy. We were working on behalf of a democratic society. In a democracy you can have any goddamn belief you want. When does having an idea make you an enemy?

But his beliefs were apparently in service to a country that was at war with a democracy.

What the hell was Stockman up to? With Germany. With my mother.

"What are you saying?" I asked her.

"I don't know what I'm saying. Except he wept for that dead man in the courtyard and I felt something for him. He is a hard man. I've seen that too. But he is equally a soft man. A vulnerable man. Do you know what that does to me?"

"You can back off from straight talk now," I said.

She stopped.

"I'm sorry," she said. "But this is all very difficult in ways I never expected."

"Then the best thing is to figure out exactly what he's doing here," I said.

One moment of silence passed between us, our eyes on each other, our circumstance settling in.

Then she said, "Yes."

This one was not soft.

She said, "He's meeting someone at four o'clock this afternoon. I wrote down what I know."

She dipped into the pocket of her knickers and handed me a piece of note paper with the Adlon crest. It read: *11 Schlesische-Strasse, Osthafen, Heinrich Reinauer Gewerblicher Einführer, 4 pm.*

I stared at this for a moment.

Heinrich Reinauer, Industrial Importer. An address in the East Harbor district.

Mother said, "He spoke German. That was all I could get."

I lifted my face. I didn't say anything as I shifted my gears. She was trying to make clear to me that she'd been a diligent spy, in spite of her feelings for our quarry.

I hesitated another moment.

She said, "He wrote that down and I had a chance to see it. Then I wrote it for you later. I didn't touch the note he made to himself."

"Spoke where?" I said. "To whom?"

"I don't know to whom. On the phone. He received a call late last night."

She didn't have to add "in the hotel room." His room or her room or their room. He received a call late. She was there. She was still there even later, when he stepped away, giving her the opportunity to read what he wrote.

Did he think he was in love with her, as well?

"I need to get as close to this meeting as I can," I said.

"You've come to the right place," she said. "Sit here." She pointed to the wooden chair next to hers.

I knew how to do this for myself, more or less, but it had been a long time and she was very good at it.

I rose. I sat.

She motioned and I turned the chair to face her.

The table and the mirror were a good seven feet long, the mirror rimmed in electric bulbs. She reached behind her to the far end of the table and pulled her makeup case in front of her. It was the shape of a miniature steamer trunk, the sealskin rubbed and scuffed and stained by thousands of nights at the theater. The case was an object of wonder from my childhood.

I needed this done. It was her case, her art. I could not refuse. How old was I when she first opened this case for me and made me up into some other child? I could not remember. I could not refuse. I waited with delight and with dread.

She lifted the lid and squared her chair around to me. With the tip of a forefinger she tilted my head to one side and then to the other, lifted my chin, lowered it. "We should do as little as we can get away with," she said.

"I agree."

"You may have a near encounter. We have to balance naturalness with a large enough adjustment he won't find you familiar."

"The meeting is near the docks."

She hummed a soft assent.

"You could use a different nose," she said. "Wash up."

She nodded me to the sink at the far side of the room. I took off my tie and my shirt. I washed with Castile soap. The water was warm. I dried.

When I returned and sat, she was bending into her case, looking hard at her choices. Her grease sticks were new and bought in London, with the English theater system of numbering.

While she pondered, I faced the mirror and rubbed on a thin coat of cold cream to my face and neck. When I was ready and facing her again, she'd made her choices. Using her left palm as a palette, she stroked down a large amount of Number 3, a skin color slightly darker than medium. Then she took up a stick of Number 13, reddish brown, and she began to incrementally blend and blend and blend it into her hand, darkening the Number 3.

"We'll give you some extended sun," she said. "It's August on the docks."

And she put her right hand to my face and began to apply my new skin, her fingertips working at my forehead, my cheeks, my chin, my eyes, my throat.

I thought: *I should have put on my own stage face. But the makeup has to be done well. I need to remember what she's doing, in case it needs doing again. For now, though, there's limited time and a lot at stake. She needs to do it.*

I clung to the necessity of it.

I hid in *thoughts*, in that chattery, abstract voice that you can talk with on the surface of your mind.

But the straight thing was: I didn't like her touch. Not this much of it. Boys have to come to that, at some point, where they stop their mothers from grooming them, dressing them, fussing over them, remaking them. And they have to stick to it. At some point it's all or nothing: I am what she wants me to be, or I am me.

I tried not to flinch.

I expected her to be talkative. She said nothing. I was grateful for that.

I thought about the Chicago Cubs.

Then she was rubbing mascaro into my beard, cutting its blackness with auburn, making it the color of certain black cats if you see them up close in the bright sunlight. This was done with a small toothbrush, for which I was also grateful.

She'd left my nose for last, which she'd been thoughtfully glancing at since the beginning. Now she built me a broken one with paste.

She said her first words through all of this. "I'm giving you the nose of a boxer," she said. "You wanted to be a boxer once, when you were thirteen and skinny."

I didn't reply.

She said no more.

She finished with the nose paste and blended it with my new skin tone, and she put a light coating of powder over everything she'd touched.

She sat back. She nodded at the mirror.

I turned. She'd made me into someone else. A half brother she birthed in some dressing room somewhere along the circuit before I was born and she gave it away. He'd boxed some but not well. Maybe he'd just brawled in bars. Not surprising.

I turned back to her. "Thanks," I said.

She nodded.

And then she said, "Look. You're a big boy. You know the score. However things turn out, I figure I had to do this." I knew at once she was talking about Albert. She said, "I'm either doing it for love or I'm doing it for my country."

# 26

Mother didn't expect that half brother of mine to have straightened himself out. She was ready to go off to the costume room for some stevedore's clothes. I thanked her for the offer and for the new face and I wished her well for her rehearsal, but I returned to the hotel, figuring to change into a two-piece blue-gray flannel suit Trask's boys had given me with the label of a Berlin tailor. Stockman hadn't seen Joe Hunter in this one. And it befit the way my brother had gotten on in the world, in spite of the knocks that gave him his nose. In the taxi back to the Adlon I settled into this character I'd become. What was his name? What was *my* name for the next few hours? Isaac. The hardworking stagehand and his wife knew whose baby he was, of course, receiving him straight from her hand. They called him Izzy, thinking of his mother by blood.

I slipped into the Adlon lobby, keeping my face down, and I went up to my floor and approached my room. It was early afternoon. The floor was quiet. Most everyone was out doing what they were visiting Berlin to do. I unlocked my door and pushed through.

A man was standing in the center of the sitting room.

He was my Cassius of the lobby, the lean and hungry, hollow-cheeked, staring man. He was facing the door, his hands folded before him just below his rib cage, as if he'd been waiting for me, though my actual impression of him was that only moments before I confronted him he'd sprung into this posture at my imminent entry.

I had no doubt he was discreetly searching my room. He was probably attuned to just such interruptions and had assumed this position at the first faint whisper of my approach along the corridor.

I made this rapid assessment in a comfortable, self-assured frame of mind, which vanished instantly when I realized I was standing before this guy with another man's face.

Hollow-Cheeks had even tilted his head a little as he contemplated this vaguely familiar but unexpected visage before him.

I had too many factors to think out—what should I say about my nose, if anything? could he see it was fake? what was this guy's frame of mind in being here? routine because of my connection to Stockman? staunchly suspicious, that being the attitude of the Foreign Office operatives at the Adlon no matter who the guest?—so many factors to think about that to hesitate long enough to think effectively would itself make me seem guilty of something. I recognized all this in the briefest of moments and I chose to wing it.

"Who are you?" I asked, faintly aggressive, in the most formal German I could muster.

"I am with the hotel," he said.

"I am staying at the hotel," I said. "In this room."

He hesitated a beat. He was doing the thinking now.

But it was about my nose, my complexion. He'd seen me pass through the lobby last night. He tilted his head again, in the other direction, and looked at me carefully.

"May I ask what brought you to the center of my sitting room floor?" I said.

His attention snapped from my nose to my eyes. I thought I saw a flicker of uncertainty in him.

Give him a punch, give him a pat. I stepped to him and offered my hand, making my voice go warm. "I'm Joseph Hunter."

He took my hand and shook it, still looking at me, still hesitating behind his eyes. Mother's makeup was good. He was trying to accept what he was seeing before him as me, given his impression from yesterday, when he'd directly seen my face only briefly and from ten or fifteen yards away.

I knew I'd eventually have to pay the piper if I didn't address this issue now. Izzy's face would vanish by tomorrow. The question was when I'd encounter this guy again.

"I am the assistant manager," he said.

We ended the handshake and I gave *him* a quick, overt once-over, saying, "*Herr* . . ." and leaving it for him to fill in his name.

"Wagner."

"Herr Wagner," I said. "What can I do for you?"

"I am here to make sure everything is correct in your room," he said.

He did not twinkle at the ambiguity. He kept his little joke to himself.

I did not let him know I was in on the gag. "That is very kind of you," I said. "Everything seemed to me to be in order."

He clicked his heels, but his eyes stayed fixed on my face. And then he said, "Good day, Herr Hunter."

I stepped aside for him and he went out of the room and closed the door softly behind him.

# 27

I did not check the room. Thanks to the Hotel Baden, I had no secrets here. I regretted showing my altered face; I could have used the chance to think a bit before reacting to Wagner. I was suddenly afraid I'd winged it into a threshing machine. I probably should have dealt immediately with the whole issue of my appearance, one way or another.

But it was done. I changed my suit and slipped watchfully through the Adlon lobby again, more than an hour before Stockman's appointed time. There was no sign of Herr Wagner.

Outside, I put on a charcoal-gray, snap-visored golf cap, and I stepped into a taxi and told the driver simply to drive down Unter den Linden till I said otherwise. I watched out the back and made sure we were not being followed, and then I directed us to the address on Schlesische-Strasse.

The street ran parallel to the Spree near the old Silesian Gate, which was now an elevated railway stop. Number 11 was a large brick building on an even larger lot at a corner, and I instructed the driver to pass it by and drop me at the next corner, at Ufer-Strasse, a hundred yards farther on.

I stepped out of the taxi. At my back was the harbor's train-track-laced jumble of grain elevators and package freight terminals and petroleum tanks, the whole area oddly pristine for a dock, having opened only a couple of years ago. Before me, Schlesische-Strasse emerged from the upriver shadow of the massive brick Oberbaum Bridge, which carried the elevated across the Spree.

The street was a little sleepy at this hour, only a few local boys passing through on foot. Both sides were lined with variations on Reinauer's joint, blood-clot-red brick boxes holding trade offices and light warehousing.

I pulled my Waltham.

A quarter after three. Forty-five minutes to go.

I crossed the street to approach his building from the opposite side. I had to find a way to watch the building, for now and maybe for later. And just in case, I had to find a way in.

The frontage was all private business with simply a narrow stoop in the center going up to double slab doors. The facade's array of windows suggested a very high ceiling on both the first and second floors, and two more standard office floors above.

I walked past, crossed at the intersection, turned at once to the left and crossed Schlesische-Strasse, heading south, away from the river, on Cuvry-Strasse. This western side of the building had the same pattern of windows as in the front, though without a doorway. I approached its southwest corner and slowed my walk after I could tell in my periphery that I was just clear of the building.

I stopped and pulled out a cigarette, and I twisted away to light it, before looking where I wanted, just in case I was being observed. Before me was an alleyway that ran along the back of this block of buildings. The big brick box immediately at hand had half a dozen sixty-gallon galvanized refuse cans lined up at the closer of two alley doors.

My cigarette was lit and I casually straightened and turned around, waving the flame from my match. As if incidentally, I looked toward Number 11. The alley had ended at my feet. On the other side of the street was a large, macadamized delivery lot. It lay behind Reinauer's building, which comprised two wide bays of loading docks, with raised concrete platforms and metal canopies.

On the nearest platform a couple of Reinauer's boys in overalls slouched against a stack of pallets. They were also taking this moment to light up, sharing a match.

They hadn't noticed me yet.

I'd seen enough for now.

I turned back the way I'd come, in the direction of the river, and strolled off.

At Schlesische-Strasse once again, I realized I'd been so concentrated on Number 11 a short time ago that I'd walked by without noticing the ongoing enterprise in the corner storefront. The signs along the Cuvry-Strasse wall spoke of keeping an orderly line and detailed the hours for work calls. I stepped around the corner. The place was an employment center for temporary day laborers on the docks.

The daily calls finished at noon. This was a reasonable place for a guy with a job handing out jobs to take a slack-time break to have a smoke. I leaned against the cornerstone, putting my profile to the front doors of the Reinauer building. I had plenty of Fatimas and a fretful, let's-get-on-with-it need to do some uninterrupted smoking.

I didn't like the daylight. There was no effective way to get into the building. I was beginning to think this was a waste of time, though I'd had no choice but to come down here. Stockman would arrive, the real stuff would happen inside, and I'd be a futile, distant observer of bricks and mortar. But it was all I had.

I smoked the pack down low but kept a few back for props and I gave my watch fob a workout, and then it was four o'clock, and on the dot a taxi pulled up and Stockman got out.

I nipped my cap down a bit on the right side and watched him in my periphery. He was focused on the stoop and then the door and then he was gone.

I shuffled my feet and waited some more. And some more.

And then I was reconfirmed in my faith in sometimes just hanging around and waiting. Muttering its way up Schlesische-Strasse from the docks came a three-ton Daimler truck. It approached, and its gears ground, and it turned in front of me, into Cuvry-Strasse.

This was a late model with high wooden sides on its bed and a canvas top. I looked around the corner and watched it turn once more into the back lot of Reinauer's building. He rated, this import guy, to command a truck like that in wartime Berlin.

I strolled along after it.

One quick glance to the left: the truck was backing up to the near bay; Reinauer's boys continued to slouch and smoke.

I turned right, into the alley, and hustled a little into the closest doorway, which was recessed and provided the refuse cans to run interference for any casual glances in this direction.

I leaned back against the door, took off my cap, slid down to a touch more than refuse-can height, and I leaned forward just enough to put one eye on the loading dock.

A hundred feet away, the slouchers were unslouching as the Daimler stopped at the platform edge. One of them flipped his cigarette butt and disappeared into the back of the building. His colleague reslouched,and the driver appeared on the platform and the two men spoke casually, the driver bumming a cigarette. I leaned back into the doorway for a few moments.

New voices now, and I leaned forward carefully once more to look.

Stockman had appeared on the platform with a short wisp of a steel-haired man in a three-piece suit. Heinrich Reinauer himself, I presumed. The two loading dock boys disappeared into the bed of the truck, and the driver approached Reinauer and made a stiff little bow. He presented a clipboard, and Heinrich signed.

The boys emerged.

Stockman took a step toward them.

They were carrying one of the packing boxes I'd seen in the courtyard at Stockman House. One of the two upright boxes the size and shape of a three-drawer filing cabinet. They were keeping it upright.

Stockman stepped to them, stopped them, patted the box, and spoke a word. They sat it at his feet. He examined the label, the steel cord binders, the four sides.

He nodded at Heinrich, who spoke a word, and the two boys took up the box again and carried it into the building.

Stockman and Reinauer spoke and the driver came down off the platform.

The two loading boys reappeared and disappeared into the truck. The second box came out, got a once-over from Stockman, and vanished into the warehouse with its twin.

And that was it.

Stockman and Reinauer followed. The driver circled his cab, and he and the Daimler ground gears and rolled into Cuvry-Strasse and away.

I stood up, put my cap on, leaned against the door, and lit the last Fatima in my pack.

I didn't have much.

But at least I knew my next move.

Only these two boxes from the castle were involved in this rendezvous with Stockman and the importer. He'd seen to them personally. The truck was sent away, but the boxes remained. This late in the day I figured there was a chance they'd stay till tomorrow. Surely there was no good reason to offload them here at this hour otherwise. If they didn't remain, I was helpless anyway.

When the dark came, I'd have to pay another visit—a more intimate visit—to Number 11 Schlesische-Strasse.

But first I had a rendezvous of my own. At the *Kabarett* called Zum Grauen Köter.

# 28

The Gray Dog. South of the Stettiner train station on Borsig-Strasse, it was twenty yards down a side alleyway, in the cellar of a *Braten und Bier* joint. A perfect place for a Zeppelin blackout party.

My brass eagle boutonnière in place—my actual face restored as well, with cocoa butter and Castile soap—I descended into too much smoke and noise, in a room that would fit on the stage of the Duke of York's and was jammed with tables and Berliners. Some rooms demand you read their bouquet like a wine, and this one was beer and roast meat and sweat and mustard and tobacco and lavender perfume and even a waft of femaleness, coming, I guessed, from the line of half a dozen kicking chorines in negligees who had to work hard not to fall off at each end of the tiny stage.

A pianist banged away in the far dark corner and the girls were singing about a lusty husband dancing around a rose bush with his wife. The headwaiter in a tux took a look at my lapel and guided me to a small back row table and sat me down, pressing the second chair tight into place. The girls kicked high and belted out an untranslatable "*KlingklanggloriBusch.*" They were loud and shrill in the way chorus girls often seemed to think was alluring but they were competing with a few dozen ongoing conversations in the room.

A girl came to my table in a tux and asked what I was drinking. I had work to do later tonight, so I ordered what the Berliners called a *kühle Blonde*, a cool fair maiden, a wheat beer that Germans used for sobering up. The girl gave me a sly look as if to ask what I'd been doing the last few days. She brought the *Weissbier* in a pint-sized stone bottle and poured the contents into a massive, half-gallon-size glass goblet, which the pint of beer nevertheless filled to overflowing with an inordinate amount of foam.

I paused to watch it froth away and I became abruptly aware of a presence beside me. Before I could look up, a man's voice said in German, "That is Monday beer. No authentic man should drink wheat beer on a Thursday."

I knew the voice.

I lifted my face to look into the boxer's mug that belonged to Jeremy Miller.

I was very glad to see him alive, but I repressed the urge to jump up and clap him on the shoulder.

"What if I had a bad Wednesday night?" I said.

"Then you should stay away from a place like this," he said. "Too much smoke and noise."

I nodded him to the other chair.

He sat.

The girl in the tux came up and bent to Jeremy and took his order, which I didn't hear.

We leaned near each other and spoke in English, audible to each other but walled in by the noise of the Gray Dog.

"How'd you get away on Friday?" I asked.

"Briefly I joined the search for myself," he said.

"Your blue suit," I said.

"My blue suit. There were several lately hired Blue Suits that evening. I had a convincing reference."

"Are you sure?" I said. "I thought perhaps they'd let you in on purpose to trap you."

"The thought did occur."

"And?"

"It still occurs."

Jeremy's drink arrived. A stone bottle and a glass goblet. He was drinking light too.

"We're a couple of fine dudes," I said, nodding at his wheat beer.

"I look forward to someone reading us wrong and picking a fight," he said.

The girl finished pouring and slipped away.

"How do we toast with these?" I said, thinking of the awkward shape and size of the glass.

"It's hardly a toasting sort of drink," he said. "Perhaps to recuperation."

I looked at my own glass. "There seems to be no safe alternative to two hands," I said.

"You are correct," he said.

So we agreed together, on the occasion of this fortunate reunion, to accept a milder meaning for two-fisted drinking.

We sipped through the foam and it was light and it tasted more of banana than of malted wheat; I presumed from the yeast.

"The headwaiter seemed to know you were coming," I said, thinking of his meaningful glance at my buttonhole adornment resulting in what seemed to be the only available table in the place and then his securing the second chair.

"We have friends here and there."

"Pro-Brits in Germany?"

"Ask me again when we are alone," he said.

"We have an opportunity for that tonight," I said.

"Good," he said. "Does it involve our friend?"

"Our baronet. Yes."

We sipped again at our cure for a hangover as the chorus kicked its last kick and its girls fluttered away through a side door off left. While the crowd still applauded, the emcee bounced onto the stage in monocle and tux.

As soon as he was squared around to them, the applause died and most of the conversations died and the emcee cried, "*Gott strafe England!*"

God punish England.

And the crowd roared back, *"Er strafe es!"*

May he punish it.

I'd heard this already several times in the street. It seemed universal in this town. No doubt in the country. Part quotidian mutual greeting, part liturgical call and response.

The emcee seamlessly rolled on into his introduction. He was sorry, he said, but the next scheduled singer had died last night from a broken heart. The crowd let out a moan, but it was instant and exaggerated and as the emcee went on in faux eulogy, the curtain at the back of the stage, which to the eye seemed flush against the wall, opened in the center and a woman in cadaverous whiteface and a tight black dress emerged.

The crowd made a collective sound once more, part horrified gasp, part incipient laugh.

Jeremy leaned toward me. "You mentioned an opportunity?"

The crowd was laughing outright now.

I leaned toward Jeremy. It was well past sunset outside. "I did."

# 29

We emerged from the Gray Dog without any further word until Jeremy pointed south on Borsig-Strasse with his chin and we walked off in that direction.

"I have a motor car," he said.

"Glad to hear it," I said.

A few steps later I said, "You don't strike me as a cabaret type of guy."

"I didn't choose," he said. "You were right about our having friends in the place. The orderly minds at the Foreign Office see the threat there from Bohemians, not foreign agents."

"Hide in plain sight."

"There was a time," Jeremy said, "when the woman in black would have sung her death-by-boredom from the idiot speeches of a parody Kaiser. A *Quassel-Wilhelm.*"

The constructed German word meant a "gibberish-Wilhelm."

"Now," he said, "the censors only have to worry about keeping the girls' private parts hidden."

The political satire period of the *Kabarett* ended more than a decade ago.

"Were you a cabaret type of guy back then?"

"Back then I was already a British pub type of guy."

"We are alone now," I said. "I asked you inside about the pro-Brits."

Instantly, flatly, he said, "There are no pro-Brits in Germany."

We went another couple of steps, with me waiting for him to elaborate.

He stopped.

But he simply said, "This is it." He nodded to a Model T tourer, its canvas top latched in place, sitting at the curb. Henry Ford, quietly conquering the world.

Jeremy made no move to get in. He lifted his face a little, looking away from me briefly, finding words. "Not in the way 'pro-Brit' sounds," he said. "Those who would help us here are not disloyal. They are not working *for* the British. They are working *against* the gibbering Kaiser and the world-conquering *Pickelhauben*."

He identified the German military leaders by their ridiculous, polished-leather, brass and silver-trimmed, spiked helmet—the *Pickelhaube*—that sat up over the ears, protecting very little except the feelings of inadequacy of the officers beneath them.

"Is that you as well?" I said. "Aren't you pro-Brit?"

The question lifted him up by the chest just a little. It had taken him by surprise.

"I *am* a Brit," he said.

"Born?"

"No," he said. "But naturalized."

"Do you have people in Germany?"

"I boxed as an Englishman. Every professional fight."

"Then you are English," I said.

"My mother lives in Spandau," he said. "For her, the Kaiser can do no wrong."

He was speaking softly now. Making no move to his Ford. "My brother, who has lived with our mother—she is a widow—my brother is now an artillery lieutenant. His mind is fiercely opposed to the gibbering Kaiser and the world-conquering *Pickelhauben*. But he thinks there is no other way to be a loyal German."

We thought about this, both of us, for a few moments.

I said, "Didn't you have to become an Englishman to truly fight the Kaiser and his generals?"

He did not hear me. We had each come to a thought. I had merely spoken mine first. Breaking his own separate silence, he now said, "In spite of our past, we are capable of a republic."

I heard the *we*. I did not challenge him on it. I didn't have to. I trusted this man. In spite of his blood.

"Where do we go from here?" he said.

I was not sure which *we* he meant.

"The East Harbor," I said.

"In our American car, imported through London," he said. "Pre-war. It's had a few years of hard use, but it will be loyal to us."

He circled to the driver's side, reached in to the coil box, and switched the battery into its chattery readiness.

"I'll crank," I said, heading for the front of the Ford.

At the steering wheel levers, he retarded the spark and advanced the gas just a little. I bent below the radiator and clutched the crank with my left hand, carefully tucking my thumb alongside my fingers. I gave the crank of this worldwide symbol of American industry a sharp tug, and it rattled into life.

On the way to Reinauer's, I briefed Jeremy on my afternoon. We crossed the Spree and approached the East Harbor on Schlesische-Strasse, passing under the Oberbaum Bridge.

"Slow now," I said, and we rolled by the front of Number 11. I saw no lights.

I directed Jeremy around the block and we approached on Cuvry-Strasse, from the south.

We parked and shut down in front of the building at the edge of Reinauer's delivery lot. We could see the left-hand loading dock from where we sat.

There were no lights at the back either.

I said, "I'm guessing he's got a man inside."

"Probably," Jeremy said. "Tonight at least."

"But if he's in there, I'd rather confront him on our terms."

"Agreed."

"I'll be right back," I said. I opened the door. "A little reconnaissance."

I closed the door and beat it softly across the macadam toward the loading dock. The air smelled of grain and diesel and creosote.

I pulled my tungsten flashlight and went softly up the side steps. I cupped the beam end with my other hand and shined it low, though I was very aware now of my Mauser and of any sound from inside, just in case. I shined the beam all around the dock surface, starting where I watched the two mugs smoking this afternoon. The stack of pallets was gone and so were any butts they might have dropped.

I moved along past the big steel-slat rolling entrance, and as I neared the access door at the end of the dock I started scanning the light in front of me.

I found what I was looking for. I crouched to a couple of cigarette butts. Flattened but unscuffed. Unswept.

I beat it back to the Ford.

"We need your good right hand," I said.

So we set up to wait with Jeremy at one side of the door and me just down the steps at the other side, my Mauser drawn, in case things went wrong somehow. His fist was our first choice. Which he got a chance to use pretty quick. I was looking off the other way when the door clicked and its hinges chirped and then there was a little choked what-the-hell sound and the crack of bone and a major thud.

I went up and Jeremy was already coming around to drag the guard's body back inside. I followed.

The place was deeply shadowed, but across the main floor the guy had turned on the electric light in the windowless shipping office.

Jeremy slipped off in that direction. I closed the outside door and took a little tour. The main floor was mostly empty, but beyond a row of packing tables, my flashlight found an arrangement of wooden boxes and crates and shipping drums. All large. Bigger than Stockman's two boxes. I was convinced this wasn't the part of the haystack we should be looking in anyway.

I returned to Jeremy, who had the unconscious guard on his face and was binding his ankles and wrists behind him. "Not much of a bout," I said.

"He was fighting out of his weight class," Jeremy said.

He said it dry, so I kept my laugh and even my smile to myself. The guard was out of Jeremy's class all right; he was a good twenty-five pounds bigger, all of it apparent muscle.

"Did you look in the shipping office?" I said.

"Just the packing tables." He cinched the hog-tie tight.

"The office is the most secure spot on this floor."

He nodded and finished with a gag job using a couple of oil rags, and we strode across the warehouse floor to the office.

Not only were the lights on, the guard had left the door standing open. He had easy access to the office. It wasn't promising as a place to stash Stockman's precious boxes.

I stepped in first. Jeremy lingered just outside.

A desk.

File drawers.

A safe. But it was half the size of even one of the boxes we were interested in.

A work table with ledger books. A small bookcase.

Nothing.

I wasn't surprised.

I stepped out. "Not secure at all, really," I said.

We both thought for a moment in silence.

"The boxes aren't that big, really," Jeremy said. "They could be anywhere in the building."

"How special are they?" I said.

A rhetorical question.

Jeremy nodded and I said the thing we were both thinking. "We should find this man Reinauer's office."

At the end of a corridor on the third floor was a mahogany door and a brass plate: *Heinrich Reinauer, Geschäftsführer.*

Our man, the managing director.

"Shall I assume you can deal with this?" Jeremy said, in that cultured British tone he sometimes put on.

"You shall," I said. I handed him the flashlight.

He illuminated a friend of mine from the Great Fraternal Order of Tumbler Locks, of which I was an honorary member. I took out my tools and raked this one quickly and I opened the door for Jeremy as if I were his butler, finding myself very pleased to have shown him my own good right hand.

He grunted admiringly.

We went in and closed the door behind us.

Jeremy immediately switched off the flashlight.

Pitch black.

"Good drapes," I said.

He lit the flashlight and found the electric light key next to the door.

Reinauer's corner office, secreted away in a bland brick warehouse building at a come-lately urban river dock, was paneled in oak with glass-doored bookshelves and an oil portrait of himself hung behind a West Wing–size desk. Each of its four windows was draped in a black single panel with a massive gold Imperial Eagle in the center sinking its claws into the planet earth. All befitting a *Geschäftsführer*.

But the most striking feature of Heinrich Reinauer's office was the pair of steel-band-strapped wooden boxes sitting in the middle of the floor. Once again I was struck by their size and shape. They were standing with their long side upright. I half expected each of them to contain a three-drawer filing cabinet, the drawers filled with every German secret known to Albert Stockman.

Jeremy and I approached them, however, as gingerly as if we expected them to contain ticking time bombs. We stood side by side before them, silently, without moving, for one beat and then another.

In the center of each of the facing panels was a shipping label. The two labels were set at slightly different angles and showed fragments of previous labels beneath.

Jeremy and I each moved to a box and knelt before it.

The label was an *Umladungsformular*. A transshipment form. The new address was written by hand.

Jeremy read his aloud. "FVFB. Kalk. MDH."

I read mine. "Krupp. Essen."

# 30

We looked at each other.

We didn't need to speak.

Krupp, of course, meant steel. The House of Krupp was what Lord Kitchener and the Brits desperately needed, a homegrown industrialist producing more artillery shells than the rest of the world combined.

Jeremy squared himself to the box, crouched, put his arms around it, and lifted.

Only six or eight inches.

He put the box down again.

He nodded at me to do the same.

I did.

The box went up very heavy, but it didn't feel like a three-drawer cabinet full of files. Not nearly heavy enough. And the distribution of the weight didn't feel right. And, of course, there was the matter of its destination.

I put the box down.

I said, "So either Sir Albert is getting Krupp into the milk can business or Krupp is getting Sir Al into the artillery business."

We took a step back.

Then Jeremy had a thought. He crossed to the box before me, crouched, and lifted that one as well.

He put it down, nodding, and stepped back. "The same weight."

"A couple of shells," I said.

"Likely," Jeremy said. "Empty ones."

"Then they're a special design. Stockman, the idea man."

Jeremy nodded.

We both turned our eyes to the box going to FVFB. Or to MDH.

"Where's Kalk?" I said.

"Near Cologne."

The question now hung in the air between us: what was our next move? Which pushed a question on stage that had been lurking in the wings. I said, "My man said the Brits were sending me some help. What did your people say?"

"I was the help."

For a moment I wondered how Trask had negotiated his way into our running this British show.

Then Jeremy said, "I'm to help the two of you."

Mother was how. Her crucial access to Stockman was what Trask brought to the table.

But I said, "As far as I'm concerned, you and I are simply in this together."

Jeremy gave me a single, sharp nod.

I said, "For the record then. We want to figure out the full extent of what Stockman is up to and stop him. Agreed?"

"Agreed."

We both looked at the boxes.

"They're nailed and steel-banded," I said. "Can we look inside and then restore them so Reinauer won't notice?"

It was a rhetorical question.

We stared at them some more.

"We open them, that's all we're going to get," I said.

"I think we have a good notion what's in there," he said.

I was glad to have Jeremy along for this. I kept thinking aloud with him. "How clever can that design be? Is looking at it worth putting these guys drastically on their guard?"

The silence of Reinauer's office hissed softly around us.

And then I finally put two and two together. I said, "Not an artillery shell at all."

I'd forgotten it until this moment, but I'd dreamed last night, in my mahogany bed at the Adlon, about the great whirring beasts passing over me in the night, as if I were sleeping on the ocean floor and these were vast creatures of the deep.

"The Zepps," I said. "He's about the Zepps and he's dealing with Krupp. Those are aerial bomb designs."

Jeremy looked at the boxes as if to confirm this and then back at me.

"No doubt improved," he said.

I asked the big question. "How badly do we need the design?"

We quietly consulted the boxes again.

They weren't talking.

"Essen is Krupp's main foundry, isn't it?" I said.

"Yes."

"This is where they'd turn out a million of these."

"It is."

"So what's in Kalk?" I said.

"That's our more interesting question."

"I think I was getting pretty close to Stockman last night at the Adlon bar," I said.

I considered that for a moment. My reporter self had indeed caught a whiff of something. Things were roiling in Albert.

I said, "I can't shake the feeling he's up to more."

Jeremy and I let my hunch hang between us for a moment.

I nodded at the boxes. "The first dud they drop and our bosses have this much. You and I grab these now, Stockman still has his designs, and we can do no more."

"Then shall we let this be?" he said.

This needed no answer. Together we turned and crossed the room. He switched off the lights, and I reset the lock on the door.

On the way to the main warehouse floor we devised a little ruse for the guard, who could have recovered his mind by now.

And so Jeremy and I ransacked the shipping office, arguing in German about which of us stupidly suggested the money would be in something other than an actual safe.

I'd earlier noticed some cases of what looked like a pretty damn good bock and we stole one of those, for appearances sake, and we argued some more—out of the hog-tied guard's line of sight—with me insisting on searching him for cash so we'd at least leave here with a little ready money and with Jeremy talking me out of it, saying this guy was just here doing his job and his aching jaw was enough trouble for him for one night.

Then we beat it out the loading dock door and back to the Ford with our case of beer.

We stopped at the curb a block before the hotel. From the wide median, the streetlights were shining through a scrim of linden trees.

"How do we meet again?" I said.

"You still have a room at the Baden?"

"I do."

"I can leave a message there for you," he said.

"And if I need to get *you*?"

There was an odd hesitation in him, which I wished I could read. But it was dark inside the Ford and he turned his face away. Whatever it was passed quickly.

"For the next few days you can reach me at this telephone." He reached quickly inside his coat. If he were anyone else I'd be drawing my Mauser.

His hand emerged with a piece of paper, which I took from him.

"They listen in on the phones at the Adlon," he said.

"I know."

"The lobby of the Baden has a telephone kiosk. You can call from there. Say as little as possible."

"Let's decide on a place that need never be mentioned."

"Yes," he said. "Make it the Hindenburg statue in the Tiergarten."

"But we speak of beer."

"Or brat, depending on the time of day."

"One other thing," I said. "I don't know who you are."

"A pretty good middleweight who once upon a time almost beat Tommy Ryan."

I'd meant around Berlin. On the phone. This answer came quick and dry. His German sense of humor. Or his German *Angst*. Or both.

But he played neither, giving the line only a brief beat before appending, "I am Bruno Obrecht. A Swiss businessman."

I started to get out of the still idly quaking Model T.

He put a hand on my arm. "But not for the next two days."

I sat back down.

"I am Erich," he said. "Erich Müller."

"Was that your birth name?"

"It was."

I stepped out of the T, and he said, "You want a couple of our bocks for your room?"

"Take them all," I said.

He pinched the brim of his hat to say good-bye and drove off.

I looked at the paper in the streetlight. His telephone number. *Spandau 4739.*

He was going home to his mother.

# 31

I stood for a moment on the street. An El train was softly clacking through the median lindens. I considered this roll of the dice, the opportunity we'd just left behind. Perhaps the content of the two boxes was all I'd come to Berlin to find. What we felt certain was in there could be everything there was to know about the sotto voce declaration I'd finessed from Stockman last night. If the bombs the Zepps were dropping could somehow be improved, made more accurate, more effective, the airship attacks might become far more than isolated, neighborhood disruptions. They might bring the war-changing terror to London that many people on both sides felt was possible from these machines. The Brits deserved to know the details of what they were up against as soon as possible. They needed to start making their own.

So why weren't those two boxes on their way to the American embassy right now?

Instead, I'd stolen some beer.

"Shit," I said.

No. "Shit" was what was in my head, certainly. But what I said aloud there on the Unter den Linden, what rang in the silence following the passing of the El, was *Scheiße*.

I was thinking in German and maybe I was just a little too close to this place right now.

However.

The British had no aerial attack of their own. They'd see plenty of this design long before they'd have their own airship. Surely it was better for now to keep the Germans confident about their security inside the Fatherland.

And I still had a reporter's niggling hunch.

I instantly questioned even that. Maybe that hunch was simply the feature writer in me. Stockman intrigued me. I wanted to get into his head. I had one foot in already. But maybe the only hard news he had in there was still sitting in Reinauer's office.

I tried to shake all this off.

I made myself walk. I let the blandly neoclassic, granite ashlar face of the Education Ministry scour my mind clean.

Spinning in the Adlon's front door I left the doubts behind. I had no choice but to play my hunches now. And I played one more.

I turned to the left and stepped into the doorway of the bar. In the far corner, drinking alone in an evening suit, was Sir Albert Stockman. He was sitting where he'd sat last night, his back to the rest of the bar.

I began to cross the floor, and he turned in his chair. It was an odd moment; I felt, chillingly, that he somehow sensed my approach. But he was actually seeking the bartender's attention. I drew near and now he did see me and he instantly rose, turning to face me. He said, in German, "Please. Yes. Come sit."

We shook hands.

I sat in the chair where I'd sat last night.

Stockman motioned to the bartender and sat down as well.

On the table before him was an empty whiskey glass.

Stockman saw me looking at it.

He said, in English, "They have a splendid American rye. Not to the taste of most Germans. They don't drink whiskey. But I have acquired some British tastes. I wanted this tonight."

The glass was empty, but now that Stockman was sitting and speaking, an afterwhiff of spirits floated past me. He'd been drinking for a while.

Last night's bartender appeared.

"Don't feel obligated," Stockman said.

"Not at all," I said. "I'll drink American with you."

"The bottle, Hans," Stockman said to the bartender, who nodded with a click of his heels and did a smart about-face.

Stockman instantly asked, "Were you with Madam Cobb?"

I still found it difficult to trust how I stood with him. I had a quick pulse of worry. This morning she had made me up into another man so that I could spy on Sir Albert. But he'd delivered the message himself, that I was to see her. Then why was he asking?

"This morning," I said. "At the theater."

"So. Yes. She and I had dinner tonight." He was speaking German again. "An early dinner before she returned to the theater. Were you at the rehearsal?"

"Not this evening," I said. "They are very busy. Working late. She has two casts to deal with, you realize. One German-speaking."

"I know," he said. "It wearies her."

Hans the bartender appeared beside us.

He put a glass in front of me and poured two amber fingers of rye in mine and two in Stockman's glass.

He put the bottle down between us.

A Pennsylvania whiskey. *Sam Thompson Old Monongahela Pure Rye*, with an etching of Sam's riverside distillery in Pittsburgh.

Stockman and I touched glasses.

"To the hardworking Isabel Cobb," I said.

"To Isabel," he said, putting as much into her name as my mother had put into her eyes about *him*. He was in love.

At that, I took the bolt of rye gladly, took it in full, relishing the burn down the throat, like a Pennsylvania summer noonday sun. And it bit with the spiciness of a pure rye, this particular one mixing cloves and pumpkin and cracked pepper.

When I lowered my glass and my face, I found Stockman looking at me. He'd sipped his. He was smiling a little half smile at me. "Were you ever a soldier, Mr. Hunter?"

"Can you call me Josef?" I said.

He cocked his head.

I said, "When I was brought as a child to America my name was Josef Wilhelm Jäger."

He smiled. "Of course," he said. "Josef."

"Never a soldier," I said.

"And if you'd stayed?" he asked.

"In Germany?"

"Yes."

"Perhaps not for the sake of the colonies. But for this war, I would have been in a trench in France by now. There is no doubt."

He nodded.

"With joy," I said, picking up on his observation from last night.

He lifted his glass to me and shot the rest of his rye.

He put three fingers in each of our two glasses.

I'd take this one slow.

We both lifted our glasses.

No toast this time. We were just two guys doing some serious drinking together. I liked that.

I sipped.

Off to my left, there was movement. I let the rye slide down my throat and I casually looked.

A German officer and a woman were arranging themselves at a table. His field gray tunic had a high turnover collar, and his shoulder boards were cornflower blue with two pips. A cavalry captain. I saw him in left profile. His cheek was imprinted with the crescent scar of his university fencing days. A *Schmiss*.

The scar caught my eye and held my gaze for longer than I'd intended. I could see, in my periphery, Stockman turning to look as well.

The woman was a peach, wearing a green silk and organdy evening gown with a high waist that lifted up and presented her ample bosom as if on an invisible platter. She was in the process of stripping off long, white kid gloves.

I looked at Stockman and he was still watching the couple. Then he turned back to me. He leaned across the table and flipped his chin to have me bend near.

"*Nicht Gesellschaftsfähig,*" he said. He caught himself. For this observation, he hadn't meant to speak German. He shot the couple a quick glance. They only had eyes and ears for each other. He returned to me and said it again in English, speaking even more softly, translating the euphemism literally. "Not fit for society."

I looked at her.

Perhaps.

As I watched her—they too bent near each other—Stockman said, "Not that I criticize him. He has earned this privilege."

The captain said something and the woman smiled softly. She lifted her right hand and brought it to his cheek and gently began to trace his *Schmiss* with the tip of her forefinger.

"She is his fiancée," I said. I looked back to Albert. His face was blank. He wasn't used to being contradicted; I feared I was overplaying our growing rapport. I angled my head for him to look. "The gesture."

He looked.

She was still moving her fingertip over her captain's scar.

Stockman chuckled softly, and he and I turned to each other, still leaning near. "You're right," he said. "But he will never have a moment of peace when he is apart from her. For fear her tenderness may stray."

I thought: *Like you with my mother.*

I nodded in agreement.

And then he surprised me. He lowered his voice still more. "Nor will she," he said.

Briefly I thought he was still talking about sex. But he said, "So many good men will die."

We took up our drinks. We sat back. This time I was the sipper and he immediately took the shot.

I knew if I was to justify those two boxes remaining in Reinauer's office, I'd have to get closer still to Albert. I'd never do that if I started thinking out each move. As he lowered his whiskey glass after his emotional bolt, I understood all this. And so I stopped thinking. Which allowed me to say, "Can I tell you a secret?"

Stockman leaned forward again. Rather abruptly. "Of course," he said.

I leaned in slowly.

I said, "I too have a *Schmiss*."

His eyes moved slowly, deliberately, to my bearded left cheek and then returned to mine.

"I think I told you I grew up in America," I said, leading us back to German. "My father made sure that I spoke the mother tongue. I was not allowed to say even a single English word in our house. And he wanted me to have an education. I also wanted that, but I dreamed of the University of Michigan. My father had other plans. He insisted I go *home* to university."

I paused very briefly, to let the *home* sink in. Stockman said, "He is a good man, your father."

"So I came to realize," I said. "In 1902, when I was eighteen, I packed a bag and I came to Heidelberg and they welcomed me and they disciplined me and they allowed me into their inner circle and I took up a saber and I earned my badge of honor."

He glanced at the place of my presently invisible scar.

I'd said my piece.

He looked at me closely for a long moment, reassessing me one more time. Then he said, "I must ask you why is this a secret. Why do you cover up this mark?"

I said, "For the same reason it is necessary to write newspaper stories for the people of America to explain the real Germany. This is something not in their blood."

"I understand," Stockman said.

He leaned back. He palmed the ends of the chair arms. "But you are in Germany now," he said.

"I am."

"Josef," he said. "Would you do a favor for me?"

"Yes."

"Would you go upstairs to your room, right now, and shave off your beard?"

This took me by surprise. But the reflex feeling I would have had even a few minutes ago did not occur. I did not for a moment hear this as the calling of a suspected bluff. He was mellow, avuncular even, in his manner and tone. He was encouraging me to come even closer to him.

"I will," I said.

"Good," he said. "You must wear this scar with pride. It is a rare thing. It is a precious thing."

"I shed my German blood for it," I said.

He smiled.

# 32

I stood before my mirror. The last thing he said as I'd risen to go was that he would wait, that he was looking forward to speaking this evening with Josef Wilhelm Jäger.

I found my hand severely steady as I worked the lather into my beard, as if I were about to pull a trigger. This was a badger-hair shaving brush, not a .32 caliber Mauser, but my body had invoked my conditioned response to a spy's stage nerves. It had been bad enough this past spring, confronting the scar for the first time since the wound had healed and I'd let my beard cover it up. Now this second revelation was odd indeed: I was fully asserting my cover identity to a German spy by showing him my actual face, which was, however, forever altered by the first German spy I'd ever confronted. And rubbing the cream into my cheeks summoned up my mother from this morning, her hands rubbing color into this beard, turning me into my battered doppelgänger to disguise me from the very man who was now waiting downstairs to see my naked face. Which would convince him utterly that I was someone I was not.

I'd had no idea spy work would be as unsettling as this.

I stropped the razor and I cut and I cut and I was clean and I was scarred and I was Josef Wilhelm Jäger.

I went back downstairs.

I expected that Stockman had continued to drink. I half expected this whole shaving event to have been in vain, that he would have reached his limit, that he would have forgotten even sending me upstairs.

He was sitting very still when I approached and he heard me and turned. The level of rye in the bottle had receded no farther since I'd left, and a cup of coffee was sitting before him on the table.

He rose.

He extended his hand to me. He spoke, of course, in German. "Herr Jäger, I am Albert Stockman."

He had shaved himself as well, by offering his first name without the title. Given who he was, it was an odd and unsettling thing for me to feel—as I now briefly did—a twist of barroom affection for this guy.

But I held off from using "Albert" to his face, though I'd thought it a number of times already, in disrespect. "Herr Stockman," I said. "May I ask a question?"

"Of course."

"Was your name once Stockmar?"

He threw back his head and laughed, and when he was done, he cuffed me on the shoulder. "You are a shrewd man, Herr Jäger. You are correct. It was done before I was born, however."

"That makes no difference," I said. "In your blood, you are still a Stockmar."

He laughed again and nodded me to my chair.

When I sat, I motioned for the bartender to come. He did, briskly. I said to him, "I'll have what he's having."

"Coffee?" the bartender said.

"Coffee," I said.

The man vanished.

I faced Stockman now, as the truly revealed Josef Wilhelm Jäger.

His eyes moved to my scar and lingered. "Please?" he said, lifting his hand, waving it as if turning the page of a book.

I turned my face to the right, fully showing the *Schmiss*.

I felt grindingly uncomfortable, but I understood my job would be made easier by all this. Nevertheless, the examination, though probably brief, felt endless. I focused on the thought that it was a good thing I would never know my own father. At our first meeting I'd be subjected to this same ordeal. *Here, let me take a look at you, my son.* To hell with that.

Then Stockman said, "Thank you."

I faced him once more.

"You did not pack it with horsehair?" he asked.

The dueling sword of the friendly, prearranged duels, the straight-bladed *Korbschläger*, had a blade as fine as my straight razor and did not bruise when cutting. Some duelists packed their cuts with horsehair to irritate them and keep them agape as they healed so as to create a more prominent scar. Mine was plenty striking on its own.

"I did *not*," I said. "That would be a lie and a sacrilege."

"Good," he said. "It's interesting how those of us who have grown up in exile sometimes have a purer sense of these things."

"Perhaps this war will refocus all Germans," I said.

"I greatly envy you, bearing this mark," he said. "I was in a different circumstance, of course, going off to university. My father had complex commitments. His son could go nowhere but to Oxford."

He paused. I had the impulse to keep improvising onward. I even thought to say: *A true German soul bears this mark invisibly from birth.* But even without thinking it out, I knew I was on the verge of going too far, of turning this into melodrama.

So I simply nodded sympathetically and was glad to find the bartender suddenly beside us, giving us pause, presenting my cup of coffee and topping off Stockman's from a carafe.

After the bartender had vanished again, Albert said, "Of course, it is the same with the British as the Americans. There is so much they do not understand."

I sipped at the coffee, hot and bitter, and I remained plausibly silent. Let Albert follow his own internal path.

He lifted his coffee, cup and saucer together, and looked at it steaming before him, and he said, "I'm afraid the British will *never* understand."

He sipped. But his voice had already turned hot and bitter.

"Not by reason, they won't," he said. "Not in a civilized way. They are waging this war against us by using their navy to starve Germany slowly to death, every man and woman and child. *That* is the act of terror. And they do it with their damnable outward restraint, as if its incremental effects civilize it. But they are not rational. They are cold-blooded, which is a different thing. Civilization cannot exist without passion."

He'd placed the cup back onto the saucer, but kept them both suspended before him. The cup was chittering lightly.

His hand had begun to tremble.

He seemed aware of it. He looked at the cup.

And the sound abruptly stopped.

He returned his eyes to mine and said, "I still have hopes that the Americans will come to understand."

"It's why I write," I said.

"I admire that," he said.

We drank our coffee for a time. Stockman seemed to turn inward. But whatever he was aware of in himself, I was apparently the point of reference. He would sip and think and look at me and look away and then do it all again.

Finally he said, "I am meeting a German scientist tomorrow who has created a process that will eliminate famine from the face of the earth. He did this six years ago. You do not know his name. I have read essentially every issue of your most important newspaper, *The New York Times*, for the past decade. His name has never appeared. Not once. Nor his discovery."

Stockman paused. Inside my head I'd paused several sentences ago. This guy had a way of veering off and surprising the hell out of me. He seemed to want me to comment now.

"What is his name?" I asked.

"Fritz Haber."

I had always read very widely. I possessed a very good memory. But Stockman was right.

"I have never heard his name," I said.

"You see?"

"What is this process?"

"He can convert the inaccessible nitrogen in the atmosphere into ammonia, which contains extractable, usable nitrogen. Do you know what this means?"

I knew some science. The air was mostly nitrogen. But I'd never heard of anyone figuring out how to use it.

"Perhaps," I said. "But tell me."

Stockman said, "Nitrogen is in everything we eat. Meat, bread, anything with protein. The nitrogen comes from the soil, through the crops. The wheat, the corn. The rye you and I have drunk together. But there is only so much nitrogen. The earth can be sucked dry. Fertile land can become exhausted from use, and it is the nitrogen that vanishes. Before the Haber Process, the only way for man to create large quantities of nitrogen to put back into the soil was by using the nitrogen in saltpeter. No one has saltpeter but the country of Chile, and even there, the supplies are finite. But you can make fertilizer from nitrogen-bearing ammonia, and if you can turn the air into ammonia, you have an infinite amount of fertilizer. The world has nearly two thousand million people. This is nearly twice as many people as a hundred years ago. It will not take another hundred years to double again. Already millions starve. But Germany will never starve. America need never starve. No one need starve. A *German* will feed them all. Fritz Haber will feed them all forever."

I sat in silence with that abrupt, vast, visceral feeling that a reporter gets when he picks up on a story that nobody has reported.

About the feeding of millions, now and into the future, of course. But the thing Stockman wasn't saying was that nitrogen was also essential in making explosives. Nitrogen created from the air meant *killing* millions as well.

The Allies controlled all of Chile's saltpeter.

How much did our government and the European Allies' governments know about this?

"This was six years ago?" I asked.

"Yes, when he demonstrated the process."

"And they're doing this now on an industrial scale?"

"Twenty-five tons of ammonia a day. For two years already."

I wanted to ask where. But I flipped the crank on my reporter's instincts and they started up instantly. I knew this was a fragile moment. An inappropriate, pointed question could shut Stockman down.

The links forward from where his mind had started were clear, from his having hopes that America will come to understand Germany, to his admiring my journalism in pursuit of that very aim, to his abruptly waxing rhapsodic about German nitrogen someday feeding a hungry world. He had it in his head to arrange for me to do a story. A grand one. The one with a humanistic face. I needed to be careful.

"If only America knew," I said.

"Perhaps that can be arranged," he said.

"I'd do the story full justice," I said.

"Have you seen Baron Mumm von Schwarzenstein at the Foreign Office?"

I had that phony letter from the baron who controlled the press, courtesy of the American-occupied German embassy in London. I had to assume whatever Stockman might have in mind would run afoul of the bureaucracy. It was still unclear to me how much high-ranking, maverick authority Albert actually had. Or how naive he might be about the ways of the German publicity machine. I had to ask a delicate question.

I created a warm little insider laugh. "Do you know the baron well?"

"Not at all," he said.

I tried not to show my rush of relief. "I've had my obligatory *Kirschwasser* with him from his crystal decanter," I said, improvising the details. "And all is well."

"Good," he said. "Meet me here in the bar at two tomorrow afternoon," he said. "Wait for me if I am late."

"Thank you," I said.

"And now," he said, "I must take a pot of coffee to my rooms to await Hamlet's entrance."

I had nothing to say to that.

I rose and offered my hand.

He rose and took it.

He inclined his head toward my scar. "This is who you are," he said.

# 33

I told Stockman I wanted to finish my coffee before I left and he bade me good night and consulted with the bartender—I presumed about having his pot of coffee delivered—then he walked across the floor, pretty steadily for all the drinking he must have done tonight, and he vanished into the lobby.

I gave him a couple of minutes to negotiate the elevator, and I emerged into the grand reception lounge of the Adlon ground floor. I stepped clear of the overhanging mezzanine, held aloft by square columns of yellow sienna marble, and I moved into the center of the lounge, with its frescoed ceiling vaulting high above me.

I carefully checked the scattering of people in the lobby. No eyes turning to me. No Herr Wagner.

To my left now was the reception desk, and there were empty settings of overstuffed chairs before it, but I moved on to the nearest chair and table of the Palm Court at the south end of the reception lounge. I sat in the center of three chairs closely arced around a small round table. I faced north across the central floor with a clear view of the stairs from the Unter den Linden doors. I ordered a pot of coffee. And, just in case, two cups.

The coffee was still warm when Mother swirled through the revolving door. She was surely tired after a long day of rehearsal, but she could do nothing other than make a dynamic entrance into such a public space as this. I knew that she would instantly, though covertly, assess her effect on her impromptu audience. I rose from my chair and began to applaud in broad, smooth undulations, though making no sound whatsoever. She was still fifty yards away and the sound was irrelevant anyway.

She saw me.

She fell out of the *Grande Dame* role and strode my way. To a viewer she was simply another woman walking across an open space. But I knew that this throttling back on her stage star aura meant she was all business.

She arrived.

"I'm having coffee," I said. "Would you like some?"

"Good evening to you as well, my darling Christopher," she said.

She used my real name but she spoke it low. When she wanted to be all business with me, she had to be the one who initiated it. Thus her umbrage at the missed niceties of greeting.

"Good evening, Madam Cobb," I said, also low. "Who are you thinking of, may I ask? I am still your humble and eager scribe, Joseph Hunter."

She stiffened. I realized she'd been unaware of the name she'd used.

And now I stiffened a little from the same twist of fear she'd just experienced. Her lapse had not been heard, much less understood. But she was capable of forgetting like this in a crucial moment, a crucial circumstance.

"I'm so sorry, Mr. Hunter," she said. "What did I call you?"

"Christopher."

She laughed lightly.

"Well, you see," she said. "That's my son's name. He's been much on my mind lately."

"You may have good reason not to recognize me."

"I'd say so," she said.

We were speaking very low now, and it was safe, but she kept up the pretense a little longer. She said, "When I last saw my son, he had stitches in his cheek in that very place."

"Did he indeed," I said. "I got this from my college days in Heidelberg."

"You went to Heidelberg, did you? You never mentioned this."

"I revealed it only tonight, to Sir Albert," I said.

"I'm sure he was impressed," she said.

"He's having coffee himself at the moment," I said. "We can chat for a few minutes if you like."

She began to sit on the chair to my left but glanced again at my scar and circled the table to sit on my right so as not to see it. I settled into my center chair and we leaned toward each other.

I could smell the orange blossom and violet of her Guerlain perfume. And the familiar musk of my mother herself, from her dozen hours on the stage, which the French scent was intended to cover. And the licorice bite of her Sen-Sen, covering the whiskey, which she always took in true moderation after a long day of rehearsing but for which she always felt guilty.

She looked with seeming casualness around her. So did I. As I'd thought, no one was near enough to have heard a syllable of this. And we were clear of the vaulted ceiling, so the acoustics remained local.

We could speak privately like this.

"He drinks too much," she said, gently.

"For which I am grateful," I said.

"It must make you look like a real pal sometimes," she said. There was a cat-tongue rasp to her tone, as if I were being a hypocrite, taking advantage of him.

I leaned closer. "Do you remember why we're risking our necks?" I said.

She sighed.

"What the hell is that sigh all about?" I said.

"You're right, is what it's about."

I never could quite figure out how she was able to switch me from irritation to guilt in the time it takes for an electric light bulb to go from dark to bright.

"How was rehearsal?" I asked, trying to soothe things.

"This is terrible, wearying work," she said. "A never-ending assault on your mind and heart."

It was never like that when she was still perceived to be a leading lady. I didn't say this. "Two casts at once, in two languages," I said.

She looked at me. "Not the theater, child."

She'd flipped on another light. She meant the spy work.

"You got into this all on your own," I said.

"I'm not blaming you."

"You didn't have to fall in love with him," I said.

She turned her face from me, as if she were hiding something.

"Are those real tears or fake?" I said.

She plucked a handkerchief out of her lizard skin bag and dabbed at her eyes. "Both," she said.

"Look," I said. "I'm sorry this has gotten complicated."

"I need to go," she said.

"Have you gone through his things?"

She turned her face sharply to me. "It hasn't gotten that far," she said.

I wasn't sure what distinction she was drawing.

"I don't have a key," she said.

"I'm not prying," I said.

"I know you have to ask."

"I'm asking if you can do this, given your feelings."

"I'm gathering as much information as I can."

"I appreciate that."

"I can do this," she said.

She was no Hamlet.

She said, "How was your adventure at the docks?"

I had to make a decision now about my mother and this role she'd taken on. The more she knew, the more she could inadvertently reveal, especially to a man she had feelings for. But the less she knew, the less she might recognize as useful information. I stalled for thinking time by leaning forward and topping off my coffee cup from the *Adlon Oblige* pot.

Her feelings for men. They came and they went. Readily. How deeply could this Albert possibly be touching her?

"Coffee?" I asked.

"Yes, dear," she said.

I filled the second cup as well.

She knew what was at stake for her and for me and even for the country she wanted to serve.

She took up her cup and sipped. As did I.

She was a smart woman. Trask trusted her with Stockman. I could use her help.

So I told her most everything that had happened on this day.

Among the omissions: I didn't tell her about the cadaver act at the *Kabarett*. She didn't need more ideas on how to reinvent herself.

When I'd finished, she said, "I should go now. I have things to listen for."

She rose.

I rose with her. "Just be careful about asking leading questions," I said.

"I understand," she said.

She turned, but she paused and turned back. She touched my arm. "Thank you," she said. "For trusting me."

"Even when you're in love." I said it as a declaration. In fact, I said it to try it out, to try to hear if it was true.

She said, "Love only makes me stupid in one way. My *mind* is always untouched."

And with this, she whisked away as if she were making an entrance into a swank hotel through a revolving door.

# 34

I sat where I was.

I thought of what my mother had said, about Albert's drinking helping me to befriend him. He was a common figure in a profession that was still figuring itself out for the twentieth century. He was officially in the employ of the German Foreign Office, certainly. Secretly so. He was powerful, clearly. But he seemed an amateur at heart. The Huns hadn't sufficiently accounted for people like my mother and me being able to get this close to a man like him. That was good for us. But I realized his amateurism made him less logical, less predictable, more dangerous in his work.

It had been a long day.

I stopped thinking.

I had two places to sleep.

It was too late to call Jeremy's mother's house.

I chose the Adlon.

I rose, crossed through the reception lounge, and neared the desk on the way to the staircase behind it. The steps led to the mezzanine and the hotel elevator.

Just before passing beneath it, I glanced up to the mezzanine.

Grasping the ironwork balustrade there, standing upright with his arms straight, his eyes fixed on me, was Herr Wagner.

I did not hesitate but nodded at him and went up. It was time to try to deal with him.

I emerged on the mezzanine landing. He had already turned around to confront me.

I was well aware that I was showing him my third face in two days. But I made sure he got a good look at the scar on my cheek as I approached. He was working hard at maintaining the opacity of his own face.

"Good evening, Herr Wagner," I said.

He nodded. I was no doubt a unique challenge for him. From the intensity of his gaze, from the faint, incipient shaping of his mouth, which waxed and waned and waxed again, I knew he was struggling to find words to say.

I was concerned, however, that if he failed to find any words for me, he'd decide to leave the task for some boys in a back room at the Foreign Ministry.

"I am sorry to keep confusing you," I said.

He stiffened a little. "Sir?"

"Do you know what I'm doing here?"

He stiffened some more. "Doing?"

I could only play the cards in my hand. I said, "You are no doubt aware that a special and powerful friend of Germany, Baron Albert Stockman, is staying at the Adlon. And that he is accompanied by the great American actress, Madam Isabel Cobb."

I paused. Wagner was keeping his face blank and his mouth shut. I waited him out.

Finally he said, "I am aware of them."

"I daresay you know that Baron Stockman arranged for me to stay at your lovely hotel. I am here to write a major story for the American newspapers on Madam Cobb's performance of Hamlet. As part of the story, I am—in my ignorance of these matters—experiencing some aspects of the life of an actor. Putting on makeup, for instance. Changing a face to become a character for the stage. Do you understand?"

"I'm not sure, Herr Hunter."

"The face that puzzled you yesterday afternoon. It was not mine. It was makeup that Madam Cobb herself put upon me so that I might experience, for a few hours, what the actor experiences. Being inside another person's skin. I regret making you an unwitting part of our little experiment."

Wagner struggled to take all this in.

His eyes moved sharply now to my scar.

I said, "The *Schmiss*, however, earned in Heidelberg, is real. I write for American newspapers. I am technically an American citizen. But I am, in fact, German."

His eyes remained on the scar.

"Would you like to touch it?" I said.

He flinched his eyes away from my cheek. "No sir," he said.

"To verify its reality. Go ahead," I said.

"No thank you, sir," he said, growing as uncomfortable as I'd intended.

"The experimenting is over, Herr Wagner. I will cause you no more confusion."

He summoned the power of his formality. He straightened. He clicked his heels. He said not a word. He moved past me and down the steps.

This might all have gone well.

This might only have bred distrust in him, and therefore, as well, in the men he worked for.

I could only hope my own work would go swiftly in Berlin.

I waited and watched Wagner shortly emerge from beneath the mezzanine, stepping smartly, his backbone flagpoled into his butt, his chin lifted.

I thought, *A goddamn Hun.*

The elevator door opened on the fourth floor, and I padded along the dense Ushak hall carpet to my room.

*Huns,* I thought. It was a little too easy for me to use the epithet. It was just a word. But I had to make sure it didn't induce a reflex *feeling* about the Germans, as well, or I could miss their equivalents of Mother and me. Or Jeremy. Stockman was no simple Hun.

And twenty minutes later, with my balcony door open to the upspill of street light and to a wisp of a night breeze, with the linen top sheet draped over my bare feet, the Huns lingered with me. The irony, of course, was that Kaiser Willie himself stuck the label on his people. As I drifted off to sleep, the quote—suppressed in the German press at the time, but lately resurrected among the Allies—rattled around in my head, words he spoke fifteen years ago to his troops heading off to China to crush the Boxer Rebellion. *Prisoners will not be taken. Whoever falls into your hands will be put to death. Just as a thousand years ago the Huns, under their King Attila, found a glory that shines even today, may you exalt the name "German" so that no one in China will dare to look askance at a German again.*

Which was just fine as an American spy's lullaby, a drifting away on a reminder of why I was here, doing what I was doing.

I woke to light and automobile horns from beyond the balcony. An hour later, braced with its good coffee and fresh eggs, I went out of the Adlon and headed for the Baden, walking briskly, though I immediately turned off Unter den Linden onto Wilhelm-Strasse and then turned again onto Behren-Strasse. I stopped immediately in front of the National Bank and lit a cigarette, waiting to see if anyone came around the corner following me. No one did. I went on east and made my way back to Unter den Linden and the Hotel Baden. And finally I stood in an enclosed wood and glass telephone kiosk in the Baden's lobby. I asked the hotel operator to put me through to Spandau, number 4739.

A woman answered the phone. "Müller," she said.

His mother. "Mrs. Müller," I said. "May I speak with . . ." I hesitated very briefly. I had three of him to choose from. ". . . Erich?"

"Who is it calling?" she said.

"Josef Wilhelm Jäger," I said.

"Please wait, Mr. Jäger." She spoke German very formally, with every *r* carefully trilled.

The phone clunked, onto a tabletop no doubt, as the line stayed open.

After a few moments Jeremy's voice said, "Josef. Good morning."

"Good morning, Erich."

"I'm sorry I am in Berlin only briefly," he said. For his mother's consumption, I figured.

"We should have lunch," I said.

"What time?"

"To meet, let's say eleven o'clock."

"Good," he said.

And he hung up.

I stepped from the booth.

I went to my room at the Baden and found the fragment of a matchstick, which I'd left wedged, unseen, halfway up in the jamb of the door, still wedged there.

I lay down for an hour, resting better than I had all night at the Adlon.

At about ten o'clock I walked the three hundred yards back to the Kaiser's favorite hotel. For the hell of it, I gave my room a careful look. Wagner or his boys had done a pretty slick job with their search. But the last item I checked showed their hand. My portable combination tool had been laid back into my latched toilet bag a hundred and eighty degrees off. The two ends were reversed. I wondered when this had been done. Sometime before or sometime after my confrontation with Wagner on the mezzanine? Was this a bit of clumsiness on his part? Or was Wagner sending me a little message that he was still watching?

Either way, I'd done all I could, and I would continue to be mindful that I was surrounded by some of Willie's best Huns, who'd reserved a place against a wall at Spandau for guys like me.

Ten minutes later a note in a hotel envelope skiffed its way along the carpet and into the room at the bottom of my door.

Before picking it up I opened the door and looked right and then left and I saw a flash of Egyptian blue turning the corner at the end of the corridor. An Adlon page boy.

I closed the door and opened the envelope.

Stockman worked fast.

I was to meet him at four o'clock, not two. And I would go with him to see Fritz Haber at the Kaiser Wilhelm Institute for Physical Chemistry.

# 35

The lindens of the boulevard before the Adlon flowed like German blood into the vast forest of the Tiergarten. I entered through the Brandenburg Gate and along the Charlottenburger-Chaussée, which was lined with plane trees and marble statues of the Brandenburg-Prussian rulers, the Margraves and the Fredericks and the Joachims. All of these monarchs were dramatically outranked, however, when I turned into the Sieges-Allée.

He asserted his authority at once, though he was still two hundred yards away and though another goddess Victory floated behind and high above him on a red granite column. This was a military monarch, four storeys high, shaped from khaki oak, the massively square-faced Field Marshal Paul Ludwig Hans Anton von Beneckendorff und von Hindenburg, in great coat, leaning on his sword, and facing down this "Victory Avenue."

I approached him.

He was a Nail Man. He was the latest in an odd German revival of an old Austrian custom of putting up a heroic wooden statue and then ceremonially driving nails into it for luck, for a blessing, for charity.

Hindenburg was brand-new, dedicated only recently and with the wooden platforms still girding him up to his waist to facilitate the first assault of nails. Berliners were asked to drive nails into their military hero for charity, the rehabilitation of East Prussia, overrun by the now expelled Russians in the first months of the war.

I began to circle him. The nails were mostly iron but with a notice-able scattering of silver-plate and very occasional spots of gold-plate. The kiosk by the front of the marble base had displayed the donation rates. Iron was one *mark*, silver was five, gold was a hundred. For your hundred *mark* you got a lapel pin, replicating the iconic Ger-man Iron Cross, done in onyx with gold-plated trim and a golden **H** in the center.

I paused at Hindenburg's backside, where he'd already been nailed a good hundred times. All in iron.

"That's where I'd put one," Jeremy said from behind my left shoulder.

Still pondering Hindenburg's backside, I said, "You figure those hundred guys had that German sense of humor about it?"

"Of course," he said.

I turned to him now. "Good morning, Erich," I said.

Very briefly his eyes went as wide as they might have when Tommy Ryan caught him with an unexpected shot to the ribs. He recovered fast, but now he was driving a nail of a gaze into my *Schmiss*.

"I had no idea," he said.

"So what's your idea now?" I said.

"I still don't have an idea."

"It's a war story I'd be happy to tell you over lunch."

"It looks like . . ."

"So they say. That's why I'm showing it to my new German pals." I glanced back up at the oaken Field . "You know, it just occurred to me. That Chicago journalist I once was had a pretty shrewd strategy when interviewing local dirty politicians. He always made a point to wear the lug's buttonhole campaign pin when he wanted to finesse incriminating quotes out of him."

Jeremy had stopped looking at the scar, but his usually stoic face was still furrow-browed with puzzlement.

"Trust me," I said.

"Carry on," he said, briefly dropping into English.

So we circled back around to the front of the statue. I gave the Field Marshal a last glance before taking him on with a hammer. He had a faraway look and the stiff posture of a man with hemorrhoids. But maybe it was just the hundred nails in his ass.

I asked the elderly, bristle-haired attendant for a hundred-*mark* golden nail. He clicked his heels and bowed, and I paid him two ten-dollar gold liberty heads from the money belt I'd worn since I'd first gone to war as a correspondent. Once newspaper money, now government.

With elaborately grateful heel clicking and bowing, he gave me a hammer and a gold-plated inch-and-a-half nail.

I clicked my heels and bowed a thanks, and Jeremy followed me to the foot of the scaffold.

He said, "The British have had their way with me, I'm afraid. My first thought was you are a fool to pay such a sum. But the German in me looks at that pin and I know what you're doing. That says you opened your heart and gave to them in difficult times. They have warm hearts, the Germans. They will count you as one of them."

"For that, given what we've got to do, twenty bucks is cheap," I said.

And I went up the first level to stand as high as Hindenburg's knees and the second to reach his waist. His arms were crossed loosely before him, parallel to the ground, resting on the sword, and I climbed up onto the railing of the scaffold and grabbed his left elbow and hoisted myself up and crawled into his arms and I hammered a golden nail into the center of Field Marshal Paul Ludwig Hans Anton von Beneckendorff und von Hindenburg's chest.

Applause rose up to me from a gathering of passersby.

When I came down, Jeremy met me at the bottom of the scaffold. He clicked his heels and bowed.

Then we walked away, past the southern edge of the Reichstags-Gebäude, the Hall of the Imperial Parliament, the legislators inside as ornamental as the building's Italian Renaissance flourishes. We left the Tiergarten and found a café along the Spree and we had our beer and brat and I told him about the scar and my late drink with Stockman and the upcoming interview.

"Have you heard of this guy Haber?" I asked.

"Fertilizer?"

"You have. How?"

Jeremy shrugged. "The German newspapers. It's been a while. He's respected. They try to make him a bit of a hero, but fertilizer doesn't play a big part in the German mythos."

"So this afternoon Sir Al wants me to mythologize manure for the Americans."

"German manure."

"The critical thing is the conversation those two boys will have after they kick me out of the room."

"Bombs starve without nitrates too," Jeremy said. "If Stockman's working on big-scale bombing from Zepps, Haber's process is critical."

True enough. But things still didn't quite add up, a thought I voiced with a "However" that I let stand on its own for a moment. And then I said the thing I couldn't get straight: "Haber's active role in nitrates for bombs is long since done with. Why the personal meeting?"

Jeremy nodded. "So how do we listen in?"

Over the rest of lunch, he and I failed to come up with a plan for that. All we could conclude was that more improvisation would be called for.

He did stop me, however, as I turned to leave him outside the café. "Remember this about us," he said.

He heard himself. Us.

"About the *Germans*," he said. "They are difficult to fool. But they are often easy to bluff."

# 36

I took the elevator to the lobby of the Adlon a few minutes before four o'clock and emerged next to the front desk. I expected to meet Stockman in the bar, but he was talking to the frock coat at reception. He saw me out of the corner of his eye and glanced my way to wave me over with a little tilt of the head. As I approached, he was giving instructions for the envelope he was holding nose-high between his face and the clerk's. Both men's hands were still on it. Stockman hadn't let go yet, a gesture of emphasis to accompany his wishes.

"I want this delivered to Madam Isabel Cobb at the Lessing Theater. Personally. By hand." He paused dramatically after the "Personally." And even, briefly, after each word to follow. No mistakes. *Persönlich. Mit der Hand.*

"Absolutely," the clerk said, clicking his heels and bowing.

Stockman released the envelope to him.

"You may rely on the Adlon, Baron Stockman," the man said, still speaking to the English baronet in German.

The meeting time with Haber must have altered his dinner plans with my mother.

I'd trained myself as a reporter to take in every detail with a fresh eye and ear. Trask and his boys had only sharpened that. But sometimes it took a few details to pile up for me to finally notice. What I'd just witnessed had to do with a delivery. A delivery of something important. And it had to do with the mode of delivery. Stockman's emphasis clanged again in my head. And again. *Mit. Der. Hand.* And then I got it. MDH. The box to Kalk, near Cologne, the box to FVFB, was to be delivered personally. *With the hand.*

Stockman was clicking back at the frock coat. Of course he'd trust the Adlon. Now he turned to me and offered his hand. I shook it. And I wondered: *Mit dieser Hand?* With *this* hand? Given his obvious connection to the device in the box, I figured it was likely that the answer was yes. Stockman himself was going to deliver the Zepp bomb to Kalk.

We were soon in a taxi and heading toward Dahlem, a villa colony eight miles southwest of the city center. It was also the home of the Kaiser Wilhelm Society for the Advancement of Science. Four years ago Willie lent his name and gave big money to do a grander Berlin version of the Institut Pasteur in Paris. Instead of just biology and medicine, Willie's little *Gesellschaft* was hiring the big dogs—the German ones—to set up separate institutes in all the major sciences, where they could do what they damn well pleased without having to teach students or answer to bureaucrats or politicians or other government operatives. I figured maybe that last principle was getting a little shaky now that Germany was at war, which maybe was why Stockman was having this meeting.

The Tiergarten had barely vanished from the back window of our Daimler taxi when Stockman squared around toward me a little in the seat and said, "There are a few things we should talk about." He said this in English, the first English we'd spoken in quite a while, I realized. Though the driver's compartment was separate from the tonneau and the engine noise was loud, the partition window was partly open for the summer heat.

I shifted in my seat to match his angle toward me.

He said, "I am accepting Madam Cobb's faith in you. But I will be frank. From our conversations I can fully understand that faith."

He paused. Sober, he had nothing of the sentimental, the vulnerable about him. So I understood that this restrained pause and these somewhat indirect words were significant in Stockman's unintoxicated range of emotional expression.

"Thank you," I said.

"Your story with him must regard his process *only* as a benefit to humanity."

I heard the command and so I filled the brief silence that followed: "But *not* to include the benefits to humanity of our quickly ending the war."

He laughed. "You understand my full meaning."

"That's my job," I said. Indeed. I repressed that thought, however, a reflex sense of irony being a dangerous trait for a spy.

But he heard it the way he needed to. "If only all journalists had that gift," he said.

"I understand your *intended* meaning," I gently corrected. Surely he didn't want even a trusted journalist to know his *full* meaning.

He got it. He laughed again. "So if he volunteers anything else . . ."

"I will treat him as I do you," I said. "Nothing will ever appear in print that would embarrass him or Germany or will reveal anything that will aid Germany's enemies."

"I have already given him that assurance," Stockman said. "Now, a few incidental but problematic things, as you might naturally be inclined innocently to make small talk or to enhance the human elements of your story."

"As indeed I may," I said.

"Little more than three months ago, Doctor Haber's wife took his army-issued revolver into their garden and shot herself to death."

He said this flatly.

He said no more for a moment.

"So no questions about his family," I said.

"Best not."

The Daimler shifted gears and so did Stockman. He said, "Doctor Haber is a Heidelberg man, like yourself. And like yourself he bears a scar on his cheek. But I understand it is not a scar of honor. Forgive me. As the bearer of a true *Schmiss*, you no doubt would have recognized it for what it is. But I thought I should mention it."

"Yes, thank you," I said.

"He is a Jew," Stockman said.

He let me absorb that for a moment. The haters of Jews—often those who have leaned close and revealed this sotto voce—assumed the following moment of quiet was filled with an agreement on the subject that needed no further expression.

But Stockman said this as uprightly and flatly as he'd spoken of the suicide of Haber's wife. I kept my manner and face as neutral as his. I hoped he'd show more of himself now. A man who, in his ignorance, showed his prejudice, about whatever sort of subject, was a man who gave power to others. He showed the way his mind tended to stop working, his sensibility tended to shut out the real world. That was always useful, to a reporter or to a spy.

And Stockman said, "He converted to Christianity more than twenty years ago. So he is a Christian the way I am an Englishman."

He let me fill in the meaning of that. Clear enough. He was still a Jew.

Stockman said, "He has been a German from birth. As was his father and his father's father. Do they not bleed? I am one of those who thinks that Shylock was justified in seeking his revenge. And that Shakespeare intended so. But the Jew has his own blood. His people were born to wander. As things are, the Jew who has a legacy like Doctor Haber is certainly a German. He overtly proclaims his strong allegiance to Germany. You and I will take pride for America to learn what this German has done for humanity. Doctor Haber is my stepbrother, Josef. Certainly that. But does one trust a stepbrother as he does his brother by blood?"

Stockman shrugged, as if in answer to his own question.

I did not reply.

Stockman looked away briefly, at the passing shops along the Kaiser-Allée, and then back to me.

"I don't know what you should make of that," he said. "Perhaps just to understand the man."

Once again, he looked beyond the taxi that carried us.

He said, still looking away, "I suppose I trust a loyal German Jew more than any London Christian."

This ended the conversation between us for the last few miles to Dahlem.

Haber's Institute for Physical Chemistry was a large but only lightly ornamented four-storey, nine-bay Greek Revival building, its central three-bay section sporting mid-floor Doric columns holding up a bare-bones pediment, which was adorned with nothing but a central, circular window. The one striking feature, however, was hardly classical: a circular tower attached at the building's northern end with a *feldgrau* metal dome and a high-spiked spire making the thing look unmistakably like a massive, field-officer *Pickelhaube*.

The place was surrounded by barbed wire. It had two soldiers, draped with Mauser G98s, flanking the central door beneath the Doric columns. These boys were not features of the institute when it was pursuing the hundred-year quest to pull nitrogen out of the air so the plants could grow.

A soldier led us up the two central flights of marble stairs to Haber's office. At each floor I glanced right and left and there was a quiet, ardent urgency about the place: white coats flashing, intense words from the end of a hall, a canister rolling on a hand truck with a gray-hair in a three-piece suit hovering over each turn of the wheels.

You walk into an institute of chemistry, especially a bustling one, and you expect the place to bray in your nose from the smells of things whose names are unpronounceable and whose purpose can be understood only in formulas. But the place smelled like a Boston Brahmin boarding school, all floor wax and ozone.

I did not have a chance to walk down one of these laboratory corridors. Immediately at the top of the third-floor staircase we turned into a short hallway back toward the front of the building and were ushered straight into a conference room with windows looking into the tops of the plane trees on the Thiel-Allée. I figured Stockman would get a grander tour when the interview was over and I was beyond the barbed wire.

The room had an oak table for ten and was hung with Holophane reflectors and tungsten lamps, illuminated now, in the afternoon light, for the sake of the wall facing the windows, which held a twelve-foot blackboard festooned with equations. If the corridors of the institute smelled like those in a boarding school, this was the faculty lounge, redolent of chalk dust and tobacco smoke.

Stockman and I sat down next to each other along the lengthwise center of the table, facing the blackboard. The soldier vanished.

We both stared at the equations for a moment, the flow of constants and unknowns, coefficients and parameters. As if on cue we looked at each other.

I said, "We needn't worry so much about his saying something he shouldn't. I just hope he says something we can understand."

Stockman glanced once more at the equations, but only briefly. "I know some basics, from metallurgy," he said. "But far downstream from this. Far enough so I could make useful things in the world."

*Like milk cans and Zepp bombs*, I thought.

We nodded knowingly at each other.

Then we had one of those silently agreed upon shifts in a conversation where the two parties understand there is nothing more to say about the current subject but aren't ready to stop talking. We had to wait here together, so we consciously turned our minds elsewhere.

In so doing, Stockman's eyes fell to my lapel. "I meant to say earlier. I admire your pin. I'm sure there's a story behind it, which I'd like to hear sometime."

Stockman didn't know about the Nail Man, or at least about the reward for a big donation, and the Iron Cross was a powerful icon for this country. Good.

"The story's a simple one," I said, making it sound like humility masking bravado.

And Fritz Haber strode into the room.

He was a stocky man, wearing a bespoke summer wool suit, a high wing-tip collar, and a necktie knotted tight. He had a round face, with a pince-nez clamped to his nose, and was determinedly bald, having shaved off every last hair, slick as a chemical canister. The scar on his left cheek was of the South Chicago saloon-brawl variety, too short and too severely curled at the end ever to be rendered by a saber stroke.

Stockman and I jumped to our feet.

"Please, gentlemen, please," he said. "We shall be informal with each other, yes?" Nevertheless, he placed himself across the table from us to reach and shake our hands. "Can I have my assistant get you some coffee?"

Stockman and I declined with thanks and we all sat.

Haber had known from the jump-off to speak German with this Brit and this American.

"It is a pleasure to see you again, Baron," Haber said to Sir Albert.

"For me it is an honor, Privy Councilor Haber," Albert said, using the honorific *Geheimrat*, an open acknowledgment that Haber had the ear of the Kaiser or at least of his high minions.

Haber turned his face to me.

I thought, for just a molecule of a moment, that the mysteries of chemistry were no greater than the mystery of the pince nez hoop-spring, which held the damn fool thing in place.

"And Mr. Jäger, I am pleased to meet you," Haber said. "Baron Stockman has told me very good things about you. That you should find it as preposterous as I do that your country has ignored what we have accomplished here, this is encouraging for me."

"I have a forum to dispel that ignorance, Privy Councilor Haber," I said.

He smiled. "I appreciate both of you recognizing my status, but please call me *Doctor* Haber."

He said this with a magnanimous flare of the hands, as if he'd just sanctioned *Fritzy.*

I took out my notebook and my Conklin, and *Geheimrat Doktor* Fritz began, no initial question necessary. He talked for a while—lectured, more like—about the challenge of the locked nitrogen molecules in the air: the delicate balancing of very high temperatures and very high pressure for extraction; the need for an effective catalyst for the project; the frustrating search for precisely the right one, with Haber eventually moving from osmium, which was good, to uranium, which was more abundantly available, and then, when BASF made an industry out of it, finally arriving at iron, though iron alone was a failure and needed a subtle blend of the oxides of aluminum and potassium and calcium to make it work. He called what he'd done a kind of alchemy, as if he'd figured out how to make gold from the air. These limitless nitrates meant, after all, that *Geheimrat Doktor* Fritz had saved the world from starvation.

I took dutiful notes.

And all the while, my mind sought the delicate balance of heat and pressure so as to extract, from the rush of highly charged molecules of air in this room, a fertilizing clue or two about Stockman's full intentions.

Haber wrapped up his lecture and folded his arms, in satisfaction, upon his chest. "Those are the basics," he said. "Perhaps you have some questions, knowing better than I what it is that Americans have failed to grasp."

"Thank you, Doctor Haber," I said. "What you've said is very clear to me and very compelling. Please understand that Americans in general have not even had the chance to grasp any of this. The failure has been among a very small group of Americans. The journalists."

Haber nodded his head at the validity of my point. To his credit.

"And journalists," I said, "need a catalyst. They are—on their own—simple iron. May I seek now, for a few minutes, the aluminum, the potassium, the calcium oxides to mix with them?"

Haber smiled and nodded as I appropriated the terms of his mini-lecture for my request, as if he were a teacher and gave a damn about his teaching and a student from the back of the lecture hall had raised his hand and made a smart comment.

I had a fleeting sense of him. Not so much what he was as what he wasn't. Or didn't seem to be. In mourning. He was nothing like a man whose wife blew her brains out with his own pistol a couple of months ago. He seemed animated without mitigation. He gave off energy and focus and devotion.

Either this was one hard son of a bitch or his anguish was so strong he'd dug a hole for it and threw it in and all this energy was him shoveling dirt. I hoped for the latter. That would make him even more eager to talk about what was presently preoccupying him.

It was time now to suppress my scoop-seeking reporter's gag reflex. Which I did. And instead I recited my already twice-refined Stockman Doctrine, my fawning assurance to this guy that he could say anything that was on his mind and if it was the last thing in the world he'd want to tell a newspaper reporter, it was okay because I was there to protect him against himself.

In the midst of this, Haber had glanced once at Stockman, with a little flex around the eyes that appealed for reassurance. I'd kept my own eyes on Haber, and it was clear from the abrupt relaxation in his face that Stockman had come through for me.

When I finished, Haber said, "You may seek."

"Thank you," I said. "First, I'd like to return to a phrase you used—and naturally so—a few moments ago. 'Your country,' you said to me, referring to the United States of America. You are, strictly speaking, correct. But now I ask that you grant me the same assurance I have given you. I will tell you a thing meant only for the three of us. *My* country is Germany. It was the country of my father, and of my father's father."

I paused.

I did not need to say *Just like your father and your father's father.* I could read his face. The ever so slight firming of his mouth. The minute nod.

"That is perhaps the aluminum oxide," I said. "The American re-porters who came to hear about your discovery lacked the . . ." I hesitated very briefly to find just the right word.

Haber intervened. "Promoter," he said.

I cocked my head at him, and he elaborated.

"These compounds are called *promoters* of the catalysis."

"Thank you," I said. "Yes. These journalists lacked the promoter of an existing connection to our country. I come to this story able to energize it for my readers by my pride in Germany."

Now it was time for a little catalytic self-deprecation, with an embedded appeal for him to spill his own beans. "I confess I'm in-timidated interviewing such a great thinker as you, Doctor Haber. But at this moment in history, great thinkers need to step forward. I hope I'm saying all of this precisely. Am I making sense?"

"Perfect sense," he said. "During peace time a scientist belongs to the world. But during war time he belongs to his country."

I took a sudden, deep, seemingly admiring breath. "May I write that down?"

"Of course."

I did.

"Your discovery will help feed our country," I said. "Particularly in the face of this barbaric blockade of food by the British."

"It will help," he said.

"'Barbaric,' of course, is our private word."

"An appropriate word for our private use," Haber said.

"Are you continuing to refine the Haber Process for agricultural uses?"

"It is no longer a matter of science," Haber said. "It is a practical matter, for industry. They are the ones who seek refinements, mostly to do with increasing output. You should speak to the people at BASF in Oppau."

"The war must be making very heavy demands on them," I said, walking a high wire now with Stockman next to me, trying to lead Haber by rhetorical indirections.

"Carl Bosch, for instance," Haber said. "At BASF."

"Excellent idea," I said.

"Very heavy demands," Haber said.

He was circling back.

"It frightens me, in retrospect," I said. "If it were not for your process, our dear Fatherland could be running out of all that it needs."

I was referring to explosives, of course, not food. Ammunition. Bombs. I kept it vague, to keep Stockman quiet for as long as possible. But Haber instantly knew what I meant.

"We would have run out six months ago," Haber said.

Stockman jumped in. "We are all frightened of that in retrospect," he said. "But we have come through. And the subject of explosives falls outside of the story we wish to do."

He was staying vigilant.

"Sorry, Baron," I said. "These are emotional issues."

"I am well aware of that," he said.

I turned back to Haber.

I was glad to be in my reporter's frame of mind. I knew if you couldn't get something out of the guy you wanted to expose, you might at least get him to rail at his enemies. Whose names you made careful note of.

I'd even had a whiff of collegial conflict from that earlier quotable proclamation.

I figured it would take Stockman a little time to assess this line of questioning. And that he wouldn't hold it permanently against me. It was worth the risk.

"Doctor Haber," I said, "your fine observation still sings in my head. The responsibility of a scientist during war. Do all of your colleagues feel the same way?"

"Some. Most."

I could see him stiffening. Not against me. Against somebody in his head.

"I'm sure you of all people could persuade anyone who would waver."

"Not always." His face was turning red. Catalysis.

"If they are German," I said.

"German? Yes, German."

"And loyal."

Haber turned to Stockman, put his hand onto the tabletop in his direction. "I've spoken to you of this man," he said.

I could feel Stockman stirring.

This was a touchy issue between them as well.

Haber's face swung back to me. "Albert Einstein," he said.

# 37

This was another scientist whose name I did not know, but from the tone of Haber's voice I was expected to.

"I myself brought him from exile to the Institute," Haber said. "I overlooked his personality for the brilliance of his mind."

Fritz was going red in the face again.

I had to assume Stockman was about to intervene. Haber was in the grip of a powerful desire to talk.

"That exile was self-imposed," Haber said. "Though he was born in Germany, as was his father and his father's father."

He paused, letting this irony sink in.

I looked to Stockman, who was poised to speak. He glanced at me. I furrowed my brow and nodded to him, fleetingly, a gesture of reassurance. I lifted my notebook from the tabletop, while still looking at Stockman, and I turned to Haber and closed the notebook before him and put it back down, making a little show of it, more for Stockman, of course, than for Fritz. Though Fritz took notice.

"How distressing," I said.

Haber said, in crescendo, "Perhaps you are unaware, from living presently abroad, that ninety-three important figures in German science and culture, ten Nobel Prize winners included and more surely to come—Max Planck, for example—and even including a great figure from the world of your other subject, Isabel Cobb—I refer to Mr. Max Reinhardt—we all signed a manifesto declaring our support for our government and our opposition to the lies and calumny being spread about us abroad. Doctor Einstein was invited to sign. Not only did he refuse. He signed a scandalous counter-manifesto that gave credence to those very lies."

Haber was nearly shouting now. Shouting and quaking. He stopped. He calmed himself.

"Forgive me," he said. And then, almost gently: "Albert is fortunate that his position was so ludicrous. Only four of the invited hundred intellectuals signed, and the manifesto was never published. He was spared."

Haber removed the handkerchief from his breast pocket and patted his head. "I otherwise admire his mind greatly," he said. "However, for what one may call a cosmological physicist, he knows very little about the real world. How sad."

"Perhaps," Stockman said, matching Haber's abruptly subdued tone, "it is time for us to excuse Mr. Jäger and for you and I to discuss our business."

Haber pulled a watch on a fob from his vest pocket. He said, "I told Colonel Bauer four-thirty."

It wasn't four-thirty yet and Haber clearly had more steam to let off.

But Stockman was getting nervous. "There are a couple of matters to discuss before he arrives. You have enough for the story, Josef?"

It was still critical that I appear eager to obey Albert. I stood up at once. "Of course, Baron Stockman. You know I am here simply to serve you. I can do a fine story with what Doctor Haber has officially given me."

"Excellent," Albert said. I remained his man. He even shook my hand at once. This led to Haber's offered hand and bowings and heel-clickings all around.

And so they were done with me.

The soldier was summoned and I was respectfully but efficiently escorted from the Kaiser Wilhelm Institut für Physikalische Chemie, placed in a waiting Daimler taxi beneath the plane trees, and sent away.

I got out at the Adlon and lingered on the sidewalk long enough for the taxi to drive off. I turned west and walked the three hundred yards to the Hotel Baden. I strode through the lobby and straight into the telephone kiosk. I'd barely gotten the receiver into my hand when somebody knuckled the glass pane directly behind my head.

I turned.

It was Jeremy.

I replaced the receiver and opened the door. "I was just calling you," I said.

"I supposed," he said.

"How are things in Spandau?"

"The factories never rest, thanks to your man Haber."

"They make shells?"

He nodded.

"Are they Krupp's?"

"Government factories."

"Your mother is well located."

"She is. I keep my eyes open. How was your improvisation?"

"That remains to be seen."

So we sat in the Baden coffee shop, in the corner farthest from the Unter den Linden windows, and I brought Jeremy up to speed, from Stockman at the Adlon reception desk to the taxi at the Adlon front door.

He said not a word till I'd done. Then he went straight to my interpretation of the writing on the second box in Reinauer's office. "I've not seen it used before, but your reading of MDH seems spot on."

"You agree it's likely mit *Stockman's* hand?"

"Seems so."

"Ever hear of Einstein?"

He shook his head no, even as he tried to think. "I don't believe."

"We need to find him."

"Around the Institute, perhaps." As soon as Jeremy said this, he shook his head again. "But how to approach him there."

"And this Colonel Bauer?"

"About him, I've got people to ask," Jeremy said. "Berlin is densely populated with colonels and 'Bauer' is common. No first name?"

"It wasn't spoken."

"If he's a third party to Haber and Stockman, maybe we can sort him out."

"How late can I call your number in Spandau?"

"Very late," Jeremy said. "My mother takes a long while going to sleep. What's your next move?"

"I have a hunch I can find Sir Albert tonight."

# 38

Jeremy and I went our ways, and I had dinner alone in the Adlon Pariser Platz, the red walnut–walled à la carte restaurant off the lobby, and then I retired to my room to give Albert a head start on his drinking.

At nine I entered Stockman's favorite watering hole. I strode automatically toward the far corner and in a few steps I could see past the end of the zinc bar to his table of choice. Three strangers in evening suits were confabbing there, two with Willie mustaches and one with a fez.

I stopped, roughing myself up in my head for not trying to formalize a drink with Albert for tonight.

But then a familiar voice said my name. "Mr. Hunter. Join us."

Even Mr. Hunter immediately recognized Isabel Cobb's voice.

I looked to my left.

Along the full width of this western wall ran a Bacchanalian mural, an unbroken, dancing, leaping, swooning, embracing flow of naked flesh and diaphanous gowns and goat parts under which were three arrangements for drinkers, two chairs each, their backs to the bar, a table before them, and a two-seat settee against the wall. In the center of these settings, nuzzled up shoulder to shoulder on the settee, were my mother and Sir Albert Stockman.

He was dressed in his evening suit. She was wearing a front-buttoning shirtwaist with intricate sylvan lace inserts and an apricot silk scarf thrown round her neck. She was straight from rehearsal, I presumed.

I approached.

As I did, a man rose from one of the chairs before them.

It was Madam Isabel's director, Victor Barnowsky.

He turned to me.

"*Herr Regisseur*," I said.

"Mr. Hunter," he said.

We exchanged another strong handshake. I was reminded of my first impression of him, how like a roughhouser he seemed.

"Won't you stay?" my mother said.

"Alas, I must go, Madam Cobb," Barnowsky said, sounding very formal. I figured they knew enough to hide their stage-star-and-present-director warmth in the presence of her beau. "A pleasure to meet with you, Baron." Barnowsky bowed to Stockman, who nodded at Barnowsky but said nothing. I figured Albert wasn't quite buying all this formality between his beloved and this theater director.

Barnowsky vanished and Albert loosened a little and motioned me into the empty chair.

I sat.

This wasn't going to be easy.

I had a front row seat before a very small stage with two lovebirds snuggled up and a great deal at stake and some messy personal issues in the script.

One of which was: *I may someday need to put a bullet between this guy's eyes.*

Another of which was: *He might need to do the same to me.* Indeed, the only thing that was keeping his finger from squeezing a trigger was his ignorance about me. The only inhibition for me was knowing too much about him. His restraint was more apt to change abruptly than mine. That put me at a severe disadvantage in any likely showdown.

We all looked at each other for a moment in a sort of dazed silence. I didn't know if I could talk about the Haber meeting in my mother's presence. Had their intimacy gone far enough for that to be okay? She didn't know what had transpired between us two men since last night and she was smart enough to let us set the tone and pace. Stockman had his airship überagenda mixing with his jealousy over his woman.

We were relieved by the bartender, whose arrival I realized by Albert's eyes shifting abruptly up and over my shoulder. He looked back to me. "What are you having?"

I looked down at the table.

It was Sam Thompson again, though if this was still the first bottle of the evening, the two of them were drinking their way forward quite moderately, judging by the amount of whiskey remaining. Their glasses were presently empty.

"There seems to be plenty of rye left," I said.

"A third glass, Hans," Stockman said to the bartender.

And we were silent for another moment.

Stockman was going to have to start this.

I took out a Fatima and gestured the pack to the snuggly couple.

Stockman waved it off with a thanks and dipped into his evening suit inner pocket and took out a silver cigarette case, going after his own brand.

My mother also declined the Fatimas, with a little shake of the head and a focusing of her eyes on mine and a surging of something in them that I read as, *Well, here we are, my son, in quite a melodrama together.*

Stockman lit his cigarette and offered his match across the table. I bent to it and sat back, as did Stockman, and we blew smoke together.

"I was telling Isabel about our impassioned Jew at the chemistry institute," Stockman said.

So they'd gone *that* far in their intimacy.

Then he made his more important point: "She has her own Jew to deal with."

Barnowsky was still weighing heavily on him.

I glanced at Mother. She was no doubt grinding her teeth, but she was a fine actress, after all, and, indeed, since she was already pressed shoulder to arm to hip to thigh against Stockman, she even crossed her free right arm over her body and placed her hand gently on his forearm. While wishing, instead, I would've bet, that she could slap him in the face.

But maybe not.

She was, indeed, quite convincing. Maybe she forgave him this attitude. She was, after all, presently in love with him.

"Herr Barnowsky is a sad, driven man," Isabel Cobb said.

Stockman took another drag on his cigarette, turned his face sharply away from us both, and blew the smoke toward the door, apparently releasing his jealousy, for his face swung back to Isabel and he put his hand over hers. "You work very hard for your art," he said.

"Don't I though," she said. She was looking into his eyes for this line, but I decided she was talking to me, telling me not to worry, she wasn't so smitten as to lose her secret way with him.

He patted her hand again and looked at me.

"This Albert Einstein was a touchy subject for our impassioned Doctor Haber," I said.

Stockman nodded.

I deliberately slowed down.

I took a drag on my cigarette. I blew the smoke.

My glass arrived.

"May I?" Hans the bartender said.

"Sure," I said, and Hans poured me a couple of fingers of rye.

Only when all this was done and the bartender had disappeared did I say, "You know anything about Einstein?"

"He's a Zionist," Stockman said. "I believe in the sincerity of Doctor Haber's allegiance to Germany, as far as it is possible for that to go, but this other man is a dangerous man. Made even more acutely so by his apparent genius."

"Albert was asking Herr Barnowsky about Herr Einstein," my mother said.

Stockman turned his face sharply to her. "Are you sure this director isn't a Zionist?"

"Of course he's not," she said. "He is a citizen of Shakespeare and Ibsen and Shaw."

"This Einstein likes his Shakespeare as well, apparently," Stockman said. "That doesn't prevent him from despising the land that gave him birth."

My mother patted his hand. "Victor Barnowsky is no Zionist, my darling."

"I say you deserve better, is all," said darling Albert.

She patted him some more. "I've dealt with this all my professional life."

Stockman's voice mellowed a little. "How difficult for you."

He turned to me now. He was, of course, trying to make a case for *himself*. As her exclusive lover. Perhaps even as her husband. I was his foil. I was the jury. I was the impartial public in obvious, silent agreement with him. He said, "This is widely overlooked by lovers of the theater, the terrible sacrifice a great actress must endure for her art. That she must inevitably surround herself with actors and directors and other men of that world, unprincipled men, emotionally tumultuous and unreliable men, morally weak men."

I could see her jaw clench at this, great actress though she was. Her hand stopped patting, but it stayed on his forearm.

Man oh man, was he ever trying to make a case. He even started to swerve back to Einstein.

"And these revered scientists. These outsiders."

He paused dramatically.

She must have said something admiring about scientists along the way.

He said, "This Einstein has a wife and two children. They were with him when he came to the Kaiser Wilhelm Institute, and he drove them away. She fled to Zurich because he began an affair with his own cousin in Berlin. This cousin was no doubt the reason he returned to his despised Germany. Not his vaunted research."

He paused to present us a moue of pained disapproval. Even Stockman could not miss the blanching of Mother's face. He just didn't have a clue what was behind it.

"I'm sorry to mention these scandalous things," he said. "But there are many men of this sort in the world who can be very attractive to women. I just believe in a different way of living."

As different as Stockman felt himself to be from the men of the theatrical world, he was, however, their kin. By something stronger than blood. By an instinct for self-performance. Little did he know. And little did he know that it was perhaps the deepest hook he had in my mother.

I could sense her gathering her actor's strength now. She said, "This is why I've come so quickly and strongly to rely on you, my darling."

He put his hand on hers. "I know," he said.

She grew urgent. "Must you leave me next week?"

"We've spoken of this," he said, lowering his voice a little. This was something he *didn't* want to discuss in front of me.

Mother was playing her own, woman's version of Albert's earlier strategy. A man used the public setting to display his plumaged worthiness. The woman reopened a private argument with her man. I was foil. I was jury.

Of course, Mother was also doing her job. She was giving me information.

He'd told her he was going away.

This was, I assumed, the *Mit der Hand* trip.

"I know we've spoken," she said. "But you have only reminded me now, with your characteristic eloquence—oh how I would miss that too, for even a few days, your lovely words—you have reminded me how bereft I will be."

"You must rehearse," he said.

"Opening night is still two weeks off. I can take a few days."

"It's strictly business."

"I won't interfere," she said.

"I'm not sure how long I'll be needed."

"But at least I could come for a few days."

"There are complications I cannot speak of."

"I will happily stay out of your way, in any nearby hotel you wish. Just come to me at night." She put her head on his shoulder.

He glanced my way, lifted his eyebrows to me.

I smiled a comradely smile.

He rolled his eyes.

Women.

He and I understood about that.

"I might be out until very very late," he said.

"I will rest."

"And your days will be empty as well."

She lifted her head. She made a show of trying to think of a solution. She came up with one and brightened. "You have spoken so warmly of Mr. Hunter. Perhaps we can bring him. During the day he can finish our story for the American papers. And he and I might even find a chance to discuss my memoir."

Stockman did not reply to this. His lover's head returned to his shoulder.

He looked at me.

I leaned forward and poured two fingers of rye into his glass.

I offered it to him and he took it with his free hand, in exchange giving me a muted reprise of the comradely smile.

He drank it down, not in a quick shot but in a steady, uninterrupted draft.

I took the empty glass from him and put it on the table.

He gently extricated his right arm without letting her raise her head and he put it around her shoulders. She snuggled in. "We'll discuss this later," he said.

She lifted her face to him.

If I were not sitting across from them, they no doubt would have kissed at this juncture. As it was, they goo-goo-eyed each other long enough that I was forced to look away and concentrate on my Fatima for a drag and blow.

I hoped she hadn't overplayed her hand. In spite of my encouraging Sam Thompson to help out, Albert would confront all this soberly in the morning.

They'd begun to murmur things to each other.

I thought, hopefully, about Albert Einstein's love for Shakespeare. I figured there might be a way to approach him.

I checked out the loving couple, and Stockman was withdrawing his arm. He'd suddenly turned downright shoulder-rollingly, tie-straighteningly furtive. He seemed finally aware of the public setting. Maybe he wasn't all that akin to theater people after all. Maybe it was just the power of my mother. The spell she put on any man.

He reached for the bottle and began to pour.

My mother sat herself up straight. She arranged the bodice of her dress. She looked at me. *Calm* she was, or she was simply portraying that. *Confidently in Control.*

Okay. She'd pressed all this forward. I'd come a long way with Albert myself. I thought I, too, could push him a little. Carefully.

"Did the rest of your meeting go well at the Institute?" I asked, while reaching for my own whiskey glass.

Maybe he'd talk a little more readily about this because it offered a clear shift away from the wheedlings of his lover.

I grasped the glass and looked at him.

He lifted two more fingers of rye. I straightened and offered my glass for toasting.

He leaned to me and we touched our Sam Thompsons. "It did," he said.

We sat back. I sipped. He took his whiskey in one quick shot.

"I hope Doctor Haber calmed down for the colonel," I said.

There was a brief stopping in Stockman, a flicker of something. I was afraid this was about me crossing a line. I hoped it was still about Haber. Maybe Albert had to remember how I'd learned about there being another person in their meeting. A colonel, no less. Whatever it was, it seemed to pass.

"Max wouldn't tolerate it," Stockman said.

*Max.* Nothing like a good bolt of whiskey sliding down your throat to get you to speak familiarly about your pals.

But the burn of the rye cooled and he corrected himself, made things properly proper. "Colonel Bauer," he said.

"Is he someone I should meet?" I said.

"I can't imagine why," Stockman said. Quickly and firmly. I was afraid *suspiciously*.

I'd gotten careless.

"Sorry," I said. "I'm just increasingly frustrated, wanting to help our cause and not knowing how."

Stockman waved this off.

But he said nothing.

I hoped it was the apology that he'd brushed aside and not the explanation.

He was staring at the bottle.

"Can I pour for you?" my mother said.

Stockman looked at her and then at me and then at her.

"No," he said. "Let's retire."

"All right," she said.

I waited for some look, some gesture, some word from him that could reassure me he'd not become suspicious.

But he rose and she rose and she hooked her arm in his and they turned to go.

"Good night," I said to them both.

"Good night," my mother said.

Stockman said nothing.

# 39

I left the Adlon bar soon after the retiring couple, and I went out of the hotel and headed for the Baden. I worried every step of the way that I was starting to lose Stockman. But I'd needed to press things forward. I had to let this play itself out.

I rang Spandau from the lobby telephone kiosk. The mother answered instantly. "Müller."

"Hello, Mrs. Müller," I said. "It's Mr. Jäger. May I speak to Erich?"

She said nothing, but the phone clunked and then Jeremy answered.

"Is your mother all right with me calling?" I asked.

"Don't mind her," he said "We've been talking about the Kaiser."

"Is she disaffected?"

"Far from it."

"How's your brother doing? I meant to ask."

"He's presently alive and unwounded."

We both fell silent a moment.

Then I said, "Max."

"Max?"

"His first name. Colonel Max Bauer."

"That will help," he said.

"I have a thought to find the other gentleman."

"Good."

And we both reminded ourselves that a telephone was still a telephone, even in the lobby of a relatively safe hotel.

We bade each other good night.

I hung up and hesitated only a moment before going out of the Baden and back to the Adlon.

In the lobby, Wagner was nowhere to be seen. In my room, nothing seemed to have been reexamined.

My laundry was waiting on the foot of the bed, wrapped in brown paper and folded neatly therein and giving off the faint, fresh, broken-rock smell of Persil. I had a clean set of summer-cotton BVDs and I put them on to sleep.

I opened the door to the balcony but pulled the drapes closed.

I put my Mauser in the drawer of the night table, went to bed, and fell instantly asleep.

And I awoke abruptly in the dark to a knocking.

My bedroom door was open to the sitting room and the knock had come from in there, at the door to my suite.

It was soft.

And then it came again, a little less soft.

I rose.

I switched on my bedside lamp.

"Please," a voice said outside. A heavy, feminine whisper.

A stage whisper.

I brisked across the floor and looked through the peep hole.

It was my mother.

I opened the door.

"Quickly," I said.

She slipped in.

She was wearing her shirtwaist but not her scarf. All the button-to-hole matches were off by one.

"You shouldn't be doing this," I said.

"I didn't know when I'd get to talk to you. No one saw me."

"There's a floor attendant."

"He's sleeping."

"German agents on staff."

"I'm telling you I wasn't seen," she said.

"I need pants," I said.

"I'll wait," she said.

I left her in the dark and disappeared into the bedroom, pushing the door partly closed. I put on my pants from the wardrobe, cinched the belt tight, and took one step back into the sitting room. "Come in here, away from the door," I said.

She entered the bedroom.

She sat at the dressing table and I sat in a side chair.

Her hands were clasped tightly in her lap, fingers intertwined. Her upper arms were drawn tightly against her.

"You dressed in the dark," I said.

She looked down.

She looked at me. She said, "He travels to Cologne on Monday."

"He told you the details?"

"Yes. Of course. He didn't think I'd make that fuss in public."

"Did that compromise his trust?"

"I don't know for certain. I don't think so."

"It was worth trying," I said. "You did well. And Monday to Cologne is very good information."

Her hands unclasped, her arms fell away from her lap. Her tension drained instantly, completely away, a tension I'd assumed was over her secret visit to my room under the sleeping nose of Albert and all the rest of the German secret service at the Adlon. In fact, she was tense because she was afraid I'd disapprove of her handling of his declared trip. I'd applauded. So all was right in her world.

Now she had to make a swift exit.

But I did need to speak with her privately, and here she was.

"Are you sure you weren't seen?" I said.

"It's three in the morning," she said.

"Mother . . ."

"I know. I know. I'm sorry. But I was careful. I came up the stairs. I saw no one."

"It's not just strangers I'm worried about," I said. I nodded at her skewed buttons and holes. Dressing in the dark meant one thing. "Did you come from *his* room?"

She didn't answer.

"You did," I said.

She stayed silent.

"How did you expect to get back in?"

She shrugged a so-what shrug.

I repeated the question with a tilt of my head.

"I have a key," she said.

"You took his?"

"No. That would be risky."

I clucked at this.

"I have one of my own," she said.

Of course.

"This whole complication is dangerous for us," I said.

"'O time, thou must untangle this, not I,'" she said. "'It is too hard a knot for me to untie.'"

Whenever she began to speak with lines from her favorite roles— this one Viola from *Twelfth Night*—I knew the topic would drag on. But this conversation was not worth the clock tick of risk. I needed to say the critical thing quickly.

"Look," I said. "This guy Albert Einstein may have some crucial information. He's a Shakespeare fan. He may be an Isabel Cobb fan as well. Your man Barnowsky may know him. I need for you to see Einstein and I need to go with you and we need to do this as soon as possible. Before your Albert heads for Cologne."

I was just trying to keep the Alberts straight. Mostly. But she played the phrase big, to tweak my nosiness. "*My* Albert hates that man," she said. "If he found out . . ."

"He won't. You won't let that happen. It's worth the risk."

246

She looked down again.

She started to unbutton her blouse.

"Look away," she said. "I need to fix this."

I rose and turned my back on her. I walked to the bed and I sat down on the edge, very near the night table.

"He has a dinner tomorrow night," she said. "At the Ministry of War. He's talking that openly to me."

"He didn't want you on his arm?"

She didn't reply.

I had to be careful how I spoke of him.

She cursed low. About the buttons.

I rephrased. "You're not going?"

"I tried," she said. "Boys only. You should come to the theater around seven. I'll see about the other Albert."

And from the dark at the far of end of the sitting room came four swift, hard knocks at the door.

I jumped up.

The following silence rang in the room. Only briefly.

Another two knocks. And Stockman's voice. "Josef."

I turned to Mother, who had succeeded merely in totally unbuttoning her shirtwaist, exposing a lacy vest brassiere.

She was wide-eyed. Her hands had fallen straight down at her sides.

I put my forefinger to my lips.

I looked in the direction of the door.

Two more knocks, louder still. "Josef," he said, in English. "I'm sorry, but I must come in."

I thought of the Mauser.

I turned to the night stand.

No acceptable solution presented itself in the maelstrom of my brain that involved my pistol and this hotel room at the Adlon in the middle of the night. I figured it would be best not to have that option.

"Sir Albert?" I called. "Is that you?"

"Yes."

"Give me a moment."

I looked at Mother.

She was standing now. I wondered if she'd played this scene before in one of those theatrical tour hotels.

She blew me a kiss, with a death mask face.

I breathed deep and stepped through the bedroom door, closing it behind me.

I turned to the desk, found the table lamp, and switched it on.

I moved to the suite door.

I looked through the peep hole and reared back. He was standing very near.

His hands were not in sight. But if he was holding a weapon, surely he'd have stepped back a little so he could at least raise his arm in preparation.

I opened the door.

Stockman had dressed in haste and only partially: his black evening suit trousers with a braid stripe; his white shirt, properly buttoned, but no collar.

At his side, fisted in his left hand, was Mother's apricot scarf.

I'd already observed that Albert was right-handed. To carry this in his off-hand was a conscious act. Was he keeping his pistol hand free?

"May I come in, old man?" he said.

A very friendly phrasing and tone for a presumptuous request at this hour.

Stockman felt very dangerous to me.

But the slightest hesitation would only make him more suspicious.

I stepped back instantly, opening the door wide.

"Of course," I said.

He stepped in.

I watched his eyes. He rapidly checked every corner of the room. His gaze lingered for a beat on the closed bedroom door.

I shut the suite door behind him.

"Drink?" I said. "The Adlon attendant has kept the side table nicely stocked."

"No thanks," he said.

We were standing in the middle of the floor.

"Would you like to sit?" I motioned to the divan and the chair.

"I'm sorry to bother you like this," he said, still in English.

I nodded at his left hand. "Isn't that the scarf Madam Cobb was wearing tonight? Is she all right?"

His eyes had fixed on the bedroom door again. At my voice, he looked at me.

"I don't know," he said. "May I step into your bathroom?"

It was the one place where she could hide outside of the bedroom. "Of course."

As soon as he looked away and began his first step past me, I focused on the pockets of his trousers. Left front and then, as he crossed the floor, both back pockets.

He vanished into the bathroom.

The prime pocket, right front, had eluded me for the moment.

Water began to run in the basin.

It would be quickly obvious that she wasn't in there.

After only a few seconds the water shut off again. He'd made a cursory attempt to hide his suspicion. But his patience had quickly run out.

He emerged from the bathroom. One step and he stopped.

He looked at the scarf in his hand. An anguished little gesture.

If he was not still actively drunk, his head was surely pounding with the afterclap of rye.

I had to believe, from the look of his right front pocket, that he was indeed armed with a small pistol.

He drew near me.

I knew he would have to search the bedroom.

I had two thoughts. If I let him initiate the search, he might draw the pistol first. And whatever my mother was planning for this situation, she was ready by now.

"Sir Albert," I said, very gently. "My friend. You will not insult me if you'd like to look in my bedroom."

His eyes focused on mine but in that restless way of darting back and forth, back and forth, from one eye to the other.

"Yes," he said. "Thank you for understanding, Josef."

It had been the right thing to say.

He moved past me.

I turned.

In my periphery something caught my eye on the floor, where he'd been standing. He'd dropped the scarf.

Stockman wanted both hands.

He opened the bedroom door. The light was still on.

He stepped in and I followed, as quietly as I could.

He went first to the wardrobe. I stopped in the doorway.

He twisted the handle and opened the wardrobe door. Slowly now. He was using his right hand, his pistol hand. Good. It would mean a few moments of delay for him to be able to shoot.

I took another small step toward him, determined not to seem threatening, ready to lunge at him.

The door was swinging wide.

No rustling in the wardrobe.

No words.

He closed the wardrobe door and turned.

We looked at each other.

I offered him a gentle smile. "Whatever you need to do," I said.

He turned away from me. Looked across the room.

I followed his eyes.

The drapes at the balcony door.

He knew. I knew. The other likely place.

He moved past me once more.

I edged my way toward the night table and the Mauser.

He reached the drapes, hesitated.

The temptation in my fingertips was to ease the drawer open. But the room was quiet. The sound would make him turn and what he would see could be understood in only one way.

I stayed put. If he stepped out and there were sounds, I could have the Mauser pretty quick anyway.

He put his hand to the drape. Still he hesitated. He loved her. He did not want this to be true. But he loved her. So the possibility of this was roaring in his head.

He wrenched the drapes aside.

The door was open.

He stepped out.

He vanished to the right.

There were no sounds.

He crossed by the open window and vanished to the left.

Nothing.

He appeared in the doorway.

Even across the room I could sense the quaking in him.

My own mind was roaring now. There was only one other possible place. But could she even fit under the bed? I did not let my eyes go there. I knew that the sheets and the light quilt were untucked and hung low. I thought I even remembered a dust ruffle down to the floor.

Would Stockman go so far as to get down on his hands and knees to make sure about this last possible place?

He stepped into the room.

He stopped.

I tried to read his body. There was an aura of release about him: his shoulders had gone slack; his hands, which were prepared moments ago even to kill, hung limp at his sides.

"Can I get you that drink now?" I said. Very softly.

He hesitated.

Surely he wanted to believe what his hands and his shoulders already believed.

My last gesture of innocent confidence would be to step out of the bedroom before him. If he did energize his hands in a final burst of suspicion and he got down on his knees after I left, there would be sounds at the discovery—Mother would surely engage him—and only then would he come after me. I could maybe get back into the room in time to prevent his weapon coming into play.

"Yes, you can," he said.

I turned. I stepped from the room.

The drink table was against the wall just to the side of the bedroom door. I put my hand to the bottle of Scotch. I did not take the top off. I turned my hand and grasped it by its neck. A weapon.

But almost at once I heard Stockman's footsteps approaching from inside the bedroom.

I let go of the bottle and he emerged and passed on across the floor.

I glanced over my shoulder.

He was collapsing into the scroll-armed chair.

I poured two sizable shots of whiskey and crossed to him.

He took one with a murmured thanks.

I sat on the divan.

We did not toast. He shot his down. I sipped only a very little bit of mine.

"She's in her room," he said.

I waited for more.

"She must be in her room," he said.

"I'm sure she's safe," I said.

"She left my bed," he said. "We can speak as men together, you and I, can we not?"

"Of course," I said. Now I shot my whiskey down, and before he could say any more I rose and moved toward the side table. I needed a refill.

"For me too," he said.

I awaited Albert's men-together talk in much the same mood as his when he approached the balcony a few moments ago. I had to throw the drapes back but I really did not want to find what was on the other side.

I picked up the bottle of whiskey, a fine old Dundee, though it could have been a Chicago-saloon, two-bits-a-shot, squirrel whiskey for all either of us cared at that moment.

I returned to Stockman and poured us some more and I sat down.

My only revenge was that she was probably in the next room listening to every word.

"I woke," he said. "We had been man and woman together, you understand."

I understood. I pushed him along. I said, "She was gone?"

"She was."

I glanced across the floor to the apricot-colored pile of silk.

I had an inspiration.

"If she were going to another man, she would have taken her lovely scarf," I said.

He looked over his shoulder and then back at me. Then back at the scarf. Then he looked me in the eyes as if he'd suddenly realized it was *me* he was in love with.

"Josef," he said, in a commensurate tone of voice. "You are *right*, my friend."

I realized how tightly coiled a metal spring there'd been in my chest, because it now suddenly eased. I didn't have to hear his man-talk so he could convince himself he was still okay in bed with my mother.

"Of course," I said.

"Thank you."

"It was simply evident," I said.

"She is in her room. But she must be angry with me."

"Which is why she did not answer when you knocked."

"Exactly," he said. He looked at the drink in his hand, which he'd not yet touched. He took about a third of it now, as if it were his own choice and not a physical necessity.

"Yes," he said. "She must think she has cause to be angry."

He lifted his shoulders and let them fall as if to say, *What can you do?*

"You heard the issue tonight," he said. "I have to go south for a while. I don't know for how long exactly. A few days. A week. She has her play, after all."

I took a good bolt of my whiskey. Maybe half of it. Not from choice but from necessity. So I wouldn't choke on the irony of having to now say the things I needed to say. "But she has something more important to her than *Hamlet*."

His drunken brow furrowed in puzzlement. The dope.

"She has you," I said.

I wanted to keep on drinking while he figured this out. But I was already feeling a little too warm in the face, a little too reconciled with the stuff that had to come out of my mouth.

I looked for a place to put my glass down.

I may even have remarked at this point at the inappropriate absence of a table near this chair and divan.

If I did, the remark was lost on Stockman, whose face was crimped in thought.

I placed the glass on the floor.

*All right*, I thought. *Say it.* "She's a woman in love. When she told you she couldn't bear to be away from you, she meant it. She aches. You understand, Albert? She aches, my brother. For you."

I'd raised my voice for this whole proclamation. Grandly. So she could clearly hear that I knew what I knew.

I'd stopped drinking in time to manage the important things. I was coherent. I knew I'd remember everything we said. I was in control of my words and focused on their hidden rhetorical intent. Perhaps, though, the theatrical flourishes had a bit of a life of their own.

"She aches to be with you," I said. "And if there is any sense in her that this is an important trip you are making, that only causes her to ache more urgently. She wants to be there with you. Beside you. Don't you see?"

His face was uncrimping now.

"You are a lucky man," I said.

He nodded faintly.

"Chancellor Otto von Bismarck was a great leader," he said.

*Ah, Albert*, I thought. *This is your response to my invocation of Isabel Cobb's love? What the hell does she see in you?*

"Perhaps the greatest of all German statesmen," he said.

*But what the hell did she see in any of them?*

I was glad he was speaking nothing but English. I wanted Mother to hear him clearly.

"There would be no Germany, in all its present glory, if it weren't for him," he said.

I was tempted to pick up the drink from the floor, but I did not.

"He is the quintessential figure of diplomatic moderation and balance. And those qualities were often useful. But he had to learn a lesson from an American general. Did you know that?"

"I did not," I said.

"The great Union general from your Civil War, Philip Sheridan, dined with Chancellor Bismarck during the Prussian war with France. The critical last war that united us as a people. Sheridan said at table that the proper strategy of war consists not only in telling blows against the army of the enemy, but to cause the enemy's civilians—and I am quoting Sheridan now—'to cause so much suffering that they must long for peace and force their government to demand it. The people must be left nothing but their eyes to weep with.'"

At this he paused to drink. A natural pause for a man whose drinking was driven by a darkness in him that needed management, or encouragement.

"He had it in him, our dear father Otto," he said. "But he needed to hear that. He dealt properly with the French from then on. He had no further qualms to shoot every prisoner, burn every village, hang every man, dispose of any civilian at all who might conspire against us. And such measures ended the war far more quickly. Won the war. Allowed us to become the people that we are."

He paused again, looked at the empty glass. I thought to fill it, but I did not. Nor did he. He bent down and, with meticulous care, set his glass on the floor, beside the leg of his chair.

He lifted his face once more to me. "It's ironic," he said. "Our Kaiser himself dismissed Bismarck for failure to appreciate the call of God to create our German Empire. Wilhelm despised Bismarck's moderation. And yet the same flaw resides in him. Particularly with regard to England. I sympathize. There is blood involved. But his grandmother the queen's most powerful connection to all of us was her husband, and his pure blood did not actually flow in her veins. Her own Germanness, from her forefathers, was greatly diluted. Too much of England coursed in her. For our Kaiser thus to waver in his will because of his sentimental attachment to Victoria is madness. He will prolong this war. He will lose this war."

Stockman grasped the two knobs of his chair arms, straightened his spine, lifted his chin. "It is time for heroism in our Germany, Josef. Time for a new hero."

And the thing that was nagging at me, puzzling me, over this apparently drunken digression suddenly became clear. What leap had his mind taken from the adoring love of my mother to Otto von Bismarck and then to Kaiser Wilhelm? These men were the precursors for the new hero. The hero being Albert. The hero who needed a witness, a woman, my mother and her adoration.

I even bet that this chain of association had not yet snapped in Albert's head.

Softly as his own voice whispering inside his own whiskey-heated brain, I said, "She needs to be with you for this."

He lowered his heroically lifted chin and looked at me. "I should go now," he said. "I will let her sleep."

He rose. I rose. He was surprisingly steady on his feet. I was somewhat less so for a moment.

"*Eisen und Blut,*" he said, the first German he'd spoken since he entered my rooms. I recognized it from Bismarck. His most famous speech. Not by speeches and majority decisions would the great issues of the day be settled, he'd said. But by *iron and blood.*

It would have been a good exit line, his *Eisen und Blut.* But instead, Albert moved to Mother's apricot scarf, bent, and took it up once more. He put it to his face and breathed deeply in. At *this* he grew unsteady, swaying a little until he lowered the scarf and blinked his way back to his purpose.

I, on the other hand, in witnessing this gesture, grew suddenly quite steady afoot and it was all I could do to restrain my right hand from fisting and knocking Stockman down.

But restrain, I did.

Indeed, I put my hand on his shoulder and said, "Don't forget what I've said."

"You are my friend," he said. And he was gone.

After the click of the door I stood in the center of the room and did some blinking of my own.

His declaration of friendship was the first thing to blink away.

Not so easy, I found.

But I blinked.

Then there was my mother.

I turned to face the bedroom.

And she was standing in the doorway.

She was not looking at me. Rather, she was studying her hands working at the buttons of her shirtwaist. She was half buttoned and I waited.

She did up every button to the top before she lifted her face to me.

I could not read her expression. I therefore assumed it was real.

"Where were you?" I said.

"Under the bed."

"How?"

"Barely," she said. And she looked down and took her two hands and fluffed her lately compressed breasts.

I looked away.

"Hamlet prepared me," she said.

I gave her a moment and looked back to her. She'd finished with her breasts. I said, "Hamlet has not prepared you for what's next."

"'I will screw my courage to the sticking-place,'" she said.

"Good," I said, though it didn't turn out so well for Lady Macbeth.

"Victor knows all the splendid Jews in Berlin," she said. "Especially the theater lovers. I will find this man Einstein."

# 40

And she did.

At six o'clock that evening I arrived at the Lessing and the old man on the chair nodded me through at once. I crossed the lobby and stepped into the back of an auditorium ringing with the sound of hammers. On stage the utility lights were lit and men in overalls were upstage center, building a wooden archway flanked by parapeted platforms. Barnowsky was no painted scenery man.

He was nowhere in sight. It was Saturday night. I figured rehearsal was finished already. I twinged in concern that she'd made no progress in finding the other Albert, but Mother had specifically said seven o'clock, and so I went along the side aisle and through the door that led past the wings staircase and down the corridor to her dressing room.

I approached the closed door. I drew near and laughter rolled into the corridor, my mother's familiar bray—the one laugh of hers I could never quite identify as real or fake—and a man's unfettered, alto laugh.

Was that the laugh of a man who faced down the mysteries of the physical universe? If it was and he was capable of this laugh, maybe things weren't so bad, cosmologically.

I knocked on the door.

The laughter stopped.

I heard a murmur of my mother's voice to her visitor, and then she called out, "Come in."

I opened the door.

She was sitting in her makeup chair in an informal dinner gown of pale-green taffeta. She'd been waiting for a while, having already changed from her rehearsal clothes. I wondered how long the guy in the room had been here. A while, certainly. The pervasive greasepaint and cold cream smell of the room was actually beginning to yield to his pipe tobacco, a bland but insistent blend of burley and Cavendish and something vaguely nutty.

He was rising to his feet to greet me, a trim, medium-sized man with upstanding, dense, faintly wavy black hair and an equally dense mustache that neatly shrouded his entire upper lip from laugh line to laugh line. His chin was deeply cleft and his eyes were nearly as dark as his hair but they came brightly alive as he rose.

"This is Doctor Albert Einstein," Mother said.

He offered his hand with my name on his lips even before she could formally announce it. "Mr. Hunter. I am very pleased to meet you." He spoke in English that was proper but German-accented as heavily as if by a ham actor.

I thought I saw his eyes flick toward my saber scar. But if so, it was so quick I could not say for sure.

Mother said, "I told the professor that you're working on a story about the Kaiser Wilhelm Institute and you need to speak with him."

"I am pleased to assist you from the urging of Madam Cobb," Einstein said. "She is pressing boldly outward our boundary of understanding. She tries to do for the immense William Shakespeare what a great physicist tries to do for the physical universe. So I comply with anything she asks."

He laughed that high, ringing laugh.

Mother laughed with him. Not the bray. His overriding laugh made hers harder to read, but I looked at her and her eyes were locked on him in appreciation.

"The story is narrower than the Institute," I said in German. "And I ask only to more deeply understand what I already know. You and your words will not appear in any newspaper. I ask for something perhaps like one scientist objectively testing another's work."

He brightened at my analogy, at my understanding of the process of scientific discovery. He laughed again. "A peer review," he said.

"Forgive us for speaking German, Madam Cobb," I said.

"Not at all," she said. "I want you two to communicate fully."

"As shall you and I," Einstein said, in English, turning to her. "Over some little food."

"Yes, Professor," she said. "I look forward to learning from you." And to me: "When you and the professor have finished, he and I will dine nearby."

Perhaps I showed a glint of concern in my face.

She said, "You will recall that our previously intended companion tonight is dining at the Ministry."

"I do recall that," I said.

She rose. "I'll leave the two of you alone so you can speak German without regret."

"You need not go, dear lady," Einstein said.

"I have to consult for a time with my director. I won't go far."

Einstein took up her hand and bowed over it and kissed it.

Mother shot me a look as if she blamed me for not regularly doing this myself.

As her physicist rose from her hand, he said, quite ardently, "*Soll ich dich einem Sommertag vergleichen?*"

And she shot me another look, this one approximately *You see how they adore me?* This look seemed unrelated to any apparent understanding of the words, though she was certainly correct about its intent.

She swooped from the room and the door clicked shut.

I said to Einstein, returning to German, as he'd just used with her, "You only asked to compare her. Are you saving the comparison itself?"

He laughed.

He had quoted Shakespeare's sonnet to her. *Shall I compare thee to a summer's day?*

"I am afraid," he said, "that I cannot remember the comparison. Only the request."

"Thou art more lovely and more temperate," I said. *Er ist wie du so lieblich nicht und lind.*

"I am indebted to you," Einstein said. "I shall finish the verse over dinner. Do you think she will understand?"

"She'll understand, all right," I said. "If not the words, certainly the intent."

He beamed and I smiled in return. I managed only a wan smile, however, as I felt once again, inevitably, inextricably—perhaps even cosmologically—drawn into my mother's flirtations and wooings and beyond.

Though I expected this Albert's intent was no more than courtly flirtation.

Einstein and I sat down on the two chairs before Isabel Cobb's makeup mirrors.

"May I?" he said, lifting his pipe.

"Of course," I said.

He drew out a box of matches from the side pocket of his tweed jacket, and as he did, he glanced at me. Brief though it was, I was certain this time that the glance had sought out my scar.

I knew Einstein had once abandoned Germany. I said, "My father exiled our family from this country, but he sent me back to Heidelberg for an education. When I was young and stupid," I said.

He smiled. "That is the state in which we all enter university," he said.

He tamped his tobacco with his thumb and lit the bowl and drew at it and lit again and finally was producing sufficient smoke for me to speak.

I knew he'd exiled himself, and I knew his politics. I tapped into them at once. I said, "I am writing for a syndicate of newspapers in the United States. These are newspapers whose readers are largely German-Americans. The gentleman Madam Cobb and I just referred to is an English baron with deep roots in Germany. Very deep roots. He feels the German cause is misunderstood in my country. He feels Germany is justified in this war. More than justified. Righteous. He wants me to write a story that will help advance that theory in America."

Einstein had just taken in a deep draw of his tobacco, and he turned his head a little away and blew the smoke to the mirrors. He turned back to me. Slowly now. The bright energy in him was gone.

He lowered his pipe.

A good reporter makes every person he questions think that whatever they say will be welcomed by a sympathetic ear, will be heard as true and persuasive and wise. Not only was this easy to do with Albert Einstein, it was a great relief. I'd been working in this way far too long and unrelievedly with Albert Stockman.

I said, "I have learned that you are someone whose sensibilities and values I might trust. Though given the people I've been involved with, I learned this about you indirectly, like an experiment where you cannot observe a thing directly but must infer it from its effects."

In spite of his sudden gravity, Einstein smiled at this.

"The English gentleman is named Albert Stockman. Baron Stockman is subtle in his approach. The article, as he has conceived it, will focus entirely on the great humanitarian accomplishments of your colleague Doctor Fritz Haber. I am to write exclusively and glowingly about the Haber Process feeding the hungry of the world."

I paused.

Einstein looked at his pipe, thinking, no doubt, to draw from it.

I said, "I will never quote you, Professor. But I feel as if things are going on that I need to know, and if I don't know them, I'll become part of a terrible deception."

Einstein stared at his pipe a few moments more and then gently placed it on the makeup table, watching it all the way.

He lifted his eyes from the pipe but did not move them to me.

I turned my head to the mirror.

We looked at each other there.

He was silent still.

We continued to look at each other, our directness an illusion, bent together by the silvered surface.

His silence worried me. I decided to lead him a little. I said, "I realize that the same process produces explosives. Without limit."

The face in the mirror looked away.

As did I.

And so our eyes met directly.

"Your intuition is correct, Mr. Hunter," he said.

He did not let go of my gaze but he searched for words. I had to be patient now. I held very still.

"I am indebted to Professor Haber," he said. "He brought me to the Institute. I have freedom here."

He stopped.

I wanted badly to challenge any sense of loyalty he might have to Haber. Did he know how Haber spoke of him? But I waited.

Einstein said, "Do you like an irony? At this institute that bears the Kaiser's name, within a country and a political system and a philosophy that reserves its right to repress whatever freedoms it chooses and that nurtures a violent disdain for the fundamental freedoms of anyone not of their nation, I am nonetheless free to think about what matters most. I suppose the deepest workings of the physical universe do not seem to them a threat."

He stopped once more.

I held very still.

And then he said, "This does not have to do with the Haber-Bosch Process. This does not have to do with explosives. All of that is a matter for the industrialists now."

He looked at his pipe, put his hand upon it. He said, "Fritz Haber has an excellent brain. But his nationalism is contemptible. He does not need a brain for that. The spinal cord would be sufficient."

His hand returned to his lap. His eyes returned to me.

He said, "You know what happened in France in April."

It took me only a moment. "Ypres."

"Yes."

"The German gas attack."

"Chlorine gas," he said. "A persuasive case could be made for the intrinsic moral superiority of physics over chemistry, judging them by their factors of risk, by the relative difficulty or ease of their doing terrible harm to humanity."

He picked up his pipe now and brought it to his mouth.

My mind at this moment was suddenly like those Allied troops in the trench as the first pale-green cloud of chlorine gas drifted toward them across no-man's-land. They knew this looked bad. But they had not yet been overwhelmed. They waited.

I waited.

He shrugged. "Ah, but no doubt physics will catch up someday. Humans will always find a way to pervert the beauty of knowledge. Our technology will soon exceed our humanity. No. I misspeak. It has done so already."

Einstein drew in vain on his pipe. He took it from his mouth and looked at it. And as if making this observation to the object in his hand, he said, "Fritz Haber was responsible for the beginning of modern chemical warfare. *This* is his science now. This is who he has become."

My own breath stopped. Briefly. I would put this all together later. Right now I had to focus on listening.

Einstein removed his matches once more and relit his pipe. "Do you know his wife committed suicide?"

"I heard."

"Do you know why?"

"I do not."

"She was herself deeply schooled in chemistry. She attained a doctorate degree in chemistry at the University of Breslau. She knew enough to adore Fritz. And enough eventually to despise him. She took her own life shortly after that unleashing of the beast in April in France. Against her pleadings, Fritz went to Ypres to personally observe the event. He returned exhilarated, unhappy only that the fools in command failed to understand this great opportunity. That they failed to have sufficient forces to take full advantage of the inevitable break in the front lines. Fritz thinks Germany could have won the war from this single, dramatic event if the military had been bolder."

Einstein paused. Then he shook his head, very slowly. "For him to think like that, more brutally than the professional brutes. Oh how he and I have argued. So much so that there is nothing for it now but to be silent before him, before the madness. He proposes that making wars more monumentally cruel will shorten their duration. And he makes the proposition to me that in war, death is death. If it is by the suffering of the eyes and the lungs and the brain and the heart from chemistry, it is no different than the suffering of limbs and head and torso from metallurgy."

Einstein drew in a deep draft of pipe smoke, taking it even into his lungs. He let it out slowly. And he said, "Clara put a bullet in her brain to advance the theory that Fritz was wrong."

We let the silence sit between us for a time.

I allowed myself to take a shallow breath or two of the toxic reality: Stockman and Haber were working together on a poison gas attack.

Einstein was considering Clara's theory. He said, "The isolated argument Fritz makes about the two modes of death is perhaps, in some ways, sound. Shrapnel and bullets and fire could be seen as already maximal in brutality. But he leaps to a ridiculous conclusion."

His next silence brought a calm draw on the pipe. He'd said all that he assumed he needed to say.

I needed more.

I said, "So Doctor Haber is no longer in the business of feeding the hungry. But his present business. How does it go?"

"I am no chemist," he said. "He and I collide at the Institute and interact and he always must tell me some little thing or other. I am afraid that in his mind my listening to him co-opts me into his work. But from respect to him personally, and from futility, I simply listen. He has moved beyond chlorine gas to phosgene. Phosgene is more toxic than chlorine. And it causes less coughing and so remains un-expelled from the lungs. He is quite proud."

My mind worked and worked at all this, even as I kept my attention on Einstein's words.

But I had to ask the right questions.

And I thought of the box in the export office.

"Has he spoken of bombs?" I said.

Einstein hesitated. He thought.

"Not artillery," I said. "Something that a Zeppelin might deliver."

He straightened abruptly. "More chemistry," he said. "Those infernal machines filled with a chemist's gas."

"Did he say anything?"

"Not that I can recall."

"In the light of Doctor Haber's philosophy of war, would an aerial bomb be an advance?"

He thought for a moment. "I am no military man."

"Just the science of it."

"Of course," he said. "The same wind sufficient to carry the poisonous gas across a battlefield also blows the gas quickly away. A bomb would greatly reduce the force of a necessary wind to a level just sufficient to stir things about."

"Would such a bomb need a special design? Would any bomb do?"

Einstein puffed briefly at his pipe, considering this, his brightness returning a bit, I presumed in the pure scientific puzzle of it. "Not any bomb," he said. "Certainly not. The perfect bomb would perhaps be something of a challenge. As I understand it, phosgene and similar gases boil at relatively low atmospheric temperatures, below the present summer temperature, for instance. So they will be transformed from the liquid inside the bomb to the killing gas immediately upon exposure to the air. However, there is the matter of the bursting charge. This would have to be carefully managed so that the shell will burst open but not, as well, consume the gas too quickly at the point of impact, which would greatly reduce the footprint of toxicity. And also so that the shell will not bury its striking end in the ground, trapping much of the liquid there unvaporized. The bomb maker would have to be very clever."

He paused, hearing his own implicit admiration. He clarified: "That is to say *despicably* clever."

"What would Doctor Haber see as the right conditions for an attack?"

In spite of the moment of self-awareness, Einstein leaned forward, bright again. "It would be at night, with cloud cover, to minimize the daylight-warmed ground from creating upward currents of air. These would otherwise quickly dissipate the gas."

I too found myself on the edge of my chair. I sat back.

I felt I had heard enough.

But Einstein added, "And of course the best target would be a large city. A nighttime crowd. The streets of a city would further temper the upward currents, and the buildings would tunnel any movement of air to its victims. The gas would linger to kill."

At this, my mind asked to shut down. His mind seemed to rear back from itself, abruptly alarmed at its own cleverness in working out this attack as a hypothetical.

He said, softly, "You see how we are all vulnerable."

# 41

Einstein and I made our good-byes and I rose and he rose and we shook hands. I offered to find Madam Cobb and I urged him to wait, as I knew where to locate her in the theater. He thanked me and sat down and I stepped out of the dressing room and softly clicked the door closed behind me.

I turned to head along the corridor to the auditorium.

Mother was standing a few paces away, alone, leaning against the wall and smoking a cigarette. She looked at me and hastily dropped the cigarette to the floor and tapped it out with the toe of her shoe.

I approached her.

We spoke low.

"It's been a long time since I've seen you smoke," I said.

"It's been a long time since you've seen me frightened."

"Are you?"

"Yes."

She said no more than that in answer to what she would usually take to be a juicy theatrical cue line. I believed her.

"What is it?" I said.

"I'm going with him."

"Stockman?"

"Yes."

"When?"

"Monday morning. Early. He asked me to go with the most tender of entreaties. Albert the vulnerable, the tortured, the needy. Then he swore me to secrecy with a whispered vehemence that scared the living bejabbers out of me."

I didn't respond at once. I tried to figure out how much I should tell her, in her present state, of my own recent fright. For *fright* it was quickly becoming. My mind had only just begun to work out all the implications of what Einstein had told me. Stockman was heading south to somehow expedite an aerial poison gas attack. And thinking this far now, I thought to add *against London*.

"He's not going to invite you," Mother said.

"He told you that?"

"Yes. I'm to play the *Grande Dame* to Victor *and* to you. The story is that I'm going away alone for a few days to a spa. I must. I'm not telling you where."

"Will Barnowsky tolerate that?"

"I'm ill. I need to go away for a time. He'll tolerate it. We're still two weeks from opening. I'm doing swell, my son. Swell. Let a stand-in rehearse with these locals. I can be ill for days and still play Hamlet in my sleep. In two languages? Not a problem for Isabel Cobb. You know I can do anything on a stage. Anything I want. My mind. My will. My heart. My mind. Did I mention my mind? It can do anything."

Abruptly she stopped speaking.

She heard herself. "What the hell was that little monologue all about?" she said. "That doesn't sound good."

"You'll be fine," I said. "The third act has begun in our play. That's all."

"Yes, my darling. Yes. You're right."

I reached under my coat and into the small of my back and I drew my pocket Mauser from its holster. I brought it out before her. Too quickly. She drew a sharp, lifting, stiffening breath and reared back.

"I want you to take this," I said.

"Is it necessary?"

"You tell me. It's to calm your fear."

She looked at it.

"Do you know how to use it?" I asked.

"Don't you remember my Lydia Justice in *A Woman Wronged*?"

I didn't. "Do you know how many plays I've seen you in?"

"Well, I learned to shoot for Lydia. And though on stage they were blanks, they were precisely shot."

"Fine." I offered the pistol.

She waved it away. "Do you actually think I could kill him?"

I'd even asked myself the same question not too long ago. The last ten minutes had given me my answer, I realized. I thought again to tell her about the gas. But after that one brief, clear-headed admission of her fear, she'd been thrashing around to deal with it in every way but honest. These much higher stakes might only frighten her more, and she could inadvertently betray herself to Stockman. She needed to know, but not now.

"You may not approve," she said. "You may not believe me. He may have terrible flaws. But I love him."

I clamped my mouth tightly shut and looked away.

She read the gesture. Partially. "Don't worry," she said. "I'll stop him. I know I have to stop him from whatever it is we're all worried about. I'll bring him down. But that's all I can do. There is no possible circumstance where I'd shoot him to death."

I said, "People other than Stockman could be a danger to you."

I offered my Mauser once more.

She looked at it.

"Believe me," I said, quite softly. "There are things we can't anticipate."

She took a deep breath.

She took the pistol from my hand.

She held it like she knew what to do with it. Like she was the wronged Lydia Justice six nights and two matinees a week.

# 42

Jeremy was waiting for me outside the Hotel Baden. He was a shadow and a flaring red tip of a cigarette and a plume of streetlight-gathering smoke from under a linden tree in the median. I saw him at once as I got out of the taxi.

I went to him.

"What are you smoking?" I said.

"Murads," he said.

"Close enough," I said. "I'm out."

He gave me one and a light.

"I have a feeling you know something," Jeremy said.

"You develop that intuition in the ring?"

"Doubt if it's intuition. You're telegraphing your punch."

"They call it the lead in my other line of work," I said. "Sir Albert Stockman, a member of the British Parliament, is masterminding a nighttime Zeppelin attack on London, employing a bomb of his own design filled with a deadly gas called phosgene. It will target civilians with the purpose of heralding enough terror to force a quick end of the war in favor of Germany."

That was the lead of our story.

I let it sit in him for a moment.

He took a deep drag on his Murad.

"It's all pieced together and circumstantial," I said. "But that's the business we're in. I'd bet my bankroll on it."

"I believe you'd win," Jeremy said.

"We have every reason to assume the attack will take place next week. And Stockman will try to put his own personal stamp on it somehow. He sees himself as a great German hero in the making."

"With the help of Colonel Max Hermann Bauer," Jeremy said. "What I've been told about *him* fits the puzzle. Last month Bauer was appointed chief of Section One in the German Department of the General Staff. His main task is to identify and test new weapons and tactics. Even before the official posting, he was the man who got Haber's gas to the front lines at Ypres."

"So he's being instrumental again."

"Bauer's also a political maverick," Jeremy said. "Despises both General Falkenhayn and Chancellor Bethmann-Hollweg."

"Then why did Falkenhayn promote him?"

"He probably figures shunting Bauer to new weapons keeps him on the fringe. So Bauer would be keen to counterpunch."

Jeremy let me finish the thought. "With a surprise strike by a new weapon that could win the war."

"Just so."

"He'd need a powerful buddy to get a Zepp to do his bidding."

"Erich Ludendorff would do," Jeremy said. "Bauer got his weapons credentials in artillery. He had a hand in the general's big-gun victory at Liège after the rest of the German command ate crow for two weeks at the start of the war. He and General Ludendorff are known to be very close."

"Our Albert would be drawn to a maverick," I said. "He was sharply critical of the Kaiser this morning."

"Most of the German high command is critical of the Kaiser."

"Willie's soft on the Brits."

Jeremy nodded. "Notwithstanding, he's duly tough after the fact. He never dreamed his U-boats would catch a target like the *Lusitania*. No one really did. But he was keenly vigorous in defense of its sinking."

"So Bauer and Stockman figure they can safely act on their own, as long as they pull it off."

"If you listen to Germans argue with each other," Jeremy said, "no one is ever wrong about anything. Collectively too. If the poison gas bomb goes off and England effectively suffers, then the High Command certainly was right all along. Every one of them, from the Kaiser on down."

"This makes sense of the tower at Stockman House," I said. "The wind studies. They were thinking about poison gas in British streets."

"My other bit fits as well," Jeremy said. "I decided FVFB had to be comparable to Krupp. I just couldn't sort things out in my head from the companies I knew. So I consulted the Berlin Stock Exchange. Farbenfabriken Vormals Friedrich Bayer. Pharmaceuticals. Dyes. Chemicals."

"I think we know what they make in Kalk," I said.

"Did Madam Cobb persuade Stockman to let her go along?"

"I persuaded him on her behalf, I think."

"And you?"

"Not invited."

"We need to invite ourselves," Jeremy said.

At this, we smoked for a few moments.

Across the street was the hotel where another identity awaited me behind the baseboards of a wardrobe. Colonel Klaus von Wolfinger. I'd already shaved for him.

"Time to bluff," I said.

"This is good advice."

"It was yours."

"I am never wrong," he said.

"Since you're so German, can your people fit you out as an officer? We're talking about getting very close to an army base."

"Yes."

"Trask has me set up as a colonel attached to the Foreign Office," I said. "Secret service."

"Your uniform complete?"

"The only officer headgear I could pack was a crusher," I said. "Can you get me a peaked field cap?"

"Size, if I have a choice?"

"Seven, British," I said.

"When does Stockman leave?"

"In about thirty-six hours."

"With that box, they have to be driving."

"As much as I'd relish the irony," I said, "I don't think your Ford will pass for a German staff car."

"I can arrange a car. But the people I draw on for support are all of them around Berlin. In Spich we'll be on our own. Any special needs you can anticipate?"

"In other words, what's our plan," I said.

"In other words."

I thought of what we knew about Albert and about Spich and about his wooden crate. What the likelihoods were.

Jeremy said, "I suppose the argument could be made that we simply need a bullet. For Stockman."

I shook my head *no*. "We let the boxes go in order to keep us in the game. And because those presumed prototypes are replaceable. The plans are somewhere. Several somewheres, I'm sure. But Albert's replaceable too, at this point. His work is done. The Zepps and the gas and the shell design already exist. What you learned about Bauer is the thing. We need to interfere in a striking enough way to prevent the maverick attack and also openly discredit the attempt. We need to get the half-British Kaiser's attention. The only cruelty he'll disavow is failed cruelty."

Jeremy nodded. "So what do you need?"

I was improvising now. Without a real plan. But from the realities I'd just voiced, there was a basic act that seemed to be called for. Indeed, I could think of no other.

I said, "I don't know exactly how to employ it, without our knowing Spich, but I think we need a bomb of our own. A portable one."

He thought a moment. About either what I had in mind or how to get one.

In case it was the former, I said, "If we can blow up the Zepp with Stockman's untested shell armed, either on the ground or very shortly

274

into the flight, we can spectacularly poison an air base inside the Fatherland. The whole maverick plan will come out and look bad."

"I can arrange this," Jeremy said.

"And a dispatch case to fit the thing," I said. "I'd need to carry it close."

He dropped half his cigarette at his feet and stubbed it out. "I'll pick you up tomorrow at six. Here at the Baden. Dress like you are now and bring what you need for the south."

Jeremy pulled his pack of Murads from his coat pocket. He handed them to me. "In case you can't find Turkish tobacco in the hotel."

I took them. "Thanks."

Maybe it was the moment of leave-taking after a serious talk that suddenly brought this to mind, but I thought of Stockman in the Adlon bar.

I said, "That drink I had with Albert the first night in Berlin. He criticized the Zeppelins for bringing only isolated disruptions. That's what I was focusing on. But it was his other criticism that really mattered. *Commonplace.*"

"This is anything but that," Jeremy said.

"Stockman is a terrorist," I said.

And I was letting him sleep with my mother.

# 43

When I got back to the Adlon, there was a note waiting for me, in a sealed hotel envelope slipped under the door. My mother had simply written *Hotel Alten-Forst. Spich.* Its brevity, its mode of delivery, the risks and suspicions of yesterday early morning, her place now, near the center of Stockman's plans, my exclusion from those plans: all this meant I should not—*dared* not—see her again before the time of my rendezvous with Jeremy.

Would I have tried to talk her out of all this? I wished I'd told her about the poison gas. But maybe it was better she didn't know. She was committed to her role. The most dangerous thing for her now would be to try to withdraw from him. Still. As a woman, would she continue to love a known terrorist? As a son, how could there be even a match-spark of doubt about the answer to that? But there was.

Spich.

I'd brought my Gladstone to the Adlon. I gathered the things I needed for travel and packed them. I stepped off the elevator and paused at the mezzanine balustrade and looked for Herr Wagner.

He'd kept his distance since I'd confronted him in this very spot, but I didn't want the Gladstone to set off any alarms in his head. He was standing just beyond the reception lounge, in front of the Palm Court. He was watching someone cross the lobby. I followed his gaze to a small man, dressed in a dark, three-piece suit. A Far

East Asian. Wagner openly observed the man as he marched with clear and oblivious purpose into the Palm Court. Wagner turned as if to follow.

I beat it quick down the stairway but emerged cautiously from behind the reception desk. Wagner was indeed following the Asian man, out the doors to the Goethe Garden. I strode away in the other direction, across the lobby and the vestibule platform, and then I was spinning through the revolving door onto Unter den Linden, feeling happier with each step to be leaving the Adlon behind.

I returned to the Hotel Baden and stopped inside the front door and asked the *Hausmeister* where Spich was. He touched the tip of his nose in thought and then led me to the front desk and a book of maps.

Kalk was just across the Rhine from Cologne; Spich was just nine miles farther south.

When I stepped into Jeremy's Ford in front of the hotel the next evening, *Spich* was still nagging at me in vague familiarity.

As soon as I'd closed the door, Jeremy throttled up the T and we drove off, and he said, "I didn't mean to be mysterious last night. I'm taking you to my mother's house in Spandau."

"I promise not to argue with her about the Kaiser," I said.

"You'd lose anyway," he said.

"What do you know about the town of Spich?" I said.

He glanced at me and then back to the street ahead. "It's a major army Zeppelin base."

Of course.

I told him about Isabel Cobb's note.

He glanced my way again. But he made no immediate remark.

He was thinking.

I was thinking. If Stockman was taking Mother along to share his triumph, then the choice of hotel was significant. It was in tiny Spich, not urbane Cologne. It was the hotel nearest the Zeppelin's ascent on the heroic day. She was going to be part of that. But the other witnesses—be they press or just a few influential people, including the greatest actress and most fascinating paramour in the world—these witnesses would hardly be present at the start of a secret military mission. The successful return would be another matter. And in that event, Stockman's standing as a hero would be greatly diminished if he was simply one of the crowd, cheering. Strategic advice and technological creativity and a place in the bedazzled crowd were not quite the stuff of statues in the Tiergarten. Not for the leading man. I bet he'd talked his way onto the Zepp for this thing. He was planning to step down from the gondola triumphant.

I looked at Jeremy. He sensed it. He looked at me.

"He's going up with the gas bag," I said.

It took him only one breath of thought. "Of course."

We kept quiet now as we drove through the linden forests of the Tiergarten, emerged on the broad central boulevard of Charlottenburg, and then passed into the villa colony of Westend. A few minutes later, with the northern sky striated in stack smoke from the arms factories and the western sky rimmed with the conifers of the Spandauer Stadtforst, we crossed the Charlottenburg Bridge into the narrow streets of Spandau city-center.

Jeremy's family was or had been well-to-do. His mother lived on Hohenzollern-Strasse in a stretch of very nice, scaled-down villas. Her two-storey house was stucco-finished with the window moldings cut into the rough stone in the German classic style. The place sat on an acre or a little more, thick with pine and birch. A beaten-gravel drive curved behind the house where we now parked the Ford.

Jeremy's mother emerged onto a flagstone veranda to greet us.

He stepped in front of me and bent to her and they hugged. Then he moved aside and she extended her hand and we shook. She was small and as sinewy-solid as corded wire. She had the grip of a retired bantamweight who once could throw a hell of a right cross.

"Welcome to our home, Herr Hunter," she said, her German formal in person as well, leaving no trillable *r* untrilled.

We went in and sat in her immaculate parlor, Jeremy and I on side-by-side matching wing chairs covered in unpadded leather and she on a plank chair before us with a cut-out heart floating behind her head. I imagined that she addressed her two sons on matters of motherly importance in this very setting. Her husband hung over the fireplace. I presumed it to be him. He was clean-shaven, a state far rarer in an earlier era, and I figured I could see his eyes in Jeremy's, though by this pose they would be the son's eyes only as he danced into the center of the ring ready to do some damage. And this guy's mouth was compressed hard, even as he sat for a portrait. A hard mouth and a harder gaze, such that it led me to recall: Jeremy's only allusion to his father was a reference to his mother as a widow.

The mother rose now and moved to a vast ebonized walnut buffet whose upper panel was laid with marquetry hunting scenes of leaping horses and fleeing elk. From the buffet she served us tea and buttered bread and we sat and ate and she spoke ardently about the price of the butter—two *mark* fifty a pound—and feared it would soon go to three *mark*. She took care to blame the British and the French.

And later she fed us a dinner of boiled beef with horse radish sauce and *Spätzle* in her dining room on a heavy wood table with a vast, spotless linen cloth that demanded every bite I took be an act of desperate carefulness.

As we ate, she asked me a little about the articles I wrote in America on Germany's virtues, but mostly she monologued, though with each bite of dinner she fell primly silent until her mouth was empty. Jeremy and I kept our own mouths closed while she chewed, digesting with our food each of her just completed segments of thought on such things as British iniquity and international ignorance and Wilhelmian inspiration and Bismarckian virtue, the breadth and depth of the latter winning, for the first chancellor of a unified Germany, a place at Martin Luther's right hand in heaven.

All this transpired with still another portrait of her husband looking down on us, this time standing with hunting rifle in hand and a brace of dead rabbits beside him and a look on his face that suggested he was, here in the dining room, as disapproving of the rabbits as he was of his sons in the parlor.

This I figured I knew: Jeremy's mother was a woman who not only acknowledged her son's father but enshrined him, lived with him openly every day in every room. A woman who was never touched by any man but him. A woman who played only one role forever. Nevertheless, in spite of our obvious differences in father and mother, Jeremy and I had been catalyzed into who we were by heat and pressure from a single unifying principle that would elude even Albert Einstein.

We sat on the veranda after dinner, Jeremy and I. The night had come and the horizon before us burned brightly from the munitions factories on the eastern bank of the Havel. He said, "She will drink *Kirschwasser* now until she can no longer pour it. And then she will sleep very soundly."

I thought to say something about his mother and my mother. But I said nothing.

I offered him a cigarette, from the pack he'd given me. He took one with a nod. We lit up and he said, "From the way we reckon it, this thing could go quickly, down there."

"If the weather is right."

"I'll make us a pot of coffee," he said. "Then we need to steal an automobile."

"Do you have one in mind?"

"I do," he said. "A few minutes' walk from here is the house of the longtime commandant of Spandau Prison. Colonel Walther von Küchler. He's shot more than a few chaps in our trade. He keeps a staff car. A good one."

I understood.

Jeremy took a drag on his cigarette.

And he added, in a voice that rasped away any sense of offhandedness, "He's also known in a few houses in the neighborhood as *Kuschelbär*."

Snuggle Bear.

That this colonel had executed some of the boys in our own trade was plenty of leavening for our little project. For Jeremy to add the man's exploits with the local women made me suspect I'd been wrong about his mother. Maybe I didn't have to look so deep for the familial chemistry I sensed he and I shared.

"Did you bring your lock-picking tools?" he asked.

"I did."

"Good," he said.

So when we were jittery with coffee and Jeremy's mother was kayoed from *Kirschwasser* and it was past midnight and the neighborhood was sleeping, he and I dressed up in our German uniforms—the peaked field cap Jeremy's boys got for me was a fine one, with red crown piping and a skull badge between the cockades—and with my Luger strapped to my waist and with our Gladstone bags in hand, we stepped out of his house.

Two guys with a common uniform have some kind of electrical charge between them. It might be low-wattage at times, but it's always there. The circuitry of an army. Of a police force. Of a baseball team, for that matter. This sudden thing between Jeremy and me made us stop just across the threshold and look at each other.

A dark energy was coursing in us. From our being Allied spies in disguise together, of course. But our uniforms also made us German army officers. So inevitably the German army crackled in us as well. That was a strange part of the personal bond forged by a uniform. You can be bound by blood. But also by skin.

And since we were military men, our eyes fell to the pips on our shoulders.

I was a colonel. He was a major.

Jeremy shot me a salute. With a wink.

I returned them both.

Then I introduced myself. "Colonel Klaus von Wolfinger." I offered my hand.

He thought for moment, finding a name for himself, and he grasped my hand. "Major Johann Ecker."

We shook.

We walked off briskly, heading north on Hohenzollern. A few minutes later we turned west on Pionier-Strasse, which was sheltered, even from the pervasive glow of the factories, by a dense run of plane trees. Almost immediately, across from a drill ground, Jeremy stopped us. He looked around. We were alone in this part of the street, and we slipped quickly up the lawn of a darkened, two-storey, half-timbered and gabled house.

We cut around the side and into the back yard, where we found a good automobile indeed parked near the door. As with most of the German staff cars, it was a civilian vehicle appropriated for military use. Dressed up in *feldgrau* camouflage was a late model Mercedes 37/95 double phaeton touring car, its cloth top unfurled into its secured place. This model was often called the "Torpedo" from the distinctive V-thrust of the radiator, which was echoed by the shape of the headlamps tucked inside the front fenders.

I found myself treading lightly now, as I approached. As befitted the most powerful production automobile ever built. Ah yes. Let us steal this fine thing. Especially from the spy-killing commandant of Spandau Prison.

Jeremy was a couple of steps ahead of me. I drew near and stopped. He peered in, put his bag into the back seat, leaning for a moment to open it and emerging with a leather portfolio case.

He lifted it so I would take note, and he stepped to the front passenger side and placed the case in there.

"We'll need your flashlight for the maps," he said.

I put my bag into the back seat and retrieved the light.

"But first, let me in at the back door," he said.

He was looking up to the darkened windows on the second floor.

Before I could reply, he added, "We don't want him to wake up."

We didn't. One way or another.

I did not clear up the ambiguity of his exact intentions, however. I would find out soon enough.

I put the flashlight in my pocket, took my tools from the Gladstone bag, and led him to the back door, which had a tumbler lock. I opened the door.

He stepped past me, saying, "No need for us both."

Which seemed to me to clear up the ambiguity. Jeremy would arrange for Snuggle Bear *never* to wake up.

# 44

I stood in the yard, smoking a cigarette.

Jeremy was gone longer than I'd expected him to be. Long enough that I began to think about going in after him. But the house was quiet and dark, and I trusted Jeremy's skill at this. I wondered if he was having some preliminary conversation with the man, a necessary explanation of why it was keenly appropriate for Jeremy to be the guy who ended his life. I would do likewise, I figured, if I had his particular combination of motives and this opportunity.

Then there was movement at the back door. I straightened and took a step in that direction.

The shadow striding across the yard was Jeremy.

He arrived before me.

From the starlight and the glow to the east I could see him just well enough to read his state. At least roughly. He gave off a quietude, almost an inertness. He did not seem like a man who'd just killed another man. Anything but. Which made me all the more certain he'd done that very thing.

"I brought you something," he said.

He held out his hand and I received a palm-sized, cast-iron object. Flat with a pinback. I drew it up, away from the shadows of our bodies, and I could see the German Iron Cross, first class. The flare-tipped Maltese upright and crossbar were edged with silver.

"You deserve a better bluff than a phony lapel pin," he said.

I pinned it high up on my chest.

"The major drives the colonel," he said, and he circled the car to the right-hand driver's seat. I headed to the crank while he flipped the ignition switch. It took only a small, sweet pull to start up the immense engine, ninety-five horses worth.

When I slid into the passenger's seat, Jeremy said, "Someday, we'll need your lock-picking tools to steal an automobile." He reached outside the cabin—the gate change shifter was mounted to the car's body at the running board, just inside the upright spare tire—and he notched us into gear and we rolled away, the Mercedes' chain-drive grinding softly, deep inside its corridor of oil.

We doubled back down Hohenzollern-Strasse. I recognized his mother's house up ahead. It approached, it drifted past, he did not move his eyes from the road before us.

I took out my flashlight and thumbed the slide button. I opened the portfolio. It contained a sheaf of maps. I recognized them. They were part of the KDR 100, the *Karte des Deutschen Reiches*, the finely detailed set of large-scale maps of Germany done up over the past three decades for the General Staff.

"Our route to Cologne," Jeremy said.

I took out the first two we'd need. Map 268, *Spandau*, the thousand square kilometers of Germany in which Spandau was the major city. And Map 293, *Potsdam*.

We turned south on Wilhelm-Strasse and Jeremy throttled up and we surged ahead into the night. On an accommodating road, the Torpedo could do seventy miles per hour, could do a hundred with its chassis stripped down. Germany was fast asleep and dark, but shortly there were arc lights ahead and we flashed past a straight, cobbled road leading to a brick wall and twin, loopholed towers flanking a massive door that was as pale and jaundiced as a face from solitary. The main gate of Spandau Prison.

Then we were in the dark again, with just our headlamps before us. I thought we were on our way, but a few minutes down the road Jeremy slowed abruptly.

I looked to him.

"The last of our preparations," he said.

He pulled off the road and we rolled over gravel past a low wooden house with a kerosene lamp burning in the window. There'd been no hesitation, no searching to find our way here. Jeremy knew the place.

Our headlamps lit up a wide-mouthed garage. From within, the radiators and darkened headlamps of half a dozen vehicles stared out at us. A man in overalls emerged from the depth of the garage into our light. He'd been waiting.

We made a sharp right turn, passing an open-topped automobile stripped of tires and windshield and sitting on stone blocks. We stopped. Jeremy switched off the engine.

"Another good German," he said.

We got out.

I lingered by my door while Jeremy circled the car and strode to greet the man in overalls, who was carrying an acetylene lamp.

They shook hands and they turned their backs on me and leaned close to each other, speaking low.

I knew to stay where I was.

They had some intense, private matter between them.

I thought for a moment of the covert group Jeremy drew on, worked with, in Germany, wondered at the role he played for them, wondered how he explained his Britishness.

But they clearly trusted him. He clearly knew how to use them.

Then he and the man in overalls turned my way and I stepped to them.

He was Evert. Jeremy said just his first name. And he said, of me, simply, "Christopher."

I shook Evert's heavily callused hand. He smelled of graphite grease. He held his lamp low and his face was in deep night shadow. But his eyes were even darker than the shadow, were startlingly visible. "*Ein herzliches Dankeschön*," he said, bowing a little at the waist. He gave me heartfelt thanks, though he didn't elaborate. But I could surmise. He was working for a different sort of Germany. Jeremy was still very much a German in the eyes of men like this one, was furthering that cause. As, therefore, was I.

Evert turned to Jeremy now and said, still in our shared mother tongue, "I'll get your device. Do you need the lamp?"

Jeremy looked at me. "Do you have your flashlight at hand?"

"Yes," I said.

"See your own way," Jeremy said to Evert, nodding at his lamp. The man moved off toward the garage.

"Over here," Jeremy said.

I switched on the flashlight and followed him.

He'd stopped the Mercedes with its back end even with an upright gasoline pump.

I shined the light first on the pump, which Jeremy cranked, and then on its hose as he inserted the nozzle into the Torpedo's gas tank, which sat low beneath the rear-deck luggage rack.

As we topped off the tank, Evert arrived carrying a closed canvas bag. Jeremy looked up from his hose and they exchanged a nod and Evert put the bag into the back seat of the car.

The makings of our bomb, I assumed.

And now Evert had returned and Jeremy was replacing the gas pump hose. Evert kneeled at the back of the Mercedes and was working with a tool at the license plate. Off it came. And he was putting another in its place. The one removed and the one affixed were both prefixed with *MK. Militärkraftwagen*. Military vehicles.

At last we were ready.

Evert thanked me again. He said, "I would have expected no less from a German reared in America."

"Of course," I said.

"We will create a true republic in our country," he said. "Soon."

In response I pumped his hand a bit more vigorously and bowed a little at the waist, as he had initially done, and we broke off and I got into the fastest staff car in the world and we hit the road again. As we pushed south from Spandau into the deep dark of the heath country, I thought how the mission ahead of me was as vague and difficult as Evert's. And I wondered if the right thing wasn't to clarify the goal as Jeremy had done tonight and simply put a bullet in Sir Albert Stockman's brain.

# 45

Before the heath yielded to Potsdam we turned west. The road was accommodating and Jeremy throttled up the Torpedo and we raced on through the Brandenburg Forest, skirting the city, and we ran fast through the forest at Tucheim, and he said I should sleep, he was fine and the way was clear to him for a few hours. And though I'd had as much coffee as he and knew from other wars how to keep awake, I let myself sleep, and somewhere along the way I dreamed about drawing my Luger and shooting it into the dark. I couldn't see a target but I knew I had to keep shooting, and the clip in the handle kept feeding 9mm Parabellum shells, endlessly, and I fired and fired, and in the darkness I never saw who I was trying to hit or if he had fallen, and so I just kept firing.

I woke at dawn as we decelerated into a street of folk-tale houses and shops, bright-painted bossage or half-timbered white stucco, and with froufrou gables and roof edges. This was the Weser Renaissance style, born along the river that gave it its name, the style of the brothers Grimm. The city was Hamelin.

We were passing from the main street onto the bridge over the Weser before Jeremy realized I was sitting upright.

"You awake?" he said.

"I am," I said. "Are you?"

He was, but on Hamelin's western bank we stopped at a small café with the logical but unfortunate name *Der Rattenfänger*, the ratcatcher, from the name of the Grimm tale based in Hamelin and translated more vapidly in English-language books as the Pied Piper. We ate our breakfast—avoiding the *Wurst*, just in case they were having a joke on us all—and we received ongoing glances and bows of respect from the working men who ate there with us. We were high officers in their army. And I was more. One man with a vast gray mustache rose to full attention before me and saluted. He then inclined his head toward my Iron Cross. "Hail to your bravery," he said. I nodded in the supercilious manner of a son-of-a-bitch young secret service colonel, rehearsing the character I would need to play in Spich.

The owner tried to foot our breakfast bill but we declined, with thanks, and we stepped outside. Without having to say anything, we moved off fifty yards or so from the café where we could face the nearby upswell of mountains, the eastern edge of the Weser Uplands, and smoke a cigarette.

"About five hours to go," Jeremy said. "As long as the dirt-road bits stay dry and the cows keep to the fields."

"Spich has to be small," I said. "In a small town and a tight military community, these uniforms aren't camouflage. We're going to stand out."

Jeremy blew smoke toward the mountain. It was covered with a mixed-growth forest, pine and spruce, oak and hornbeam.

"So we'll have to strut," I said.

He looked at me.

"The colonel and the major have to be there with a purpose," I said.

Jeremy took in a thoughtfully slow drag on his Murad.

"They're in Spich about *him*," I said.

Jeremy exhaled sharply, in agreement. "Who do you expect knows his intentions?"

"The commandant has to."

Jeremy nodded. "And an airship commander."

"They could be the only ones," I said. "And I bet neither of them knows what the bomb contains."

"I bet you're right," he said. "But they do know the whole thing is on the sly."

We said no more for now. The point was to smoke and stretch our legs, and then we walked back to the car.

One last salute. A guy old enough to have fought for Moltke at Gravelotte was approaching the café. At the sight of us, he stopped and snapped us a brisk one. "*Gott strafe England,*" he said.

Jeremy and I answered in unison, "*Er strafe es!*"

And we drove off.

But at a garage on the southern outskirts of Hamelin, we topped off our gasoline tank to get us easily through to Spich, and Jeremy let me drive the Torpedo, breach of rank though it was, so he could sleep for an hour or so. She was another skin, my Mercedes, a great steel body about me and I was its heart, my own heart beating fast from the roar of the engine and the whip-grind of the chain drive and the sense of torque beneath me, the great unseen spin of things flaring out to the four wheels, hurtling us along.

I drove a stretch of the route that brought us through the center of small town after small town—Arzen and Reher and Herrentrup, Meinberg and Kohlstädt and Marienloh, Hemmern and Rüthen—and every time, I had to slow down for the narrow streets, the cobbled streets, the horse-cart and hay-wagon streets, and that was fine, for I could throttle down and shift down my Torpedo and then fire her back up again.

Jeremy got his hour of sleep and more, nearly two, and he woke and I let him have the Mercedes once again, and he was chest-puffingly pleased at the transfer of her; he was a man reunited with his mate after a trial separation during which she'd dallied with another guy. He forgave her. And he drove her fast.

It was early afternoon when we saw a wide stretch of factory smoke before us. Mülheim, with the Rhine invisible just beyond and Cologne nearby, south around a bend of the river.

We soon turned south ourselves, before Mülheim, and I said to Jeremy, "Time to start the bluff."

He and I were relying on the unthinkableness, in the heart of the Fatherland, that two Germans who looked and sounded like ranking officers of the *Deutsches Heer* could be anything but what they seemed. We all had the same blood. Even the three million socialists. So surely these two splendidly portrayed German officers were legit. Consequently, the more dramatic our public strut, the better.

So we stopped at the side of the road, surrounded by cabbage fields, and we lowered the cloth top on the Mercedes. Let the Spich locals and the air base army men know that two high officers from Berlin had come to town. Let those boys start to talk; let them start bluffing themselves.

The main street of Spich ran about a quarter mile along the highway, which had lately turned east-west. We slowed to a crawl and made our way through, the houses and shops bright with whitewash and scarlet geraniums in window boxes. We turned local heads, all right—at cobbler and grocer, at butcher and inn—and the military heads turned, as well, a couple of enlisted men wearing undress uniforms, who snapped to at once when they saw us. They saluted. I returned the salute casually.

At the eastern end of the main street we approached a town square with a four-spout fountain in the middle and a cobbled market area and a tidy three-storey, dark wood and white stucco *Rathaus*, the town hall. As we circled the fountain, a staff car passed us, heading in the other direction—a camouflaged Horch phaeton—and I exchanged a very precise salute with what seemed to be another colonel, out and about in his *Pickelhaube*.

"I wonder if that was our man," Jeremy said.

"I hope it was," I said.

We'd reached Spich's eastern-most cross street, Wald-Strasse. A sign urged us to turn left for the Hotel Alten-Forst. We did, and ahead was a great wall of pines, the southern edge of the Alten Forest, and notched into the trees was a clearing where the hotel sat, a white-stuccoed, hip-roofed building with two unequal wings joined in an L, the long wing at the rear, parallel with the line of trees. I twisted

around to look down Wald-Strasse. South was flatland as far as I could
see. The airship base was in that direction.

I turned back toward the forest.

Jeremy had slowed to a near stop.

Though we had not discussed it, I stated the obvious. "We're not
checking in there."

I could not chance encountering Albert.

"Just reconnoitering," Jeremy said.

"Even if they come straight here, we've got a good six hours on
them," I said.

Jeremy accelerated a little, and we approached the hotel, entering
a circular driveway that curved around a tightly manicured lawn with
a flower clock in reds and pinks and yellows, how time passed in a
town where every window was studded with geraniums.

As the driveway bent back to run in front of the hotel, with the
option of turning into its courtyard, we both focused on the settings
of tables in a small, canopied *Biergarten*. We rolled on past and completed the circuit, and we headed back south.

Jeremy had noticed an inn on Wald-Strasse just north of the town
square. The Boar's Head. It had two upper stories above the street-
level bar. We'd passed it as I'd been looking south. We stopped there
and parked our Mercedes off the street in a side yard.

We entered the ground-floor saloon. In the thick afternoon dimness that pressed against our eyes and seemed the same in drinking
joints the world over, a young man, who was no doubt on the cusp
of conscription, was wiping the long zinc bar. He took one look at
us, threw his rag aside, stood up straight, and faced us. His Adam's
apple bounced a couple of times. He was thinking to salute but was
feeling unqualified and inadequate for the job. So instead, he turned
sharply on his heel and beat it through a door at the back of the place.

A woman emerged. The young man's mother, I supposed. She was
wiping her hands, working kitchen and front-of-the-bar both, and I
would've bet her husband, the boy's father and boss of the inn, was
off in the trenches already. She'd be running this place completely

alone in a year or so, with husband and son in uniform, and she'd be waking in a sweat night after night, sure she'd lost them both.

Jeremy was speaking with her, as my subordinate, asking about rooms. She had only a single lodger on the second floor and the two other rooms were free there. Jeremy was about to engage them, but I intervened.

"And the third floor, madam?" I said.

She looked at me as if I'd leaped from the shadows.

"It is a longer climb, Colonel," she said. *Herr Oberst.* She was flustered, as intimidated by rank as was her husband in a trench in France.

"Is anyone booked there?" I said.

"No, Colonel. It is empty."

"How many rooms?"

"Three," she said.

"We will rent them all," I said. "And absolute privacy with them."

"Yes sir," she said.

The entrance was from the back garden of the inn. Jeremy and I climbed a tightly winding staircase and emerged in a musty corridor. He carried his Gladstone and also the canvas bag with the makings of our bomb.

Climbing, Jeremy asked, "Three rooms?"

"Our being at the inn instead of the hotel is suspicious," I said. "Renting the floor explains we did it for privacy. Any rumors about that would even be useful."

"*Der Bluff,*" he said.

"*Der große Bluff,*" I said.

The big bluff had begun.

# 46

Before I left him at his door I asked for the dispatch case I'd requested.

"I'll bring it to you," he said.

I moved off.

My room was high-ceilinged near the door but it followed the steep pitch of the roof so that I had to crouch to actually look out my window.

A man with too heavy a coat for the August afternoon was passing slowly by on the far side of the street. The coat was patched at the shoulder. His shoes were scuffed badly enough for me to notice the fact from this distance. As willfully costumed-up as all this seemed, he did not turn his face from the fountain square toward which he was headed, nor did he miss a step till he was gone from my sight.

A light knock at the door.

I opened it to Jeremy.

He handed me a russet leather vertical bag with a shoulder strap and a buckle fastener at the bottom of the weather flap.

"They will never see me without it," I said.

He nodded.

If and when the time came to do something with our bomb, I would carry it while appearing to be only what I'd always been.

"That little beer garden at the hotel," he said.

"I noticed it."

"In three hours?"

"Good."

We would rest. Then we would sit and nurse a few beers and wait to watch Stockman and my mother arrive. We had to know his vehicle. I had to know their room.

"Mufti or military?" Jeremy said.

"Military. Did Stockman ever lay eyes on you?"

"He did. A couple of times. But he'd catch me out only close up. In uniform, tucked away in the beer garden, we should be all right."

So we each slept our three hours and then we settled in at a table under the *Biergarten* canopy at the Hotel Alten-Forst. We ate, we drank, slowly, and the sky darkened and the electric lights came on in the hotel. We were sitting across from each other, Jeremy with the driveway before him, I with my back to anyone arriving at the hotel and able to turn my face away at his nod.

The nod came a couple of hours into our wait.

I angled my face past Jeremy's right shoulder, rendering myself unidentifiable to a passerby, but I moved my eyes sharply back toward his, watched him watching them. He tracked them past, and then he nodded at me again.

I looked out into the courtyard.

Albert's broad, tweeded back. My mother's darkly besilked body, her arm hooked in his. She seemed small. Very small. Had she always been this small? She could fill a stage. She seemed enormous on a stage. But tonight, as she pressed her body close to this man as they maundered toward the hotel doors, toward their room together, she seemed impossibly small.

I should have told her in Berlin. About the poison gas. I should have told her exactly what sort of man this was.

"I'll watch the check-in," Jeremy said, rising.

I rose too, swinging around to see the vehicles.

Two Opel touring cars, their tops up.

"They were in the lead car," Jeremy said. "He was driving. Just the two of them. But the car behind is with them."

Even in the night, in the spill of the electric light, I could see the lead car's deep red color. Dark-uniformed bellmen were pulling suitcases—mostly my mother's—out of the vehicle.

The Opel behind was in camouflage. A burly man in *feldgrau*, wearing a peakless field cap, was taking up a place to stand as a barrier to the tonneau door.

"We know what's in the back," I said.

"They didn't have time for Bayer. The thing is still empty."

"Watch the wall of keys," I said, turning my head a little bit toward him.

He slipped away to get me a room number.

I sat down in his chair, facing the automobiles.

The bellmen finished stacking a baggage trolley. One of them wheeled it up the courtyard while the other went to the red Opel, cranked it, and drove it off, heading for the parking area beside the hotel.

The guy in uniform guarding the camouflaged Opel remained at parade rest. Motionless. Waiting. Waiting for Stockman. Albert was going back out tonight.

You could bet he'd be heading for the poison gasworks in Kalk.

I looked out east, into the night sky.

The air was still. The sky was full of high overcast. The moon was down. Flying weather. The Zeppelin wouldn't go tonight, not this late. But if this weather held, if it was the same across the channel, then soon.

A few minutes later, Jeremy arrived.

The mug in field gray was still standing guard, and Jeremy gave him a last look before turning his back to the driveway and sitting in the chair I'd occupied for the past few hours.

I leaned a little across the table. I said, low, "Our man is gassing up tonight."

Jeremy nodded. He switched our steins, retrieving his own. Both of them still held some recently drawn beer.

He took a draft.

I didn't.

Jeremy said, "Notwithstanding all the reasoning we've done, as much as we trust it, I should go watch a piece or two fit into place."

He would follow to Kalk.

"Careful," I said.

"I'll wait ahead of them. Near Bayer. And then near the air base. Won't try to go the distance."

He rose.

There was one more thing. I figured he'd forgotten.

But before I could ask, he said, "Room 200."

# 47

Not even ten minutes later Stockman strode past, and the guard snapped to attention at the sight of him. As Albert approached, the man opened the passenger door. He stepped back as if to wait, but Albert waved him on to start and drive the car. Albert stepped in and closed the door, but before he settled, he gave a single, focused glance into the darkness of the back seat.

They drove away.

A grinding took up in my chest. I was anxious to do this next thing. I was grateful for the chance, the only one I could expect to have in Spich. But I feared this. For reasons I would have been hard pressed to fully specify. It was enough to say it was about *her*.

I drained the rest of my beer.

Warm and flat.

I rose.

I put money down and I walked into the courtyard and through the hotel doors and into a lobby of chestnut paneling and mounted elk horns. Inside, I walked as if I knew something secret and damning about every turning head and they had better realize it and keep to themselves. The heads turned quickly away.

The Alten-Forst had an elevator and I stepped in. The operator snapped to, a boy who would likely be inducted alongside the innkeeper's son sometime next spring.

I stepped off on the second floor and went down the dim corridor to the door at the end. Room 200.

I was in character now. I was the American spy Christopher Marlowe Cobb playing the German spy Klaus von Wolfinger. I would maintain that role-within-a-role for the next few minutes, if I possibly could, focusing just on those two layers and not the full set, not little Kit Cobb, Isabel Cobb's forever-young son, playing Christopher Cobb the war correspondent playing that American spy playing that German spy. That was the grinding in me. Those *four* gears. Meshing now. Slipping now. Binding now.

I lifted my hand.

I knocked at the door. Sharply.

It yielded instantly, swinging a little away from its jamb.

It had been ajar.

I drew my Luger.

I pushed through the door and into the sitting room of a suite full of carved oak and leather furniture draped and stacked and strewn and be-vased with roses, dozens and dozens of roses, the place reeking of nostril-flaring sweetness, and in the midst of it Mother was rising up from a chair, still in her deep-purple silk evening dress, her head bare, her hair undone and tumbling down. And her hands were flying up and she was choking back a cry and she was wide-eyed from seeing, in this first burst of the sight of me, only my uniform and my pistol.

I stopped, lowering and holstering the Luger and whipping off my hat and saying, "Mother, it's me."

Her hands fell, her face twisted away. She slumped back into the chair.

I moved to her.

"Mother," I said. "I'm sorry. The door. I thought something was wrong."

I could see now that her face was wet, her eyes were red from weeping.

"It's all right," I said.

I kneeled before her, took her hand. The tears had long preceded my entry, I realized.

"What is it?" I said.

She was breathing heavily. She took her hand away from mine, pressed it to her throat.

She struggled to control her breath.

"I'm sorry I frightened you," I said.

She waved this away.

I stayed bent to one knee. I waited. She snubbed a long breath into her body. She let it out as if it were smoke from a cigarette.

She lowered her face. Took another slow breath.

She lifted her face once more.

None of this felt like an act. The tears were real. They'd been shed alone.

"It's all right," she said. "I should have known it would be you . . . That uniform."

"I had no choice," I said.

She waved me silent once again.

Tears were still brimming from her eyes.

They catalyzed in me.

I stood up.

"What has he done?" I said, my tone going hard, going nearly fierce.

She pressed back a little in the chair. Snorted softly, as if in scorn.

She wasn't answering.

She wasn't looking at me.

"What?" I barked.

She lifted her face to me, lifted her hand, swept it to the side, indicating the room, the flowers. "He has *done* all of *this*."

They were joyful tears. They were tears of goddamn love.

I backed a step off.

Two steps.

I made sure my Luger was seated properly in its holster. I thought of the suite door. I looked. I'd left it partly open. I turned and moved to it.

"Are you going?" she said.

I reached the door, simply closed it, as I had intended.

I stared at the closed door, putting space between myself and my mother, as I had also intended.

"You've always been like this," she said. A rebuke.

I turned now to her, taking it slow, deliberately taking it slow. I would not alarm her. Not by my actions.

"I love roses," she said. "Do you even know how much I love roses?"

I did. But she said it as if she knew the answer was *no*.

I said nothing.

"*He* does," she said. "I count at least five different cultivars in this room. Bon Silene, the dark pink here behind me," she said.

I said nothing.

"And Doctor Grill. Over there," she said, pointing with a nod of her head. "Pink tinted with copper."

I took a step now, to cross the room, to return to her, still taking it slow.

"Exquisite," she said.

With my second step she began to speak more rapidly.

"And Safrano. From the French for saffron. In its bud the color is the color of saffron."

Even moving slowly I was frightening her.

"Four Season Damask," she said. "And *Veilchenblau*. Can you believe it?"

I drew near.

"The nearest thing to a blue rose in this world. He found that for me. There are two dozen of those."

I stopped before her.

She lifted her face. "How did he find it?"

I said nothing.

"*Why* did he find it?" She said this as if I should know the answer.

"Don't you understand?" she said.

She seemed very small sitting there, my mother.

I crouched before her again, dropped to my knees so our eyes were level with each other.

"You must listen to me," I said.

She drew her mouth tightly shut. She straightened at the spine.

"He is a bad man, Mother. More than what we've always known. Much more. Bad in ways he's hidden from you."

She said, very softly, "You would have said this of everyone who has loved me."

"This is about Albert Stockman."

"They never had a chance with you."

"Mother, you need to listen now."

She stopped.

"He has come here to make a Zeppelin raid," I said.

She cut me off. "He's restless being so passive in the defense of his people. We may not agree . . ."

"Shut up now and listen." My hand did not move, would *never* have moved, no matter what, but I had the impulse to slap her across the face. For her own good. She would have done as much to me.

She reared back. The words were slap enough. I had her attention.

I said, "He will drop phosgene gas on London. Poison gas. Do you understand?"

Her face had gone blank.

"This is his plan," I said. "*His.*"

I'd never seen her face blank. Not just her face holding inscrutably still, making it impossible to read. Blank.

I said, "He's even built a special shell to hold the gas, to release it in the streets of London to kill as many as he can."

"Impossible," she said.

Her blankness shifted ever so slightly with this. How? Around the eyes. Just the eyes. *Something* there. They seized the blankness and slammed it into my face like a brick.

"I'm telling you the truth," I said.

"It's not possible," she said, each word enunciated like a boxing jab.

303

"Doctor Einstein told me."

"He doesn't even know my Albert."

"He knows Fritz Haber," I said. "At the Institute. He knows Haber better than anyone. Haber is the German father of poison gas. He and your Albert are working together in this."

I tried hard to read her face for some trace, some flicker, something, anything, to suggest she was at least opening to the possibility that this was true. I saw nothing.

"Has he spoken of London?" I asked.

She looked at me as if I'd not said a word.

I advanced the spark in my voice. "Has he spoken of London?"

"He loves London," she said, her face suddenly flashing alive. "Of course he speaks of London." She was going to seize on this sort of question as if it were the basis of my beliefs about him, typical of my flimsy thinking. "He loves the city. Loves the theater."

My breath caught.

"He fell in love with me in a London theater," she said.

"Has he lately spoken of the London theater?"

"You're not listening," she said.

"The theater *district?*" I said.

She leaned forward and slapped me across the face.

"You're not listening," she said.

I rose.

Of course. What they called "Theatreland" in London was still robustly defiant of the Zepps, the Huns, all of it. The streets would be full of people leaving shows at the prime striking hour. And there would be the spill of plenty of light.

I said, "Sometime soon. Perhaps tomorrow night, if the wind and sky are right, your Albert will bomb the theatergoers of London with poison gas."

She jumped up.

I retreated a step.

"Go away now," she cried. "Go away."

I turned my back to her.

"I can't do this anymore," she said.

I moved away, toward the door.

"I won't go on," she cried after me.

I approached the door.

"You're a liar, Christopher Cobb," she said.

I put my hand to the doorknob.

"You lie like a jealous lover," she cried.

And I was out the door and careening down yet another hotel corridor.

# 48

I walked to the Boar's Head and went in the front door and straight to an empty table in a far corner, sitting with my back to the wall. Not that I wanted to entertain the admiring glances of the half-drunks in the room. Jeremy would surely look in here for me when he returned from Kalk and I wanted to make sure he saw me. I avoided eye contact with the men in the bar and kept my left hand on the tabletop for a time, simply flicking it upward, from my still-planted wrist, to show my palm when anyone started to approach. A subtle gesture, really, given the context and the warm intentions of the inebriates. But I needed to do it only twice, and both times it worked instantly. The whole roomful, being German and quick to follow orders from on high, shortly understood and kept away. For this, I felt a warm feeling for these guys. An admiration even.

So I kept my stein awash in a nice black *Köstritzer* for an hour or more—the time sliding away after the boys in the bar learned to keep their distance—and then Jeremy was before me. He sat. Our innkeeper appeared almost instantly. Jeremy simply nodded toward my drink and she went away and shortly returned with the same for him.

We touched steins. He drafted long, and I drank not at all now but returned the stein to the table when he put his down.

"They met him at the gates of Bayer," he said. "Near midnight, but men in suits. They all went in. He drove out an hour later. Big event. Big, special, secret event."

He took another drink.

"Then to the air base," he said. "Then to the hotel. The drivers and the truck went away. Probably back to Berlin."

We sat in silence for a time.

Jeremy finally asked, "Did you speak to our actress?"

"Yes," I said.

I knew there to be only a few swallows of my *Köstritzer* left, and I finished them.

After that, I stayed silent long enough for him to prompt me.

"Anything?" he asked.

"Perhaps his target is Theatreland."

Jeremy humphed a that-makes-sense humph.

"I don't think we can count on her from this point forward," I said.

Jeremy fixed his eyes on mine and twitched his head a little to the side.

He wanted me to explain. I thought to say, *She's sweet on him.*

But that would have only led to more difficult explanations. Beginning with: *Don't worry. I cannot imagine her working against us.*

Which, I now realized, I couldn't entirely vouch for.

Instead I said, "I can't see her in any plan we might make from here on."

Jeremy shook his head faintly *no*, disputing my assessment. "Your man and mine in London think highly of her."

Hell. It even occurred to me to say, *She's my goddamn mother. I should know what we can and can not count on from her.*

But I said, "I've got a bad feeling about her."

"She seemed a tough bird."

"She's too much an amateur. Trust me on this."

Jeremy flipped his head a little. "Have it your way," he said.

Another of my mother's theatrical triumphs. Impressing tough guy Erich Müller.

I *would* have it my way.

"Thanks," I said.

And so we drank a bit more together, Jeremy and I, almost entirely in silence, and then we went up the back stairs to our rooms and we slept.

The next morning we sat at the same table and the innkeeper served us eggs and *Wurst* and black bread and her boy served us coffee. As we ate, Jeremy and I spoke of how short the hours had become. If the weather was right, this would likely be the night.

He said, "I'll spend the morning in my anarchist's workshop."

But before we could get to the matter of my next move, a figure appeared in the door, at first in dark silhouette backlit by the morning light on the threshold of the dim bar.

A man in uniform.

He hesitated there, squared around to us, and then he approached.

Two pips on each shoulder. A captain.

He arrived before our table, straightened smartly to attention, and saluted us.

Jeremy's hands happened to be free and he returned the salute, though casually.

I was lifting my coffee cup with my right hand. The cup had been rising when he arrived, and I continued on to take a sip.

The captain patiently held his salute.

I lowered the cup and placed it on its saucer.

I saluted.

He snapped off a finish to his.

"Colonel," he said, bowing his head to me. "Major." A bow to Jeremy. Then back to me: "I am sorry to have intruded on your breakfast."

"Not at all, Captain," I said. "Would you like to sit?"

"Thank you, sir, but I am simply to give you a message and wait upon you."

I lifted my chin a little to encourage him to proceed.

He said, "My commanding officer, Colonel Franz von Ziegler, commandant of the airship base, has taken note of your arrival, and he sends his warmest regards. He offers his personal assistance in any way that might be useful to you."

"Thank you, Captain," I said. "Perhaps I can visit with the colonel on the base at his earliest convenience."

"Of course, sir. If you would like to do so this morning, he has instructed me either to wait for you or to return for you."

"His schedule?" I asked.

"Is flexible at any hour till noon."

"Return in an hour," I said.

"I will wait outside with the colonel's automobile."

The captain straightened and clicked his heels and saluted once more.

I returned it. He did a sharp about-face, and he strode across the barroom and out the door.

Jeremy and I watched him go. Then we looked at each other.

"As we'd hoped," Jeremy said.

"The commandant's eager," I said.

"He expects to fear you."

# 49

The captain was leaning against the commandant's camouflaged Horch phaeton when I emerged from the inn with my Iron Cross on my chest, my dispatch case over my shoulder, and my Luger on my hip. He snapped to attention at my approach.

He made a move to open the front passenger door. I recalled his commandant sitting in that position when we passed yesterday on the main street. But I was an arrogant son of a bitch named Klaus von Wolfinger, a secret service colonel from the Foreign Office in Berlin, so I narrowed my eyes at him. He instantly recognized his mistake. He slammed the passenger door shut and opened the rear door in the tonneau. He would be made to act the proper chauffeur for me.

"Sorry, sir," he said.

I gave him a minute nod and climbed in.

The door clicked gently shut behind me.

We drove in silence down Wald-Strasse, across the railroad tracks, and out into the barley fields on the road to Uckendorf. Less than a mile later we turned onto a two-lane macadam leading into the air base, a thousand acres of flat, cleared, fallow farmland stripped empty for airship landing and maneuvering, but with a cluster of structures a half mile ahead, the centerpiece being a Zeppelin hangar, growing larger by the moment, clearly outsized, massive.

Measureable now: longer than the greatest Atlantic steamship and twenty storeys high.

We drew near. End on, the hangar was an octagon cut off at the knees and with a slight pitch to its upper edge, the squared-off frontal outline of an airship. The doors were shut. Along each flank sat wide, low, corrugated steel buildings. Storehouses and barracks. A telegraph station. And an administrative building, where we now parked.

As I stepped from the automobile and into the shadow of the hangar, its vastness seized my chest and lifted me. Like I once felt walking State Street in my Chicago, passing beneath the Heyworth Building and the Mandel Brothers Building, Marshal Field and the Masonic Temple.

The air base administrative building was steel and plain but it was smaller than the other buildings and had a brick chimney in the side wall. We went in. Two enlisted men at desks in an outer office leaped to their feet, shooting off salutes that the captain and I returned, and we went down a narrow corridor and straight into the main room of the place.

From behind a large, quartered-oak desk rose the commandant, a full colonel like me, but having arrived at the rank at a more traditional pace. He was perhaps sixty. He was clean-shaven except for a sword-blade gray Wilhelm mustache.

I waited for the office door to click shut behind me, and I stepped to the front of the colonel's desk, stopping between two oak chairs that were arranged to face him. He and I straightened and shared a simultaneous salute. I'd watched him take note of my Iron Cross as I approached. He did not have one or was not displaying it.

And then, as our saluting hands fell, we both glimpsed something that we now subtly displayed to each other, by very slightly and very briefly turning our faces to the right.

We each had a *Schmiss*.

This was good.

I offered my hand. "I am Colonel Klaus von Wolfinger," I said.

He offered his. "Colonel Franz von Ziegler," he said. "Commandant of His Imperial and Royal Majesty's Airship Station at Spich."

We shook.

Ziegler said, "Colonel, you have a fine medal there."

My hand moved to my chest beneath the Iron Cross. "Thank you," I said.

He smiled. "Of course that. But I meant your scar."

I returned the smile, though faintly. "And you, sir."

His was particularly wide, as broad as my thumb.

He figured he knew how to read my look. He said, "I drank foolishly long and much upon that night and inflamed it."

He was a purist. And he was solicitous of my goodwill. He did not want me to think he'd exaggerated the wound with horsehair.

"Mine was badly mended," I said.

We flashed a quick, comradely smile at each other.

"Bonn," he said, identifying his university.

"Heidelberg," I said. "Borussia?" I asked. The university fencers all were members of clubs, each school having a variety of these, differentiated in a de facto caste system by occupation or wealth or nobility of blood line. Borussia was Kaiser Wilhelm's club in his Bonn university days, the most elite in the country.

"You honor me by the question," the colonel said. "But no. Guestphalia."

"Also splendid," I said.

"And you?"

"Rhenania," I said.

"Excellent," he said.

We paused now for a beat.

This thing was forever shared.

He ended the pause with a deep intake of breath and a straightening. "I took the liberty of approaching you," he said. "If you are here for some purpose that is none of my business, I apologize."

"Not at all, Colonel," I said.

"It is early," he said. "But the occasion warrants. May I offer you something to drink?"

"It is early," I said.

"Coffee then?"

"No thank you."

He made a very small but abrupt lift of the chin, as if he'd been righteously rebuked. I was all business. He was a man who respected that, who was just that sort of man himself, and he regretted giving any other impression.

"Would you care to sit?" He lifted his hand only very slightly to indicate the chairs.

I sat in one. He sat. I opened my dispatch case and removed my letter of introduction from the foreign minister.

"My purpose here is very much your business," I said, extending the letter toward him.

He took it from me with a face gone grimly tight.

He opened it. He began to read.

The German foreign minister himself was vouching for me.

"Minister Jaglow's introduction is general," I said, "because the specifics are for your ears only."

Ziegler took a short, quick breath at this.

He read on. He finished. He looked at me. "I'd *thought* you might be Foreign Office," he said, softly.

He was intimidated.

He began to fold the letter.

It was time to open the throttle on the big bluff.

"You may keep it for your files," I said. "If you have any concerns."

He finished folding the letter, slipped it back into the envelope, and handed it across to me. He would show no fear.

Good.

I opened the weather flap on the dispatch case once more and replaced the letter. I closed the case.

When I returned my attention to Colonel Ziegler, his hands sat one upon the other on his desktop.

His face was fixed in a stoic calmness. Placid, almost. This was his imminent-battle face, when all that could be done to prepare had been done.

"My people are not precisely clear as to what you know," I said. "But our inquiries reveal that you are a respected and trusted officer. No doubt that is why certain parties chose you and this base."

I paused.

I watched his calmness harden into a mask.

I said, "You and perhaps a single airship commander—and perhaps no one else—understand the unusual circumstances of the imminent mission to London."

I hesitated only slightly to give him a chance to leap in and clarify how many others knew of the mission. He didn't. I didn't press it. I said, "You are taking a civilian aboard. And within your arsenal on this raid, there will be a single, special bomb. For its very existence, the civilian is responsible, which is why he has been authorized to accompany it. I suspect you do not know the exact nature of that bomb's specialness."

I paused again.

Ziegler's face had not changed in the slightest.

I waited one moment more. And another.

He realized I expected something from him. The calmness collapsed into a brow-furrowed sincerity. "You are correct, sir," he said. "I do not know why this bomb bears its privilege."

"Good," I said.

It wasn't quite the word he'd expected. His eyes flickered with the temporary relief I'd intended: he'd said the right thing to disavow a conspiracy.

"I believe you," I said. I let him feel good for a moment and then I tweaked him again. "You met with him last night."

"Sir, he came to me as I was informed he would. I was instructed to receive the bomb from him and place it in safekeeping until its loading for the mission."

"Perhaps you do not know the irony attending him."

"I do not, sir."

I said, "He is an Englishman."

Ziegler lifted up slightly from the chest.

"You did not know," I said. "Good."

His eyes flexed in surprise. He understood that I'd read his reaction. He was not used to this.

And then he made a quick confession. "I knew he had an Anglicized name."

I waved my hand, absolving him.

He nodded his head faintly in gratitude.

"The man who directed you," I said. "I presume it was Colonel Bauer himself."

"Yes sir," he said. Very softly. This was *softly* from a man not accustomed to using that tone. "Though strictly by dispatch," he added. "I have never met with him."

"Colonel Ziegler, you do understand that our conversation here is strictly confidential."

"Yes sir."

"This is not a matter of treason," I said.

He stiffened at the mere mention of the word.

"Not strictly speaking," I said.

Ziegler launched a beseeching hand into the airspace above the desk. "I have only responded to orders."

I nodded.

He said, "Transmitted to me under the seal of the General Staff."

"I accept your innocently obedient role in this, Colonel. Otherwise, I would not be speaking to you like this. I am enlisting your help."

He withdrew his hand. Restacked both of them. He straightened as if sitting for a portrait. He was ready for further obedience. He was trained for this.

I said, "General Falkenhayn was himself unaware of the details of this mission. Though I do not suggest treason."

Colonel Ziegler braced himself.

"The Kaiser has *certainly* been unaware of the mission about to depart from Spich."

I could hear Ziegler's breath catch in his chest.

I said, "Though the officers in our High Command all yearn for victory over our enemies—and England is certainly the most heinous of these enemies—there is much dissension as to methods and targets. You are surely aware of this."

He nodded.

"This is very difficult for loyal and obedient officers in the field," I said. "Men such as yourself."

"I serve the Kaiser," Ziegler said.

"Just so," I said. "And we all serve our shared blood. The blood of the German race."

"Germany above all," he intoned. *Deutschland über alles.*

I gave him a paternal smile.

And then I made it vanish instantly. "This Englishman," I said.

The colonel's eyes narrowed a little. Yes, this Englishman.

"I do not suggest treason," I said. "The man is of German forebears. Though he is a prominent man in the English government, he works secretly for our cause."

I let this sit for a brief moment in Ziegler.

"Nevertheless," I said. "His blood is not purely ours. Do you understand?"

He did. He nodded.

"Should not our trust for a special mission be pure?"

One more beat to let the rhetorical question answer itself in his mind.

"He must not fly, this Englishman," I said. "Do you understand?"

"Yes sir," Ziegler said in his heel-clicking voice. "And this special bomb?"

I flickered now. I'd made a snap decision back in Berlin, in Reinauer's office. I'd compounded that decision later. To let this go forward. To sabotage Stockman's intentions in the riskier way, with the mission launched, so as to draw full, failed, discredited attention to it at the highest levels of the government. With the Kaiser himself. Otherwise I would only briefly delay things. I still believed that.

But the terrible moment I'd arranged was now upon me. The moment when I myself would order a poison gas attack on London.

"The bomb and its mission will go forward," I said.

# 50

"What would you have me do about the Englishman?" Colonel Ziegler asked.

I had two tasks now. Planting the bomb was one. But first I had to get Stockman out of the way. I briefly considered using Ziegler to accomplish this. But the crucial thing was to keep Berlin ignorant. Short of having the commandant arrest Stockman and prevent him from any outside communication, I had to expect Bauer would quickly become involved in any change of plans.

"I will take care of that, Colonel," I said. "In due time. Meanwhile, you can serve the Kaiser and our country by speaking to no one about any of this. No one."

"Of course."

"I may even allow the Englishman to proceed for a time in ignorance of our suspicions." I paused, leaned forward in my chair. And I added, "So we may be sure there are no matters of treason involved. Do you understand me?"

"Yes sir," he said.

"If there are, then we must determine how far the crimes extend. Both up the chain of command and down."

"Yes sir," he said, his voice gone tight. It was best to let him continue to worry about his own behavior.

Which he began at once to defend by going on the offensive, good officer that he was. He said, "May I say, Colonel, that I am relieved this man will not fly with our brave crew?"

"Yes, Colonel, you may say that."

"We choose to carry no parachutes, even though our airship has fixed launching hooks for the latest Paulus model. But each chute weighs fifteen kilos. We carry more bombs instead. And the men scorn even the temptation. If they cannot save their ship, they prefer to perish with it. But this man insisted on having a parachute."

I thought how this was Stockman, all right. He admired my *Schmiss*. He wanted to fight the war against England somehow. But his satisfaction was to have me shave and so to share the honor vicariously. And his fight was to sneak in and dose them with poison. Of course he'd figure out how to save his own skin.

"Just so," I said. "He is English." That was for Ziegler's consumption, but in my head: *Just so. This is the man my mother loves. Another professional pretender.* "Tell me, Colonel, what arrangement did you make with him last night? For his flight."

"We are ready each day," Ziegler said. "We await our final weather information. This comes to us by telegraph at about three o'clock each afternoon. If the weather seems favorable, I will contact him at his hotel."

Even as I improvised along now, new challenges were presenting themselves. The weather. As far as I knew, the weather today looked good for the mission. But I had no idea what it was in England, which was the crucial question. And the weather could quickly change, could stop the mission. If I eliminated Stockman and then the flight was suddenly canceled, his fate would quickly come to light—surely before the next opportunity for the mission to fly—and my only chance to expose the poison gas strategy in a bad light to Berlin would be lost.

Ziegler said, "We must be in the air by five to arrive in London at the target hour."

Another problem. Whenever I'd visualized planting the bomb on the Zeppelin, my mind had seen it as nighttime. But of course it couldn't be night. The flight to London was upward of five hours. I had to do my work in broad daylight.

Ziegler and I sat for a moment, fretting in parallel, showing none of it to each other.

"Will you load the bombs at three?" I said.

"Yes."

"But I presume the mission could be canceled in those last two hours."

"Yes sir. If the weather changes abruptly. We'd be advised of that."

So much could go wrong in all of this already. I didn't want to be forced to destroy the Zeppelin on the ground. I didn't know how far the phosgene would reach or how quickly from the larger explosion. Far enough and quick enough to be nasty. Far enough and quick enough, perhaps, to be inescapable. But if I'd already eliminated Albert and the weather changed and the Zepp didn't fly, I would have no choice.

First things first.

I had to be sure of access to him.

"Are you picking him up when it's time?" I asked.

"I am to telephone him. He wished to make his own way here."

I thought: *He's bringing her to see him off.*

I set that thought aside.

"You will telephone me first at the Boar's Head Inn," I said.

"Of course."

"There is no instrument in my room," I said. "You will make sure the innkeeper finds me. Leave no message. You must hear my voice."

"Yes sir." Colonel Ziegler punched each word.

I sat back in my chair.

I fixed my gaze firmly on him. I let him work all this over in his mind for a few moments under my steady scrutiny.

Then I said, "Perhaps it's not too early, Colonel."

His face muddled up. The gears ground in his head.

I gave him a faint smile. "To have that drink."

He fairly leapt from his chair. "Sergeant Götz," he boomed, happy to be back in command.

The door banged open behind me. "Sir!"

"Schnapps," the colonel said.

And so the colonel and I drank together for a time.

He grew intensely nostalgic and even sentimental about the military action he'd seen, regretting having missed, because of his age, most of the wars of unification; cherishing the bit he had finally experienced as a freshly minted, nineteen-year-old lieutenant at the Siege of Paris; doing his most ardent fighting later on, in the African colonies. I listened quietly and he talked volubly and when I felt we'd secured our bond of uniform and rank and shared secret mission, I asked to see a little of the base.

He was eager to comply.

We stepped out of the administrative building.

"Our airship is only lately delivered," Ziegler said. "The LZ 78. Modeled after the navy's newest."

And he led me first through a door in the freight-train-long row of contiguous lean-tos at the base of the near wall of the hangar—where maintenance supplies were kept and the ordnance and flying supplies were staged for the missions—and then through a sliding door into the hangar and into the presence of the Zeppelin itself, its long bullet-body darkly glowing from the massive bank of yellow-tinted windows in the ceiling.

The size of the airship staggered me even more than the hangar it sat in, as on the morning in New York a few months ago I was staggered by the *Lusitania* as I stood at the foot of its gangplank. These things were not simply vast, fixed objects. These things took you inside them and then raced upon the face of the sea or through the sky. This thing now before me, colossal as it was, actually flew. It was as if the Great Pyramid of Giza could suddenly lift up from the earth and soar away.

It seemed invulnerable, this Zeppelin. Even noble, somehow, intrinsically so. Apart from the terrible intentions its owners had for it, the airship itself seemed innocent. I was sad for what I had to do.

And terrified that I might not be able to do it. I was tiny in the world of this thing. The bag on my shoulder—more importantly, the single device I intended to carry in it—was tinier still.

The air smelled of hydrogen. Even here. Even with the Zeppelin at rest. It was filled full already, its twilight-gray skin stretched taut with two million cubic feet of gas, anticipating this night. LZ 78 was ready to fly. And I had to find a way to destroy it at the very last moment.

# 51

The doors at the upwind end of the hangar were partly open, about the width of the central guiding rails. Ziegler walked us in that direction. He spoke of the ton-and-a-half bomb payload and the four latest-model Maxim guns in the gondolas. I noted heavy-duty branch valves along the floor, bespeaking the deeply buried hydrogen conduits; wheeled distribution tanks for gasoline with heavy-duty pumps and safety cocks, the fuel itself also buried underground; two-branched water hydrants every hundred feet; three dozen ventilating chimneys in the roof; signs everywhere with warnings about smoking, about matches, about sparks; the dampness beneath our feet, the floor kept constantly wet by a sprinkling system. Everywhere around us were markers of the fear of fire. Fear of the explosive flammability of hydrogen.

"Good," Ziegler said. "Here's Major Dettmer."

We were passing the forward gondola, and ahead, standing in the center of the rails, arms akimbo, darkly silhouetted against the tall corridor of morning light at the open doors, was the commander of LZ 78.

We approached. He turned and took a step toward us, his face suddenly rendering itself, in the light from the windows, into clean-shaven, cleft-chinned stolidity.

He saluted us both.

Ziegler introduced me. And he explained me: "Colonel Wolfinger represents the Foreign Office. They have interceded about the civilian."

Dettmer's eyes cut instantly in my direction.

"He won't be flying with you," I said.

I patted my dispatch case, as if the written order for that was inside. I wanted the major to take note of the case so when I needed access to his airship, he would not question its presence over my shoulder.

I paused to let Major Dettmer reply if he wished.

He realized I was waiting.

He said, "It was not my idea to bring him, sir."

I smiled at him. "I did not imagine it was."

"I have clear instructions about his bomb," he said. "We do not need his presence to drop it where they wish."

To demonstrate my authority and validate my identity, I'd played the safest cards in my deck of deductions so far. I took a little gamble with one now.

"They do still light their theaters at night," I said.

Dettmer smiled.

I was right about the target.

"I would like to see you off," I said. "To see for myself that the bomb is secure," I said.

"Yes sir," he said.

"They have given you special handling instructions, I presume."

"They have."

"Have they told you why?"

I sensed Ziegler stiffen beside me. He'd answered this question already. I was checking up on him.

"We have speculated," Dettmer said.

Ziegler said, sharply, "He asked if they *told* you its specialness, Major. Not if you have a speculation."

Dettmer looked at his colonel and then back to me. "I'm sorry, sir. No, sir. They have told us only how to handle the bomb."

I said, "But that clearly suggests something to you, speculative though your thoughts may be."

He looked at his colonel once more.

I turned to Ziegler. I let him off the hook, mercy being as intimidating an assertion of power as severity. "You quite properly answered the question that I asked, Colonel. I am now asking for your speculation."

Ziegler said, "We assume the bomb contains a poison gas."

"Do you accept a war of terror upon a civilian population, Colonel?"

He straightened. But he was not composed. He had no idea what I expected him to say.

"I follow orders," he said.

"And you, Major?" I turned to him.

"Yes sir."

"Follow your instructions carefully with this device, gentlemen. We obey. We do our duty. All of us. As we must."

Including myself in the invocation of duty, I was reminded of the weather. How its fickleness could test that duty. Once I'd dealt with Stockman and planted the bomb, the Zeppelin had to fly.

And then I had a thought.

I turned to Ziegler.

"This matter of the weather," I said. "Once armed, this special bomb becomes even more dangerous. We should abort the mission only under extreme circumstances."

Ziegler did not reply.

I looked at the major. He was standing at attention.

The burden, the dangers, of what I was suggesting would fall on him.

Too bad.

And then my brain caught up with a thing I had been shunting aside, a thing I'd learned some months ago to shunt aside. I thought of the men I have killed, the men I had yet to kill, in doing my duty.

Unless I failed in my own mission, the man standing before me would not have to brave a flight into bad weather this evening.

He would be dead.

He and his whole crew.

By my dutiful hand.

I shunted this aside again.

I said, "This special bomb is very volatile. We do not wish to poison the air base and all of Spich."

"No sir," Ziegler said, his voice thick with what sounded like misery.

I looked at him.

This did not resemble war as he'd known it, as he'd relished it, for his long career. Not in any way.

I turned back to Major Dettmer. "I will not ask you to attack London if the weather is against you. But you must at least fly to the Strait of Dover or the North Sea and dispose of the thing. You must fly. Do you both understand?"

The commander of the LZ 78 executed a very slow, very precise salute and held it.

He was a good soldier.

This was necessary work, my work here. He was such a good soldier that he would otherwise poison London from his goodness. My work was necessary. Wretchedly so.

I looked at the colonel.

I lifted my chin slightly.

He snapped into a quick salute, also holding it at his temple.

I saluted them both.

And that was that.

# 52

Jeremy was waiting in what had become our place in the Boar's Head bar, the marble-top table in the far corner. He'd left me my preferred chair with its back to the wall. The man noticed things.

I sat.

He nodded.

I nodded.

The innkeeper arrived beside us. Before we ordered a little early lunch, I said to her, "I will receive a phone call this afternoon around three o'clock. I will be sitting here. Please find me. I want to speak to the man personally."

"Yes sir," she said, with the crisp snap of ingrained obedience, which seemed to be as natural a manner for Germany's women innkeepers as for its career army officers.

Then her face flashed into thoughtfulness and instantly into revelation. She'd just remembered something.

She looked to Jeremy. I looked with her.

He was sitting stiffly upright, playing the Foreign Office major.

"Did you find your telegram?" she asked.

He did a minute shift of his head sideways. A Cracker Jack flip book of a boxer's feint.

She went instantly on. "I knocked, but you didn't answer. I slipped it under your door."

"I did find it," Jeremy said. "Thank you."

He glanced at me, then back to her.

Jeremy and I ordered. She went away.

He turned to me, and I didn't have to ask.

He said, "The groups we must work with inside Germany—the *Republikaner* particularly—we've used their help for this, their resources, their bomb, and they feel invested in it. I'm obligated to stay in touch with them."

"Do they know of the special nature of the threat?"

That minuscule feint again. As if I'd just thrown a left-hand jab. But then immediately he said, "Not at all. We keep them informed. But only as much as we want them to know. To them, we're simply bursting balloons."

I figured I knew why he felt like dodging when the *Republikaners* came up. "You not real comfortable with those boys?"

He smiled at me. "You don't miss much," he said.

"It's their bomb but none of their business."

"Precisely."

"We okay for this?'"

"We're okay," he said. "And as to the pin for this particular balloon, everything is ready but the hour."

He still needed to set the clock on the time bomb he'd been assembling while I was at the air base.

"The bomb was one of the resources provided by the *Republikaner*," he said.

"Make it five minutes after five," I said. This was guesswork. How prompt would they be? Ziegler had stressed the importance of that hour to make it to the target on schedule. These were Germans. Their trains ran precisely. All this whistled through me quickly and I said, "No. Let's give ourselves a little more margin. The Zepps climb slowly anyway. Seven after five."

"Seven after," he said. "And you leave the inn at three?"

"If the weather's right."

"Then I have time to eat the sausages," he said.

I began to brief him on the events at the air base, and in the midst of it a man entered the inn and headed for the bar. The innkeeper, who was wiping down the zinc top, saw him come in and she instantly took up a stein, turned to the tap behind her, and filled the vessel. She moved to the newcomer and put the stein before him, even as he was still taking off his peaked field cap and laying it on the bar.

A large, late-morning beer was this man's routine.

Though perhaps only on flight days.

It was Major Dettmer.

He and the woman spoke together for a few moments, low, their heads angling toward each other.

I doubted he flew drunk. But he needed some fortification.

The innkeeper moved away.

I had no interest in speaking to him, seeing as I intended to kill him this afternoon.

Jeremy was watching me watching something over his shoulder.

When I brought my gaze back to him, he flipped his face very slightly to the side, keeping his eyes fixed on mine. *What is it?* he was asking.

In a low voice I finished telling him about Ziegler and then about Major Dettmer, ending with: "Dettmer came in while we've been speaking." I slightly angled my head in the major's direction.

I looked over Jeremy's shoulder.

The man was heading this way.

Beyond him the innkeeper was clearing his stein from the bar.

He'd made quick work of it.

I pushed back a little from the table. Preferring to flee, but recognizing the need to make everything seem normal, I rose.

Dettmer arrived, saluted.

I returned the salute, and I formally introduced Jeremy to the major.

"I do not wish to intrude," the major said, "but may I ask to sit with you for a few minutes?"

I could have said no. I was Colonel Klaus von Wolfinger, after all. Turning Dettmer abruptly aside would have been consistent with the character I'd created.

But if the man I was to kill felt the need to talk with someone in a bar before a mission that was plenty dangerous on its own, then it might as well be with me.

I nodded without comment at an empty third chair that placed him between the two of us.

He sat.

He put his peaked cap in his lap.

"Commander Dettmer will fly the LZ 78 this evening," I said to Jeremy.

"God punish England," Jeremy said to him. *Gott strafe England.* "May we order something for you?"

"Another beer?" I said.

Dettmer looked at me.

"You're drinking this morning," I said.

"Only what I allow myself on these days," the major said.

Outwardly I offered nothing for him to read at this. No smile. No frown.

Then I realized I was deliberately trying to make him uncomfortable.

"Merely one long beer," he said.

I was too much in character. I owed him better than that.

"We admire what you do," I said, making my voice go as warm as I dared without drastically altering my necessary persona.

He nodded once, in thanks.

We waited for him to speak. I realized he had nothing particular in mind. He simply needed a little conversation on the day of a mission. There'd been the words with the innkeeper. The brief pose, their two heads angled toward each other, suggested a closeness between them. Perhaps even more, something only a woman could give. But there were things on his mind a woman couldn't speak to. And the men were locals. Drunks or bores. He'd seen two of his own sitting here, and so he'd come to them.

"How do you keep warm up there?" I asked.

He laughed softly. I understood what he was about to go through. At the Zepp's operating altitude two miles above England, it would be a Chicago-winter fifteen below even in August. And it would be a slashing cold, with the head wind beating into the command gondola.

He spoke happily for a time about their woolen underwear and their leather overalls and their fur overcoats and the sheep's wool lining in their leather gloves. And their scarves and their goggles and the ineffectualness of all that.

He was happy to speak as if these were the things that brought him to his morning ritual of a beer and conversation on the days he flew.

He moved from goggles to dreams, however. A seamless transition. "I often freeze in my dreams," he said. "I can wake in a midsummer sweat in my rooms in Spich and continue to shiver from the cold in my dreams. In my dreams I have forgotten my overcoat or my gloves and I pay dearly for that."

Dettmer paused. He turned his head toward the bar, as if thinking he should have another beer.

But he looked back to me.

He said, "Or the opposite. I am on fire. We all have these dreams, you know. The day is soon coming when their planes can climb fast enough to catch us. Or when they create an incendiary shell that can reach us, and the first one to touch our airship's skin will turn us into a fireball. We will have a brief time to decide then, each of us. We carry no parachutes, you understand. And so my men and I have each made a decision. Some of us will leap and some of us will stay. Some will die falling to earth and some will die consumed by fire in the heavens."

Dettmer stopped speaking. His eyes moved to mine and then to the Iron Cross pinned to my chest. He smiled a faint smile at me. He figured I understood. He figured men could talk like this to each other if they each understood.

I did understand.

I wished it were for the reasons he assumed.

I wished I were fighting this war in a way that earned this moment between us.

Instead, I was barely able to remain seated in the chair.

But I stayed.

The innkeeper's boy arrived. He put the plates of sausage and kraut before us.

"Perhaps some food?" Jeremy said to Dettmer.

"Thanks," he said. "I have to go now to prepare."

Having remained in Dettmer's presence, I'd come back to my own obedience, my own place in this war that wasn't quite yet an American war. But things were being done in the world that should not be done. And as an American I was dealing with that.

Dettmer, at least, had established preparations to make. A clear and specific path to the completion of his mission, however arduous or frightful that might be. I was still improvising.

So I said to him, "What *are* the preparations to fly your airship?"

He was glad to come back from his dreams and to focus on the routine.

"I will put my men to work," he said. "The chief engineer, the helmsmen, the radioman, the gunners, the bombing officer, the sailmaker. The engines are to be examined, the elevator and rudder controls tested, also the telegraph and the Maxims. The bombs must be loaded precisely. The gas cells must be checked for leaks."

"When do you board?" I asked. "When are all the checks completed and you go to your stations?"

"We board in the hangar," he said. "The final taking on of gas and ballast and ordnance is a delicate thing. The balance of lift and load. That is part of the preparation. Our very body weight must be accounted for. Only the watch officer remains outside to oversee the ground crew at the launching."

The timing seemed terribly off.

My physical presence on the airship during preparations, which I'd blithely assumed to be possible, would throw off the weight adjustments. I would have no access to the interior. But there was nowhere outside to effectively place the bomb. Nor the opportunity to do it, in plain sight.

I'd trusted too much on my ability to improvise.

"I must go now," Dettmer said.

He rose.

I rose too.

He started to salute.

Instead, I offered my hand to him.

We shook.

He held my hand for a moment, even after I'd stopped the shaking. "Thank you, sir," he said.

My mind thrashed.

Dettmer turned to walk away.

And then I thought of the ground crew and their supervision.

"Major," I said.

He turned back.

"Does the watch officer fly with you?"

"Yes, of course."

"How do you account for his weight in your preparation?"

"He is the last to come on board, once the ship is outside the hangar. Till then we have a man with us to take his place."

My mind settled.

"May I have the honor of sharing the last hour before your launch? Perhaps I could take the place of your watch officer's substitute."

Dettmer straightened instantly to attention. Of course.

But he had a practical matter first.

He broke from his uprightness to give me a once-over.

Apparently I was close enough in size. He stood at attention again and snapped me a salute. "It would be *our* honor, sir."

Perhaps it was the sudden impression I had of myself as a fraud that prompted the question that came then to my mind. A fraud especially to this man before me. Perhaps the question was prompted by the way I dealt with that, thinking I was no fraud at all, that I was no more a fraud than any actor in any role, that my role in this drama was crucial, that I had lives in London to save and I had no alternative. Perhaps this most important reality led me back into the character of Colonel Klaus von Wolfinger and it was he who prompted me to ask the question. Or maybe it was my true self—the newspaper reporter looking for the arresting personal detail in a story of life and death—maybe it was Christopher Cobb the reporter, who could be as hardened as any secret service officer when necessary, who prompted the question. Whatever or whoever it was, to my shame, I finished with Major Dettmer by asking, "If the day comes that you dream about, which are you? Earth or sky?"

He did not hesitate. "I am afraid of fire," he said. "I will jump."

# 53

Major Dettmer saluted me smartly. I saluted him. I did not watch him leave.

Jeremy ate. I did not. We neither of us said a thing.

Then he rose.

"May I borrow your case?" he said.

It was sitting on the floor at my feet. I retrieved it and handed it to him.

We nodded at each other and he went off to activate the bomb.

I touched the handle of my coffee cup and I let it go. I did not know my way forward. Not yet. Which was the nature of improvisation, after all, not to know the next thing to do until the present thing is done. For now, sit here. That was clear. Receive a phone call. Passive things, however. The other actors in our little drama were the ones presently at work. The plot went forward only if the weather was clear. Which it likely would be. So after the waiting, my own next move would be to make sure that Sir Albert Stockman—British parliamentarian, crypto-Hun, aspiring poisoner of London, and paramour of a world-famous actress—was prevented from arriving at the Zeppelin air base this afternoon.

Did we need to kill him?

Was he intrinsically dangerous?

If either Jeremy or I made it out of this alive, Stockman would never be able to return to his phony life in England. He would be known for what he was and Germany would be stuck with him. And if our plan to expose and discredit the poison gas air attack worked, his dangerous usefulness would mostly vanish.

There were, of course, other considerations on this question, personal to me, that would fit into either pan of the balance scale. But, in fact, I did not have to decide right now. We couldn't kill him this afternoon anyway. Not in the hotel room, certainly. Not in broad daylight in a German town. We couldn't effectively remove him from the hotel, either living or dead.

Then I thought: The body could stay in place. Isabel could play the role of terrified witness and grieved lover with ease. But the deed might get noisy in the doing. And word of his killing could make it to the air base before the mission and stymie things.

I picked up my cup of coffee and drank from it. Thick and bitter and no longer hot. It was clear to me that Jeremy had to sit with Albert till my part with the Zeppelin was done.

That decided, I ate my lunch.

And soon thereafter Jeremy returned.

He presented my bag to me with both hands.

I took it into my lap and opened the weather flap.

Wedged inside was a dark blue tin that once held *Stollwerck Chocolade*. It nearly filled the dispatch case.

Jeremy sat in the chair Dettmer had occupied, nearer to me, and he drew it nearer still.

He said, in almost a whisper, "You're free, of course, to admire my handiwork in private, but I'd strongly recommend you let it be. I've packed it all tightly in cotton wool."

In answer I closed the flap and set the case gently on the floor.

Perhaps it wasn't answer enough. He added, "The connection from the clock to the device is delicate."

"I understand," I said.

"I wish we didn't have to trust it," he said.

"We have no choice," I said.

We let that be for a moment.

He remained near; we could still talk low; the bar was empty. I said, "We need to speak of what's next."

"Stockman," he said.

"Stockman."

Jeremy said at once, "It would be difficult to kill him this afternoon."

"I entirely agree," I said.

"You have a thought?"

"I do. As soon as the bell rings on the London raid, we go to the hotel, take the room, and you hold Stockman at gunpoint till I return."

He'd been listening to all this with his ear turned my way, his eyes averted. Now he looked at me. There was a grim fixedness about him.

I figured I knew why. "The *Stollwerck Chocolade* part is a one-man job anyway," I said.

He nodded. The grimness loosened. Then he had a sudden thought. He said, "You're putting the actress in the center of things."

That was true.

I said, "Can you think of another way?"

He tried for a moment, though I was sure he'd already been working at the Stockman solution for a while. "I can't," he said. "But I'm not the one who has problems with her."

"She'll know enough just to sit and look terrified," I said. "She'll be fine at that. She can act."

Did I believe myself? I had no choice.

Jeremy rose. He said, "Bring your lock tools."

He was right, of course. But a very dark shadow passed through my head. I would have to slip unbidden and unwanted into a hotel room that held my mother and one of her men.

Jeremy went away to sleep, and I ordered a beer.

Merely one long beer.

Dettmer's limit.

When I lifted it, I paused as if to touch steins with the major.

# 54

Over the next few hours I looked at my watch a dozen times.

My twenty-one-jewel, railroad-grade Waltham.

I had time to admire the watch.

The minutes went slowly.

At last it was three o'clock but no call came and then five more minutes went by without a call and then at last, at ten minutes past three, I heard the ring of a telephone from the direction of the kitchen.

I stood up.

I waited.

The innkeeper appeared at the doorway.

As soon as we made eye contact, she turned and disappeared.

I put the strap of the dispatch case with the ticking bomb over my head and onto my shoulder and cupped my hand beneath the case and pressed it against my hip. And I followed.

She was standing in the doorway to a small office immediately before the entrance to the kitchen. She stepped aside.

I went in and took up the telephone and put the receiver to my ear. I said, "Wolfinger."

"Colonel." It was Ziegler. "We have good weather."

"Thank you," I said. "Allow me to deliver the news to the English gentleman."

"As you wish, sir."

We rang off.

And I stood before Jeremy's door and I knocked and the door opened only moments later.

He was putting on his peaked cap.

We went out of the Boar's Head and into the Torpedo and we drove to the Hotel Alten-Forst.

We parked the car and I left the bomb on the floor of the tonneau and we strode through the lobby of the hotel and into the elevator and we arrived at the second floor.

And things slowed down.

The flower-wrought-iron door clanged open. The elevator boy spoke some chirpy words that I did not hear. Jeremy and I stepped onto the long Turkish runner carpet. We turned toward Room 200.

We moved off. One long stride and another, and then together we knew to slow down, to walk softly, one short soft step and then another, and I would not let myself remember anything, creeping toward my mother's hotel door. Not remember, not anticipate. I focused on the details at hand. Had I told Jeremy along the way that I'd drive the Torpedo to the air base? Or had I only intended to tell him, running the words in my mind as I approached his room at the inn but forgetting to say them? No. I said them as we got into the Torpedo in the side yard of the Boar's Head. I'd said that I'd take the car.

My mind thrashed on to find some other preoccupation. But now we slowed even more in our walk to Room 200. We trod more quietly still. And the door before us loomed large, squeezing everything else out of my head.

And we stood before it.

Jeremy gently drew his Luger. I gently drew my lock-picking tools.

We looked at each other. We were both ready.

One of us needed to listen at the door.

Not me.

I nodded for him to do it.

Jeremy turned his head and brought his ear near to the door. His face was angled toward me.

He listened.

Then he smiled a small, wry smile.

And so it took all the will I could muster to open my leather pouch of tools and work the pick and the torque wrench gently into the lock. I manipulated the pins one at a time, choosing silence over maximum speed, though I was plenty fast, happy to focus unthinkingly on this task of the fingertips.

But the distraction of professional concentration vanished with the click of the lock and my withdrawal of the tools and my reflexive step back from the door, my body ready to run away. Jeremy pushed in front of me and wrenched the knob and threw the door open and rushed in.

We dared not fail at this. I had no choice. I followed him, not pausing to put the lock tools away but dropping them on the floor, drawing my Luger. He'd turned sharply to the left and was lunging through the bedroom door and my mother screamed—in her authentic, unperformed voice—and though my legs were leaden and my chest was clamping shut I also pressed through the doorway as well, even as Jeremy, inside, cried "*Halt!*" and then again "Stop!"

I took my place beside him and let myself see.

The bed was strewn with rose petals.

Whose idea was that?

Stockman had halted. He was standing beside the bed and was squaring around, his hands rising, showing us his palms. Showing us more, perhaps, if I'd looked closely, which I did not, but at least he was not naked. He was wearing his union suit. His body did, however, register on me as athletic in the tight throat-to-ankle cling of his underwear.

And I had no choice now.

I turned my face to my mother.

I released a breath I had not known I was holding. Nothing utterly private was visible on her either, though barely so—she wore a peach silk and lace chemise and matching corset with black stockings gartered at its hem—did we interrupt them just before or just after?—and in spite of her scream, she was now arranged in an alertly sitting, arm-braced, chest-forward pose worthy of a cigarette card. Her eyes, however, were wide in *Shock and Terror*, wide enough to play to the back row of the Duke of York's.

Was this what I'd feared all those years?

This scene?

This pose?

It was no more than what I'd imagined whenever I tried to imagine it as mundane.

At some other specific moment in the half hour just past or in the half hour to have come, perhaps it would have been different for me. Worse for me. But this was how it finally had happened.

We stared at each other, my mother and I. She glanced away for the briefest moment—to check out Stockman—and then she looked back to me and let the *Shock and Terror* mask fall from her face.

And this face was naked.

This was perhaps the most utterly private part of her body, this face.

I wanted to turn away from it but it held me.

This face was weary.

This face was old.

This face was mortal.

This was the face of a woman who would hold very tightly to a man of skills and looks whose love she had lately won, having feared never to find such a man again.

Having sorted through a lifetime of such men.

And she held all the more tightly to this one because he was also a man of great means, a man of significant power, a strewer of roses.

He was, however, also an aspiring mass killer.

341

I was done looking at her.

I turned my attention back to Stockman, whose own eyes were wide as well. Legitimately so. His new pal Josef Jäger was holding one of two pistols that were presently pointed at him. And Jäger was in a new guise.

Everyone was very quiet for a few beats, all of us taking in the scene.

I said, speaking English, "You can put your hands down, Sir Albert, and join Madam Cobb on the bed. Chastely, however, at this opposite edge."

I flipped the Luger in the direction I wanted him to go and he obeyed without a word.

As he adjusted and arranged himself, I said, without taking my eyes from his face, "And you, Madam Cobb, can relinquish your fetching pose and relax at your end of the rose garden."

I could see her movement in my periphery.

She complied.

"Allow me to introduce myself," I said. "I am Colonel Klaus von Wolfinger of the *Auswärtiges Amt*." I hesitated for a moment, having used the German phrase, as if I were in the process of remembering there was a non-German speaker in the room. I did not look at her, however. Not a glance. I said, "That's the *Foreign Office*, Madam Cobb. I am willing to think you are an innocent outsider in all of this. Naturally so. You have some other function in Sir Albert's life. But for now I am sorry we must insist you be subject to certain restrictions along with him."

Through my little speech, Albert and I were focused on each other. His eyes were subtly dynamic, however, with tiny narrowings and widenings and brightenings and darkenings as he listened to me, as he absorbed my new manner, assessed my surprising appearance, reread all my words and actions since we'd met. He was having trouble with all this.

My mother said, "I'm sure there has been some terrible mistake. With regards to Sir Albert as well as me."

I turned my face to her.

And for a second time I found her to be blank. As blank as when I'd told her about Albert and the poison gas.

I said, "Forgive me, Madam Cobb. You are used to a starring role. But I'm afraid you have no lines in this scene."

Not even that could stir up a reaction in her eyes, or around her mouth, or with her nostrils, or upon her skin. Nothing flickered or twitched or flared or stretched.

So perhaps even the blankness was an act.

It made no difference.

I looked back to Stockman.

His eyes grew steady. He found his voice. He said, "If you are who you say you are, you must put your weapons away at once, you must accord Madam Cobb and me the dignity of our privacy, and you must instantly call your superiors. Ask them to contact Colonel Max Hermann Bauer of the General Staff. He will put you straight."

Though the words themselves were measured enough, he had mustered his full umbrage and toughness for these instructions. He paused now for them to have their effect.

I smiled faintly at him and made my own words sound sickly sweet in tone. "Surely, Sir Albert, you are not under the illusion that Colonel Bauer received higher authorization for your little escapade. Even as we speak, he is also being detained."

Stockman had no answer for this. Once again his mind began to grind behind restless eyes.

I said, "Did you really think you could poison the ancestral home of the Kaiser's English mother and grandmother and expect him to approve, even after the fact? It is a matter of blood, Sir Albert."

I gave that line a moment of silence to play in his head.

Then I invoked his own invented word from our first discussion of blood. "*Der Überglaube*," I said. The overarching belief.

And his restless eyes grew still.

Had he just capitulated?

It was his own argument. Albert knew the risk he'd taken. Like the manly university swordsman he admired and wished he'd been, he seemed to stand straight and lower his saber and accept the wound. That odd respect I'd occasionally felt for him nibbled at me for a moment.

*Only* for a moment.

"I will leave you now," I said. "Sir Albert, I think you know Major Ecker. He worked for you briefly."

Stockman finally took his eyes off me. He turned his face to Jeremy. He looked at him closely for the first time since we burst in. He recognized him. "You were the one," he said, the killing tone of his voice reminding me that Stockman had actually wept for his man Martin. He glared at Jeremy, though he seemed to address me: "So does the officer corps of our Foreign Office tolerate a common murderer?"

"That's quite enough, Albert," I said. "The Foreign Office is more concerned with *uncommon* murderers."

Stockman shifted his glare to me.

But he said nothing.

"Make yourself comfortable, Baronet," I said. "Major Ecker will sit with you, and he is authorized by the highest Foreign Office authorities to shoot you dead if he deems it necessary."

Stockman sniffed and turned his face away.

He understood.

I looked at my mother for the last time in this scene. "I do not mean to alarm you, Madam Cobb. And surely it will be unnecessary. But he has the same authorization regarding you."

She straightened a little in the torso and played a defiant heroine worthy of her Duchess of Malfi: "He may shoot me if he chooses, but I will follow Sir Albert to the end."

I had no idea what part act, what part truth was in this declaration. I doubted that even she knew.

I made no reply.

I turned my back on her.

Jeremy and I exchanged a nod and I passed into the sitting room. I gathered up my lock-picking tools and I put them in my pocket and then I was striding down the hall, wrenching my mind away from the fact that there was one more confrontation to come with Albert Stockman and his lover.

# 5 5

I leaned into the Torpedo and lifted the dispatch case from the floor of the tonneau. I stepped out, holding it close. I opened the passenger door and laid it gently on the seat.

Inside the case was the ticking of the clock, but I could not hear it. The ticking was muffled into silence by the cotton wool and the tin.

I looked at my Waltham.

It was five minutes to four.

The matter of Stockman and my mother had taken too much time.

I started the engine and drove away fast.

At the air base I was tempted, because of the time, to drive up to the place where the colonel's driver had parked this morning. But if something went wrong, if the bomb went off with the Zepp still on the ground—by a delayed takeoff perhaps—I wanted the car in a place away, a place I could run to and not have to throttle and spark and crank while phosgene rolled immediately over me.

So I stopped in a stand of birch trees near the entrance to the air base grounds, just off the road to Uckendorf. There was no security out here and the camouflaged Torpedo was inconspicuous among the trees.

I hung the bag over my shoulder and walked away from the Torpedo, taking my watch out to see the time and hearing it tick—the Waltham had a loud tick, muffled by my watch pocket but audible in the open air—and I thought of the ticking in the bag, and it was five minutes past four o'clock.

I hustled on, wanting to jog the half mile to the hangar area, but slowing myself to a brisk walk for the sake of the bomb under my arm, its delicate wired connections. I reached the administrative building in a little less than ten minutes.

Ziegler was in his outer office, on his feet, and he spun to me, strode to me at once. "Good," he said. "Come."

I followed him out of the administrative building and into the hangar through the same side door we'd used this morning.

LZ 78 loomed instantly above me. And *against* me, its gray vastness feeling like a palpable weight upon my eyes, my face, my chest. It staggered me, made me work hard to steady myself on my feet. It made the thing hanging from my shoulder feel dangerous only to myself.

"The commander is forward," Ziegler said.

I dragged my body away, moved my legs, followed Ziegler along the length of the ship, the upwind doors wide open now, the sky going pale white from a thin spew of clouds, a breeze funneling into the hangar and into my face.

The breeze made me think: The Torpedo was well away from here, but it was downwind. Gas released in the launching zone would roll my way. I would have to run fast, if it came to that. I would have to start the car fast.

But if the flight went off on time, I would surely have time to get away. Where exactly would LZ 78 be at seven minutes past five?

"Colonel," I said, "are we still on schedule for a five o'clock launch?"

"From what I gather," he said.

"Good," I said.

All along the airship's length there was the bustle of ground crew, in gray shirt sleeves and soft caps, unfurling the handling lines.

The lines were slack. The hangar ballast was still on board.

We reached the control cabin, a long, boat-shaped, enclosed gondola suspended a man's body-length beneath the great gas-packed hull. An exposed aluminum ladder went up from the gondola and into the keel walkway.

"Here we are," the colonel said.

He stopped at the foot of a rope ladder leading to the forward compartment of the gondola.

He motioned for me to go up. "I'll leave you here. They don't want extra weight. They're expecting you."

We snapped off a simultaneous salute to each other.

He said, "When you've finished, would you care to join me at my office to watch the launch?"

"Of course, Colonel," I said.

And I went up the ladder into the major's command area.

The place felt unfinished, with the web of aluminum braces visible overhead and along stretches of the lower walls. The focal working parts were prominent panels under the windows at the front and along the sides, holding gauges and instruments for heading and for incline, for altitude and for speed, for hydrogen pressure and for fuel level, and standing before the panels were wheels and levers for rudder and elevator and ballast.

The place bustled with half a dozen men in leather jackets and heavy scarves doing their pre-flight checks. In the midst of them was Dettmer with a clipboard in his hand, speaking intensely with one of his officers.

I waited.

I was prepared to insert myself into his awareness. But I felt the need to seem casual about all this, to plausibly portray a benign observer. I had a few minutes of margin. Ideally I'd plant the bomb somewhat nearer its detonation to minimize the possibility of its being discovered in time to disarm it.

Another officer approached the two men, and his arrival drew Dettmer's eyes up and over to me. Immediately he excused himself and stepped my way.

He saluted.

"No need for that, Major," I said. "This is your domain."

His chest lifted and he smiled, grateful for the sign of respect.

I wished I could order him to use the parachute they'd put on board for Stockman, if something were to happen.

But he was a dead man.

All these men around me—I'd roughly parsed them as executive officer and helmsman, navigation officer and chief engineer and telegraph operator—these were all dedicated professional soldiers in obedient service to their country, and all of them were dead men if I did my obedient service to my own country and to my country's ally. As was the watch officer a dead man, whom Dettmer now temporarily nodded off the ship to execute his duties with the ground crew. I was there to compensate for his weight.

"How long do I have on board?" I asked.

Dettmer looked at his clipboard. He looked at his own watch, which he drew from his tunic pocket on a dull gold chain. "Half an hour certainly. Perhaps more. We can wait till the weighing off to reboard the watch officer."

I said, "My official duty is to check on our special bomb. But I'd like to see some of the ship."

Dettmer nodded and went immediately thoughtful. I presumed he was trying to think of someone to spare as my guide.

"I know your men are busy," I said. "After being led to the bomb rack for inspection, I'd need only a little orientation from someone. You wouldn't mind my respectfully and carefully looking around on my own, would you?"

"No sir," he said. "Of course not."

He summoned one of the other officers nearby.

He introduced Lieutenant Schmidt, his telegraph operator, a lanky young man with hollowed cheeks and calloused hands, the perfect image of a rube off a farm in southern Illinois, down where you couldn't tell the difference between Illinois and Kentucky.

"This way, sir," he said.

He stepped to the aluminum ladder in the middle of the floor and I followed.

We climbed through the gondola roof and into the open air for a few steps, the smell of hydrogen suddenly strong around us, and then into the hull.

We emerged on the wood slat floor of the keel walkway. It stretched the length of the airship within a tight A-frame of aluminum girders, but this end of the ship was in darkness at the moment, with only swatches of self-luminous paint defining the path. The lieutenant switched on a tungsten flashlight.

"We won't have light in here till we are under way," he said. "The generator."

"I'm fine," I said.

"You would be astonished," he said, "how carefully insulated all the electrical devices are."

He led on, heading aft. He shined his light here and there, identifying whatever his beam fell upon, trying to be a proper tour guide: the vast flanks of the gas cells, covered in goldbeater's skin to prevent leaks; the wiring and the cables, for rudder controls and engine telegraph and speaking tubes; the containers for ballast, full of water laced with alcohol to keep it from freezing at ten thousand feet. He even pointed out the tools and spare parts and the rigging ropes. He loved his airship, this apparent rube of a Lieutenant Schmidt, who was not such a rube after all. He had a mechanical turn of mind.

I tried to ignore him.

I had my own agenda.

I took most careful note for myself of the eighty-gallon aluminum fuel tanks clustered like cave-growing mushrooms along the walkway, their flammable contents piped down to the Maybach engines below, kept away from any engine spark.

Behind these tanks would be a fine place to deposit my dispatch bag and its bomb.

We were in a dark stretch. The lieutenant kept his light forward. I could hear a faint ticking.

It was my own watch.

But I was very aware of the ticking I could not hear.

And now there was some daylight ahead, coming from the floor.

We approached, and the defile of the walkway opened up, the planking vectoring around an open keel hatch.

In the upspill of light I took my watch from my pocket and checked the time. Twenty-five minutes after four.

"We take on supplies here," Lieutenant Schmidt said.

The hatch also had another function. This was clear to me. Directly over the opening was an array of iron hooks welded into a horizontal level of girders. The hooks were within easy reach, outward and upward, just above one's head. This was where a man could hang the break-cord tether of his Paulus parachute and then leap through the hatch. The tether was attached to the top of the silk canopy of his chute, which was folded with its lines into the rucksack on his back, the top of which was closed by another break cord. His plunging bodyweight reached the end of the tether, which grabbed at his parachute, which broke through the top of the rucksack and billowed open and snapped the tether. And the leaper was free and floating. He escaped. He did his duty as best he could and then he lived.

And yet all the men on LZ 78 had refused parachutes.

I could understand why.

They were brave and they were dedicated and they were professional. They were soldiers. To make their way here and do this thing successfully, they would have to abandon their ship early in its distress. Which they refused to do.

I was killing men like this.

But Albert was not a man like this.

He'd insisted on being one of them to share their glory, but he'd also insisted on a way to escape them if they were to die.

At last I realized it would be easy for me to kill Albert at the end of this night.

A bullet in his head.

Simple.

At my hip, the bomb ticked on.

I'd stopped to ponder all this.

The lieutenant drew near.

I was staring at the array of hooks.

"You know what that's for?" he asked.

"I do," I said.

"This is where they are supposed to be kept," he said, and he flashed his light into a rack in the dimness beyond the hatch.

He snapped his head back.

He'd clearly expected the parachute storage rack to be empty, a testament to the crew's scorn for any plan to abandon their ship.

But a single, rucksack-shaped bundle lay on one of the shelves.

Albert's.

And then Lieutenant Schmidt surprised me a little. He was a shrewdly practical man, as guys stupidly mistaken for rubes often were.

"Someday," he said. "They will make a parachute that needs no anchoring in the ship. It will be light and easily worn and you can simply jump. Even at the very last moment, when you have done all that you can do. You will jump from wherever you are and deploy your own canopy."

Briefly—not as Klaus von Wolfinger, not as America's secret service agent, not even as the Cobb who wrote news stories—but briefly, as one guy hearing another guy and knowing what he means, I thought to say to him, *May you still be flying when they start issuing those.*

But the words snagged on a goddamn irony in my head, and instead I said, "We should see the bomb rack. Time is growing short."

"Sorry, sir," Lieutenant Schmidt said, and he led me farther, to midship and another open hatch, a large one, with the walkway skirting it.

Over this opening, however, the cross girders supported a tenement-garden-size release mechanism. The bombs bloomed in neat rows, fins unfurled, awaiting their headlong harvest.

Beneath them, crouched low and leaning head and shoulders over the hatch opening, was an officer in the uniform common to the command gondola.

Below him was the watch officer I'd displaced.

I did not hear the words they exchanged but the watch officer saw me in the shadows and nodded the crouching officer's attention toward me. The man turned his head and leaped to his feet. He saluted.

I returned it.

"Sir," he said. "Lieutenant Kreyder, bombing officer of LZ 78, awaits your command, sir."

"At ease, Lieutenant," I said.

"Thank you, sir," he said, and he spread his legs a little and clasped his hands behind his back.

"That's not enough at ease, Lieutenant," I said. I was out of character now. Too soft. I was going a little out of my mind meeting and naming these men one by one.

"Sir," he said. "It's not often I have the honor of showing a colonel my little garden."

He was repressing a smile. He was seeking my permission to laugh a little with me.

I wanted to tell him that he and I had the same image of his bombs. I wanted to have a little laugh with him.

This was no way to fight a war. For either of us.

This all had to stop, this saluting and naming and talking together.

I had to think about the people in London who were, at this very moment, dressing for the theater. Not soldiers at all.

I knew I had to make quick work of this phony rationale for standing inside the LZ 78.

I had to plant my bomb and walk away as quickly now as possible.

# 56

So this officer pointed out Albert's bomb, hanging with the others. It looked different from the rest only in subtle ways. The shape of its striking point, the angle of its fins, the sheen of its metal body.

I saw these things and I let them go.

The lieutenant spoke reassuringly on and on to this special colonel who was taking a special interest in this special bomb. "We will drop no others until that one has done its work," he said. "We have studied the target area carefully, the navigation officer and the commander and I. We have flown over this district before. It is relatively well lit even when it is farther down our route. But tonight we will go straight there."

I backed away. "That's enough, Lieutenant. I am satisfied. Thank you."

He was beginning to salute, but I turned away from him.

The rube was still near me.

I said to him, "I will examine the ship on my own for a while, as your commander mentioned."

"Yes sir," he said.

"You can return to your post now."

His hand came forward. He was offering his tungsten flashlight.

I had my own in my pocket. But I needed to continue acting like Wolfinger, who would have made no such preparation.

The lieutenant said, "I know this ship like the back of my hand."

The rube figured he'd read my thoughts in my brief moment of hesitation. Figured I'd give a damn about his finding his way in the dark.

I took his flashlight.

What matter did it make now if I dropped out of character to let this boy think Colonel Wolfinger would care about his welfare? So I said, "Thank you."

He straightened and lifted his hand into a salute and he held it there. I waved it off. "Go," I said.

"Sir," he said, and he vanished into the dark of the walkway.

I shifted the flashlight to my left hand and put my right hand beneath the dispatch case and cupped it and drew it against my hip.

I gave the lieutenant time to distance himself from me along the walkway.

I switched the flashlight on, and I headed forward. My destination was the mushroom garden of fuel tanks feeding the engine at the rear of the command gondola.

But moving through the dark I could not stop thinking about these good Germans all around me.

And I thought of my own good German. Jeremy Miller. No. Erich Müller. *Müller* was the German. I was lucky to have him on my side.

My side. But I was American. And I was killing the men on this airship in defense of England. For Jeremy. Who was not a German, in reality. Jeremy the Englishman, he said. Jeremy the Brit.

I heard his own words: *There are no pro-Brits in Germany.* The Germans in this country who were *his* allies, and therefore my allies, those Germans might wish to defeat the Kaiser and his generals and their way of governing; they might wish for a better Germany, a democratic Germany, a bona fide republic. But they were *not* pro-Brit.

And there was Jeremy's mother. His own mother. She loved her Kaiser, who took them to war against the Brits. The Kaiser who hailed the sinking of their great passenger ship in the North Atlantic. Who justified a thousand dead civilian Brits. She was certainly not pro-Brit. Not like her son.

And I saw that little echo of his boxer's move in my mind. The head feint.

What was the punch his old reflex made him dodge? A question from the innkeeper. *Did he find the telegram she'd slipped under his door.*

*Sure*, he said. And to me: *These were the groups we worked with inside Germany. The* Republikaner. *We were obligated to stay in touch with them.*

I remembered his back turning away with the *Republikan* at the garage where we fueled up the Torpedo. Their intense conversation. Backs turned.

We were *obligated* to them?

Having to provide a little easily censored information to a tractable collaborator would elicit a *shrug*. Not a feint. It was the question itself, spoken in my presence, that elicited the feint.

And he'd slipped one other punch.

*Did they know the special nature of Albert's bomb?* I'd asked.

And he did his little head feint to me. *Not at all*, he'd said.

I stopped now.

I switched off my flashlight.

I stood in the dark.

He'd gone out of his way to make sure I didn't open the bomb.

He gave me good reasons.

But he said it and he knew I understood those good reasons and yet he said it again by stressing its delicacy, and again, by regretting our need to trust the device at all.

*The lady doth protest too much, methinks.*

I knelt down on the walkway.

I would be careful. Just in case I was presently being a fool, I would handle my box of chocolates carefully and look carefully. But I would look.

I could not hold the light and do what I had to do, at least for the first part. I needed both hands.

I remained in the dark.

I pressed the lieutenant's flashlight into my tunic pocket next to my own.

I pulled the strap over my head and set the dispatch case easily, easily down before me. I opened the weather flap. I put my hands inside and pulled at the tin box. It did not yield.

I turned the case sideways and held it gently between my knees.

I squeezed the case just a little and pulled at the tin and it rose slightly and I squeezed a little harder and pulled and again and again, and doing this inch by inch I finally was holding the bomb invisibly in the dark before me.

I rotated it so that it was level.

I grasped it tightly with my right hand.

With my left hand I moved the dispatch case from between my knees and placed it to the side.

I dipped into my tunic pocket and withdrew one of the flashlights. My own, I thought.

I switched it on and held its beam on the tin box. *Stollwerck Chocolade.*

I used the light to guide the box to the planking of the walkway before me.

I could work with one hand now.

I put my thumb in the small lip at the center of the lid. I lifted. The lid rose. It was hinged on the opposite side and I opened it all the way back and let it go.

The white beam from the tungsten bulb showed a faint yellow tinge upon the white of the cotton wool.

He had indeed packed it tightly. I had to be very careful now. If he was, in fact, the Jeremy Miller I'd come to rely on, I had to take heed of his warning. I did not want to disturb the bomb.

I needed two hands again.

The hinges were holding the top of the tin box parallel with the floor. I laid my flashlight there, its beam shining back toward me.

I hesitated now.

And listened.

I could hear a clear ticking from within the box.

All right.

I leaned forward, turned my head to listen at the surface.

The ticking was coming from the left side.

I sat back up.

I looked at the dense surface of purified raw cotton. I tried to visualize the arrangement within. The stick of dynamite would be nearly as long as the longest dimension of the box. The clock was small. A travel clock. I figured the dynamite was laid in close to one of the long sides.

The safest way not to disturb the connection from explosive to clock was not to pull the packed fibers apart. I'd go in at the very edge and try to lift up the covering layer as a unit.

The stick of dynamite could be laid out at either edge. I chose the bottom edge, as it now sat before me.

I ran four fingers gently in, pressing against the side wall of the box. And then I touched the curve of the dynamite stick.

I backed my hand up a bit, found the lower edge of cotton wool, ran my fingers underneath. And I pulled.

The top layer of cotton wool began to rise up, mostly as a unit. I brought my other hand into play, gathering and recompressing and lifting back the clinging batches of wool fibers.

And then the business contents of the tin box were exposed.

Darkly, at the moment.

The lifted layer of cotton wool was blocking the beam of light.

I held up the cotton wool with one hand now, as if it were a second lid.

I took up the flashlight with my other hand and shined it into the tin box.

The clock was there. Ticking away. The stick of dynamite was there.

The wires from clock to dynamite were missing.

The two objects lay in the tin box utterly separate.

I flipped the flashlight beam toward the bottom edge of the layer of cotton wool, my mind lunging forward to figure out how to reattach the wires, how to make this work.

But there were no wires. No wires at all.

I flipped the beam back to the dynamite.

The blasting cap was also missing.

Jeremy's exact words about the bomb slithered through me: *I wish we didn't have to trust it.*

After the bomb I planted failed to explode and the Zeppelin flew on successfully to London, he wanted me to blame the device.

But it was him. Erich Müller.

# 5 7

I sat back on my heels.

I wanted to figure him out.

But I didn't have time.

I was down to my last fifteen minutes or so before I'd have to get off the Zepp.

I had no bomb.

I thought: *I'm sitting inside one.* I was surrounded by two million cubic feet of explosively flammable hydrogen.

But how could I both detonate it and escape it? Especially since the explosion would also instantly release a tempest of poison gas.

Was I ready to die for tonight's theater crowd in London?

A reflex voice in me cried *yes*. Faintly though, coming through a welter in my head. I knew the answer would be louder and clearer if it was Broadway. If it was my own country. Or if my mother was playing Hamlet at the Duke of York's.

But I had to believe that even tonight I'd be dying for more. I'd die for a chance at exposing and discrediting poison aerial attacks themselves.

Seemed like a good cause.

But no. I wasn't ready for that. Not the dying part. I had to work hard now to try to have it both ways.

Which made me think of Albert's plan.

His parachute.

I had a way to survive if I could figure out how to blow up the LZ 78 while it was in the air.

But the *how* had to include a long enough fuse.

First things first.

A few hours before takeoff, Dettmer had a man subtracted from his ship. For this, he'd be thinking to take things *on* board—compensating ballast—not off. Maybe that's why the parachute was still sitting there. But I couldn't depend on it remaining. I needed to secure the parachute.

I stood up and closed the lid on the tin box and picked it up with me. As if it were still useful. Without something to serve as a blasting cap, the dynamite wouldn't blow. Not till the airship did. Still, by reflex, I kept the box. I had few enough resources. It was all I had. Something might come to mind.

I opened the dispatch case and slid it back in.

I shined my light and strode forward.

At least for now I could get around the ship without anyone's close scrutiny. A Zeppelin had a crew of about twenty. At least half of them were mechanics. They were all with the engines. More than half the rest were presently in the command gondola. Everybody on board had a focused task. That would probably last till the ship was airborne.

A footlight shone ahead.

The hatch was still open.

I arrived.

No one was around.

I took the parachute from the shelf. It was heavy, a good thirty pounds. I put it under my arm.

I skirted the hatch on the walkway and walked forward, keenly aware of the distance I was covering, my distance from the parachute launching hooks and the hatch.

I was instinctively heading for the place I'd targeted when I still thought I had a time bomb: the run of tanks piping fuel forward and downward to the engine compartment of the command gondola.

That was still a volatile spot.

And it was only about a third-base-to-home sprint to the hatch.

I arrived at the fuel tanks and shined my light on them.

I lifted the light to the bloated clouds of hydrogen bags hovering overhead.

I looked back toward the hatch, a distant glow.

And back to the bags.

Gas.

A flame burning low and gas leaking in. The pace of the gas could provide its own fuse.

I had my Luger. For a quick, tight cluster of shots high up in one of the bags above me.

I had matches.

I needed something to burn slow and low.

I didn't know if my gasp made me clutch the tin box tight against me or if clutching it made me gasp. But I knew there was something inside. Sweetly, it was a thing Erich Müller never thought to render useless.

Cotton wool.

Cotton wool burned slow. Especially compacted tightly.

Of course, the first stroke of a match might ignite the fumes that already scented the air.

Or the contrary problem might assert itself. Cotton wool could burn itself out.

It was all timing. Timing. And I had no idea what the timing might be.

But the ticking in my watch pocket was the only time that counted now and it was reminding me that I needed to act.

I struck out forward along the walkway, moving as fast as I could into the dark with the beam of tungsten before me.

I had to get back to Dettmer and ask permission to stay aboard. He would surely let me fly with them tonight. After all, he'd been prepared for an Englishman to do so. Instead, he'd have a chance to impress the Foreign Office.

He'd want me to watch the takeoff of his airship with him. But I needed to get off his bridge and go to work as soon as possible afterward. For my larger aspiration in this mission, vivid, unmanageable word had to get out. The ball of fire should be seen at Spich, at least distantly. The Zepp and its phosgene had to fall on German soil.

I'd pull the trigger on the LZ 78 soon after takeoff. But long enough after to put jumpable distance between that hatch and the ground.

And then there was the scene from limbo being played out at the Hotel Alten-Forst.

I stopped abruptly, even though I needed to rush. This was a complication that only now reminded me of itself.

Who was Jeremy? What was his intention? He was sitting in Room 200 with a pistol on Stockman and my mother. Or at least he was when I left him. The two men could have been working together. Or they had lately begun to do so. They certainly had the same immediate objective: the gas bombing of London.

But I knew the truth wasn't simple.

And whatever it was made no difference to my actions in the next half hour or so.

I moved on.

Another hole of light in the floor was growing bright up ahead.

And then I was down the ladder and through the roof of the command gondola.

I landed and found Major Dettmer handing off his clipboard to his executive officer. The cast on the bridge was a little different now. The navigator and the telegraph lieutenant were off to their posts. The helmsman was at the rudder wheel and a junior officer was at the elevator control.

The executive officer crossed before me, caught a glimpse of me, and paused to salute.

"No saluting," I said. I would put them at their oblivious ease around me. "I am a fly on the wall."

But I realized I'd just translated an American idiom into German. It sounded odd in my mouth even as I spoke it. "As they say in America," I quickly added.

The executive officer laughed.

"The place is full of flies," I said.

He laughed again and Dettmer did too, having drawn near.

"They are all rubes in America, I think," Dettmer said. Not an exact equivalent of "rube" in German, but close enough.

The executive officer continued on his way and I turned to face Dettmer. "Major," I said, "may I ask a favor? Not only for myself personally, though it would certainly be that as well, but as a favor to the Foreign Office. We have removed the English amateur from your midst. Please allow me to take his place. Berlin has telegraphed me to ask for a firsthand report on the work the airships do. Particularly, of course, on the night when you deliver this important package."

As I expected, Dettmer snapped to. He would have saluted, but I lifted my own palm quickly to stop him. He stayed his hand and said, "Of course, sir. I'd be honored."

I offered him my own hand to shake, and he took it with warmth.

Behind me the executive officer shouted an order to someone below. "Prepare airship march."

I said, "I will freely explore the ship in flight, if I may have your permission. I want to experience everything. Your Lieutenant Schmidt gave me an excellent tour. And your Lieutenant Kreyder wishes to share more of his important procedures with me."

"As you wish, Colonel," Dettmer said. "As you wish. You'll forgive me if I am preoccupied for the next hour or so."

"Of course," I said.

Dettmer's eyes shifted over my left shoulder.

I looked.

His executive officer was crossing back our way.

"Captain," Dettmer said to him. "The colonel will fly with us tonight. At weigh off, release the extra ballast. And bring the extra cold gear. Only the takeoff necessities for now."

"Yes sir," the captain said, slipping away.

Dettmer looked back to me. "We'd brought these things for the other man. The overalls and the fur coat and the felt overshoes and so forth, the extreme cold weather things, these can wait until we are at a higher altitude. Your flying jacket will immediately make you one of us."

He laughed at this thought.

Courteous words from Wolfinger came to my mind. A comradely laugh even formed in my throat, ready to employ. I could make myself say or do none of it.

I was getting too close to these boys once again.

Dettmer paid no attention to my unresponsiveness.

He said, "The woolen underclothes you should take time now to put on. To sweat with the rest of us."

He laughed again, a softer one, this one while searching my face, suddenly afraid he was getting too familiar.

I could manage nothing but blankness for him.

He cut off his laugh.

This was Klaus von Wolfinger's likely response anyway. So be it.

The executive officer arrived with two contrasting articles of clothing folded one on top of the other, one rough-ribbed wool and one soft-cured leather.

Dettmer said, "You will need to put on the woolen underclothes at once, Colonel. There is privacy in the keel. In the crew space aft."

I was glad to have a chance to get away to myself.

I began to reach for the clothes.

Dettmer intervened. He said, "But first, please allow me." He took the leather flying jacket from the captain.

He held it up and spread it open for me.

He said, "You'll need to remove your pistol, Colonel."

I hesitated. As myself, and as Wolfinger.

Dettmer picked up on the hesitation. He said, quite respectfully, almost gently, "For the jacket. Of course you will retain your weapon. Though we ourselves carry none, for safety's sake."

"I promise not to discharge it, Major," I said.

He nodded to me.

I undid my pistol belt and laid it at my feet with the dispatch case.

"Thank you, sir," he said.

The air was cleared.

He lifted the coat a little.

This was a ritual I dreaded now. The bond of a uniform. The bond of personality, of camaraderie. I dared not bond with these men.

I had to focus.

These men were the enemy tonight.

They were the instruments of mass murder.

I made myself smile. I turned my back to him. I slipped the dispatch case off my shoulder and laid it on the floor at my feet.

Dettmer put the jacket on me.

I felt it like a second skin.

That was the danger.

And my mother slipped into my head. The mother she had always been, training her son the way she always had. In and around theaters. This was not a skin upon me. It was a costume. I was playing a role. I was an actor. I was a spy.

I shot my cuffs.

I began to button the jacket. With each button, a flourish of the hand.

I did not even need to turn to Dettmer for this. The gesture was for me. Working on my character.

My qualms were quickly dissipating.

I stopped buttoning about halfway.

Dettmer said, "There. You are now senior officer on the LZ 78."

I turned to him. I doled out one more faint smile. The smile of a superior officer pleased with his inferior for recognizing the appropriate protocol in an unusual circumstance.

He saluted. He held it.

I saluted him.

"You notice that the fit of your jacket is good," Dettmer said.

It was, indeed. Nearly perfect. "I do," I said.

"We'd heard that the Englishman was a larger man."

Albert was certainly larger than me. I had a flash of that first sight of him outside his castle, towering over my mother, leaning down to buss her on the cheek.

Even more dangerous than to think on these Germans at this moment was to think on my mother.

"We did not expect the jacket to fit *him* so well," Dettmer said. He let that settle in for a moment.

They'd arranged for him never to be one of them. His uniform would not fit.

And then Major Dettmer actually worked up the courage to give Colonel Klaus von Wolfinger a small, conspiratorial wink.

Wolfinger chose to overlook Dettmer's transgression. I said, with a large dose of duty and only a faint, condescending hint of faux camaraderie, "Things are as they should be."

# 58

I pitched my airship underwear behind a fuel tank.

I thought simply to stay here in the keel for the takeoff and on through my incendiary improvisation. But Dettmer expected me. He could conceivably do something officious if I didn't show up for the launch, could send someone to see if I'd found my way all right in the dark.

The walkway suddenly shifted a little beneath my feet. The airship trembled, and I felt a twinge of uplift in my chest.

I knew we'd thrown off our hangar ballast and had lifted from our bumper blocks and outside we were surrounded by two hundred ground crewmen holding hard at the handling lines, letting us hover but reining us in, keeping us centered in the hangar doorway.

I went forward and down the ladder and onto the bridge.

Dettmer was at the front window of the gondola, his back to me, framed alone against the sky beyond the hangar door. The sky was off white, as if it were packed with cotton wool.

He scanned outward and downward, from far left across to far right. And he commanded, "Airship march!"

The executive officer, leaning from a side window, cried, "Airship march!" and the order was taken up outside to port, to bow, to starboard.

At once, almost imperceptibly, we began to move.

Major Dettmer looked over his shoulder.

He saw me. I was where he'd hoped I'd be.

"Colonel," he said. "Please join me."

I stepped forward, stood beside him on his right.

Dettmer kept his eyes ahead.

Two wide-set guiding rails led from the hangar mouth out three hundred yards into the maneuvering field. Arrayed ahead were eight handling lines stretched forward by a hundred bent and straining *feldgrau* backs.

And the movement was clearly perceptible now.

We were floating into the daylight.

And from all around us—front and sides—a sound rose up. Men's voices—two hundred men's voices—rising as one. They sang. They sang of thunderbolts and clashing swords and crashing waves. They sang loud even though they strained hard to drag this vast machine of war into the oncoming night.

And when they began to sing the chorus, the men around me, Dettmer and the executive officer and all the others, joined in. *Lieb Vaterland, magst ruhig sein!* Dear Fatherland put your mind at rest. *Fest steht und treu die Wacht, die Wacht am Rhein!* Firm and true stands the watch, the watch on the Rhine.

Colonel Wolfinger sang as well. He sang louder than them all. Indeed, I have a pretty good tenor and so Wolfinger even drew an admiring turn of the head from the commandant of the LZ 78. Major Dettmer smiled at this powerful officer who had graced them with his presence. And I nodded my head to Dettmer, even as I lifted my voice with all these good Germans and entreated the dear Fatherland not to worry about a thing.

When the chorus was done, the men outside went on for another verse, though the officers on the bridge stopped singing and focused on their tasks.

Wolfinger was ready just to keep a stoic, watchful silence. He'd been warmer to Dettmer and his men than he'd been to anyone in perhaps his whole career. And his clamming up now suited Christopher Cobb just fine. Because I wanted simply to get through the next twenty minutes and on to my business.

Dettmer was going on and on to the colonel—to me—about guiding cars and a winch and wind headings and cloud cover and the moon and we were moving inexorably forward, and even as he spoke, I took my watch from my pocket to check the time.

It was a Waltham.

An American watch.

I put it away as quickly as I could without drawing attention to it, glancing at Dettmer, who was speaking to me at that moment but looking forward. I cursed myself for all the details I had not anticipated. This one I had failed to consider long before things got tough. Though why shouldn't a high-ranking officer in the Foreign Office have a fine American watch? It was a privilege that could readily accrue to his position. But I'd overlooked it. And that made me worry about what else I'd overlooked.

Perhaps Dettmer had seen me in his periphery as I read my watch. Perhaps he'd finally realized I was not responding to him. Maybe he'd finally said all that he could possibly think of to say to keep his Foreign Office observer informed and impressed. Whatever the reason, he did stop talking to me.

And then finally we were well free of the hangar.

And the airship was set against the wind.

And the water ballast was released and the watch officer returned and the engines began to pound and the lines were cast off and I stood through all this simply waiting, hearing the orders but not listening to them, feeling the bustle increase around me but not moving, holding even more still, waiting now to do what I had to do.

The floor was quaking beneath my feet.

The engines vibrated into my legs and into my jaw and into my brain.

Dettmer commanded engine revs and elevation angles and we were moving, we were rising, the distant tree line was beginning to sink below us, slowly. There was no necessary race forward as in an aeroplane. We crept upward.

"Major," I said. "I will leave you now."

Dettmer looked at me.

I tried to read his face.

I kept mine blank, inhabiting, in my actor's brain, my character's power, his independence, his arrogance.

Dettmer's face was blank as well. Rare for him, with me. But surely natural to him with others. He had his own power here. He was the commander of this ship. He was respectful of me, of the people I represented. Fearful even. Perhaps. But the self-possession and the exercise of power and independence that I was portraying to him were, in a real sense, conferred by him. Especially now that we were in the air. The captain of a ship on the sea was God. The commander of a ship in the air was no different.

I tried to see suspicion in Dettmer.

I could not.

But this look between us went on for a longer moment than was comfortable.

"With your permission," I said, and I lowered my head to him ever so slightly.

He said, "We each have our mission, Colonel."

I said, "My mission tonight is based on a surpassing respect for yours."

He smiled. Quickly, warmly.

How ardently this soldier, this commander, this master of a German warship craved personal reassurance. Craved approval.

How sad this all was.

"My ship is yours," he said.

I brought my right hand up sharply to my right temple. He straightened with a silent gasp. He was touched by my initiating this salute. He brought his own hand up and we held this for a moment, those few beats of amplified respect between two officers.

But through this whole exchange I could not look him in the eyes.

# 59

I turned to cross the gondola, and as if the cabin knew my haste it grabbed my chest and pushed at the backs of my knees and propelled me toward the ladder. The airship was climbing, of course, and I was rushing downhill.

Manageable still. The angle was maybe ten degrees. But I was very glad the ladder would let me face aft.

I put my hand to the ladder and the executive officer said, "Careful, sir."

I nodded without looking at him.

I climbed through the roof and out into the open air.

I let the angle press me tightly against the rungs, but almost at once I was dragged to my right. I grasped hard at the left side rail and held on tight. I stopped climbing. For now it was sufficient not to be slung into the air.

We were coming round a bit, perhaps adjusting to the head wind, perhaps taking a heading. But the outward pull eased now and I climbed hard and fast and I was inside the keel.

I had to get this done long before we were at our final cruising altitude. This angle would be a constant challenge.

The hull was still dark.

I held tight to the handrail along the walkway and shined my flashlight forward and I moved as quickly as I dared let myself, with this constant tugging in my chest threatening to fling me headlong into the darkness.

I passed over the gondola engine. Along this stretch of the walkway the sound of the forward Maybach, which was straining to help lift us, jackhammered in my head. It was a bit of a struggle to think in the midst of this but I knew at once I needed to do my work close to this place. The sound of my Luger plugging a gas cell would be masked here.

I pushed on aft for now. I needed to do two things before I could get to the matter of making fire.

There was no light up ahead. The forward hatch—my hatch—was, of course, closed. When I desperately needed for this to be open, I would not have time to open it. So I pressed on, pushing my center of balance downward, down into my legs, into my knees, pressing hard at each footstep, leaning my torso backward, holding tight to the handrail, my flashlight beam bouncing before me, lifting as far out on the path as I could throw it.

And then I saw in my beam the walkway turn up ahead, where it skirted the hatch.

I arrived.

I braced myself against the starboard turning of the railing and I flashed the beam to the closed hatch and then, beyond it, to its portside. I was looking for a lever or a handle or a wheel, some way to open this thing. It wasn't there. I scanned the beam and I found it, at the forward end of the hatch, a wheel with protruding handles set in the bulkhead.

I moved toward it.

The rail along the walkway ended and I angled my body hard to my right—the ship's upward incline seemed greater now by a few degrees—and my target, clear in my flashlight, was another rail along the bulkhead.

I lunged for it.

I had it.

I made my way along to the wheel, and with my left hand I grabbed one of its handles and then, needing the wheel to both open the hatch and hold myself steady, I grasped a second handle with my right hand.

The dispatch case lifted off me. My chest clamped in panic even as the shoulder strap grabbed at my neck.

It was okay. The strap held. The bag and the tin box were safe. The angle backward was a good fifteen degrees. Perhaps more. It felt like fifty. Two powerful hands pulled at my shoulders.

I strained at the wheel. It turned, bit by bit, bearing my clinging weight with each torque of the gears of the hatch. Light was dilating into the keel behind me.

And then the wheel would turn no more.

I looked. The hatch was fully open.

I let go of the wheel, one hand at a time, quickly grabbing downward and reattaching at the handrail. And now I had both hands secure there and I dragged myself along the bulkhead and approached the corner going forward.

I stopped.

I clung hard. The pull on me was strong, trying to fling me aft. I knew the danger. The light was all around. I sensed the hatch gaping behind me. The maw of a bright-faced beast. If I let go I would tumble directly out of the Zepp.

I turned my head. I looked.

We were running over rooftops and now over a paved road, and now a dense stand of trees was passing and passing. Had we circled back over Spich? A public relations move upon takeoff?

I looked away.

We were up a good three hundred, four hundred feet. I remembered newsreel clips of parachutes being tested off the London Bridge and the Eiffel Tower, so I figured I needed about six hundred feet minimum to jump.

I inched along. And I turned the corner into the walkway.

I climbed, the spill of the light of the hatch fading behind me. I switched on the flashlight, and up ahead I saw the silver flank of the nearest fuel tank. I approached and flashed the beam into the deepest shadows beyond.

The parachute was there. I would carry it forward with me. The ticking would really begin after the fire was lit. I'd need to have this thing attached to me when I struck the match.

I needed an extra hand. I extinguished the flashlight.

I bent to the parachute, drew it out. I wrapped my right arm around it and held the rail with my other hand. The next milepost was based on sound anyway.

I climbed onward.

The hammering approached, the piston roar of the Maybach. I moved into the very center of it.

The walkway was elevated a foot or so from the aluminum skin of the keel, and the fuel tanks were welded to the keel and set about the same distance off the walkway edge. I lifted the parachute over the railing and wedged it between two tanks for now, and I moved forward one fuel tank.

I turned and faced aft and sat down on the walkway, bracing myself with a foot against the near edge of the next tank.

The engines were hammering through me not just as sound but as a bone-deep vibration, from where I sat, from where the bottom of my foot pressed against the side of the fuel tank.

But I was thinking just fine. I was thinking clearly.

If the army played a few minutes to the locals before heading out to do its business—and the German imperial propaganda machine was already as well oiled and powerful as the Maybach engine I was sitting over—then perhaps we'd level off soon and give the people a good look at the new Zepp in flight and feed their war fervor. This was the newest model, after all. Lately delivered.

I had to make a tough choice. Sit and see if my guess about our location and heading was right and risk a more remote blast if I was wrong or work in this tilt-floored Coney Island Pavilion ride and risk fumbling the tin box and letting it tumble down the walkway.

I drew the box from my case.

I opened the lid but kept the box in my lap for now, my flexed legs holding it more or less level.

I found my matches and pulled them from my pocket. I laid them on the cotton wool.

Where would I set the box so that it wouldn't slide while the cotton burned?

And what about the parachute? Trying to put the harness on and carry the chute rucksack down this incline and hook it properly for a launch would be a terrible challenge at this angle.

I had to roll the dice.

I had to wait.

And I did.

I sat for a few moments and a few moments more and I thought that the angle was softening a little, but then perhaps not.

And then yes.

And we began to turn again.

Another portside turn.

If we'd passed over Spich, as I'd thought, and then over the Alten Forst, we'd now be turning north again, finding our bearing toward England, and in lovely, level flight we'd pass once more over the good citizens of Spich, who'd been alerted by our first passage and now were crowded into the streets to wave and cheer and throw their hats in the air. *Gott strafe England.*

I had no intention of blowing up the LZ 78 and its payload directly over Spich.

But it was a small town.

We'd cross it quickly.

And the upward angle was declining.

I felt I was right.

I waited.

We were leveling.

I waited.

And now we were level.

I rose up. I placed the tin box on the walkway and I stepped aft to the parachute and unwedged and withdrew it from its place against the fuel tank.

I turned back and flashed my beam to the box sitting open there on the walkway, matches on top of cotton wool. I approached it, the parachute cradled in my right arm.

And the lights came on.

# 60

It came from above and from below. The light was muted—the bulbs and their fixtures double-contained in glass—but the hull was illuminated clear enough. Plenty clear enough for me to look far ahead along the walkway and see a figure coming this way.

I glanced back aft to see if I'd soon be surrounded.

No one in that direction.

Back to this figure, advancing rapidly now.

Lieutenant Schmidt. My canny rube.

I dropped the parachute to my side.

He was smiling. He was preparing to salute.

And then he wasn't. He was looking at the parachute as he approached and he was recognizing it and then he was looking at the box in front of me.

He was maybe thirty feet away now.

He slowed.

It would have been impossible for him to figure out anything close to my plan. But he knew something odd was going on.

He was ten feet from me and he stopped.

I lifted up to full height to stand before him as a far superior officer.

He wavered.

I could have found these things here myself. However odd they were, if their presence in the middle of the walkway was sinister, then surely his first impulse would be that it had nothing to do with me. I was a very high ranking officer in the *Deutsches Heer*. I had found these suspicious things myself.

The Maybach pounded loudly on.

There was no need to speak to him anyway. I was righteous in my rank, in my place here on the LZ 78.

I motioned him closer.

I pointed at these things. The parachute. The box. The matches.

I cried above the engine roar, "See what I've found, Lieutenant. What do you make of it?"

He looked more closely at the box.

He began to bend toward it.

"Close enough!" I commanded.

He stopped himself. Stood upright.

My rank was prevailing.

He saluted. He waited.

I had no time for this.

The engines roared around us both.

There was nothing more to say anyway.

He could not be allowed to walk off now. He would, of course, speak of this to the executive officer or the commander. Even if he was not suspicious of Colonel Wolfinger, even if they were not either, even if, instead, they thought I'd shrewdly uncovered a plot, perhaps a further plot of the Englishman, they'd still send somebody up here to me.

I could not let that happen.

Lieutenant Schmidt would be dead in a few minutes anyway.

I drew my Luger.

I pointed it at him.

His face went blank. Of course he hadn't suspected me. And he could not even begin to imagine what was happening now or why.

We looked at each other.

When he and his fellow crew members imagined their death in the night sky, what had been his choice? To burn or to jump?

His face was a rube's face now. Not canny at all. Uncomprehending. No. Not a rube. Just an overgrown kid from some backwater Black Forest town who loved his telegraph and his airship.

I motioned him to move back a few steps.

The Luger was pointed at his chest.

He was starting to get it. He began to raise his hands.

I shook my head *no*.

He took a couple of steps back and I stopped him with a flip of a palm.

A quick ending for this boy now was surely better than an extended burning ten minutes from now. Or a leaping. That terrible, time-stretching fall to the earth.

I stepped over the box and drew near him.

His face showed no fear. It showed something far worse. Betrayal. A previously unimaginable betrayal.

Betrayed by a colonel in the German army.

Too bad he wouldn't be able to put this worthwhile lesson to good use.

I wanted nothing more to do with his face. I motioned for him to turn around.

He obeyed.

He stood straight and still before me. His ears were splayed. I hadn't noticed that before.

I lifted my pistol and pointed it at the back of his head.

The engines hammered on.

This wasn't necessary.

It would be sufficient for him to sleep.

"I'm sorry about this," I said. I said it aloud. But even I could not hear the words in the din of the Zeppelin's engines.

I drew my right hand wide and focused on the center of his parietal bone and I swung hard and caught him there with the flat bulk near the Luger's breech block and Lieutenant Schmidt fell sideways into the handrail and then collapsed onto the walkway, and he did not so much as twitch a finger.

*Sleep on, young man. At least you've been spared a nasty choice.*

Mine already having been made.

I holstered my Luger.

I turned and crouched before the tin box.

We'd be clear of Spich by now.

I took up the matches and laid them aside. I expected the cotton would burn slow and low. But I wanted the flame at that level for only a minute or two. I lifted the top layer and exposed the dynamite and the clock. I took the clock out and tossed it aside, leaving a hollow there. I spread the fibers, loosened them all around in the inner space. When the flame in the slower-burning, packed fibers reached this pocket of oxygen, the fire would flare up.

I laid the top layer back in place.

I rose and moved to the parachute and brought it back and knelt again before the tin box, on its aft side. I unfurled the external harness and placed it around my shoulders and cinched it at my waist. I laid the rucksack next to me.

I took up the matches.

The pound of the Maybach abruptly reshaped itself inside me. It became the sound of my heart. It became the coursing of my blood. It was music now. It was like the piano player whaling away in front of a motion picture screen where some terrible calamity was on its way.

I could smell fuel oil. I could smell hydrogen.

Why hadn't I noticed them this strongly before?

Maybe I'd die for London after all.

Maybe all it took was the strike of this match.

I held it low, as near to the cotton as I could.

And I struck it.

It flared up and I thought it would keep flaring until all the air around me was afire.

But it didn't.

I was still here.

The flame receded a little.

I lowered it to the cotton wool.

I touched the flame there.

And I flinched back and away.

The cotton flashed up instantly.

Too fast. No explosion but it was burning way too fast.

Then this flame receded as well. The fumes immediately around it were consumed.

The cotton was burning.

Very nicely.

Get the hell out.

I stood up. I lifted the rucksack. I turned. I strode off. Fast. But controlled. My knees were a little weak, a little reluctant to hold me up. But I moved. And I moved. And the light was before me.

And I stopped.

The goddamn gas bag.

I turned. I strode back to the box.

A faint wisp of a smell, like burning leaves.

The flame was spreading.

I looked up to the gas cells.

I drew my Luger and I looked forward. I felt a slight movement of air, from the hatch at the gondola ladder. I judged the flow of air and I looked up again. I made a guess at an angle to compensate and I chose a spot in the whale-gray flank of the gas cell above me. I lifted the Luger.

I readied myself once more to go up in flames with all these boys and their airship, and I fired once and again and again and the explosion waited inside there and I fired again and twice more and it was enough, a tight cluster of six shots into the gas cell, and I holstered the Luger and I turned and I ran, ran as fast as I could and still keep my footing on the planking beneath me and the deep hole of light was before me and growing larger and I ran and I reached the turn in the walkway and I took it and I went around to the long side of the hatch and I stepped over the railing and I looked down—though I dared not wait no matter how high I was—and an empty field was passing there, a good six hundred feet below, and I grabbed the loop at the top of the rucksack and I leaned and I hooked it and I leapt.

I fell and I fell and I fell with the air pounding at my eyes, I fell though a part of me was breathlessly inert, was not moving at all, was waiting for the saving clutch of the tether, waiting. And it came, a wrench at my shoulders and at my waist and a thumping compression of my chest. And the falling abruptly turned to floating.

I floated and I floated and I breathed and I looked down to the tops of my shoes and an empty field beyond, and I was hearing the piston drone of Zeppelin engines.

I lifted my face and lifted my hands to grasp the risers and I turned my head around and looked up.

All I could see was the shade-darkened inner canopy of white silk, my parachute billowing above me, and I could see the high, cloud-smeared sky beyond.

And almost at once the LZ 78 emerged from its silken eclipse. It was dark and vast and gliding away from me. Serene, I thought. Secure and serene and murderous, I thought. I've failed, I thought.

The sound of its engines Dopplered lower and began to fade as the Zeppelin sailed on, though it was still quite large against the late afternoon sky, the forward tapering of its colossal hull, the splay of its fins making it look like an aerial bomb of the gods, flung personally from Valhalla by Odin. I had, of course, been destined to fail.

And in the flank of the Zepp, at the very bottom, the sunlight flashed briefly.

No. I craned my head. Not the sun. It was a lollop of flame and now it was a rapid blooming, a golden rush from that spot and forward along the skin of the Zepp and then came a billow of flame breaking through the hull and swelling into the air and the front third of the Zeppelin reared up like a frightened horse, the ship cracking apart, and the flames soared gelatinous now, great thunder clouds of cumulus fire. And it was all strangely silent in this first surge of things, in the igniting of the hydrogen and the inward flash of the gas cells and even in the vast uplift of flame torching the sky, there was only silence. And I remembered I was falling.

I looked down and the ground was rushing at me and I thought to keep my legs loose, ready to flex and fall away, diverting the direct blow, like jumping from a porch, like a kid who's used to jumping, and my legs jolted and instantly I diverted the fall to my left, hitting at calf and thigh and hip and side and I was down and I was all right, I could tell that my legs were okay, my body was okay, and silk was falling softly against me, clinging to me.

And now from on high came a clap of Odin's thunder pounding into my head and rattling my bones and then a concatenation of thunderstrokes, smaller sounds but sharper, and then another larger boom that rolled over me, and I pulled the silk covers around me, a kid still, awakened in the night in a terrible storm, hiding in the covers, and I waited, and the sound rolled on and away, and then there was silence.

I sat up and pulled at the canopy, dragged at it, wrenched at its insistent hold, and finally it came free and I looked up.

The sky was filled with the black billowing of smoke and the blood-orange flare of falling fragments and the back quarter of the Zepp was buoyed still, briefly, though it was starting to burn, and then it plunged and disappeared behind a distant line of trees with an upswell of smoke.

I had seen enough.

I stood up.

I turned my back on all that.

The air smelled faintly of malt.

Nearby was a stack of barley straw bales.

Stockman's bomb was dead.

But that was all I knew for sure.

# 61

By reckoning from the verging sun, whose disk I glimpsed briefly through a scrim of clouds, I struck out to the southeast. At one point early on, I skirted a copse of pine but I diverted into the trees. I found a downed and rotted trunk and stuffed the parachute into a hollow beneath it.

It felt to be a long while because of the uncertainty of my path and the fading light, but in fact I made pretty good time to a stone wall at the eastern edge of a pasturage, beyond which I found a graveled road.

I followed it south, though it was angling me back to the southwest, and I ended up walking into the little town of Liebour, where a crowd had gathered around its central fountain in the town square.

They'd assembled half a dozen wagons and were calling out for volunteers to board them.

I knew what this was about.

The nearby calamity.

They were heading to the place of the crash.

I figured the active gas was dissipating, but they would find clear evidence of the phosgene.

I stayed back from the crowd, striding with purpose around the outer edge of the square. Those who noticed me started and stared or shrunk back or saluted.

I ignored them and pushed on, and I reached the road sign leading away from Liebour. I was very glad to recognize two choices. One to

385

Uckendorf, from which I could find the road east toward Spich that passed half a mile from the air base. The other choice, which angled farther east, led to Stockem. I'd studied Jeremy's portfolio of maps well enough in our long trip to remember this town lying on the same Uckendorf-Spich road but closer to Spich. A shortcut.

I struck off in that direction, walking fast, and thinking hard, now that I knew where I was going. I tried to figure out why Jeremy had arranged for Stockman's bomb to succeed. Which raised the question of why he did so with such an elaborate first two acts in his little play, their elaborateness difficult to explain.

I didn't have an answer for that. Not right away.

I knew only that something was rotten.

And it occurred to me: maybe the explanation was not quite so difficult if our Erich Müller—stage name Jeremy Miller—was working for the German secret service. Not so difficult if they approved the attack but wanted Stockman out of the picture. Albert had control of his bombshell design, and maybe part of his selling price was for him to be directly involved in the mission. All this drama could have been intended to deflect Stockman and still use his device to attack London. They could blame the American secret service, in cahoots with the Brits. And with Jeremy appearing to help in such an elaborate way—secretly setting up the failure of the British-American plan at the last minute, with the simple failure of the time bomb to be blamed—he would effectively preserve his own central secret, that this dynamic English secret service agent was, in fact, an agent for the German secret service. The rococo acts one and two were the solution.

Was I thinking clearly?

It all seemed very complex.

But what seemed simple was the logical end of Act Three of this play. The Germans wanted Stockman alive. Of course. He was a member of Parliament, after all. Inside eyes and ears. If they'd wanted him dead, this would have been a much simpler play. Jeremy had never intended to let me kill Stockman. He was going to have to prevent

386

that now. And through Jeremy, the Germans knew that my mother was also an American spy. They knew it from the outset. So in the climax of Act Three—for a German audience very satisfying in its Aristotelian inevitability—we would have a poisoned London and two dead American agents.

I was afraid one of them was dead already.

# 62

I hit the macadam road from Spich to Uckendorf with the light beginning to dim. I turned east and pressed on and soon the land to the south of the road was denuded of crop and tree and animal. The air base's thousand acres. A wire fence took up, and then, ahead at last, was the stand of birch. I turned in at the road leading to the hangar and entered the trees.

With the light fading and the Torpedo's camouflage working, I was stopped cold at my first glance ahead. I thought the car was gone. But I stepped and stepped again, looking more closely, and there it was and I rushed to it.

I opened the driver's side door.

Upon the seat lay a Luger.

I pulled back.

Before I could even start to think rationally about this, Jeremy's voice said, "It's mine."

I spun around.

He was standing only a few paces away.

His hands were raised. As if I were holding a pistol on him.

I wasn't. I put my hand to my own Luger, but he was not moving and he even lifted his hands higher. I did not draw.

"I have no other weapon," he said.

I looked at him closely. He was still buttoned up tight as a German officer.

He nodded down to his tunic. "They don't make provisions for concealed weapons, do they."

I said nothing.

"You did it," he said.

"You sound surprised," I said.

"As you know."

"As I know," I said. I drew my own Luger now. Calmly, slowly. I pointed it at the center of his chest.

"I suppose I *shouldn't* be surprised," he said. "They all think highly of you in London and Washington, and I could see why all along."

"They think highly of you too," I said. "In London and Berlin."

"No," Jeremy said, instantly and ardently. "Not Berlin. Not the way you mean it."

In the silence now I pondered his tone. I understood performance. It was the gift of my upbringing. He sounded real.

"Our little bomb," I said.

"Our little bomb," he said. "We came to Spich. We took our rooms at the inn. We slept. We ate breakfast and I assembled the bomb. Nothing had changed. It was to go as we both had expected."

"Your telegram," I said.

"My telegram."

He paused.

Okay. True enough so far. But. I said, "It wasn't the Brits who ordered you to allow the poison gas attack on London."

Jeremy hesitated. He looked away. Not to prepare for a lie. Not an aversion of the eyes. He flipped his face a little to the side and his mind worked at something and he squared his gaze around to me again. As if I'd slapped him across the face and even though he was a man trained to counterpunch, he accepted it as just.

His hands were still up and he seemed utterly oblivious to the fact. They were natural there.

"Not the Brits," he said.

"You pulled a Stockman," I said. "You were the one dropping the gas bomb." I heard my vehemence. I'd once liked this guy.

He gave a single sharp nod, casting his eyes down.

And then he looked at me straight.

"I work for the English," he said, "but only when their goals are the same as the goals of my own country. I am German. But the Kaiser is not my country. Hindenburg and Moltke and Falkenhayn are not my country. None of the Kaisers. None of the generals. *My* Germany wishes to be like your country. A country governed by the people and protecting the people—all the people—from their government and from themselves. A republic."

I believed he was speaking the truth about himself.

I said, "And what of the people of London tonight?"

"It was not my decision to make," Jeremy said. "We have our own leaders. They know we will never remake Germany as long as the Kaiser rules and these generals are heroes. The march into Belgium. The poison gas at Ypres. The sinking of the *Lusitania*. These acts of cruelty and the government's rabid defense of them are already undermining its position. Not just in the world but here among the true Germans. The attack on London could have been decisive."

"But it would have been your attack as well," I said.

We looked at each other in silence for a long moment.

Jeremy said, "I'm glad you are good at what you do."

I could only shake my head at this.

He laid the poisoning of London upon his leaders and then did what they asked. He laid the salvation of London upon me and was passively glad it went that way. I doubted this was a viable frame of mind for an aspiring republic.

He misinterpreted my reaction. He said, "I'm here, am I not? I didn't have to come. I came with hope, even though it was scant. Hope you were alive. The explosion rattled the windows at the hotel. I was afraid you'd died in the deed. You are capable of that sacrifice. I knew that. I'm very glad you were good enough also to survive."

I still found no words.

He said, "I gave you my pistol freely. My hands are raised. For my betrayal of you, I am happy to offer this proof of my regret and of my regard for you."

He turned around.

He offered me his back.

He did not look over his shoulder.

He did not see that I was indeed still holding my Luger steadily upon him.

He said, "If it is your decision now to kill me, I am ready to accept that."

I lifted the Luger and pointed it at the back of his head.

He waited.

I waited. Not to make a decision. That was made. I waited to adequately clear my head of how dangerous this well-intentioned and obedient man was.

"Turn around," I said.

Jeremy did so, slowly.

The Luger was pointed now at the center of his forehead.

He waited.

"Put your hands down, Jeremy," I said.

He did.

I lowered my pistol.

He let out a held breath.

I slipped the Luger into my holster.

"May I shake your hand?" he said.

I thought about that. Briefly.

"Yes," I said.

And we grasped hands.

# 63

When our hands parted again, I said, "What have you done with Stockman and Madam Cobb?"

"You underestimate her," he said.

This didn't sound good.

"We had a useful chat," he said.

"When?"

"Not to worry," Jeremy said. "Stockman was out cold and tied up."

I was worried.

Jeremy had left Stockman with his lover. A woman so blind with love she still couldn't accept or reasonably assess what he was capable of doing. But this man before me was capable of at least one of Albert's most heinous intentions. And he'd been my friend. He was quickly becoming my friend again. Mother's feeling for Albert, her desperate *need* for her feeling for him: couldn't I understand that?

"We should go to them," I said.

"I'll crank," he said.

And he did. When he slid into the passenger seat, I handed him his Luger.

I drove out of the trees and turned east onto the Uckendorf road.

Jeremy said, "From what you must have thought of me, you need now to understand. I was never allied to Stockman. I am ready for us to kill him. I will do it myself if you wish. He will compromise us both."

I looked at him. It was only a glance, but just before I took my eyes from him, he glanced too.

He knew what I was thinking.

"I will not return to England," he said. "I'm asking you to keep no secrets about me."

"Good."

He said, "I will be a more serious enemy to Berlin by working here for the republic."

I advanced the throttle in this open, empty stretch of good road.

I said, "So did you leave her guarding him?"

"Not to his eye, if he wakes," he said. "She's got the right stuff, but I don't think she realizes we intend to kill him and I didn't say otherwise. She thought it prudent that she continue to seem his ally. We feigned her bonds. She can slough them off at will. But she wants him to think they were in it together."

This was all right.

Perhaps she was still taking her role as spy seriously.

I had something to do now. The thing she did not yet see coming.

It would be for the sake of Jeremy and his work. A democratic Germany could perhaps prevent another great war. It would be for the sake of my work, for the work of the American republic.

And it would be for me.

For her.

I sped into Spich.

Then I had to slow down drastically.

The town square was dense with people. As in Liebour, Spich had turned out to share this disaster and do what it could. I eased the car in among them, and when people felt others yielding, they turned and yielded too, all of them doing so willingly, readily, respectfully, many of them greeting us, officers in their army.

We crept through them and Jeremy and I found ourselves acknowledging these people's nods and waves and salutes. As if we were one with them in their loss. It went with the uniform.

And then we were free and soon we pulled into the parking field next to the Hotel Alten-Forst.

I switched off the engine.

I had been thinking this out as we drove.

I needed to do this alone. Twice today I'd put a gun to a man's head and twice I'd spared the life before me. Even if only temporarily. This would not happen a third time. Stockman would die directly by my hand. And my mother would instantly be cast in a great and complex role. I would tie her up properly. She would go on to play the devastated lover, having witnessed the death of the man she'd loved most in all her life.

"I have to do this alone," I said.

He looked at me. He did not understand.

"It's not a matter of trust," I said. "It is a thing between the actress and me."

"I'll be here if you need me," he said.

"Be ready to drive us to Berlin," I said.

I needed to visit the American embassy. It was nearly time, as Trask put it, to leave the country abruptly.

# 64

I shed the flight jacket into the back seat, swapped the clip in my Luger for the full clip from Jeremy's, restrapped my holster over Colonel Wolfinger's tunic, and with a final nod between us, I left Jeremy in the Torpedo.

I strode across the hotel courtyard and through the lobby, taking note of who might be here when I followed a gunshot out of the hotel. The lobby was singularly empty. An old man sleeping in a corner chair. One liveried man clerking behind the desk. Even the visitors to Spich were in the street on this night, being Germans together, awaiting word, sharing their righteous rage.

It was a good night for an assassination. The shot would be two floors up and at the back of a nearly empty hotel in a distracted town.

The elevator operator was also gone and I went up the staircase. I emerged on the second floor and entered the long corridor to Room 200. I slowed a little. I approached with measured, muffled footfalls on the Turkish rug.

Mother wanted to continue to play her role. So be it. I would not knock. If he was conscious, I would not invite her to reveal the phoniness of her bonds. I would use my tools to enter the room.

And Room 200 was drawing near.

I measured my breathing as well. Careful now. Professional now. I stood before the door.

I drew out my tools. Pick and torque. The lock yielded. I did not turn the knob at once. I put my tools into their loops in their leather wrap and I put the wrap into my inner pocket. I used the movements to calm myself.

This was all feeling too personal.

That could cloud my judgment.

In fact, it already had.

I put my hand to the knob and turned it and opened the door wide.

Mother was sitting directly before me, in the chair where she'd sat last night among the roses.

The flowers whose petals had not been plucked and strewn on their bed this afternoon sat meagerly in their vases.

She wore a kimono negligee. The peach-colored chemise, which was her costume for the afternoon cigarette card pose, showed at her chest.

I took a step into the room.

She was not bound. Even in a phony way.

She looked at me oddly. The expression must have been genuine, because I couldn't for the life of me read it.

I took another step.

This was way too personal. Only now did it fully strike me that she shouldn't be sitting here.

I moved my hand to my Luger even as the door slammed behind me.

But before I could draw, a pistol barrel touched me at the back of my head.

Stockman said, "Pull it out slowly and hold it to the side."

I had no choice.

I drew the Luger from its holster, grasping it as if I would use it, just in case, since he'd given no instruction about that.

I extended my arm to the right, straight out.

I had no possible move other than this.

He nudged my head with the muzzle of his pistol.

"Toss it away to the right," he said.

I flicked my wrist as little as I could and still seem to comply. My Luger fell heavily to the floor.

The steel vanished from the back of my head.

"Don't move," he said.

I didn't.

I heard the bolt slide into place at the door.

"Turn around," he said.

I did.

He looked clear-eyed but beat-up. A welt as fat as a three-hour cigar emerged from his hairline and fell across his right temple. His pistol hand was steady. He was holding a Webley break-top revolver. He and his German blood carried a very British weapon. I chose not to comment on this. That I even *thought* to comment was inappropriate under the circumstances. But he had the drop on me, and though I was toying with ironies on the jittery surface of my mind, I was thrashing around for serious options in the core of me as well. The ironies kept me a little detached. Calmed me. One of the ironies: in spite of the beating and the hog-tying, he still looked very much like my mother's chisel-faced leading man.

"Who are you really?" he said.

There were certainly some ironies surrounding that question.

"The man who blew up your poison gas bomb over German soil," I said. "Along with the LZ 78 and the rest of its payload."

The pistol wavered a little.

I said, "Weren't you conscious for the blast? It was a good three or four miles away but it rattled your windows."

I realized I was provoking him. But I had no choice.

I said, "It was unfortunate to poison some Westphalian cows and lose a Zeppelin, but I had to stop you from disgracing our Fatherland and embarrassing our Kaiser. The measure was extreme, but he had to learn about you and Bauer waging your own little war. You are traitors to the Kaiser and to the Fatherland."

Somewhat to my surprise, the pistol grew steady again.

Stockman said, "That's all irrelevant now. I don't give a bloody damn about the bomb or about the Kaiser. Not anymore. I know what's important here."

I had no idea where his mind had just leaped.

He said, "I know what's important after all these years. And you are the man who would blow it up."

I waited for more.

"Do you want to confess?" he said.

I said, "I have no idea what you're talking about."

"You think I haven't suspected from the start?" He glanced quickly over my shoulder. "I'm sorry, my darling," he said. From the angle and height of his glance, Mother had apparently risen from her chair and had moved off a little to her right.

"I'm sorry I haven't discussed this with you, my darling," he said. "But that's because I don't blame you. Not at all. It's this man. It's *his* fault. He would destroy us."

And now his eyes fixed on mine.

He said, "You are Isabel's lover. It makes sense of all the little things. You are her lover even still."

He seemed to want to say more, but words failed him. He pushed his pistol forward a little. It was holding steadily upon the center of my chest.

A heart shot.

Into a heart I heard thumping heavily in my ears.

The Webley was a double-action. I hadn't heard the cocking yet. But I knew it was coming.

Any second.

And my mother said, from behind me, "My darling Albert."

Stockman shifted his eyes.

The pistol stayed where it was.

His eyes went a little wide.

His brow furrowed.

And he began to move his shooting hand, the pistol shifting slightly to his left, in Mother's direction, moving even as his eyes had moved, even as they widened and his hand was moving faster now, the pistol was moving and I started to move as well, to my left, I thought to turn away from the line of fire and lunge and grab his arm and lift it, I visualized this even as I began to move and I was twisting away and his pistol hand was moving and we were both of us nowhere near to the place where we wanted to be and the room rang loud and the center of Albert's forehead blossomed instantly as red and as full-petaled as a rose and he flew back and his pistol jerked upward and he flew and he fell and the room rang and then it stopped. Then all was quiet.

I straightened.

Stockman lay dead on his back.

I turned.

My mother had my Mauser pocket automatic in her right hand, which was cradled in her left, the pistol still aimed, still wisping.

She looked at me.

Nothing showed in her face. Nothing.

She lowered the pistol. She squared around. She stepped to me and she reached out and took my right hand and lifted it between us. She laid the Mauser in my palm, and she looked me in the eyes.

"There," she said. "I hope you're happy."

# 65

On the way out of the Hotel Alten-Forst I put two bullets from my Mauser automatic pocket pistol into the mahogany front desk, scaring the hell out of the clerk, whose account would help convince any inquiring minds that a mysteriously untraceable German military officer was responsible for the killing in Room 200. The famous actress Isabel Cobb would be found tied up tightly on the bed, the love of her life dead in the next room. I received no reports, but I had no doubt that everyone who witnessed her performance on that terrible night was deeply moved.

In the following weeks Isabel Cobb went on to a great triumph performing as Hamlet in two languages in Berlin, though I had to learn this from the American newspapers. The London newspapers, in the summer of 1915, were disinclined to report on the night life of Berlin.

They did report, however, on the mysterious disappearance of Sir Albert Stockman, a distinguished member of Parliament, who was thought lost in the Strait of Dover on a night when U-boats were known to be in the area. He was rumored to have armed his personal yacht with a deck gun and used the vessel to lure the submarines to the surface and engage them in battle. The country mourned the presumed death of a true English hero.

A month later, a Zeppelin dropped a dozen bombs in the theater district. The second of them fell on Wellington Street in front of the

Lyceum Theatre, where a number of theatergoers were buying oranges and pastries and sweets from street vendors during intermission. Seventeen people were killed, twenty-one were badly injured. That bomb contained no poison gas. None of the bombs did, though several of them were perfectly placed for the purpose.

The first bomb had fallen before the Gaiety Theatre in The Strand, where an American musical comedy was playing by the name of *Tonight's the Night*.

Needless to say, as I tied my mother up, there were a few questions I thought to ask. Like what was in her head when she untied Albert. Was it blind love? Did she think the two of them could just run away from all this? Did she shoot him only when it was clear he was about to kill her son? Or did she let him go expressly to arrange our little climax? She would certainly see it as a far better scene for Isabel Cobb to play. But we spoke not a word. Even up to the moment of my closing the door of Room 200 behind me. Not a word. Sometimes, between a mother and a son, there were things you just didn't want to know.

A
man
in the
making

Books by Richard C. Robertiello, MD

*Voyage from Lesbos*
*A Handbook of Emotional Illness and Treatment*
*Sexual Fulfillment and Self-Affirmation*
*Hold Them Very Close, Then Let Them Go*
*The Analyst's Role*, with Bertram Pollens, PhD,
 and David B. Friedman, MD
*Big You—Little You*, with Grace E. Kirsten, MA
*Your Own True Love*
*A Man in the Making*

# A man in the making

## Grandfathers, Fathers, Sons

Richard C.
Robertiello
M.D.

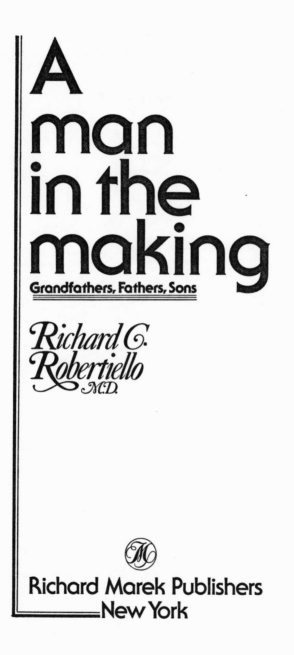

Richard Marek Publishers
New York

**Library of Congress Cataloging in Publication Data**

Robertiello, Richard C, date.
  A man in the making.

  1. Fathers and sons. 2. Men—Psychology.
I. Title.
HQ756.R6      301.42'7      79-15709
ISBN 0-399-90056-X

Printed in the United States of America

I want to thank Don Congdon, my agent; Joyce Engelson, my editor; Fred Sawyer, my copyeditor; Nancy Friday; and three of my colleagues, Dr. Terril Gagnier, Mr. Lawrence Hauser and Dr. Julius Weissman, for their helpful suggestions. My thanks to Frances Hollands, who spent many hours typing the manuscript.

To my son, Bobby, in the hope that this book will help him to understand and forgive, and that it will bring us closer

# Contents

A
man
in the
making

# Prologue

My twenty-seven-year-old son, Bobby, and I are on the Phil Donahue TV Show, a one-hour audience-participation show about father-son relationships. The producer had heard that I was writing this book and also that I was supposed to be an expert on father-son relationships. He thought it would be a good idea for my own son to appear with me, so they flew us both out to Chicago. Bobby and I had talked a lot about our relationship. It had certainly had its ups and downs, and at this point it was up. Bobby was open and self-revealing to me and I think I was to him.

Before the show, Phil and his assistant put us in a room together. Bobby was very nervous, but I was calm and cool, having gone through this many times before. Phil seemed more nervous than Bobby. He was very "up," and spoke rapidly and excitedly. He told us he did not want us to dominate the show, that it was basically for audience-participation. After the usual commercials, Phil went on, introduced Bobby and me, and said he had gotten together a group of fathers and sons to be part of the participating audience. He even had a four-generational group—great-grandfather, grandfather, father, and son. Phil stepped over to a father and son in the audience. Both looked as though they might be from a small Midwestern town.

"Are you two father and son?" Phil began.

"Yes," the father volunteered.

"Tell me how you get along."

"Oh, fine," said the son.

"Yep, fine," echoed the father.

"Have you ever had any problems in your relationship?"

"Nope," said the father.

"No, none at all," affirmed the son.

"Nothing ever came up between you that you had to discuss? You never had any disagreements?"

"Nope, everything has always been perfect between us," the father said.

Phill was nonplussed. That wasn't the way he had expected the show to begin. "Well, that's just wonderful! Good luck to both of you and thanks for being with us."

My silent translation of Phil's words was: "Why, you two dumb hayseeds are both so out of touch that you wouldn't know a problem existed if one of you came after the other with an ax!" However, one does not say such things when one is MCing a TV show.

Phil composed himself and went on to the next father and son.

"And how about you two? How do you get along?"

The twenty-year-old son replied, "Well . . . I guess we get along OK, but I have never felt close to Dad. When he isn't working, he's playing golf with his friends. We really never talk to each other except to say things like 'Pass the salt.'"

"That's true," said the father. "I've always felt a tremendous gap between us. I certainly haven't liked it, and I know John hasn't, but there doesn't seem to be anything either of us can do or will do to narrow the gap."

Phil was a little more pleased—here was a bit of controversy and interest for his viewers. "What do you think caused this distance?" he asked.

14

"I really don't know. When I was a kid, Dad was just somebody who gave me orders, told me what to do. I never talked to him about any of my feelings or my problems."

"That's so," his father said. "I hate to admit it, but that was the way it was. And now, even though we like each other, there still isn't very much talk between us. Oh, once in a while we talk about the Chicago Bears, but there isn't even much of that."

Phil then turned to the four-generational group. The grandfather said, "Dad was kind of strict. He was hard to talk to."

His father, the great-grandfather, a very kindly looking man in his seventies, added, "I know it's so. I wish it hadn't been. My son and I have never really talked much to each other."

"Yes, I agree," the grandfather said. "I've always admired Dad, but we haven't shared very much. And I've followed the same pattern with my own son." He turned toward his son, the father. "Dad, the same things you said about your father I could say about you. I know neither of us wanted it to be that way. And I see now I'm doing the same thing with my son. I take him to ball games and play catch with him, but I know I'd like to be closer to him than I am."

The fourth generation, a twelve-year-old boy, was uncomfortable and embarrassed by the interview. When Phil turned to him and asked him how he felt, the boy mumbled, "I guess that's right. . . ." But he couldn't elaborate on his statement.

Next, Phil turned to me and Bobby and asked about us. "We've really had a great many ups and downs," I told him. "There've been periods in our lives in which we talked for hours about our feelings, but then there've been entire years in which there seemed to be an emotional desert neither of us chose to or even wanted to bridge. Sometimes we've been very close and very admiring of each other, but other times we didn't even like each other."

"It's true," Bobby said. "I've always felt cheated—like there was something I should be getting from you that I was never getting, or never getting enough of."

"I know what you mean," I said. "That was exactly the way I felt about *my* father."

15

Bobby and I continued to chat along the same lines. We discussed his career choice, becoming an opera singer like his sister, my stepdaughter, rather than a psychoanalyst like me.

"Of course I was disappointed," I admitted. "I wanted him to follow me—to be a chip off the old block. But I backed his making an independent choice."

The program was drawing to a close. Phil was looking for a dynamite punchline wrapup. He turned to Bobby. "Bobby, suppose you finish this sentence: *If there is one thing I wanted more of from my father than I got, what would it be?*" Bobby reflected for a moment. Then, very simply and straightforwardly, he said just one word: "Affection." Even Phil was struck dumb. The audience—especially the women—murmured. No one said anything for what seemed eternity. I was not surprised, but I was numb. I knew how Bobby felt; I knew how much I had always felt that. All my life I had had a fantasy that one day my father would put his arm around me and call me "Richard." He never touched me and he never called me anything. Now Bob wanted the exact same thing from me and I just couldn't do it. I was paralyzed. I looked away from him and stared off into space.

Aside from occasional handshakes, I never touch Bobby. We can "talk about our relationshit"—no, that isn't a typo—but I can hardly ever show him affection. I can embrace or kiss other men easily, including other men his age. With my "adopted" sons—young men I treat, supervise, or train—I can feel tremendous affection. I can tell them that I love them and show it to them physically (no, not sexually), but I can't do this with Bobby.

As I write this, very early in the morning, I think back about another morning, over thirty years ago, when I was twenty-three. I had a loving wife and a marvelous career as a doctor ahead of me. But I was miserable so I swallowed enough pills to kill a horse. Only a miracle saved me. I feel that same loneliness this morning, even though I am loved, successful, and have everything in the world I have ever dreamed of emotionally, professionally, and materially. I think vaguely about killing myself and ending the pain. But I know now it is

16

only momentary suffering, and that after I have had breakfast and seen my first patient, it will disappear. But my father never put his arm around me—and I still can't put my arm around Bobby. . . .

# 1

# Men with Men

Why am I incapable of demonstrating my love for my son? And who, in fact, is the "I" in this situation and where did it originate? My case, of course, is common enough—many fathers are isolated from their sons in this way. Nonetheless, to accept this without question would be a cop-out; I would be letting myself off the hook too easily. If I experience genuine concern, then I must take the responsibility for my failing and try to understand its origins.

I must look back—back as far as I can—to the relationships of the men in my family to their fathers and to their sons as well as to their relationships to their women. I must return as far as I can remember—to my grandfathers. One of my grandfathers, Michelangelo, was probably the single most important person in my life, much more important than my mother or father. I lived in the same house with Michelangelo for the first fifteen years of my life, even though my parents were alive and in the same house. I slept in the same room with him and his wife from the time I was two until I was twelve. He was much more the parent who reared me than my

19

mother was. Today, of course, men are beginning to be more involved in rearing children. But in the 1920s and 1930s, I had the then rather unique experience of being a male child brought up primarily by a man. Michelangelo did not go out to work. He was always at home with me. He was in almost complete charge of my discipline and upbringing. My grandmother Bettina, his wife, and my mother undoubtedly had more to do with feeding and toilet-training me. But basically, after age two, I was a man brought up by a man. This must have had its effect on my being capable—or incapable—of being a father to my son. But Michelangelo was identifiable not only by his gender; he was in many ways a genuinely remarkable man who did not relate to me the way most grandfathers do to their grandsons. My other grandfather, Domenico, was more like a traditional grandfather in his relationship to me. He did not live with us in Manhattan, but in Brooklyn. I saw him perhaps a little more often than many children see their grandfathers, but even so it was only on weekends, occasional holidays, and summer vacations, and even then he was a busy doctor so the amount of time he spent with me was limited. He would give me an occasional smile and a quarter, but I rarely if ever had a dialogue with him. Michelangelo was with me night and day—every moment when I was at home, all through those fifteen years. I was his one and only project and his main interest in life, and I had more uninterrupted parenting from him than most children receive from their mothers. And yet, in many ways I am more like Domenico than Michelangelo. How can I explain it? What were Domenico and Michelangelo like as fathers? Domenico's only son, Jerry, killed himself when he was nineteen. Michelangelo's second-oldest son, Beniamino, killed himself in his forties. What kind of fathers were they to their sons?

One of Michelangelo's sons was my father, Attilio. What sort of a father was Michelangelo to Attilio? Was he the same way with Attilio that he was with me? Clearly not. He left Attilio in Italy to come to seek his fortune in America when Attilio was two, and was reunited with him in New York when Attilio was eight. He certainly did not treat Attilio as the same kind of human project that he considered me. And what kind of a father was Attilio to me and to my brother, Charlie, ten years my junior? Did I learn to be a father by copying Attilio or Michelangelo as a role model or did I imitate neither of them? By the time my son, Bobby, was born, I had other role models to choose from, among them three male analysts. Did I learn anything about being a father from these men? And what about other male relatives, teachers, peers? What have I taken in from them?

To find out about myself as a father, I have to discover myself as a human being, a man, a son and grandson, a husband, and a lover. What kind of a man am I? I am fifty-six years old and have had twelve analysts. I certainly have an interest in finding out who I am. I *should* have some idea of who I am, how the different parts of me were formed, what I have in me from my biological, genetic roots and from my ethnic background, from my role as a minority person in America, and from my exposure to the important people— women as well as men—in my past.

And yet as I begin this search I really do not believe I know very much about myself or that I know the answers to the questions I raise.

But I have some of the tools, the cognitive awareness, of what makes *other* people tick, namely the profession of helping, for the past thirty years, other people discover their identity. This knowledge and experience should guide me. And my twelve analysts have tried in their own, at times misguided, ways to help me discover my true Self, even though until about ten years ago psychoanalysis had only a slim notion of what a Self was. My analysts could tell me about my Oedipus complex and my need for mothering, but since they did not know what a Self was, they were hardly in a position to help me find out about my own.

In the past decade, some analysts, myself included, have begun to discover something about this Self—a person's subjective sense of his whole being in contrast to his or her drives, needs, and conflicts. This Self comprises the totality of the person's subjective sense of who he or she is and how he

21

or she relates to the world. It is a unifying concept. It does not fragment the individual into parts such as instincts, drives, conscience, intellectual awareness, or ways of dealing with reality. It has to do with one's total being and one's sense of total being, including identity and self-esteem. This is one of the newer and very appropriate ways of experiencing the Self that has emerged with the psychology of the Self in contrast to other psychoanalytic views such as the Oedipus complex or interpersonal relationships. No analyst has helped me specifically to discover my Self, so in many ways I do not know too much about it. There are, even today, many analysts who do not know much about it. I must try to be my own analyst; to fit together the parts *and* the whole that make up my Self. In many ways I am starting out with a very limited sense of this Self. I am beginning a search to try to understand who I am, where I came from, and what I pass on to my son.

How shall I approach this journey? There are several possibilities. One is a Freudian sort of free association that might bear some fruit. Another is a historical view of my specific development. I am not neglecting or ruling out either of these. But the framework I have chosen is one that was suggested by the four-generational group at the Donahue show. It also fits nicely into another new approach to personality that has emerged mainly within the past decade— that of family systems theory. One of the ways family therapists try to encourage their patients to understand their personal patterns of interaction is to ask the individuals in the family to make up what they call genograms. These genograms describe the ways their mothers, fathers, grandparents, and relatives related to one another. Understanding this and seeing it on paper often clarifies family reaction-patterns that have gone on from generation to generation. Thus, a means to understanding what sort of man I am is to comprehend the family roles of my grandfathers, my father, and other male members of the family. And one way of trying to understand how I relate to my son is to try to see how they related to their sons. One might say, the relationships in my particular family may be quite different from those of other families. Nonetheless, in choosing myself as the example, I am using the person about whom I have the most data—gathered from tales of my family, from my own memory of them, from my subjective awareness of them, and from my persistent analytic exploration of my reactions to them over a span of thirty-five years. So the choice of myself, though it may be motivated in part by a need for exhibitionism, narcissism, and compulsive self-exploration, also appears to me to be the most appropriate one. If my history and my family is unique, my method of trying to understand my Self and how I developed from my roots need not be different.

Though I am particularly focusing on my relationships with the men in my family and outside of it, I obviously was influenced very strongly as well by the women. I am a strong believer in the mother-child dyad as being the most crucial influence on any person's development. The focus on the men comes as a matter of structural convenience, not necessarily of dynamic importance. Family systems theory and its focus on roots has served me in this book as a convenient structure within which to explore the newer ideas of the psychology of the Self.

Male identity development is obviously different from female development. The old Freudian view was that in many ways men have it easier than women. The object of a man's love remains the same. It is always his mother. When he is a baby, he needs his mother to love and feed him. As he grows into the Oedipal phase, about age four to seven, he turns to his mother as a "sex object." Then, after a temporary retreat from her with more interest in his male peers and perhaps his father from ages eight to eleven, and a temporary cooling off of his heterosexual passions, puberty occurs at about twelve. Again sexual interest increases, and once again he is drawn with perhaps even more passion toward his mother. According to Freudian theory, when he must unhappily accept the fact that mother is not available to him as a sexual partner, the boy's interest turns to other women. Freud thought that men possess the advantage of having their feelings directed toward the same person during most of their childhood, whereas women must change the object of their choice for intimacy from the mother to the father. This view of male development seems basically valid to me as far as it goes.

However, nowadays we analysts think of development in many more complicated ways. First of all, what *is* a man? Even on the simplest anatomical and endocrinological level there are disputes and difficult questions. There are children born who are hemaphrodites—who have both male and female genitalia. How are they to be brought up—as men or as women? There are children born whose genitals appear to be predominantly male, but whose hormones are female. There are other people, including transsexuals, whose genitals and hormones are precisely the same as any other man's but who experience themselves so much as female (or the reverse with females who experience themselves as male) that they, like Christine Jorgensen, have their male genitals and hair removed, have false vaginas made, and have breasts implanted surgically. There are recent studies that focus on the influence of hormones on the fetus—hormones that may influence the child's sense of maleness or femaleness, physical and psychological characteristics, and perhaps even tendencies to become homosexual rather than heterosexual.

What is a man? How does one define masculinity? Clearly the culture in which we live, and even one's genetic and ethnic background, have a great deal to do with this. What is "masculine" in Samoa, or among Eskimos, or even in Italy, is not the same as it is in Manhattan. And beyond that, what is considered masculine in Manhattan's Little Italy is not quite the same as it is on the chic Upper East Side. At one time people tended to connect masculinity with physical and emotional strength, intellect, adventurousness, sexual aggressiveness, with being dominant, fearless, and in control, and with containing one's feelings. These notions are all going by the boards with the advent of women's liberation. That is, the concepts are changing in a small subculture in the United States. They may not have changed one iota in Little Italy or Harlem or Peoria, Illinois. To rigidly define masculinity makes very little sense in today's world. Sexual preference—whether

24

one was homosexual or heterosexual—was at one time incorrectly used as a measure of masculinity. It certainly is not so today. Some of the men I know that *I* consider to be the most "masculine" are homosexual. We must not confuse gender identity—one's sense of maleness—with sexual preference—the choice of the gender of one's sexual partner. In this book I want to try to explore, obviously without coming to any hard and fast answers, what makes a person feel masculine and from whence this feeling arises.

In choosing myself as my subject, I must reiterate that I am obviously not Everyman. My life has been quite different in many ways from that of most men. But just as in medicine or psychology we can often approach an understanding of the normal through observations of the pathological, I hope that my variations from the norm may help explore and explain factors in others who may be closer to the norm or different in other ways. Certainly, I am quite different from most men in our culture since I was strongly influenced in my development by the constant presence in my home of my grandfather Michelangelo. This unusual upbringing may help us focus by comparison with the norm of a very much more mother-centered rearing as a decisive factor in the formation of male identity. The out-of-the-ordinary combination I present, and will later expand upon, of a very high sense of identity and autonomy with a very low sense of self-esteem, may clarify factors in both these areas. There are enormous differences between me as a man and my father as a man; perhaps these can be explored and in part explained. Then I may be able to tie this knowledge into helping me understand my relationship to my son, Bobby, and perhaps enable me to improve it.

# 2

# Michelangelo

Laviano is a town of about two thousand people situated on the side of a steep mountain that is part of the Apennine range that runs down the middle of Italy. At the highest point of the town stand the ruins of a Norman castle. The castle is fairly intact, although it has been used as the town latrine for about five hundred years. What is a Norman castle doing southeast of Naples? The warlike and barbarian Normans conquered the town and left northern European imprints on its people. My grandfather Michelangelo had fair hair and blue eyes, and a temperament far from that of the warm and emotional southern Italians. Though no one in the family had left Laviano to any extent for centuries, he looked and acted much more like a Norman than like a southern Italian, and so did the rest of his family. Everywhere else in southern Italy my relatives hugged and kissed me the first time they saw me; my grandfather was stern and exacting.

Laviano is all hills. There are no level roads. The town is only a group of stone buildings huddled together in typical medieval fashion, and the roads are mainly large stones laid side by side. Most of the buildings are one-room huts. Occasionally one finds a larger dwelling, with two or three stories, more modern, like the one the Robertiellos own. The town is surrounded by farms on which the peasants work the sparse soil. Everywhere one looks there are mountains and valleys, and forests on the sides of some of the mountains. In July and August the air is clear and cool and the countryside is beautiful. Even the wealthiest townfolk, like my grandfather's family, must struggle for existence. The winters are bitter. Many years the land yields poor crops because the soil is not fertile. Aside from a few landed gentry, most of the people are peasants. Ten years ago their earnings averaged fifty cents a day, but they worked only about two hundred days a year. The peasants are tiny, less than five feet tall, and resemble the rustics in Brueghel paintings. They are bent over from tilling the soil, physically ugly and disfigured—a different breed from the landowners. There is almost total segregation between the two classes—perhaps nearly as much as between blacks and whites in southern American towns at the turn of the century. I had a cousin in Laviano who died about ten years ago. Even though I had been to Laviano three times during my life, I never had any idea that he was married. I had always thought of him as a bachelor. He lived with his sister in the three-story family homestead on the side of a mountain. The house was centuries old but did have running water and a not very adequate plumbing and heating system. When Luigi died, a very well hidden family secret came out. He had had the temerity to marry a peasant. His wife had never been allowed in the house. The secret was kept even from close family like myself. I had never met her or heard about her. All their married life he met his wife clandestinely in her hovel.

The peasants in Laviano live in one-room caves with dirt floors and no running water or toilet facilities (hence the use of the castle as a latrine). They share their caves with pigs, chickens, and donkeys. The only sign of spirituality in Laviano is a rather large church, which always seems to be closed for repairs. On my first visit to Laviano I was so appalled I left after two days, one reason being that the cobblestoned streets were so covered with donkey manure that I was literally sickened by the stench. My second visit occurred about the time of the festival of the Madonna, and the streets were clean, so I could enjoy the stark beauty of the place. Today I consider Laviano to be one of the most lovely, unspoiled places I have ever seen. I feel transported back into the middle ages, and experience a sort of peace and connection to mystical roots that I never have found anywhere else except in the garden of St. Francis, in Assisi, and in the Cloisters, near Manhattan, on days when this museum is not crowded with visitors.

Laviano is austere; the good feeling there is not one of joy or bounty or love. It is one of coolness and containment and tranquility. But in spite of the idyllic atmosphere, I am sure that many peasants do not survive very long. A thirty-year-old woman looks as if she were sixty. The members of my family, who are landowners and town officials, have a certain ruddiness of complexion and look of strength and determination—a will to survive against heavy odds, a no-nonsense approach to life, like my paternal grandfather, Michelangelo. He was tall, aristocratic, and fair-skinned, with a thick, light-colored mustache. He was the second child in his family. I have heard two versions of the family story about his youth. One is that the firstborn was a girl and that the family gave her all their money as a dowry in order for her to marry into a "wealthy" family in town. The other is that the firstborn was a son and that he was given all the family money to go to Naples to college and he promptly squandered it on wine, women, and cards. The latter version does not sound like the Robertiellos; the first seems more credible to me. In any event, Michelangelo was deprived of his chance to get an education, and was bitter and disappointed. In those days, the southern Italians thought the streets of America were literally paved with gold—I have heard this from untold numbers of them. So, around the turn of the century, Michelangelo left his wife and four children in Laviano, took the train to Naples, and then the boat to New York. There he found a room on Carmine Street in the Italian ghetto. Eventually he found work as a tailor at the elegant wage of $5.00 per week and saved enough money to bring his family, including my father (then age eight), to New York in 1900. If I didn't know my grandfather, I would be amazed at how a man could save enough money in such a short time on such a low wage to be able to bring five people across the ocean. He had to be the most passionate miser of all time. When I was five years old, even though my father was a very successful doctor, though we lived on one of the most elegant blocks in New York, and though I went to an elite private school, Michelangelo would rant for hours if he found out my mother had spent a nickel on an ice cream cone for me. Whenever she did that, or took me to a movie for a quarter, I had to vow not to let my grandfather or my father (who in this regard followed in his footsteps) know about it. Instead of handkerchiefs my grandfather gave me old flour sacks to take to my rich WASP private school, in which I sat next to the daughter of the president of the board of Metropolitan Life. Instead of "R," the monogram on my handkerchief was "Pillsbury." I can remember the humiliation I, the "poor Italian Kid," was subjected to for that! And in addition, old Michelangelo would not allow my mother, who was terrified of him, to buy me new clothes, so I went to school wearing short pants with patches while the other kids had knickers. Grandpa was as rigid about wasting time as he was about spending money. When I was four and he caught me listening to the fifteen-minute "Jack Armstrong, the All-American Boy" radio show, he would yell and hit me, telling me I was a loafer and would grow up to be a no-good bum. As part of being a saver, Michelangelo collected stamps, coins, string, and aluminum foil in giant balls. I followed his lead and was proud of my giant ball of aluminum saved from wrappers from my father's cigar boxes.

Michelangelo apparently decided the day I was born—and was a male—that he would take me over, raise me, train me, and help me to become all the things he had always wanted to be. Everyone else in the house was too frightened of him and his temper to offer any opposition.

Besides, my mother was in many respects incapable of being a mother. She breast-fed me for the first four months of my

30

life, but this ended abruptly when she became ill and had to be hospitalized for a week. After that sudden and premature weaning, I was bottle-fed by her or by my grandmother Bettina. I was also probably toilet-trained by my mother and Bettina. My mother was and is a very passive, compliant, insecure woman, who was dominated by her own mother and father and then completely cowed by my father and grandfather. Her anxiety about her ability to cope was so great that despite the best of intentions she was not able to give very much affection to me or anyone else. However, she was not intrusive or domineering, possibly because she had enough difficulty dealing with her own narrow world. She certainly wasn't very capable of taking on anyone else's problems. She was too busy trying to learn to adapt to the people she endowed with the power to run her life and make her decisions. She lacked much power of her own, including over me. She did her minimal duty toward me, but passed any real care off to anyone who volunteered. Since she depended so much on my father and he was so jealous of any attention she showed to anyone, including me and my brother, Charlie, even if she experienced an inclination to show me attention or affection, she had to stifle it. She was a short, dark, rather attractive woman, always a bit on the heavy side, essentially placid but with so much insecurity about her survival that this temperament was peppered with constant spurts of anxiety when she was in danger of not pleasing her masters. Most of her life she was depressed. She rarely if ever had any interests of her own. Her life was spent trying to comply first with her tyrannical father, then with my tyrannical father and with my paternal grandfather, who lived in her home for the first fifteen years of her marriage. It apparently never occurred to her to complain about living with her in-laws. In fact, they were surrogate parents who effectively relieved her of the responsibility of cooking, cleaning, and much of child rearing. So childlike and dependent did she become, that when she was forced to invite some nonfamily member to the house— even for afternoon tea—she would panic and call on a maid, her sister, and my wife for assistance. At holiday dinners she would quickly get up from the table, as had my two grand-mothers, and hide in the kitchen, pretending to busy herself preparing the food. Any interaction with a stranger frightened her. She rarely expressed an opinion—personal, political, artistic, or other. She was only really contented when she was alone or with her mother and sisters, and my father would not permit much of that. When I was a small boy she occasionally read newspapers and popular fiction. After all, she had graduated from a training school for teachers, as had her four sisters. She was not illiterate like my paternal grandmother, and had even taught kindergarten for about a year, before her marriage at age twenty-two. But my father put an end to her "intellectual" activity, which threatened his control of her. Most of her life her only "interest" was listening to the radio— to talk shows. She rarely watched television; it was too disturbing, too stimulating, for her. Mother kept her energy and aliveness down to a minimum by being constantly depressed—a depression that lasted through much of more than fifty years of her marriage and lifted totally and appar-ently miraculously—but understandably—when my father died when she was seventy-six. My mother was collusive in being totally squelched as an individual by him. She still is anxious and does not manage her affairs too well without help, but she is now, for the first time, lively, interested in newspapers, movies, plays, and opera, enjoys seeing friends and relatives, and travels fairly frequently to all corners of the world in which there are relatives. And now she is much more *giving* to me.

Because of the aforementioned reasons, my mother was unable to be much of a mother to me. She sent me away to relatives at almost every opportunity. I, of course, was delighted to escape, and she welcomed the thought of being relieved of her responsibility for me. She especially failed me in several very important ways. A child needs the primary relationship with his or her mother to teach him or her how to be human—how to negotiate the day-to-day transactions in a relationship with another person, how to be close, to love, to care about another person's feelings. to empathize. And a child needs to learn how to share joy with another person, for the anticipation of joy helps a person transcend some of life's cruel blows. My mother, as well as the rest of my nuclear family with the exception of my sister, was anhedonic—joyless—depressed, and anxious. When a child feels anxious, he or she needs to go to a mother who can soothe and say in words, and in nonverbal ways, "There, there, now—everything will be all right." The child can then internalize the mother's comforting function. When I ran to my mother with some problem, the effect was to make her even more anxious than usual. Instead of making me feel better, she escalated my fears, and instead of being solaced, I had in addition to bear the burden of the anxiety I had caused her. Thus, because I was unable to anticipate closeness, caring, or surcease of anxiety, I did not learn at that age to withstand either attacks on my self-esteem or the strokes of fate that the world would in the future deal me.

My father was so busy glorifying himself as a doctor that he was rarely at home. When he was, he spent his time yelling and screaming and feeling sorry for himself. He couldn't have cared less about me. Michelangelo's wife, Bettina, was as silent about this as she was about everything else. She was a short, stooped-over, wrinkled old woman who looked more peasantlike than the other members of the family. She was so completely dominated by my grandfather that she never learned to read or write, and she literally never stepped out of the house during the fifteen years I lived there. People referred to her as a saint, but today I could suggest a few more accurate psychiatric labels for her. She was so unobtrusive that she hardly existed. She cooked, cleaned, and washed, but rarely uttered a word. She was never mean to me; she was never *anything* to me. I remember sitting at her wake in the parlor of our beautiful home, which looked to me like the Palace of Versailles, with its Renaissance paintings and sculpture, spiral staircases, and enormous chandeliers. I had lived every day of my life in the same house with Bettina, but I felt absolutely nothing. The only thing I recall about her wake was that I tried to look up the skirt of one of my cousins who was sitting across the room. Twelve analysts have failed to uncover a single emotion on my part directed toward "my grandmother, the saint." I had another saint in my family, my sister, but my feelings about her make quite another story.

So there I was as an infant, the first son of Attilio, handed over to Michelangelo for him to train to be what he, Michelangelo, was supposed to be but wasn't—the world's greatest genius and intellectual achiever. My grandfather was very Pavlovian in his methods. He used behavior modification—rewards and punishments.

He worked with me constantly. When I was in second or third grade, I remember his sitting at the kitchen table with me for hours. We would go over my homework, spelling the words again and again until I knew them perfectly. We would study the multiplication tables even before they were assigned to my class. When I made a mistake, Michelangelo would scream at me, usually in Italian, though he knew English: "Stupido, imbecille, non capisci niente (stupid, imbecile, you don't understand anything)!" When I was especially slow, he would crack me across the hands or the bottom with a ruler. I could tell time when I was two and read when I was three. I was bilingual in English and Italian. I began to recite and then write poetry when I was four. I practically never played. My grandfather trained me to learn and work constantly. When I displeased him, he took off his belt and hit me with it. I remember running around the dining room table with him in hot pursuit. I was terrified of him and his belt. I did not displease him too often.

Michelangelo actually overcome his penuriousness to push my father to send me to Friends Seminary, an elite and academically excellent Quaker private school in a beautiful eighteenth-century building located on our block in Manhattan. I was five when I was sent there to kindergarten. Much to my bewilderment the children spent the whole day playing. I went to my teacher and announced to her that I had no intention of wasting time playing when I could and should be learning. One can imagine her astonishment; nonetheless my position seemed logical to me. She took me to the principal

34

and I reiterated my complaint. Apparently they were so nonplussed by this determined five-year-old intellectual that they agreed to put me in the first grade. This was the first of several such moves that resulted in my graduating from high school at fifteen, college at nineteen, and medical school at twenty-two. Once, in the seventh grade, the class was punished with an extra hour of Latin instead of art for one week. I told the teacher I would much rather take Latin instead of art every day, and that it was not a punishment but a reward for me.

But returning to five-year-old Richard, who was now in the first grade, one of my conditions for attending school was that my mother would sit in class with me all day. I can't imagine how I was able to induce the principal to agree to this request—I must have been pretty convincing even then. I am frequently told today that I have extraordinary persuasive powers—a great asset to a psychoanalyst, and one that also helps with women. If, as a child, I could persuade my teachers, principal, and mother to agree to my entering first grade and having my mother sit with me as well, I must have had that gift early in life, as well as a very strong sense of my Self, my identity. Even then I wasn't afraid to be idiosyncratic and individualistic, to deviate from the norm of my peers. I remember a few things about the first grade. I was terrified to be there without my mother, so she stayed. I recall that even with her in the room I rocked back and forth on my chair—no doubt the same rocking motion that infants, psychotics, and very anxious people indulge in. The teacher told me to stop, but though I was a very good boy and extremely obedient, I couldn't break the habit for more than short periods.

After a week or so the teacher decided she had had enough of my mother's sitting in the room, and tried to convince me to let her leave. But each time I begged, cajoled, and threatened enough so that she gave in and allowed my mother to remain. I had not internalized a soothing mother. I needed her physical presence, but even that wasn't enough. The teacher had capitulated, but one day she brought reinforcements—the principal of the lower school. Miss Thomas was a short,

35

intense, dark-haired woman of forty who wore horn-rimmed glasses. I did all my numbers on her, but they didn't work. She insisted that Mother leave, which she very reluctantly did. In a foyer next to Miss Thomas' office, I threw the granddaddy of all temper tantrums. I yelled, kicked, screamed, and banged my head on the marble floor for what seemed to be hours. (More sophisticated, adult versions of these temper tantrums have almost always worked. My adult version, when all else failed, was to threaten suicide.) But Miss Thomas was relentless. I finally had to give up—just as I do now when everything else fails—and accept the grim reality of being in the first grade without Mama. Being without my adult version of Mama is still difficult for me, since I do not have a very good internalized mother, and I still often have an internal temper tantrum when my Mama-designate leaves me. Mother's unavailability to me has left its mark. At times I may even go into a deep depression, though today these are short-lived; I can understand them and stop them. But while I was working through this material in my last and best analytic experience, the pain of being abandoned was so intense that I could—if I permitted myself to—actually weep when my wife or lover stepped into the next room. And even today, when my wife goes to the bathroom I half-jestingly ask her to send me a postcard. Now, I am not *only* an infant—the adult part of me can tell the child part that my wife will indeed be back and I don't need to panic. Nonetheless, I have to and do recognize that there remains a very vulnerable child in me who is terribly frightened whenever his "mother" walks away, and who feels certain she will never return. That occurred at school that day, and it occurred throughout much of my childhood when my mother went out in the evening with my father, even though Bettina and Michelangelo were there as baby-sitters.

Almost all the men in my family seem to possess that terrible need for a constant attachment to a woman and a continuous tendency toward rage over the woman's not fulfilling our needs. Michelangelo had it with his wife, Bettina. He constantly complained and attacked her for not being there enough for him even though she was so terrified of him that she never left the house. Yet he always felt neglected by her and jealous of any attention she gave her sons. My father, Attilio, also considered himself neglected by his mother, Bettina, and was furious with her for preferring his brother, Beniamino, to him. I am convinced one reason Bettina and my mother never paid much attention to me was that their husbands would have been enraged by it. My father always became angry when Mother involved herself with anything or anyone but himself. He ridiculed her for reading a book or talking on the phone to her mother or sisters. Ultimately she did all but wipe herself out, and practically become a slave to him. Beniamino ultimately killed himself partially because he felt insufficiently loved by his wife and daughters. My father's nephew killed himself after a broken love affair. My grandfather, Domenico, my mother's father, always thought himself neglected by his wife and daughters. He became a depressed a great deal, but assuaged his anger and filled the void in his life with other women. His son, my uncle Jerry, committed suicide when he was nineteen because an older woman rejected him. And I tried to kill myself at nineteen and again at twenty-three when a woman left me.

Why are the men in my family so devastated when a women neglects or leaves them? Is it genetic? Probably, in part. And, of course, a great deal of the problem arises from inadequacies in the mother-child dyad. But sometimes I wonder if an additional reason we men need so much affection from women is because we receive so little from our own sex. Having no feelings of closeness to another man puts too heavy a burden on our relationships with women, even if the woman becomes to all intents our virtual slave—as Bettina and my mother and some of my own women have become.

It is only in the past year that I have begun to realize how peripheral my relationships with men have been. I suppose my best and oldest friend is Sam. We love, respect, and admire each other, and we have done so for thirty years. Sam has taught me a great deal about how to be a person. He is open, warm, gracious, and considerate. When I met him, these qualities in me were not so highly developed. And I have taught Sam a lot about people and about the world. There are no secrets between us and there never have been—I would trust Sam with my money, my life, my wife, my children, my deepest personal secrets, and I am sure he would treat me the same way. Neither of us has a moment's doubt about our total availability to each other at a time of need. We have shared joy and sorrow together. We embrace easily. When Sam hears a good joke, he phones me in the middle of one of my analytic sessions and asks me to call him back so he can tell it to me. And I do the same for him. I have always thought what we had was a really idyllic man-to-man friendship.

Then, this year I entered an all-male peer group devoted to exploring the possibilities of emotional closeness between men. There are six men in the group. All of us are psychoanalysts. Four of us are straight, two are gay. Our first few meetings were "love" meetings in which we felt a great deal of closeness, warmth, and solidarity with each other. Then we began to do numbers on each other. Two or three sadomasochistic relationships began to develop. Just before this occurred, I had been repeating to myself the Rex Harrison line in "My Fair Lady" lamenting that women can't be more like men. I had actually believed that men related to men in an honest, open, loving, straightforward, guileless, non-manipulative manner. After all, that was the way I related to my friend Sam, and he to me. I thought that this was different from the way men related to women, or women related to women or to men. In a way I was correct. What I did *not* realize is that there is no special male-to-male mystique that makes it happen that way. It is merely that men have a "gentleman's agreement" to keep a comfortable distance from one another. That is what keeps their relationships so pure. In thirty years, Sam and I have never exchanged an angry word or glance. When we have disagreed even mildly, or disapproved of the other's behavior in some way, we have been so polite and considerate about communicating this to each other that there hasn't been a really honest exchange of negative feelings. In some respects I feel closer to the people in my men's group after a year of meeting twice a month than I do to Sam. Some of them have told me directly that despite my

38

warmth, sensitivity, real caring and their affection for me at times I can be a selfish, manipulative, controlling person. I am sure Sam knows that about me. I even know it about myself. But Sam has never told me this, and I have never told him his faults. We keep our gentleman's agreement and our illusion of brotherly love and closeness. We probably could have a thoroughly honest session of communication with each other—I am sure our relationship would not only survive it but be deepened by the experience. But I have never really communicated very well with my grandfather or my father or my male cousins or uncles or with my son or stepson. And they have never communicated very much with any male in their life—certainly not with one of their relatives. As a result, almost all of us men have been entirely dependent upon our women to provide us our feelings, or at least the outlet for our feelings. And we have been so afraid of losing that connection to our unconscious that we have been tempted by, and at times fallen prey to, the temptation of seducing our women, and controlling them so they cannot leave us. Then, when they catch on to our game and accuse us of these things, we are hurt, angry, and defensive. We then try harder to find more effective ways to keep them. If we fail in all our efforts to keep them with us, we either replace them quickly so as not to feel the pain of their loss or else we are devastated. In my family we attempt and sometimes succeed in killing ourselves. We literally cannot live without a connection to a woman. To Michelangelo and my father men were strong, hardworking, and practical; women were soft, romantic, and poetic. Women were the ones who could feel and care and love and be tender and considerate. For many men this ability has been so stifled by our society, as well as by our specific family, that we feel lost and dead and gray without it and without women to provide it for us vicariously. The homosexual men in our group as well say they seldom have been truly emotionally close to another man. Sex is one thing; feeling is another.

Did I feel close to Michelangelo? He was certainly the most dominant force in my life. He taught me all I knew. He trained me. His whole life revolved around me. He watched my every move. He checked my bowel movements and report cards. He wanted me to succeed for *him*. But he didn't care for one moment how *I* felt or what *I* dreamt or how frightened I was. Nor to any degree did Bettina, or my father or mother.

There was only one person in my household whom I loved and who loved me. That was my sister, Betty, named for my grandmother. She was two years younger than I. Her photographs show an enchanting little girl with a quality of sweet innocence. Though I was jealous of the attention she received from almost everyone—even a bit from my father—and though I was envious of her beauty and charm, of which I felt fairly correctly I was lacking, I still loved her and felt loved by her. She was my connection to the world of feelings—to love and magic and play and spirit. And, of course, to sex. I remember peeking up her skirt at her lovely vagina with adoration as we sat on the floor face to face making up stories to tell each other. Betty's was more than a vagina, it was the door to feeling and love and spirit. My rivalry with her manifested itself in my feeling that the IRT (with an "R" in it) was a better subway than the BMT (with a "B" in it). Betty was for me the Holy Grail, the Jungian symbol of all the mysterious, beautiful, soft, sweet things in life. Later in life, I tried to recapture that magic by falling in love or by attending burlesque shows in my quest for the lost Grail. I rarely if ever have found the Holy Grail in another man. Lately, at the tender age of fifty-six, I sometimes imagine I could. And, lately, I have begun to find it a little and on occasion *in* myself and *by* myself. Today I am more enthralled by the mystique of a piece of primitive African art than I am by a vagina. Sometimes I become excited by my own writing and my creativity as an analyst. But most of my life I have sought the Grail from a woman or a number of women. Sometimes they have either presented me with it or I have projected the magic in myself onto them and, for a while, imagined that they indeed gave the Grail to me. During those periods of my life in which my women could provide it, or during which I could sustain the fantasy, I felt my life to be whole. The only other times were during those few hours when I watched strip-teasers and let myself endow them with my lost magic. I never went out with one of them. I never wanted to make love to one or touch one. They were there only to provide me with the magic, when it had gone out of a real relationship with a real woman.

Michelangelo and my father had practically no magic at all. Michelangelo provided me with a structure—a way of dealing with and conquering the world. He did his best to squeeze all the magic out of me—even the magic of a child's play. Betty provided the best and only magic of my childhood—actually the best of my life. But she was there only from the time I was two until the time I was seven. Then she died, and so almost did all the magic. Her death was abrupt and unexpected. She had an infection in the mastoid bone, something that nowadays is usually cleared up easily with penicillin. She was taken to the hospital, operated on as was then the custom, and died. No one told me in any detail what had happened. I was not taken to the wake or the funeral. I should have been. I needed to mourn her death as did the grown-ups—even more than they. No one talked to me about her, her death, or my feelings about it. I remember I had a fantasy that a bad man had come into her room, taken her away, and killed her. I was aware that my mother and father suffered over her loss, but no one seemed concerned about mine. As I recollect it, I suppressed my feelings and never even shed a tear, and in so doing, I all but stifled my capacity to love and feel. Thank God, a small, flickering flame remained alive in me somewhere, in spite of Michelangelo's efforts to extinguish it. By some miracle he did not succeed, but my expulsion from the Garden of Eden when Betty died, and my fall into the hell of Michelangelo's grim, humorless, playless reality were such terrible experiences that I henceforth could never attach myself too strongly or too permanently to a women whom I thought might provide that lost magic. I could never again risk the pain of that descent from paradise into hell, so I settled for much of my grandfather's hell on earth with an occasional, mostly ersatz or plastic, illusion of my vanished world. On these occasions when I was again faced with the loss of the magic—as when I

41

left a wife or lover or she left me—the suffering was so unbearable that suicide seemed almost preferable.

I once took out some faded photographs of Betty and me. They showed us touching or holding each other, or playing together, looking at each other with affection. They are the only photographs of my childhood in which I am smiling. Recently, while I was experiencing strong feelings of love toward a woman whom I truly valued, I thought to myself that I could not bear the anxiety her possible loss would cause me, so I asked a friend to be with me while I got in touch with my tears and my grief over Betty's loss. Thus, I experienced my feelings about my sister's death for the first time in my life forty-eight years after the event! I sobbed and sobbed for almost an hour, after which I could try to go on loving my woman with a little less fear that, should I ever lose her, the experience would destroy me. I had, finally if belatedly, gone through my mourning for Betty. And I had survived it.

As a child there were no other women and no men whom I felt close enough to so that they could sustain me, and to whom I could then express my grief until I found another real or imagined Holy Grail. As I have said, there was no magic in Michelangelo—only the stern dogma of hard work and success aimed at producing a person who would make up for the bitterness and frustration of his own existence. His dreams of being a respected professional man able to utilize his really magnificent mind to create and live out his own brand of magic had been shattered. He thought he would live out that dream through me. He was also cruelly destroying my dream. Michelangelo, with his tough Norman mind, might have been a doctor or a scientist. I, constitutionally and hereditarily, must have taken more after my mother's family. I was more of a philosopher, a psychologist, or priest, and my being directed toward medical school just did not work. The most total amnesia of my life is for my time spent there. I went through medical school like a somnambulist. I got through it—in the top half of my class—by dint of the structure Michelangelo had given me, but when I actually had to practice medicine and be an intern and simultaneously one of my temporary Holy Grails left me, I could no longer bear to be alive. I made a sincere effort to end my intolerable suffering. This led me into personal analysis, and my discovery of a profession that possessed some of the lost magic. Thus, I was not left completely at the mercy of some external Holy Grail. I had found a way of incorporating some Jungian anima, some "feminine" creativity and softness, into myself. And after that, even though I have thought of it often, and came close to destroying myself when some woman or some fantasy I had attributed to a woman vanished as Betty did, I actually found the pain bearable. The tiny flame that had managed to stay alive despite Michelangelo's constant verbal and physical assaults flickered on in myself and in my work as an analyst, faith healer, African witch-doctor, Christian mystic, guru. I had managed to keep the faith.

Through years seven to twelve, I kept the faith rather literally. I replaced the angel and the spirit that Betty was for me with God, saints, and other angels. I was a devout Catholic, much more so than anyone else in my nuclear family. My father, Michelangelo, and Bettina never went to church. Mother did so irregularly, but I felt that it was more for appearance than out of faith. I attended St. Ann's, a very beautiful church on East 12th Street in Manhattan. My father's funeral service was held there when I was fifty-three, but I had not set foot in the church between the ages of twelve and fifty-three. Its claim to fame was that Al Smith, the governor of New York and the presidential candidate, went to services there. I frequently saw him on Sundays. I went for Catholicism hook, line, sinker, attaching all my magic to the priest's robes, the incense, and the organ music. I believed totally in Jesus Christ, and committed no sins in those five years. The only thing I had to confess was occasionally forgetting to say my evening prayers. I remember kneeling on a hard wooden bench until my knees screamed with pain, thinking this small martyrdom would bring me nearer to God. Perhaps it did. But when I enrolled in Sunday school at age twelve for instructions for confirmation, I soon discovered that the priests and nuns were more like Michelangelo, my personal devil, than my sister Betty, my angel. They spoke coarsely and hit us, hard, with rulers. No longer did the Catholic church represent magic for me. And certainly no one at home did. Girls had not yet become the purveyors of it, except perhaps a little in fantasy. Thus, the world of the magic I so desperately needed was practically closed to me, and I existed in a void.

My mother, in addition to having her surrogate parents, Michelangelo and Bettina, living with her, as well as a housekeeper, required even more support and assistance. She took in a girl cousin, a few years older than me. I was twelve or thirteen and she was fifteen or sixteen. When Mother treated her kindly, my jealousy was terrible. I could not tolerate being displaced again. I climbed onto a window ledge and threatened to jump five stories. This action came out of genuine pain, but it was also a conscious ploy that I knew would work with Mother. The cousin was shortly thereafter sent back to her home. My strategy had worked—for the moment. But not having any magic from a man had once again made me depend on a woman, my mother, to provide all of it. Michelangelo had done his job well. He had not given me any magic himself, and he had all but destroyed my ability to find it anywhere else, including in myself.

Michelangelo returned to Italy and shortly thereafter died, when I was about fifteen. I do not recall experiencing any reaction to the news of his death. I never existed as a person for him; I was merely his narcissistic extension. I have never mourned his death nor can I conceive of ever needing to, for in spite of his importance to my development, there was never any genuine emotional bond between us.

# 3

# Domenico

Ferrandina is a little town southeast of Naples. I have been there only once. My mother's family comes from Ferrandina; they are the Candelas, from whence I received my middle name. The town is situated on a low mound on a flat plain. Its population is about five or six thousand—over twice that of Laviano. Prior to my visit in the early 1970s, there had been a boom when natural gas was discovered. That is why I was able to stay at a very modern hotel that even had a tennis court with night illumination. Since I am a tennis player, I was impressed by this. But the hotel and the tennis court seemed out of place now that the boom had ended. Though dry, Ferrandina's land is relatively fertile. The people are not rich, but they derive enough to eat from their land. The climate, though desert-hot in the summer, is generally agreeable in the winter. There are no downtrodden peasants who have struggled for centuries to eke out an existence. There are landowners, professionals, and commoners, but the class distinctions are not as marked as they are in Laviano. When I went to Ferrandina, the family home was headed by my cousin

Pasquale, an excellent physician and a very sophisticated and intelligent man. He is married to a beautiful, aristocratic, well-educated woman. Their son is also a doctor. Pasquale is a melancholy philosophizer who feels his life has been wasted. His wife is highly emotional, even hysterical. One of her reasons is that Pasquale for years and years is said to have been having an affair with an uneducated, unattractive, lower-class woman. The story I have heard when people ask him **why** he is supposedly having an affair with a peasant woman when he has such a beautiful, elegant wife at home is that he answers, "Because she washes my feet." That simple come-back may say a great deal about his needs and his view of his relationship to a woman. Male chauvinism aside, it is possible that on some level a man needs a woman who is ready to wash his feet—or at least would do so if he requires this service of her. And on some level a woman probably needs a man who would oblige her in the same way. For both sexes apparently need someone who accepts their dirtiest parts, both physical and psychic, and my cousin's wife was probably too aristo-cratic to do that. It is **hard** to find a woman in these days of women's liberation who realizes that this is part of loving a man, and that many men will gladly reciprocate. There are of course men who use this to humiliate or enslave a woman, but many men see it as a necessary aspect of intimacy. And since they have never experienced that kind of physical intimacy with a man—their fathers never once changed their diapers—and there is such a powerful taboo against anything resem-bling this kind of closeness between men, men have to obtain it from women. Because most women did not have their diapers changed by a man, they don't ever expect to find this in a man. They feel that men will want to view them as beautiful, clean, perfumed flowers. They are ashamed of their bodies, with their odors and secretions, and never dare take the chance that men will accept their natural, physical selves, which they disguise and cover with scent. Then, when a man asks them to "wash his feet," i.e., accept his bodily and sexual "dirtiness," they feel put down and exploited, not believing

46

the man would condescend to reciprocate. But the truth is that many men would be delighted to do so if given the chance. Most of the men I know love to go down on women, love a woman to be earthy in sex. But the women are often too frightened of all this, and are offended when a male suggests it. "I love a woman who pisses and shits" is a line in a poem whose author I have forgotten. Pasquale seemed to know that line in his guts, so when he explained his affair in the way he did, he was being philosophical and wise—not just a male chauvinist. And in his capacity as the town doctor, I am sure he had put his fingers into many women's vaginas and anuses, possibly without a rubber glove, and very likely without any feelings of revulsion or disgust.

Pasquale's resemblance to my grandfather Domenico was almost uncanny. They could easily have been twins separated by a generation. I felt more of a physical, biological kinship to Pasquale and Domenico than to my father or to Michelangelo. During my stay in Ferrandina, I was shown the family album. In it was strong evidence that the Candelas were descended from the Spanish nobility who ruled southern Italy intermittently for centuries. The Candelas are shorter and darker, more intense and earthy-looking than my Norman grandfather. I take after the Candelas, am more hot than cold, more Spanish than Norman.

In Ferrandina existed a fabled eating club that put on Roman banquets that included eating contests. One of their Rabelaisian slogans was: "A sheep is for five—four men and the sheep." Days were spent devouring vast quantities of various foods washed down with every sort of available wine. Eating was a sacred ritual, taken very seriously, almost as a religious ceremony, by my grandfather Domenico. He used to sit down at the table, without companions, but with his wife and others, including me, in attendance. Next to him were his wine and his big bottle of *acqua minerale*, which was delivered to his home weekly. No one, including himself, spoke while he ate. He liked to say, in Italian, "When one eats, one is fighting against death." The plates, his napkin, and the

47

silverware were laid out in precise order. He would indicate the beginning of the meal by tucking his napkin under his starched collar, covering his tie and vest. He would merely nod and signal when he wanted food or service. For example, waving both hands in the air was a signal that they were soiled and another napkin was needed. Domenico realized more accurately than sophisticated psychoanalysts that eating is a preverbal experience, that to savor the essence of a meal, food and service must be forthcoming without the use of the spoken language, in an adult a replay of the preverbal child at its mother's breast. At the table, on occasion, I act like Domenico. I signal for salt, for more food, for a fresh napkin. This sometimes irritates the woman I am with, and I can understand why. But I can also understand Domenico. No one interrupted him for a phone call from a patient during a meal. Children like myself had to be silent or else leave the room. Domenico made eating a magic ceremony, like the mass. It was a celebration of life and a defiance of death. I have almost always felt that way about eating despite the fact that eating at the Robertiellos' was completely devoid of magic. To me, food is one of the great pleasures in life. I hardly ever dine alone, for eating is a ceremony that, if not shared, must at least be witnessed. The English psychoanalyst Winnicott called the nurturing climate in which a child is fed or a patient is treated a "holding environment," and I will never eat twice in a restaurant in which I do not feel loved or cradled in this way. I like headwaiters who are warm and open and friendly, and I hate the ones—especially the haughty French ones—who are so snobbish they make me feel as if I weren't good enough to be in their establishment. One should be greeted and shown to a table by a loving person who cares. I don't think that feeling can be faked. The headwaiter at New York's Lutece makes me feel like that, even though this is a four-star restaurant. And the owner of the Shanghai Cafe, where even today one can get a fabulous meal for a few dollars, also makes me feel loved. Service is as important to me as it was to Domenico. I can't indicate my wishes with hand signals exactly, but at Lutece I come very close. The headwaiter picks something he knows I will like and describes it. Usually I merely have to nod my agreement. Then, the service has to be quick and perfect or I become furious, an internal rage that usually results in heartburn. Domenico's anger was overt; he yelled at his wife or the maid, and caused the kitchen to shake by stamping his feet. I am sure he never had heartburn. Women I have dined with have often told me my behavior at table is, to put it mildly, irrational. When the food or service is substandard, I retreat into an internal fury that cuts me off from them and the rest of the world. Perhaps there is the analytic explanation that I am a poor, starving child who needs good mothering so badly that I have a temper tantrum when I don't get it. That may be true, but I also ascribe my behavior to my having the same genes and the same attitudes toward life as Domenico. I suspect that this is not merely from having internalized the role model whom I saw those few times at his house. After all, why didn't I copy Michelangelo or my father, Attilio? I saw a great deal more of them. To them, food was not a magic celebration or a feast in imperial Rome or modern Ferrandina. It was merely a way to survive in the struggle for existence. Father used to grab a bite between seeing patients, and sometimes I copy him in that, but for the most part I am much more like Domenico, for I love ambiance, good cheer, smooth service, and magnificent food and wine.

My tastes in wine are curious. Basically, I am not much of a drinker, and one thing I was spared during childhood was the presence of an alcoholic in my family. I am very fussy about wine, and have never enjoyed an American or even an Italian wine. I usually enjoy only the best French wines, and this is not out of snobbery or expertise. I can't imagine it is anything more than my having the same genes as Domenico. When Freud first started writing about personality, he emphasized genetics and constitution. Then, since there was obviously nothing he could do about these factors, a great deal of his emphasis was shifted to childhood experience as a determinant. Jung focused on the racial unconscious and ethnicity as a determinant, and he and Freud split on this issue. Until recently I have thought about myself mostly as a product of my early childhood. I would hardly say that this is *not* so. But now I see these experiences as essentially suppressing a "me" that seemed to be there before I was born, and today I am attempting to rediscover that prenatal being, and trying to bring the real "me" of today closer to him. I feel I am much more a Candela than a Robertiello in my genes, and am trying to scrape away the part that was painted on me by Michelangelo and reach to the person underneath. Of course, some of that person was also derived from Michelangelo— Domenico would never have taken the time to write a book, for he was more involved with sensual pleasure than with intellect or philosophy, despite the fact that he too, like my father and my cousin Pasquale, was a fine doctor. As I write this book, I do not feel I am doing it only to please Michelangelo, for there is a part of me that feels very real, very gratified, very creative, as I set down the words.

Another part of Domenico that, thank God, I received through my genes and not through my childhood training or experience is my sexuality. Domenico, as distinct from Michelangelo or my father, was always nattily dressed and clearly had an eye for the ladies. He didn't discuss such things with me, but he clearly was very aware of sex, whereas the Robertiellos ignored it. I recall that when his youngest daughter went out with young men, Domenico would sit by the door with a loaded shotgun, and that my Aunt Peggy, after an adventure, would climb to the roof of the building she lived in and cleverly lower herself into her bedroom window in order to escape her father's wrath. She also used me at the very tender age of five as an excuse to have secret romantic rendezvous with her lovers on sunny afternoons in Brooklyn's Prospect Park. She also inherited the genes from Domenico, for she was one of the most sexual women I have ever met. I think I have spent much of my life trying to find a woman like Peggy, who was as sexual as I experienced myself to be. Unfortunately, I have not had much success in this endeavor.

50

Peggy was not the magical mystical Holy Grail that Betty was, but she was a sensual version of it. But coming back to Grandpa Domenico, for many years he used to make trips back to Ferrandina, ostensibly for hunting. The story goes that not only my cousin Pasquale, but about half of that town looks exactly like Domenico, so apparently his sensuality wasn't confined to eating—or at least not eating only at the table. His two younger children, my aunt and my uncle, appeared to have inherited his healthy love of sex, as did I. Like Domenico's, my own life has witnessed periods that were extended and extensive "hunting trips," and sexuality has been one of the forces that has made my life tolerable and brought me peak experiences.

Jerry was Domenico's youngest child and first son after five daughters. I remember him as very handsome, with a twinkle in his eye, a broad smile, and a winning way. He was fourteen when I was born. I spent a reasonable amount of time with him during my first five years. He used to play with me, sing to me, and lift me above his head—things no other men had done. He was the male in my family who was closest to my age and with whom I could most easily identify. He constantly argued with Domenico, who scolded him and berated him for not studying enough and for being too much interested in women. In 1928 Jerry was given a trip to Italy on an ocean liner. On the way back, he fell in love, madly and romantically, with a blond, non-Italian woman several years older than himself. Jerry came back starry-eyed with love, believing he had found his Holy Grail. Apparently the woman jilted him, perhaps because he was too young for her. When I was five and Jerry was nineteen, he went into a small room with a gas stove in Domenico's office, closed the door, turned on the gas, and died. I learned the whole story soon thereafter. Jerry's death was my first exposure to the fatal sequence of sex, love, rejection, and suicide, but it was certainly not the last. Jerry had never received love from his father, had tried to get all the magic from a woman, and could not bear his expulsion from the Garden of Eden. Two years later, when I

51

was seven and my sister died, I learned at first hand about this expulsion.

Jerry was a very important role model for me. I felt I too was a lover and a romantic, that I too would love and lose, and I would never live past the age of nineteen. And, but for a happy chain of circumstances, I would have followed in his footsteps. I was nineteen, a college student majoring in biochemistry, as was my roommate. I was in love with a blond, non-Italian woman several years older than myself. She rejected me (or so I thought then) and I swallowed the contents of a vial my roommate had thoughtfully labeled "potassium cyanide," which would certainly have killed me on the spot. I recall thinking at the time that I had to live out Jerry's script. Fortunately my roommate, who had guessed my suicidal proclivities, had switched labels. The vial contained harmless hydrogen sulfide, so instead of ending up at the morgue, all I did was belch a rotten egg smell for the next few hours. And then my WASP blonde not only did not reject me, but was quite insistent on marrying me. I had found the magic again, so I had a reprieve from death.

Uncle Jerry's sister Peggy, two years older than he, was the light of my early sexual life. My relationship with her continued into my twenties. She too had all of Domenico's genetic makeup. (Strangely, my mother, her sister, must have taken after her own asexual mother.) Peggy was a flapper. She was about five feet two, with black hair, dark-brown eyes, a 1920s bob, and an absolutely sensational figure which she was not reluctant to advertise. I remember her especially in the period separating Jerry's death and Betty's, when I was five to seven and she was in her early twenties. She would parade in front of me in her bra and panties, being seductive and using terms like "sex appeal," which were mysterious to me but whose intent I somehow divined. I would become very excited and she would make fun of me—such a little boy—for looking at her in such a sexy way. This sequence of seduction followed by castration was one of my first sexual experiences, and later became very erotically charged for me. In later life I sometimes

52

would find a woman who really enjoyed this stimulation-castration game; on other occasions I projected this onto women who did not. But the most important sexual contribution that Peggy made was to my voyeurism. Looking at that beautiful body so wantonly displayed became a turn-on that has never left me. After first watching her perform I then took to peeking at her through the keyhole in the bathroom. Apparently I was not the only person to be excited by Peggy, for a group of her neighbors met one day and sent her a set of curtains—a not-so-subtle hint that their husbands were more interested in her windows than they should have been. In a drawer in the parlor of her home, I discovered a viewer with a set of prints of famous modern paintings. Among them was a Modigliani nude that looked not unlike my vision of Peggy. Since that and *The National Geographic* were the only way in that era for a five-year-old to gape at naked ladies, I transferred part of my voyeurism from Peggy to modern and primitive art. Much of my infantile voyeurism lives on today. I have sublimated some of it into the appreciation of nudes and other art, but my strip-teasers demonstrate that this sublimation is not complete. The Candela part of me, which Pasquale and Domenico, Peggy and Jerry, shared, and which was absent in my father's side of the family, has persisted in me—fortunately, I think, in a joyous earthiness and an open appreciation of sensuality. On certain occasions during which I have been impotent, I have been terrified that I have lost this magic. Luckily, so far the occasions have been short and always connected with the fear of losing a loved one.

I believe the reason why sex is so important to me and to others is that in addition to its procreative function, it combines and integrates the four important psychological positions in our earliest infancy. That is why, if these positions are fully integrated and incorporated, sex can lead us to peak experiences. There are four basic positions in our early infancy: the needy child, the nurturing mother, the angry child, and the punitive angry mother. The needy child is completely open

53

and vulnerable. He or she presents an open, concave part—mouth, anus, vagina—which he or she wants filled by a convex object—a breast, a penis, a finger. Opening up oneself trustingly, without guile, to the possibility of having a physical or emotional void filled is a tremendously joyful experience. The counterpart to the needy child is the nurturing mother, played out by both men and women, who fills this void, with a breast or penis or finger, an act that gives him or her a feeling of enormous power, strength, and gratification.

This experiencing of sex as a loving interchange between mother and child, with both sexes alternately playing both roles, is an aspect of sex that many people, though certainly not all or even most people, may experience occasionally. This kind of sex is warm and nice, but it lacks the element of passion contained in the reverse part of the mother-child transaction. For a baby is also a ferocious monster, a devil that wants to bite, devour, and destroy its mother's breast. Why is this? It is because the baby's need for the breast is so great that the baby envies the power of the breast and wants to literally destroy it. The baby is a sadist in the truest sense of the word—Jack the Ripper, the Marquis de Sade, the Boston Strangler. Because of her understandable retaliation for these sadistic wishes, the mother—more often than we like to admit—is both in her own and the baby's view a sadist. She wants to do away with the cruel and demanding little tyrant who is making unconscionable demands of her, is sucking her dry literally and figuratively, and is ruining the rest of her life by possessing and exploiting her. The sadomasochistic elements in the mother-child dyad, so eloquently explained by Melanie Klein, especially in her book *Envy and Gratitude*, were so frightening even to most psychoanalysts that they were largely disregarded by the mainstream of psychoanalysis for more than forty years and only recently are being rediscovered. For sex to have the fire of passion, it must be ignited by the fire of destruction. The sweet and loving part, madonna and child, is only one half of human sexuality: Sadomasochism is required to make it complete. Each partner must incorporate the angry, primitive, devouring, biting child and the vicious, punitive mother.

Most people cannot successfully combine all these elements into their sexuality—at least not with one person. Many men experience the classical madonna-whore split, in which they use one woman as the good mother/child toward whom they are the good mother/child. Then they have another, or several other, "bad" women with whom they are the bad mother/child. This compromise is certainly better than nothing, but even so it leaves a gap in their emotional life, since their original sensual experience occurred in a dyad, not a triad or an orgy. It is the exhilaration of experiencing all these roles within a dyad that makes sex a transcendental experience.

Women have their version of the dyad, often more in imagination than in reality. They marry the good provider who is kind and gentle to them, and they nurture and suckle him if he is open enough to allow it. But they fantasize about the dark mysterious stranger, the rapist; the man who sweeps them off their feet. The Judeo-Christian view of man and of sex naively postulates that we are made in the image of God. This may be so, but we are also fashioned in the image of the devil. God and the devil, the madonna and the whore, the gentle lover and the sadist, the sadist and the masochist, are all present in man and in bed. Puritanical northern Europeans have idealized mankind insofar as its sexuality is concerned. The Romans had orgies. And contemporary Italian men, if not women, seem more in touch with their devil than northerners are.

A woman patient came to see me one day. She had trouble relating to men. "In New York," she told me, "there are two kinds of guys—Italian guys and Jewish guys. The Jews are nice and sweet and soft. They have soft brown eyes and you can push them all over the place. The Italian guys have black beady eyes, They are tough and hard and they push *you* all over the place."

"And I," I asked. "Which am I?"

"You? Oh, you're Jewish!"

We both laughed. Unfortunately, during the period of the consultation I was "Jewish" in her definition of the term—sweet and loving and rarely a devil. But thankfully there have been other times in my life both before and after then when I was somewhat more "Italian," at least to the degree that I was not "pushed all over the place." Nonetheless, this split in my identification between "Jewish" and "Italian" went much beyond my sexual role, and will be the subject of a good deal of consideration later on.

Another part of a broad sensuality that I must have derived from Domenico is my interest in sports. Despite his use of hunting expeditions to carry on love adventures, he also truly enjoyed that sport. There were guns around his summer house, and I remember his shooting small game in the vicinity. Most of the Jewish role-models who influenced my later development considered hunting atavistic and barbarous, and for that matter hunting has never interested me as a sport per se. Nonetheless, just as I accept the sensuality of eating and sex as a basic part of ourselves, I also believe we must admit to an unconscious need to destroy and kill. Accept doesn't mean condone or encourage. But we need to understand that in all likelihood we are descended from predatory apes and a part of us goes on wanting to kill. Though I do not enjoy killing animals, I am a "killer" on the tennis court. This goes beyond wanting to play well, for I really have the urge to "kill" my opponent by winning. Noncompetitive sports like rock climbing and jogging hold no appeal, but I watch football, baseball, and basketball, and as I have said, I love to play tennis. Domenico not only liked to kill animals, he savored the good feeling one gets from using one's body, and he rode horseback even into his seventies. I rode a good deal into my thirties, never aware of my debt to Domenico in this matter. No Robertiello ever exercised. One day I played catch with my father for a few minutes. He couldn't catch the ball, and his arm hurt him for days afterward. But Domenico not only ate, made love and killed, he also enjoyed using his musculature, and that too I must have gotten genetically from him, for there were no role models in the family for me to internalize the love of physical activity.

When I reflect about heredity versus environment, using myself, my friends, and my patients as examples, I must conclude that my inheritance from Domenico has helped sustain the life forces in me that at times sunk to such low levels that only chance prevented them from expiring. Several patients and friends of mine have had Italian-American and Italian lovers, and almost all have said that sex with them has been a totally different experience from what they have enjoyed with other ethnic groups. I used to laugh at stories of Italians being great lovers, and when my lovers said that to me, I was sure they were flattering me, that they fed the same line to all their partners. A patient once told me that all of her numerous former lovers had remained life-long friends. When I asked her why, her answer was very simple: She had informed every single one of them that he was the greatest lover she had ever slept with. I didn't want to be similarly duped. However, a friend of mine recently took on an Italian lover and informed my wife that she had discovered sex in an altogether different way. My wife responded that she could have put her wise years ago. Too many female friends who have no reason whatsoever to deceive me say the same thing, and there must be a reason for the enormous yearly migration of northern European and North American women to Italy. I am not being either facetious òr self-laudatory, but in my opinion it is important for us take our roots and our ethnic and cultural backgrounds into account. In an epoch when it is thought unfashionable to consider race as a determinant of personality or specific talents, we have perhaps gone too far. In our justified efforts to stamp out bigotry, we are in danger of losing sight of ethnic truths that everyone knows but is afraid to say. Men are surely not the same. I do not claim that Italians are better than everyone else, or even that all Italians are champion lovers. I am sure my grandfather Michelangelo wasn't, and I doubt that my father was. And there are many parts of Italy and many different Italians. But to deny that

there are basic personality differences between the vast majority of Italians and the vast majority of Swedes, for example, is
to blind oneself to an obvious fact; thus Jung was accused of
being a racist and even a Nazi because of his insistence on a
genetic racial unconscious that was different for different
ethnic groups. If one avoids the pitfall of overgeneralization,
this truth becomes self-evident. We are born with specific
characteristics and a tendency to live out certain myths that are
repeated throughout human history. And these myths that
our unconscious causes to unfold are to some extent products
of our ethnic background. Yes, our early relationship to our
mother affects us enormously, as does our relationship to
other significant figures in our past. Certainly, my life and my
Self are testimonials to that—to my need for mothering and
fathering, to my introjections of male role models from my
childhood and my later life. But underlying early experiences
is the genetic, the biological, the constitutional, the racial, the
ethnic—factors that have been lost sight of because we have
considered them (correctly) incapable of modification, at least
during one generation, and therefore (incorrectly) thought
them irrelevant. If we understand from whom we came and
from whence, we can begin to sort out who we are biologically. This can help us shore up our identity. Finding our
roots can help us to bring into focus the parts of ourselves that
fit in with our basic being and to shed the parts that were
largely manmade accretions to that basic Self. Understanding
more about my roots has given me a much more solid feeling
about what is me and what is non-me. It has helped me to
accentuate Domenico, Jerry, and Peggy, and to eliminate not
all but some of Michelangelo's and my father's Norman
orderliness and compulsiveness—qualities I once cherished,
but today feel have displaced a more basic, essential part of
me.

I never believed in astrology and I still do not. However, the
astrologers' outlook is similar to mine. They believe that one's
basic personality is determined by the constellation of stars
and planets at the moment of birth; that if you accept this and

know your basic personality configurations, you can try to live your life in a way that best fits into your predetermined pattern. I differ from the astrologers concerning the stars and planets, but I do believe that knowledge of your racial, ethnic, and genetic roots can help guide you to a way of being that is more in tune with your uniqueness. So, the time that remains to me, I shall try, while giving Michelangelo his due—and without paying dues *to* him—to bring out more of Domenico and to be more sensual and less intellectual.

Recently a patient of mine and her brother were reunited with a father who abandoned them when they were both infants. They had been told that he had died and they had never been given any information about him. Their mother remarried. My patient was startled at the tremendous resemblance both in physical appearance and in temperament between herself and her brother and father. Neither she nor her brother is very much like their mother or their stepfather. Their genetic makeup had a more important impact on their physical selves, on the way they moved, and on their personality and character traits than did the effect of role models, internalizations, or reactions to and against the parent that was present.

I often think I am an extreme example of the round peg who was throughout his life stuck in to a square hole. There I was, an emotional, sensitive, sensual, romantic, philosophical genotype, much more feminine in the Jungian sense than masculine, much more anima than animus. And my first twenty-three years were spent training me to be compulsive, scientific, orderly, and asexual. No wonder I tried to kill myself. I had almost never been allowed to be me. The English psychoanalyst Winnicott, already mentioned, makes a clear distinction between the "real Self" and the "false Self." Masud Kahn, one of his successors, correctly points out that this distinction is somewhat vague and a bit romantic, not unlike the myth of the noble savage beneath the surface of civilized man. It is certainly true that the distinctions between where the real Self ends and the false Self begins are not geometrical. And our façade, our persona, is as much a part of our total Self as our inner Self is. But from a subjective point of view, the representation we have in our psyche of our Selves is often very different from the face we show to the world, or the person other people think we are. Our inner world is in many ways more important to us than the outer one. We are often connected to a sad, needy, lonely child that our external appearance of cool confidence completely belies. I believe that love can exist between two people only when each is in total contact with the needy, lonely, dirty, perverse, ugly child in the other. Partnerships based on interlocking façades are empty. You cannot pick your lover from a printout; you will do better to see his or her face across the proverbial crowded room and hear the proverbial bells ring. I have made romantic or friendship choices on the basis of those bells many times, and I have practically never been wrong. I picked one of my wives using the "printout" system. She was lovely, accomplished, sensual, and affectionate—all the right things—but there were never any bells. The marriage never worked and folded up in bitterness and recriminations. We had chosen each other on the basis of our façades and worldly positions rather than on our responses to each other's inner Selves. We had been friends for six months before we "decided" to be lovers. Other relationships have also broken up, but if they were formed on the basis of bells ringing, they ended more amicably, and because of inescapable realities, not incompatibility of souls. And once a person loves the child—even the grimy, evil, hungry, angry child in you—he or she can never hate you. In many countries, marriages are based on the confluence of astrological charts. In India, most partners do not even meet before they are wed. I do not trust astrology as a basis for marriage, but I trust intellect even less. The "right" person from the "right" background is the worst method of selecting a mate—unless, of course, your real Self has been so thoroughly submerged that you hardly know where to find it. In that case, you might as well match two façades. I hope and trust that human beings who are so totally cut off from themselves are rare.

Returning to my own situation, I must first clarify the feminine versus masculine concept. I am not referring to my gender identity or my sexual preference. I have never for even a moment experienced myself as anything other than a man. Because of my genetic, racial, and ethnic background, or perhaps because of my role models or other, more mysterious factors, I have always been secure about my gender identity. I have been insecure in bed; I have been anxious about my sexual performance; I have on occasion been impotent; but I have never experienced myself as a woman. Some people are not as fortunate as I am in this respect, though they may be much more so in others. Gender identity means the sureness one has about being a man or being a woman; sexual preference is another matter. In this area, too, I have perhaps been fortunate, not necessarily in being heterosexual, but in not having had conflicts about it. I have never been attracted sexually to a man nor have I had a homosexual experience. I have often had homosexual fantasies, but I was never anxious or frightened by them, nor did they ever make me wonder about my sexual preferences. I do not find the idea of a homosexual experience in any way repugnant. I am fairly sure that had I been brought up thirty years later I would have experimented with homosexuality, but I seriously doubt it would have been more than an experiment. Again I must emphasize that gender identity and sexual preference must *never* be confused. There are many totally homosexual men who are very certain of their gender identity as males. And conversely there are many totally heterosexual men who have questions about their gender identity.

When I speak of myself as "feminine," I do so in a completely Jungian sense. "Feminine" in his definition—and please, for the moment at least, try to get past contemporary feminist platitudes—means soft, warm, poetic, creative, sensitive. "Masculine" in Jung's sense means assertive, logical, orderly, direct. Jung believed that a complete person had to be

61

able to simultaneously express both the total man and the total woman in himself or herself. Women in our culture have an especially difficult time retaining and developing their "masculine" side at the same time they are fully expressing their "feminine" side, especially in a loving relationship with a man. A patient of mine, a successful psychologist, came to see me because her affairs with men were disasters. As she worked out some of her problems, she developed a beautiful, loving relationship with what appeared to be a wonderful man. She found herself caring less about her work and being irritated by its demands. She reported a dream in which she was supposed to play the role of a man in a drama. She tried to put on her tuxedo, but it fitted badly. She tried to flatten her breasts, but they kept bulging. She tried to paste on a mustache, but it fell off. Finally, she forgot her lines. My patient had, with therapy, developed to a very great degree her heretofore neglected "feminine" anima qualities, but in the course of doing so she was losing her "masculine" animus qualities! She had become the woman she could be, but was now having trouble retaining the assertive professional "man" in her she needed in order to be a complete person. She then had to work on reasserting that animus part of herself.

What Michelangelo had attempted, and to a great degree succeeded in doing with me, was to stamp out my "woman" and make me into a total "man." I was often the best student in my class. I was competitive, assertive, intellectual, and successful, but the poor little woman in me was almost destroyed. Domenico, my sensual, sexual, athletic grandfather, was much more of a "woman" in the Jungian sense than the asexual Michelangelo. So my task was to reclaim the "woman" in myself and, beyond that, to recognize that she was more a part of my real Self than the "masculine" façade that Michelangelo had constructed over her. When you search for your Self, your identity, you must not only seek out your gender identity and your sexual preference, you must look to find *both* the "man" and the "woman" in yourself, and you must decide which one is more important to your biological, ethnic, racial, and psychological self, and in what proportions. Furthermore, you must ascertain if the "man" and the "woman" are being expressed in optimal fashion in your life and your relationships to others. And most importantly, you must decide whether the Self you are expressing is the one you are connected to biologically and emotionally or whether it is a mask that has been grafted onto you in order to please the significant persons in your childhood. Are you being the good child (or bad child) your mother or father wanted you to be? Are you being the opposite of what they wanted you to be? If so, they are still choosing for you, albeit negatively. Or are you really being the Self that is most close to your subjective representation—brought about by whatever amalgamation of genes, role models, introjections—that *feels* like you? It took me almost a half century to discover I was more Domenico than Michelangelo.

# 4

# Attilio

My father. How do I write about my father? I feel a reluctance to write this chapter that I did not experience in earlier chapters. I really want to let sleeping dogs lie. My father died in 1976, when he was eighty-four and I was fifty-three. I thought after twelve analysts and more than twenty years of analysis that I knew something about him or at least about my feelings toward him and my relationship to him. I was wrong. I learned more about him during the last six months of his life, and more about my feelings about him, than I had in all the analytic sessions put together.

I always knew I hated my father as far back as I can remember. That was no news, no surprise. Practically everyone who knew him hated him—my friends, our relatives, his colleagues, the nurses on his wards. It was easy to hate him.

Attilio had the same fair skin, tall stature, and aristocratic bearing as his father, Michelangelo. He too seemed more Norman than typically southern Italian. He was born in Laviano, was left there while his father established roots in New York, and came here as a boy of eight in 1900. He went through the usual routine of living in an Italian ghetto, the son of a poor tailor. He must have been ridiculed in school since he knew no English. He had his father's fierce pride, and he was determined to succeed at all costs, so after grammar school he worked all day, went to school in the evening, and studied half the night. His older brother, Beniamino, had somehow managed to become a pharmacist and eventually owned a drugstore in Greenwich Village. My father passed his high school equivalency test, was accepted at the College of Pharmacy, and received his degree as a pharmacist. But he had much greater ambitions, and wanted to surpass his brother, whom he considered his mother's favorite. So he went to medical school at Columbia University, College of Physicians and Surgeons, without really ever having gone to high school or to a regular college. Since Columbia was one of the best medical schools in the country, he was competing with Harvard, Yale, and Columbia graduates. In addition, he had to work as a pharmacist all the while he was in medical school. His father, Michelangelo, deeply resented him, feeling that he was taking his wife, Bettina's, attention away from him. Michelangelo beat my father regularly when he was a child and never gave him a cent to help pay his way through school. This made my father even tougher and more determined. He got his MD and then his medical license. With this achievement, he was then home free, well able to earn a good living. But my father did much more than that. In some ways (not surprisingly) he was as tightfisted as Michelangelo. He could never spend money on himself. Even when he was in his late seventies and early eighties he would shop for a suit in the cheapest section of New York and succeed in finding one for under thirty dollars. (I am a bit like that too. Perhaps the most I ever paid for a suit was recently when I bought an Yves St. Laurent—on sale, of course—for $140.00.) But my father could also be grandiose. When I was five and he was thirty-six, he bought a beautiful brownstone on what was then, and in some ways still is, one of the most beautiful blocks in New York, 16th Street between Third Avenue and Stuyvesant Park. Opposite the house was St. George's Episcopal Cathedral. On the corner were some eighteenth-century buildings housing Friends Seminary and a Quaker Meeting House. But the neighborhood was nothing compared to the house. It had been owned by the most prominent Italo-American doctor in New York, a man who hobnobbed with Caruso and Scotti and New York society people. I have already compared it to Versailles. It had four stories and a basement, with two gigantic rooms on each floor. The ceilings were twenty feet high, and from each hung a giant Italian crystal chandelier. The beds were Italian Renaissance. There were life-size marble statues. We had an original Vasari in the library. There were Chinese antique tables and chairs and a large Florentine wardrobe. All of the draperies were velvet, and the upholstery was exquisite. We moved into this palace in 1928, before the great depression. My father must have been doing very well. His first-floor office seemed to me the size of a basketball court. He sat behind a huge, carved mahogany desk, and when one of his poor banana-peddler patients came into that office, he must have been knocked off his feet. My father enjoyed and also realized the importance of putting on a show of splendor and authority for his patients, for in those days doctors had little besides aspirin to offer them in the way of pills, so the value of a little sorcery and a lot of charisma in alleviating the 90 percent of ailments that were psychosomatic was enormous. He always dressed conservatively in a dark suit that undoubtedly was inexpensive but did not look like it, a tie, and a vest. He was the model of propriety and decorum. I remember wandering around the office looking at the examining table, the syringes, the needles, and the vaginal speculums as if the whole place were some kind of fairy castle. I lived in that house from the time I was five until the age of sixteen, when I left for college. The entire house, not just Father's office, has continued all these years to be a place of enchantment for me. Venice is one of my favorite cities, and the Palace of the Doges one of my favorite buildings. I think the house on 16th Street must have had the same effect on me then that the Palace of the Doges has on me and on most tourists now. I am also fond of spending the night in the hotels in India that have been converted from rajahs' palaces, like the one in Jaipur or Udaipur. As a child, I had the same feelings about my home. As I've said, everything about my relationship with my sister Betty was magic: She was a fairy princess, but we were also two tiny children wandering about in a real palace. There was a spiral staircase going up through all the four floors. From the top I could watch the patients entering my father's majestic office. Later I could slide down the banister from the second floor, with its enormous library, living room filled with paintings, and its grand piano, down to my father's office. But of course we only played or even appeared when my father and grandfather were away, for we were terrified of them.

Money matters in the palace were handled in a manner I must term as insane. I have already described how I was sent from "Versailles" to the elite Friends Seminary wearing patches on my clothes and with a piece of flour sacking in my pocket as a handkerchief. But the irrationality was more pervasive than that. Despite living in a palace, we remained poor, inferior Italians. Everyone else—Jews, Irish, and certainly WASPs—was better than we were. We were ashamed of our race and of our cultural heritage. The Jews, for example, no matter how downtrodden they were, somehow always managed to instill into their children the belief that they were God's chosen people. But, realistically speaking, to be Italo-American in New York in the late 1920s or the early 1930s wasn't much to be proud of. Most of the Italian immigrants were poor, and low achievers to boot. Nonetheless, had they made the attempt, I am convinced that my family could have found much in our Italian heritage that I could have been proud of. The entire family, including my father, who had such a lordly bearing that he was called "the Duke" at his fancy WASP medical school, was ashamed of being Italian. In his heart I am sure he identified with his lowly patients—the uneducated, uncultured, and very low economic achievers. When anyone in the family mentioned the Irish or the Jews, his bigotry was always accompanied by reverence. To Father, Jews were crooked, conniving, and untrustworthy, but they were bright, ambitious, and successful. The Irish were drunks, but attractive and socially adept. Italians, including us, were the bottom of the barrel. The fact that he was a professional and economic success, who lived on one of the most fashionable blocks in New York, had nothing to do with his view of himself or his family. We were still peasants in Laviano, ostracized from intercourse with the landowners.

The same sentiment must have pervaded my mother's family. My aunt Peggy hid as one of her most guarded secrets the fact that her real name was Filomena, and when she went out with her friends, especially her boyfriends, she pretended she was Spanish, not Italian. Those were the days before the Puerto Rican influx to New York, so Manhattan's Spaniards were really from Spain, and there were so few of them that they were not a despised and persecuted minority.

My family's shame about being Italian has unfortunately persisted up to a point in me. When, at the age of forty, I went out with an upper-class WASP woman, when I had a Harvard BA, a degree from Columbia Medical School, and considerable financial and professional prestige, I was impotent with her for the first six weeks of our liaison—but not with other women I was seeing during that period. Neither of us could understand it. Since I was an analyst and she was a therapist, I decided to lie in bed next to her and free-associate—say whatever came into my mind. I went back immediately to the first grade, to Janet, the exquisite, blue-eyed, blond WASP who sat next to me. Those first graders seemed to have a higher degree of sexual interest than the grown-ups in a contemporary swingers' club. Those proper little WASPs in their straitlaced Quaker school talked of practically nothing but their five- and six-year-old sexual fantasies as we climbed the jungle gym in the schoolyard. Most of the boys and girls would hide in a secluded corner of the stately old building and show each other their peepees. There was nothing I wanted more than to see Janet's peepee—a delight at least as enticing as finding the Holy Grail. But Janet was a rich WASP fairy princess, almost from a different planet, and I was like that peasant in Laviano who would never be allowed to enter the home of her

69

husband, my cousin. So I never dared show my peepee to Janet or risk looking at what I imagined to be her blond—in reality hairless—Holy Grail. The sight of a vagina surrounded by blond hair still excites me. When I went out with Harriet, thirty-five years later, she was still Janet, the prize forbidden to a humble plebeian like myself. I felt she would not only reject me, but would humiliate me for having the effrontery to desire her even in fantasy.

My father suffered from this same kind of self-abasement vis-à-vis non-Italians. In those days, blacks were beyond the pale, and even a liberal like Eleanor Roosevelt referred to them as darkies. But among non-blacks, Italians were the lowest rung of the ladder; Jews were one step up. I carried these feelings with me to my largely Jewish grammar school and high school, to Harvard, and to Columbia Medical. (It occurs to me that throughout my life I have practically never enjoyed a close relationship with a man who was not Italian, Jewish, or black.) After a while I began to feel somewhat on a par with Jews and blacks. I went through three and a half years of medical school hardly saying a word to anyone but Jews or blacks. Of course, this was their choice as well as mine, but I must take some responsibility for it. Harriet pointed out to me that my family was much wealthier than hers, that I had gone to more prestigious schools, and that I was more successful than she. In addition, she not only wanted to show me her peepee, but she was more than eager to have me make love to her. Once we decided she wasn't Janet, I proceeded to do just that.

Being a member of a despised minority group and internalizing this as a part of one's self-image constitutes a vitally important segment of our identity. When I read in *Portnoy's Complaint* about the idealization and pursuit of non-Jewish women, I was immediately struck by how my father, my grandfathers, and I had the same orientation. But though I have never felt on terms of equality with, or comfortable among, non-minority-group members, especially women, this feeling has not entirely dominated my behavior. For, after all, I have had two WASPs as wives and have known intimately many more of them. Nonetheless, the feeling of inferiority persists, and the fact that these women desired, accepted, and even married me has not totally alleviated it.

I am often accused of, on the one hand, being very self-effacing and on the other of, if not being vain, at least having an overly generous appreciation of my talents. This is the same combination that Attilio had. I must have incorporated these traits of his. He used to boast that he was the best doctor in New York, as I sometimes have done.

Alongside my occasional cockiness remains the fear that in reality I am only a short, ugly, gauche peasant who might be expected to drink from the fingerbowl in a fancy restaurant and has to curry the favors of the blond WASP princess. Today I am sure that Janet would have gladly shown me her peepee and that some of the Jews in high school or the WASPs and Jews in college and medical school would have befriended me if I had sought their company, for in the few instances in which I summoned the courage and risked humiliation, I was usually accepted. Attilio's fear of humiliation was much greater than mine, and he covered it with his haughty patrician stance. He never got close to many people, though sometimes he was able to approach Italians who shared his humble origins. He was the "Duke" and the peasant at the same time. I have fortunately or unfortunately never been the "Duke," but for too many years of my life a part of me felt like that plebeian scorned by WASP, Jewish, or Irish princes and princesses. This was not a paranoid obsession that has ruined my life, or even seriously affected my marital, sexual, or friendship choices, as it did Attilio's, but it had its impact. The psychological effects of being in an ethnic minority group are enormous, for ethnicity is more than just genes and heredity. Every minority-group patient I have treated has suffered psychologically—often in concealed ways—from his or her origins. If someone had asked me even a few years ago if I identified myself as an Italo-American or thought it had any effect on my feelings about myself or my friends, or on my behavior, I would in all candor have said no. I did then not consider myself much different from my friends of other ethnic

71

groups. This part of me was quite split off. There was a tremendous gap between my intellectual awareness and my feelings. I was unaware of any special identification with Italy or with Italo-Americans. I enjoyed saying that the only people I knew who weren't Jewish were my mother and my father. Almost all my friends, my colleagues, my patients, were Jewish, and I believed I was much more like them than different from them. I largely denied my feelings that I was the subject of any particular persecution or any special exclusion because of my ethnic background. Though I used to be a moaner and a groaner and extended my childhood appellation of "Mopey Dick" into middle age, I never pleaded sympathy on the basis of being an Italo-American.

Now I look at things a bit differently. I was practically the only Italo-American at Friends Seminary; at the Hunter College Elementary School, a grammar school for bright children; and at Townsend Harris High School, the then honor high school of New York City. I was one of four Italo-Americans out of a thousand in my class at Harvard, one of three in my class of over a hundred at Columbia Medical School, and the only one in my psychiatric residency and my class at psychoanalytic school. Why? Why, though I was accepted at Harvard and had one of the highest Regents grades among public high school students in New York City, graduated at fifteen, was I rejected by Williams College? Why have I rarely had a close male friend who was a WASP? When I reflect on some of these things now, I experience a certain bitterness I was never in touch with until my forties. Yes, it did occur to me when I was at college and medical school that some of my classmates were snubbing me and the Jews, but I took that as a matter of course and thought my own exclusion was insignificant compared to that endured by my Jewish or black friends. I realize now that it was not insignificant. Of course, the hurt of being snubbed was made worse by my father's and grandfather's negative view of themselves for being Italian, not being one of the chosen people or possessing a great and noble heritage. Attilio always spoke of the other doctors in the hospital and of his non-Italian patients and acquaintances with awe. He worried

72

about his lack of culture and fine manners, though in fact his behavior was the model of decorum. He did not feel he belonged on a podium, and was terrified of making public speeches or appearances, and he was uncomfortable when in a group of wealthy or well-bred people. This discomfort was accentuated in my childhood because his sister married a man who became a multimillionaire in the midst of the depression. If I lived in Versailles, *they* lived in the Vatican Museum! Their ceilings were painted like the Sistine Chapel. They had a cook, a chauffeur, an upstairs maid, a downstairs maid, limousines, and God knows what else in their city palace and country estates. They were in the Social Register, and gave huge parties with the cream of New York society that I attended throughout my childhood. Their friends included Gatti-Casazza, general manager of the Metropolitan Opera, Cornelia Otis Skinner, Luigi Barzini, and many upper-class WASPs. Instead of feeling that I was a part of this social set, I always saw myself as a poor relation, an immigrant invited to their palace. Why was this so, since I was hardly poor and had been exposed to as much good and expensive education and culture as almost any child of that era? The answer is that I must have incorporated that attitude from my father. Furthermore, the real existence of discrimination against Italo-Americans, even though it was fairly subtle, must have enhanced my feeling of being different and "less than." Do I feel that now? Yes, up to a point. I do not *think* it, intellectually, but I still feel it, though not in the way Attilio did. I joke a great deal about it, and like to show off the largest and funniest collection of Italian jokes of anyone I know. Is this a way of coping with my feelings of inferiority? I am certain it is. Some of my Jewish friends call me a "dumb wop." I laugh, never resenting this in the least, but at the same time I am sure I must be covering up something that was deeply buried until rather recently—something whose influence I have heretofore neglected to consider.

I was going to write that I did not perceive myself as having much of my father's tendency toward braggadocio. Now I am not so sure that is true. Women are often annoyed with me for boasting of my sexual exploits. I used to think this was a tongue-in-cheek act of mine, that I was actually caricaturing myself. Now I am not so sure. My uncle Jerry, cousin Aldo, and aunt Peggy certainly enjoyed telling about their amorous adventures, and Domenico probably did the same, though never within my hearing. For the moment let's leave the question open whether I too am a braggart, an exhibitionist, and a charismatic showman.

Attilio was certainly all of those things—a narcissist in the worst sense of the word. He used to brag about his climb from rags to riches, and tell dramatic stories such as how he walked on a snowy night from barge to barge on the East River to save the life of a child and then refused to allow the family to pay him. Or how a patient in his ward at Bellevue had been seen by six different big-shot WASP professors of medicine who had missed the diagnosis completely. My father walked into the ward, took one look at the patient from across the room, and made the correct diagnosis from the doorway without even talking to or examining the patient. I don't know if I have the ability to keep an audience spellbound with such tales, but I do know that at least to my secret Self, and perhaps to my most intimate friends, I readily admit that I sometimes fancy myself the best psychoanalyst in New York, that I believe myself especially brilliant at diagnosis, and that I have often treated patients for years without charging them.

Perhaps I internalized some of my father's more desirable traits as well as his tendency to boast about them. In truth, his fees were lower than anyone else's of comparable stature, and I pride myself on this. Money was never an important consideration in his attitude toward medicine or patients, nor has it been one of mine. He really was a very fine doctor who worked extraordinarily hard and studied constantly to absorb every new advance in his field, as do I. Do I brag about it? Well, not the way he did, by delivering long soliloquies of self-praise to his family or to a captive audience of unfortunate dinner guests. So possibly I have attained a little more "class" because of my fine education and my social conditioning. But am I not now showing off in these pages? For I love to exhibit myself in my writings, my teaching, my lectures, and my television appearances. I am a tremendous ham who likes to think he can roll them in the aisles with one-liners and Italian jokes. When I was younger I could tell jokes practically around the clock without repeating myself. And I must admit that in college and medical school I held the students transfixed as they listened to blow-by-blow accounts of my sexual conquests. (At times I may have exaggerated some of them just a wee bit.) Yes, I must plead guilty to having incorporated my father's tendency to be a show-off. This may be difficult to believe, *but until the very moment of writing down these words I did not know that and I would never have been able to admit it.* I feel almost relieved by the confession, for I possess the same combination of self-effacement and braggadocio as my father.

But the alternation of extreme pride and extreme humility was only one of the many elements that existed in my relationship to my father. One of the most obvious and upsetting factors was the rivalry he felt toward me and my younger brother, Charlie, vis-à-vis my mother. Michelangelo had believed his older brother (or sister, depending on the version of the story) had been favored over him, and he was jealous of both his sons, thinking his wife preferred them to him. Attilio was jealous of his older brother, Beniamino, whom he thought his mother, Bettina, loved more. And Attilio also felt my mother favored me and my brother, Charlie, over him. Attilio constantly denigrated Beniamino, and this was an important force in driving Beniamino to suicide. Attilio competed with me savagely and tried in every way to destroy me from my earliest childhood on. In attempting to kill myself, I was on one level complying with his not-so-unconscious wish. And, unfortunately, I always believed my former wife preferred my son, Bobby, to me, so I competed with him. My son's suicidal preoccupations in his young adult life were without doubt influenced by my feelings toward him. Family patterns are repeated from generation to generation—but we will talk about this subject later. At this point, though it pains me, I must return to Attilio and me. Again I hesitate. It is a story I know too well; I have told it too often to too many analysts. And yet the emotion lives on in me. I repeat it in my behavior and in my feelings toward my son and my stepson. Why can't I exorcise this dybbuk? Why do I sigh and fall into despair as I prepare to reopen the subject? I still sometimes feel like the father whom I hated and who hated me.

My first image that involves my father is of myself as a little boy of five, six, or seven. After my father had finished seeing his patients during his morning hours of eleven to one, he would rush upstairs to have a five-minute lunch so he could be at Bellevue, University, or Columbus Hospital to make his rounds. I was always terrified when I heard him approaching, storming up the four stories of the spiral staircase to the kitchen. He would be yelling and shouting that his nurse-secretary was an idiot, his patients were ignorant louts who didn't follow his advice, the housekeeper hadn't cleaned the office properly, the food wasn't on the table on time, or even that the shades on the kitchen windows were not exactly level. He did all the work, made all the money, had all the responsibility, and no one else did anything right or even appreciated him. I knew he would be there for only five or ten minutes. If I could avoid him then, I wouldn't have to see him at all, so I would try to be in the bathroom, huddling terrified, while he ate in the kitchen with his mother and his wife hovering over him. I usually succeeded, but sometimes he was too fast for me. Then he would growl at me for not sitting up straight at table or for being in his way, for he didn't want me to come between him and his women. He didn't hit me—perhaps he had had enough of that himself from Michelangelo—but he was always angry with me. He never smiled at me or said a kind word. He lived in that palace for forty years without knowing where the glasses or the silver-ware were kept, and he never bought a bottle of milk or a loaf of bread, considering it undignified for a doctor, a man of stature, to be seen carrying a brown paper sack on the street. The only bag he ever carried was his little black doctor's satchel—the mark of his eminence. (Italians worship their doctors as demigods.) Once a patient had the temerity to ask my father what he had prescribed for him. He was so insulted at the patient's "questioning his judgment" that he had the man ejected.

When I was five I came down with scarlet fever. My father had been given an experimental drug that had not yet been tried on human subjects and which he was supposed to use on his ward patients at Bellevue. He said that since he was a humanitarian, he would make the supreme sacrifice of trying it out on me instead of on his patients. I almost died. At that moment I knew that my father was not only being a hero, but that he also wanted to kill me. He didn't succeed then, just by chance, as I didn't succeed later. That same year I had to have my tonsils removed. I remember very clearly that I was certain my father and mother had decided to do away with me and I was being taken to the doctor for that purpose. And in fact I was correctly reading the unconscious mind of my father. In the case of Attilio, his wish was not clouded by any great amount of repression. Out of all the doctors he knew, he selected an alcoholic incompetent to operate on me. Throughout my life, when doctors have looked at my throat, they say that the surgeon was a butcher who took out half of it along with the tonsils. And, of course, I have been subject to sore throats since the operation.

Two years later, when I was seven, I underwent another terrifying operation—a hernia repair and a circumcision—right at the worst time—in the middle of my Oedipal period, during which castration anxiety was the most intense. Twenty years later, in analysis, I reported a dream in which my father was the surgeon who was doing my inguinal hernia repair. The knife slipped and he cut off my testicles. I .had a totally unnecessary vasectomy seven or eight years ago. Why? Was I obeying my father's wishes, just as I was when I tried suicide? I think so: There is no clear, rational explanation for the vasectomy.

Attilio castrated me in every possible way. He either ignored or derided my not inconsiderable academic accomplishments, for unlike Michelangelo, he saw me as a rival, never as his extension. Mother used to tell me that he praised my achievements to others, but that was to aggrandize himself. He never complimented me for being the first in my class or for graduating from high school at fifteen or for winning an honorary scholarship at Harvard when I was sixteen (I was too wealthy for a paid one). All he did was complain about how much it was costing him to send me to Harvard. At that time tuition was $400 a year and he was making $40,000 without heavy taxes. I was merely a burden to him—someone who came between him and his wife. In fact, I tried to come between them literally. I remember between the ages of five and nine trying to convince my mother to divorce him and stay with me. He must also have been threatened by the possibility of my spoiling his heroic image by outdoing him, and he tried to ruin all my achievements. When I had my first paper published in the very prestigious *Archives of Neurology* at the age of twenty-seven, his only comment was that it was only three pages long. He never had a paper published in his entire life; I have published more than forty. He never wrote a book in his whole life; this is my eighth. I want to beat out that son-of-a-bitch. I want to shove my success and my superiority in his face. He shoved his in my face all my life, the bastard! I hate him. The only way I could get to him or hurt him was to beat him at his own game—to be a more respected, more successful doctor than he was. I have done it and it feels good.

When I obtained my specialty boards in psychiatry at twenty-nine—probably one of the youngest doctors who has ever done that—I went to see Attilio and told him about it.

"So now you have a piece of paper that says you're a psychiatrist. So what! All you know is a lot of stuff in books. I have been—and I am—a better psychiatrist than you'll ever be! *I* know how to handle patients. *I* know psychology. *You* don't know how to deal with people. All you know is a lot of nonsense from books that doesn't mean anything. Besides, psychiatrists are the garbage collectors of medicine. If a doctor can't make a living doing anything else, he goes into psychiatry and works at a state hospital. He gets three meals a day and a place to stay. And you can't tell the psychiatrists from the patients without a score card."

There was nothing I could or did say.

Thanks, Pop. Thanks for the congratulations and the support. I did not work at a state hospital. I became a psychoanalyst. The cream of the crop of doctors become psychoanalysts, not the dregs. Drop dead. But you already have. Or have you really? Are you dead or do you still live on, in my head and in my body? Am I being the same bastard to my son and my stepson that you were with me? Oh, I'm a little more subtle than you were. You weren't exactly a master of diplomacy. But perhaps that made it easier to deal with you than it does for them to deal with me. Why did I take into me the parts of you I hated the most? Even when I understand them so well, why can't I get rid of them? My bondage to you seems interminable. I thought I had gotten rid of you when you died, but now I see that I haven't. Is there anything I don't know? Twelve analysts in individual therapy and fifteen or twenty years in "leaderless" groups, five times a week, in which I did my best to be an equal patient have not gotten you out of me. Today I am going to a peer group of male analysts. I am trying to find a father there, but I am—as usual—becoming everyone else's father. Some of these guys are as smart and as talented as I am, but I am stronger than all of them. I had to learn how to defeat the strongest, meanest man in the world, who was out to kill me from the beginning. He was Muhammad Ali, Jack Dempsey, Joe Louis. How can I find a man who is so strong that I cannot defeat him? How can I find a man whom I can look up to as *my* figurative father, someone stronger than I, who knows more, in whose hands I can put myself, whom I can trust to know the answers? I outdid Michelangelo and Attilio. Perhaps Domenico could have been my spiritual father. He was strong; I could look up to him. But he wasn't around enough. I still yearn for and need fathering. The only two times I have experienced it in my adult life were when I was on a tour with a tour leader who was wise and responsible. On one such trip I was so taken with him that my wife was, correctly, jealous. He gave me such a feeling of comfort for allowing myself to be in his hands that I gave him a fifty-dollar tip. Pop—you archetypical pop—you man I can idealize and look up to—where are you for me? I have been that figure for so many men—younger and older than myself. After completing my basic training in mortal combat with my father, I was the leader, the head of the club in first grade, the captain of the stickball team, the director of the clinic and the analytic institute, the teacher, the role model for others. Who will be the role model for me? Once I thought I had found a man in an allied profession. I believed him to be ethical and wise. A big mistake. I quickly discovered to my disillusionment that he was devious and shallow, and his books were written by ghost-writers. He was no one for me to idealize. Then two things happened: He betrayed me in my attempt to gain political power in his organization and he simultaneously began to look to me as *his* ideal. I sometimes think I have found a male role-model, but I often end up outdoing these hoped-for father-figures, and the story sometimes finishes by their looking up to me. I have an archetypical father whom I idealize at this moment, but as usual I am beginning to detect his feet of clay. For me, and for most men, idols cannot have feet of clay. Who can be my hero? At times certain sports figures. Once, between marriages, I considered leaving my estate to Y.A. Tittle, the New York Giants quarterback, because he had given me more pleasure than all the women in the world put together. When Y.A. was running the Giants, I knew they were in good hands. Y.A. was stronger and smarter and braver than I was. If I only could have known him or someone like him personally. . . . But perhaps if I had I might have noticed his imperfections and he would have become my patient or my son.

We men have such a hard time getting fathering! In retrospect I realize that alongside my hatred of my father I also idealized him in many ways. There was a real split in my feelings. I thought he was extraordinary and perfect and brilliant and I wanted to become a great doctor like he was. But he did not carry through his end of the bargain: *He should have loved me, praised me, and admired my accomplishments.* He should have seen me as a chip off the old block. Instead, he looked on me as an enemy, a rival for his mother and my mother as well

80

as the esteem of the medical profession. Idealization between father and son has to be reciprocal for it to work. A father has to be proud of his son, show him that he is, tell him that he is—and mean it! My father couldn't do any of those things with me. And in turn I have difficulty doing any of them very well with my son or my stepson.

All my life I had a fantasy that Attilio, "Pop" as I called him, would one day put his arm around my shoulders and call me "Richard." I did not even dare imagine he would tell me he loved me. He never called me Richard. He never called me anything. Once, to give him his due, and for reasons I never understood, in 1933, when I was ten years old, he took me to Chicago to see the World's Fair. I remember feeling hot, flushed, and excited as we left in a sleeper from Grand Central. It was my first trip out of New York, the first time I had ever gone anywhere alone with my father. He had never taken me to a restaurant or a ball game or a movie alone, though perhaps he, I, and Mother had gone out to a movie or a restaurant as a trio a very few times. I do not recall the train trip except that it was enchanting, with cheerful black porters, beautiful dining cars, and luxurious sleepers. When we arrived in Chicago, in line with the family policy of business before pleasure, my father and I visited the Catholic Hospital—the counterpart of one of his New York hospitals, the one where he was director of medicine. I vaguely remember seeing the nuns. That night I felt sick and hot. My father examined me. I had a full-blown case of measles. We slept over in the hotel that night, but had to leave the next morning without having seen the World's Fair. For years I felt terribly guilty, thinking that I should have known I was falling ill and should have postponed the trip. That was the first and last time my father tried to share an activity with me. And *I* had messed it up by getting sick. *I* had disappointed *him. I* had ruined the only vacation he had tried to take in thirty years. Oh, yes—my father worked seven days a week, including office hours on Sunday, for thirty years without taking even one day off. I tried to compete with that mark too, and was doing pretty well at it for a while. I still boast about how hard I work. When I am not seeing patients on weekends, I write. But thank goodness I have a few too many Candela genes to allow me to break my father's record, even though I approach it. In thirty years I have hardly missed a working day—a nonvacation day— because of illness, even when I had viral hepatitis. I certainly internalized that part of Pop. The Chicago trip was a disaster, but I doubt that its success would have made any difference. My father, even when he was not growling and putting me down, was so stiff and businesslike that nothing very much fun could have happened. And, almost a half century later, my son and I went to Chicago to be on the Phil Donahue TV show and talk about father-son relationships. Luckily this vacation was not a disaster. It brought me much closer to my son—at least temporarily.

When I was forty-seven and was seeing my twelfth and last analyst, she thought that perhaps if I had a session in her presence with my mother and father and tried to tell them what it was that I wanted from them, it might help. I was not sure they would consent, but because in some ways they considered themselves socially inferior, they tended to submit to authority. My therapist was a psychiatric social worker analyst, so my father had a few misgivings about her as an authority. But since *I* was an MD and *I* had chosen her, he was willing to go along with her advice. My recollection of the session, even though it was only about nine years ago, is very hazy, probably because nothing important emotionally happened. The analyst felt a bit awkward, as did I and my parents. (Many psychotherapeutic situations such as psychodramas, encounter groups, gestalt therapy, bioenergetic therapy, and primal scream therapy suffer from the same strained atmosphere. They are staged, and even if something that appears to be genuine feeling results, its reality is doubtful.) I began by mumbling something about my wanting Mother to say she loved me. She said of course she did. I believe she meant it, but I didn't believe her. Then I asked my father to say he loved me and to put his arm around me. He did so, awkwardly, as if given an order by a drill sergeant. I clearly remember what he said: "Of course we love you!" He couldn't force himself to say *he* loved me. One thing about Pop; he was straight. And where it really counts. I am straight too. I pride myself on being honest—without exception—in intimate situations and with patients, even though I can be political and pragmatic when necessary. My father couldn't. I consider my manipulative ability to be an excellent ego function. So I took in my father's straightness along with his inability to love his son fully.

I tried one more confrontation with him. I knew he would die shortly; his doctor had given him a maximum of six months. At the time many of my patients and colleagues were learning about family therapy, one of whose cardinal rules is to try to have an honest confrontation with your real parents. I fought the idea insofar as I was concerned, but I agreed with it professionally and had actually pushed some of my patients and colleagues into such meetings. I had even agreed several years before that if one of my patients would dare to confront her father, I would confront mine. She did so, with positive results. That was the first time in my life I ever welshed on a bet. Because she went on vacation, I managed to get away with it. This time I couldn't wriggle out of it since I was in several groups and they contained many therapists, and they just wouldn't let me off the hook. So I went to my parents' apartment (they had moved from Versailles) for my customary Saturday-afternoon visit. I was fifty-three and Pop was eighty-four. I told Mom I wanted to speak to Pop alone, and she acquiesced in her usual submissive way. I had no script. I planned to go in, start talking without prior rehearsal, and see what the result would be.

"Pop," I began, "there's one thing I've always felt disappointed about. You never gave me enough recognition for my professional accomplishments. You never seemed to appreciate my books, my papers, my teaching or my practice."

"No, I can't say that I really did appreciate those things," he said with his usual candor. "Actually, the only way you could have gotten recognition for your work from me is if you'd become professor of psychiatry at Harvard."

83

"Professor of psychiatry at Harvard! I wouldn't take that job for a million a year! What I do is infinitely more creative. And the teaching I do is with seasoned professionals, not with young medical students."

"Well, that's the way I feel about it."

I don't think the conversation went much further. I had asked Pop for what I wanted and once more had been turned down. The talk had a great impact on me, for I believe that in accepting the fact there was no possible way I could please him, I had at last partially laid to rest some of my compulsive strivings to gain his and Michelangelo's approval. I became more tolerant of my mistakes, and was less anxious to be a superstar in the office, on the tennis court, and in bed. In many ways I had been living on the edge of a cliff. Almost every major move I made had been related directly or indirectly with this need for his approval. The confrontation helped me. Am I writing this book for Pop's approval, even posthumous? I don't think so. I believe I am writing it because I have a great deal to say. I'll be pleased if I get approval for it, but I am not doing it for that reason. I am writing this book not for my father, but for myself and my readers.

Attilio's professional commitment was, to me, the most precious and important aspect of him that I internalized. I believe today that through my hatred of him I took from him perhaps the most unique gift anyone could give me. When I consider my friends, colleagues, and relatives, I see few who are as committed to their work as Attilio was—and I am. Attilio worked all day and studied all night to get through his high school equivalency test, the College of Pharmacy, and medical school. He studied and taught constantly after he started his practice. He was always available to his patients, and often went out in the middle of cold winter nights to walk up tenement stairways to see patients. I too can be seen by my patients any hour of any day. I make house calls, and always visit patients when they are in the hospital whether for psychiatric or other ills. I constantly read, write, study, and teach, and spend a good part of my weekends and vacations studying and writing. Most of the psychotherapists I

84

know are honest, ethical, and care about their patients, but few resemble Attilio or myself.

It sometimes happens that when I like a therapist personally or recognize a great talent, I at first tend to see him or her in terms of my own image, then I realize that the personal dedication that exists in me is lacking. For commitment to a cause is perhaps the greatest gift of all. People who are solely dedicated to pleasure, to self-aggrandizement, or even to another person lead shallow, unstable, and generally ungratifying lives. For one to experience a sense of wholeness, one must surrender either to God or to his or her own idiosyncratic view of God, such as a cause. A cause may or may not be socially useful; it may even be destructive. De Sade consecrated himself to an ideal of self-expression that went beyond his particular sexual perversion. Attilio's cause was not necessarily that of helping suffering humanity; it was more narcissistic. He did not really care for his patients as individuals—quite the contrary. He wanted to be the finest possible doctor as *he* defined the term. That meant sparing no effort in the accumulation and dissemination of knowledge in his field and also being of the utmost personal service in his clinical practice. It meant sacrificing everyone and everything, including his family, to this high ideal. When Attilio gave me, his son, the untested medicine for scarlet fever which almost killed me, he was not only trying to kill me. He, like the biblical Abraham, was willing to sacrifice his son to something greater than himself. The story of Abraham and Isaac is a very important one for me, as it would have been for him, for Attilio's surrender to his personal God—his profession—transcended all other obligations, including his own life and the lives of his "loved ones." When, as a physician, I entered wards filled with patients who had dangerous communicable diseases such as tuberculosis, meningitis, encephalitis, or polio, it never even occurred to me to be concerned about my own safety, just as during the terrible influenza epidemic that followed World War I, my father fearlessly treated his patients.

Between the ages of seven and twelve, I found God too—the Catholic God. I prayed to him. I never violated a commandment of the Church. I made sacrifices and even endured pain to ennoble me and enhance my faith. But when I was twelve, I met a number of Jewish classmates who were freethinkers, and who appealed to my intellect. This weakened my faith, a process that continued in high school and college. From ages twelve to eighteen I had no commitment to any specific cause. Then, like Attilio, I began to have faith in being a doctor, and shortly thereafter I found my secular calling—psychoanalysis. It is not just my profession; it is my calling, my commitment, the core of my existence, and I feel sorry for those persons who do not have a similar calling. Callings are not necessarily altruistic, though others may benefit from them, as they did from Attilio's dedication. De Sade's philosophical commitment was to the ultimate expression of his desire even if this resulted in his or in other people's deaths. The Marquis has always been one of my favorite philosophers because of his refusal to compromise. However, unlike his, the commitment I have harms few persons aside from my family, when I neglect them, is socially acceptable, and provides me with a comfortable life-style. And even if there were no rewards to being a psychoanalyst, if for example I lived in a Communist country where this profession is banned, I would either try to flee or practice underground. Because psychoanalysis is the most idiosyncratic part of my Self. People who have a Self that has not been crushed by outside force, who are fortunate enough to know something of that Self, and who are able to surrender to some idea or ideal that transcends the Self in the *narrow* sense of the word, are to be envied though they may not lead conventionally happy lives; may not be loved, appreciated, or admired. No one loved Attilio. He may at times have been appreciated by a patient, but practically never by anyone close to him. He had no real friends. He happened to be admired by many for his dedication. I am lucky. I have not had a happy life, but I have been loved and admired by many people. In the past I often failed to recognize love and admiration, but today I am sometimes able to do so, and to accept them.

Attilio, despite his commitment, dedication, and the admiration he received constantly even from his enemies, was a bitter, angry, self-pitying man. And so was I until my late forties. Commitment is a wonderful quality, but it can coexist with masochism, which was the very last discovery I made about my father. I had always viewed him as strong, resolute, dedicated, destructive, and sadistic. I saw only his power and his ability to destroy me. It was only during the last few months of his long life that I got fully in touch with the fact that he always experienced himself as a frightened, inferior, socially inept immigrant boy who was an outcast in his social group. He was terrified of being humiliated, and thought his haughty façade was fake and could be pierced at any moment by some superior, more intelligent, more polished and educated person who could reduce him to the eight-year-old greenhorn who had arrived in America at the turn of the century. When I saw this true picture of my father on the verge of his death, I had more compassion for him, and I made myself constantly available to him, even emotionally, during his last six months. But more importantly, I began to realize that I had and have internalized the exact same image of myself! The quality in me that most annoys people is my self-effacement, which coexists with self-aggrandizement. But my self-aggrandizement is more conscious and more ego-syntonic than his—more under the control of my Self. I am usually more charming and less offensive than my father was. The self-effacement and self-pity were qualities I did not recognize in him till the end, and still have not totally exorcized from myself. I was in my men's peer group recently when I was made radiantly happy by an occurrence. One of the group members said he believed my joy because my face was transfigured by it. But my voice was sad and dead and gave out a very different message, one of self-commiseration and despair. That melancholy voice had several origins—my mother, my two suicidal uncles, my suicidal cousin—but an important source was my father. Attilio never once renounced his self-pity. When he was in his thirties, a heart specialist, he told us he had a heart block that would impair his life. A lie. As a specialist, he knew the block was congenital and asymptomatic and would have no effect on his work or his longevity. Yet he used it to extract sympathy from his family and, even worse, from himself. And sometimes I imagine myself to be just a poor little immigrant boy who will never be accepted by the right people, thus lying to myself like my father did and using that nonsense to manipulate people or myself into feeling sorry for me. Why, logically, should anybody feel sorry for me? I have had some bad moments, but today I have my commitment; I have a good life; many people not only admire me but love me; I am writing this book, the quintessence of everything creative I ever wanted to do; I have a marvelous practice; I head a psychoanalytic institute in which I teach what I think needs to be taught and whose disciples listen to me. Yet I cannot altogether rid myself of that whining, sad, self-pitying part of Attilio that lives on in me.

A friend in my men's group said I reminded him of a recent Steuben Day parade on Fifth Avenue. The German-Americans were enjoying themselves, but beneath they were still the same stolid, gloomy robots they had been brought up to be. He wept uncontrollably at this parade, not out of high spirits but over a joyless part of himself. He did not weep at the Columbus Day parade, or at the Puerto Rican celebration, or on St. Patrick's day. He also wept for me, for beneath my *joie de vivre* and appreciation of life, there remain remnants of the self-pity of Attilio and others together with the anguished child whose real Self was so damaged by Michelangelo that it despaired of ever fully emerging. I am fighting very hard to get these parts of Attilio and Michelangelo out of my head. After all, our feeling of well-being is based much less on what is going on in the external world than what is happening in our internal world. So if I can exclude from my internal world the negative parts of Attilio, Michelangelo, Jerry, and Beniamino. plus the sad child *I* was, I will be OK. If I can be the good parts of Domenico, Jerry, and Peggy, and even those parts of Michelangelo and Attilio that were committed—albeit never to joy—then I will be OK. Sometimes I am those good parts, at least for a while; sometimes the other parts that populate my mind and my Self take over and I go under again. It is a battle, but I won't feel sorry for myself as Attilio did and as, truthfully, I frequently did until a few years ago.

My internal world is much more difficult for me to manage than my external one. Attilio was a pretty good model for managing the external world, as were Michelangelo and Domenico. But my father and paternal grandfather were not good models for managing their internal worlds. And obviously neither were Jerry and Beniamino and even some of my later Jewish models. I almost need to be my own model, my own "father," for that. I have found few men in or out of my family or my profession who successfully manage their internal world. I am looking for a model or a composite among my men's group, but so far none has fully appeared. Even older men need a father image. Perhaps I should put an ad in *The Village Voice* or *The Saturday Review: WANTED!—one symbolic father figure on whom I can model myself so I can have a happy, peaceful, joyous inner life. All applicants will be seriously considered. . . .*

I am tired of being my own father, being forced to construct my own model, but I will try not to say, "It isn't fair. Feel sorry for me."

Throughout much of my childhood I had the fantasy that Attilio was not really my father. My father, I thought, was his brother Beniamino. I imagined that somehow my father had adopted me because Beniamino wasn't well off enough to care for me. I recall going to Beniamino's drugstore in the Village. Despite my father's contempt for his brother's contaminating the profession of pharmacy with commercialism, Beniamino had installed a soda fountain in his drugstore. My visits there were another of those magic moments of childhood. On the counter were glass urns filled with leeches, weird, crawly monsters that in the late twenties and early thirties were still used by some doctors in America to purify blood through bloodletting. I, as a privileged character, was allowed to go behind the drug counter into the sanctum sanctorum of the back room. There were thousands of wooden drawers which I now occasionally see in antique shops, and huge brass mortars and pestles and a stepladder for reaching the boxes high up. This was the same back room in which Beniamino was found dead quite a few years later after having swallowed poison from one of those many little wooden boxes.

Beniamino was shorter and rounder than Attilio. He was soft and kind and he smiled a lot. I felt very odd in his presence. He seemed happy to see me and apparently wanted to make me happy. He would fuss over me in ways I had never experienced at home or anywhere else from a man. The beautiful, shiny new soda fountain was tended by an "American" (that is, non-Italian) man wearing a cap. Beniamino always insisted that I sit on one of the big stools and order whatever I wanted. I could never comprehend this. Michelangelo and Attilio had taught me never to ask for or even take what you wanted. I always protested to Beniamino that his offer was too expensive or that I had just finished eating. Luckily, his insistence eventually overcame my objections. I first used to order a Black and White Soda—an ambrosial concoction that I had never tasted anywhere else. Later I switched to a Rootbeer Float, which the soda man called a Brown Cow. I enjoyed my visits to Uncle Ben's drugstore, but I always felt I was doing something very wicked by taking advantage of his generosity. I still feel that way today when I buy something for myself. In 1977 I visited China, where I spent over $700 on jade and other presents for my wife and friends. I saw a pigskin jacket for $45 that I really loved and went back to look at it five or six times, trying to talk myself into buying it. Just before the plane left, I finally did buy it, using the argument that it would cost $200 to $300 in New York. On the way to the airport I was besieged by an attack from my internalized Attilio and Michelangelo. How could I have been so frivolous and self-indulgent? It was exactly the same way I felt about the Brown Cow at Uncle Ben's soda fountain.

The other strong memory I have about Uncle Ben was his playing Scopa, an Italian card game, with my father at home. They played for blood. It seemed that everyone was rooting for my father; even Uncle Ben's wife and daughters appeared to be against him. My father used to take vicious jabs at Ben for his stupidity at cards and for his inability to make a financial success of his modest drugstore. Uncle Ben was a nice guy. If someone couldn't pay for the medicine, he would give it away. I certainly have internalized that part of Uncle Ben. In family systems theory, there is often one family member who is assigned the role of scapegoat. Ben was that in his nuclear family, as I was in mine. I secretly rooted for Ben, and occasionally was rewarded, for Scopa is a game of chance more than skill. Sometimes I would play Scopa with Ben or Domenico, but never with my father. Attilio could hardly bear losing to Ben, and he certainly couldn't bear losing to me. The atmosphere at the kitchen table when Scopa was played was charged with my father's hostility toward his brother. Ben was his mother's, Bettina's, favorite; that was obvious, and despite the fact that Attilio was living with Bettina, was supporting her, was a doctor rather than a druggist, a success rather than a failure, Bettina had a soft spot in her heart for Ben that she did not have for Attilio. I know how Attilio felt. I surpassed my own brother, Charlie, professionally and financially. I live in New York and visit my mother weekly; Charlie lives in Rome and rarely sees her. Yet it is obvious to everyone, or at least to me, that she loves Charlie and not me. The reason is even the same. I am too often brusque, surly, and angry vis-à-vis my mother. So was Attilio. Charlie is sweet and kind to her, as Beniamino was to Bettina. But my envy of my brother's favored position in Mother's eyes is so infuriating that I rarely can face it squarely. It seems so unjust. I worked so hard, achieved so much, have been such a dutiful son! I manage her affairs. I make my weekly visits. And Charlie comes from Rome once every two years and is not only given a hero's welcome, but evokes a responsive gleam in my mother's eye that I have never been able to. Once, when Charlie was in his early twenties, my wife flirted with him—very innocently I am sure—in my presence. I fell into such a depression that I could hardly get out of bed for two days. At the time I didn't know what had hit me. It became clear to me shortly thereafter that my rage at my wife/mother for "favoring" my brother was so enormous that it had to be entirely directed against myself. Otherwise I suppose I might have felt like killing them both.

91

Attilio's rage was not completely directed against himself. Even though he was self-destructive to a point, it filled the room during the card games with Beniamino—the identical rage that he had toward anyone who came between himself and his wife and/or mother. It existed toward his father because of his relationship to his mother, Bettina; toward Ben, who came between him and Bettina; toward me and my brother for coming between him and my mother; toward my son, who was his wife, Eleanor's, favorite; even toward my mother's mother and her sisters, who came between him and his wife. And, as I admit, in similar situations I harbor the same kind of anger, though fortunately or unfortunately it is turned more against myself.

Poor Beniamino suffered from Attilio's persecutions too long. It was his particular bad luck to be a financial failure, and he had to be bailed out repeatedly by my father. He desperately needed my father, so he could never fight back—not even in the games of Scopa. When by chance he would win, he did not boast about it. When Attilio won, he strutted about and explained to all how his brilliant card playing had snatched victory out of the jaws of defeat. Uncle Ben's fear of and dependence on my father probably made him snatch defeat out of the jaws of victory. Just as I internalized my rage at my wife and brother for two days, Ben internalized his hatred of Attilio for decades. So early one morning, in the back of the drugstore, he took the poison that relieved him of the pain of all those years of inner-directed fury.

A few years later, when I was interning on a salary of $40 a month, forcing me to live with my father, I too was in a position in which I had to swallow Attilio's insults, humiliating jabs, and castrating remarks. I too needed him to support me financially. He knew I was helpless and dependent on him, so like a shark that smelled blood, just as he had with Beniamino, he moved in for the kill. I had at that point two good role models to follow—Jerry and Beniamino. I knew what I had to do. Early one morning at my room in the interns' quarters of the city hospital, I took enough pills to kill a horse. Only a miracle saved me. Was I more fortunate than Jerry and

Beniamino? Today I think I was. Generally, I think I am. I have learned to handle my rage better than Jerry and Beniamino did. But most of all, I have never allowed myself to become too dependent on anyone—certainly not financially, but not even emotionally or sexually. Sometimes that has kept me from experiencing a deep intensity of intimacy, but it has also kept me alive. For like Jerry and Ben, I would rather be dead than live in terrible psychic or physical pain. I know I have the comforting option of suicide. If things become too bad or too painful, I can easily end it all. Killing myself doesn't take any courage; staying alive does. The last few years the pain has been shorter-lived and less shattering, but it would be foolish for me to say it is never there, or even that some days it isn't terribly intense. It is almost always brought on by some external event that triggers a drop in my self-esteem—sometimes by some real or imagined abandonment. But it does not cause the same disintegration of my Self that it used to, except perhaps fleetingly. And I seem to be able to put myself together faster and better. If not, I can go for help from analysts or friends when I need it. Also, my pleasures and joy are more intense. Domenico is present more, giving me sensual pleasures—oral, visual, and sexual. And Michelangelo is there too, giving me intellectual pleasures. On balance, I do not think of suicide very often or for very long. Beniamino's life was not like mine. He was an economic failure, sneered at by his wife and daughters. He was castrated and humiliated by his successful brother, on whom he was financially dependent. He did not have the strength to run away. I think he did the only thing he could when he killed himself.

Now, instead of suicide, when I feel myself disintegrating, I have internalized my twelve analysts and other supportive figures to sustain me, comfort me, and say to me, "There, there now, everything will be all right, Richard." And when my internal supports do not adequately sustain, I am free enough to go to several good friends who love me and on whose total support I can count: If my inside people can't put Humpty-Dumpty together again, my outside people can. Poor Ben had neither. Thank goodness I do.

When Attilio died, I did not shed a tear for him, nor have I since. On the one hand I felt free of him, and went out and bought myself a bronze African tribal chief's throne for $5,000, by far the most money I have ever spent on a piece of art. I truly felt throughout my whole being that "The King is dead; long live the King." On the other hand I felt good about the fact that I had worked out many of my feelings about him over his last months. I had felt compassion for him. I had given up my vacations and been available to him physically and emotionally. I had been helpful to him in communicating with his doctors. It was a strange but gratifying feeling for me to know that I had been a really good, understanding, and helpful son to him during his last months. What made it even more important to me was that I had not done it for a moment out of a sense of guilt or duty, but because I genuinely wanted to. When he died, I did not feel a loss or a sense of mourning, but neither did I feel guilty or remiss. His dying and my response to it had been an important and maturing process for me. Also, in dealing with his mortality, I had to come to grips with my own. I could no longer consider myself fifty-three going on thirty-five. I did not feel old, but I stopped denying the fact of my aging. Today I experience myself as a man of my age. I had basically felt my father would never die, and I would never die. My dealing directly in an emotionally involved way with his dying helped me divest myself of my denial of my own mortality.

# 5

# Identifications in My Extended Family— Roberto and Aldo

There were two other men in my family, Robert and Aldo, who were important during my childhood and later. They were both first cousins on my father's side of the family. Writing about Aldo troubles me, so I will begin with Robert.

He was the son of my father's older brother, Antonio, who spent most of his life in Laviano. Robert had come to America with his father and mother, but for some strange and unexplained reason had been left in the care of his and my grandparents, Michelangelo and Bettina, when he was four. His own parents returned to Italy and he never saw any members of his nuclear family again. He was about ten years younger than my father, and was brought up in the home as if he were the younger brother. I knew little of his history in the family, but I am sure that being deserted by his parents and left to the devices of Michelangelo (as essentially I was) was hardly the best thing that could have happened to him. Probably with great wisdom and courage, Robert left New York in his teens and settled in California, where he completed law school and became a successful lawyer. He bought a house in Benedict Canyon that was remarkably similar to his birth-place in Laviano—situated on a mountain and constructed on several levels. He had no conscious memory, I am sure, of his birthplace, which he left as a baby; nonetheless he managed to return home figuratively if not literally.

Robert was a romantic figure to me. He never returned to Italy, but he would breeze in and out of New York every few years, having driven across the country and picked up a new car in Detroit en route. I remember his wearing a 1930s wide-brimmed hat at a jaunty angle. Robert in the course of his life had three wives. This was a scandal in the family; it also made him in my eyes one of the glamorous Hollywood set, adven-turous, traveling at will, and changing mates when they ceased to please him. Robert was rather short and dark. His mates were all tall, blond, and Nordic-looking. Robert would say that all he needed to make him happy was a million dollars and a blonde, and he got them both without any noticeable elevation of his mood. However, he was not a complainer. He was an adventurer of sorts, and under Michelangelo's tutelage was very compulsive. But mostly he was an intellectual. He taught me a great deal about politicians and their lies. He was cynical, very accurate in his predictions, and he raised my level of sophistication in politics and economics. And apparently he taught me that a little Italian boy with spirit could attract Nordic beauties. I have had my share of blond goddesses and have changed wives even more frequently than Robert. I consider myself fairly sophisticated politically, and I feel I owe that in large part to him. He introduced me to C. Wright Mills, the famed sociologist, he influenced my generally leftist views, and he certainly was the member of my family who paved the way for my later Jewish intellectual identifications. Robert died of a heart attack several years ago. Interestingly enough, within a few weeks of his death, his tall, blond wife committed suicide. He needed a woman so badly—partly because he had had so little affection from men in his family—that he married one who literally could not live without him. Robert had a way of making himself indispensable. He was the guru; the person who really took charge. But then again, most of the men in my family, with the exception of Beniamino, ran the show. And so generally do I. Thank goodness none of my wives or lovers killed themselves after I left them, but they all had a difficult time with the parting—sometimes more difficult than I did—because I had made myself indispensable.

Aldo . . . Aldo. I don't want to write about him. I have even thought of leaving him out, but that would not be scientific, and I am too scrupulous a scientist to write about the formation of my identity and to leave out one of the central figures in its development. Aldo was my first cousin, the son of my father's sister. However, genetically and temperamentally he was certainly not a Robertiello. His father was a poor immigrant who had become a multimillionaire during the depression by constructing houses in New York. It was his family that lived in what I thought of as "the Palace of the Doges" or the "Vatican Museum." Aldo, like Robert, was brilliant, an intellectual who had read everything and knew everything. But since he was enormously wealthy, he never worked for more than a few months in his entire life. He was a very handsome, very bright, extremely well-dressed man about town.

My earliest memories of Aldo are from the early 1930s. We were sitting in the luxurious, wood-paneled library of his palace listening to a radio broadcast of Hitler's speeches. I suppose Aldo understood but little German. However, even I could tell that Hitler was the most powerful orator I had ever heard. My admiration for the dictator stopped there. Aldo, on the other hand, was a Nazi supporter and a vicious anti-Semite for as long as he lived. I somehow became Aldo's audience from the age of eight or nine on for descriptions of sexual exploits. These involved a broad spectrum, from a Harlem prostitute who cost two dollars to seducing the wives of some of his best friends. He, like Robert, was especially fond of seducing blond WASPs, and some of Aldo's were in the "400." But whereas Robert was romantic, Aldo was basically sadistic and narcissistic.

As a rather shy teenager with no experience of sex—even masturbation—I was very excited by his stories. I remember the smell of his fancy after-shave lotions. That smell was erotic for me, though more in the sense of my identification with his sexuality than in a homosexual way.

I was fifteen. Aldo had been teasing me about a German blond prostitute he knew, whom he called the Baroness von Wagner. Since Aldo was always teasing and spinning fabulous yarns, I cannot say I took him very seriously when one day he said he would introduce me to her. I went along, skeptically. A frizzy-haired blonde in her thirties greeted us in her apartment. She and Aldo talked awhile, then she led me by the hand into her bedroom. I still didn't believe what was happening. She took off her clothes very mechanically and asked me to do the same. At first she didn't believe I was a virgin. I don't remember being excited emotionally or sexually. I must have put on a condom with her help, entered her, and come quickly. It was all just an initiation rite that I had to go through with. Shortly thereafter I began to seek out sex with women, including prostitutes, rather regularly. I rarely went to a prostitute after my twenties, and even infrequently before then, but my experiences with them, with just one exception, were pretty much a repeat of the encounter with the Baroness. Just once did I really talk to, get close to, and really enjoy making love to a professional.

Sex devoid of emotional overtones is empty for me, and I even try to avoid making love with my wife when for some reason we are temporarily estranged emotionally. For Aldo, sex was sex whether with a society woman or a back-alley whore. The one time I visited a massage parlor, I passed my allotted hour chatting with the girl about her experiences in group therapy.

I think Aldo became jealous of me once I was accepted at Harvard. Until that point I had been just his admirer and apprentice. When I was seventeen, I began to get my own share of WASP princesses, some of whom were several years older than I and would have been in Aldo's league. Once, when my parents were away for a few days, I invited one of my WASPs to come to New York and spend a few days with me. Naturally I shared my success story with Aldo. In one of

98

the most surprising betrayals of my life, he told my father what I had done. I was petrified. I thought I would be disinherited and wouldn't be allowed to continue at Harvard. I really don't believe that I was paranoid to think that was Aldo's plan. He wanted to be the prize lover as well as the big intellectual star of the family. He was in his early thirties and I, a seventeen-year-old pipsqueak, was already going to a more prestigious school, not only socially but academically, than he. And I had already seduced three blond WASPs, all several years older than myself. Aldo was about to lose his apprentice and take on a competitor. He would have none of that. Fortunately, my father was too embarrassed to talk about the incident. I never trusted Aldo after that. When he asked whether I made love to my wife before I married her, I steadfastly insisted I had not, for I knew he would tell my parents, who would have given me a hard time about it.

When I was in my thirties, I learned that Aldo had killed himself. He had been having an affair with the wife of one of his best friends, and their secret (which I am sure he did not keep very discreetly) was discovered. I don't know why he did it. When I heard the news, I felt absolutely nothing. I thought that he was a miserable, vain, sadistic, egotistical son-of-a-bitch, and the world was well rid of him.

I suppose I must have introjected a certain amount of Aldo's male chauvinism and his narcissistic exploitation of women. People have accused me of that at times, especially in my earlier years. When I am hurt and angry and bitter I can sometimes assume for a short time Aldo's view of himself as the hunter; women as the prey. Certainly I had that attitude at times in my teens and early twenties when I was still under his tutelage. And I can assume that attitude in bed with a woman when it turns her on for me to be dominant as part of sex play. But overall I am much more romantic, like my Uncle Jerry, am much more inclined to idealize and adore women—to make them the Holy Grail rather than Aldo's prey and quarry. In many ways Aldo was the personification of evil for me—the anti-Semite, the snob, the exploiter and brutalizer of women. It would be a lie for me to say that he did not form a part of the pattern of the quilt contained in my Self, and I suppose I still am a bit defensive about this part. That's why I didn't want to write about Aldo. For despite my righteous indignation when accused of it, I have been at times to some extent a womanizer and, in my teens, an exploiter. I like to play dominance games (very mild ones), but only if the woman wants to. I am just as willing to be dominated if that is her fancy. I liked to brag of my conquests, though hardly at this time of my life. I have awarded myself points for bagging WASP princesses. I have been occasionally a social and intellectual snob. I am not, however, an anti-Semite. There is some of Aldo in me, but it isn't *all* of me. And I resent it when the part of me that I sometimes project on others accuses me of being just like Aldo or only like Aldo. That isn't fair. Some of the passionate part of my sexuality, the part that has to do with conquering women who *want* to be conquered, comes from Aldo; that is a part of myself I would not want to be without; it would have made many women in my life unhappy if it hadn't existed. Even feminists I have slept with wanted that to be part of me; insisted on it. For love and sex are not all sweetness and light, as I've explained. They involve destruction and anger on both the woman's and the man's side. The man must at times be able to play the part of the rogue, the lustful scoundrel, or sex will be dull.

I am glad I am a bit of a snob, something I must have learned from Aldo, for it didn't come from Michelangelo, Attilio, Beniamino, Domenico, or Robert. If you are in fact part of an elite, whether it be cultural, intellectual, artistic, or social, it is very important to know it and to accept it, for it keeps you from spending time with people who seek you out because of what you have to offer them, but who have very little to offer you in return. I needed a lot of that part of Aldo to survive my later Jewish do-gooder internalizations which pushed me to spending time in committee meetings and at boring dinner parties. Too many people spend the limited amount of time that is granted them being available to those who offer them very little, but who pick their brains, exploit their feelings, or are merely after their bodies. I do not regret having cut off people like these. I do regret having sometimes donated my ideas, my time, my visions, and even my seminal fluid to persons unworthy of them.

Unbelievable—even from evil Aldo I internalized some aspects of me that I now consider valuable! They are not "nice" parts that people approve of, like my father's dedication to his work. But my Self is not, nor should it be, composed only of "nice" parts. If it were, or if I thought it were, I would be dull and colorless or else a liar and a hypocrite. I suppose in retrospect my total lack of reaction to Aldo's suicide had to do with my denial of the part of Aldo that now exists in my Self. I can't say that even now, after I have written this chapter, I feel any regret over Aldo's loss. Instead I see us standing together as we used to—before his betrayal of me and perhaps even after it—smiling at each other, recognizing what unmitigated bastards we both could be and being glad of it. We can join in our mutual contempt for the naive, sweet, flower children, the Pollyannas who are idealistic about the world and its inhabitants. In fact, they are the people I can tolerate the least—the crackpot environmentalists, the vegetarians who want to prevent all killing of animals, the pacifists and sentimentalists who actually believe man is created in the image of God—this after Hitler, My Lai, and Cambodia!

Sometimes, in group or individual therapy or even in a social discussion, when I come up with some particularly devious, cynical, or manipulative solution to a problem, people ask me if my analyst happened to be Machiavelli. No, he was not, but one of my tutors was Aldo. In the course of my career as an analyst and the director of a training program at a clinic, I have already gone through several palace revolutions—attempts on my part to purge a villain or attempts on the part of others to purge *me* as the villain. I have learned a great deal about power, about politics, and about alliances. One may be forced to use someone as a friend and ally today, then stab him or her in the back tomorrow. It has happened to me many times, and I would be naive not to anticipate it. When I recently became the head of a new analytic institue, I made it clear that I would accept the position only if I had absolute power. I always exclude any democracy, any limitations on my power, if I am valuable enough to insist on this as part of my contract. I am going to be the Godfather of any organization I belong to actively. If pushed to the wall, I can be very good at dirty politics, knife-wielding, and double- and triple-crosses. I had a good teacher—Aldo. But I am also not interested per se in these power games. They bore and pain, rather than excite me. Nonetheless I am glad I had a good tutor in that department, for there were times in my life when I might otherwise have been wiped out. All the "palace guard" coups I led were successful, and all the conspiracies against me were smashed. Attilio knew something about the uses of power, but the coup against him in one of his hospitals—which included writing anonymous hate letters against him—was successful and he was dethroned. I think the image I had of Aldo in my adolescence was that he was never defeated by woman or man. After having idealized this quality in him, I took in some of Aldo's tough resilience as part of my Self.

Another aspect of suicide occurs to me as I write. The only person who should have the power to kill you is yourself. Aldo would have shared this view. I don't think I held that thought in my consciousness in my many flirtations with self-destruction, but I do think I can harbor the thought today. I feel that *I* will be the one to decide when the thread of my life will be cut. I am assuredly not psychotic, and I am realistic enough to know that I could be killed by a truck next week. But should I contract a terminal illness, I will be the one to make the decision when I go.

Suddenly I feel good about having known Aldo, for I needed him to balance out the self-flagellators in my early and later life—the Beniaminos and Jerrys and, yes, the Attilios and even the Michelangelos. They were all sufferers; Aldo was not. Even though he killed himself, I am sure it was to avoid suffering, and if I do it, it will be for the same reason. It strikes me as a very fine reason. So I am glad I discovered that even my villainous cousin had something I want to hold on to in my Self.

# 6

# The Jews

There are snobs who like to claim, "Some of my best friends are Jews." My retort is, "The only people I know who *aren't* Jewish are my mother and father." After I left my WASP Quaker school in the sixth grade, most of my classmates in grammar school and high school were Jewish, as were the majority of the teachers. We used to say that the meetings of the Hi-Y Club (the Christian Club) in high school could be held in a telephone booth. Then, in college and medical school, there was such an accepted de facto segregation between the WASPs and the others that the only people, with an occasional exception, I had as friends were Jews and sometimes a black man. There were practically no Italians in any school I ever attended. This must say something, since my grammar school and high school were special schools for bright children in New York, and at that time the largest single ethnic group in New York was Italian. The three teachers who really stimulated me were Jewish—a high school English teacher, a neurology teacher, and a teacher of psychoanalysis. After medical school I went into psychiatry. You know what a psychiatrist is—a Jewish doctor who can't stand the sight of blood. Almost all my peers in my internship, residency, and psychoanalytic school were Jewish. Ten of my twelve analysts were Jewish. I recently attended a party at which there were four Italian analysts. The hostesses, one of them, said that if a bomb were to go off in her living room, it would wipe out the entire Italian mental health community. Then, when I started practicing, almost all my patients, students, and colleagues were Jewish. Once, twenty or twenty-five years ago, I went through my list of patients. Almost every one was either Jewish or married to a Jew. During that period I used to do psychotherapy for an Italian psychiatrist who specialized in electroshock treatment. The vast majority of *his* patients were Italian. Jews for some reason treat emotional problems with psychotherapy, whereas other ethnic groups tend to approach them through psychopharmacology or other organic types of treatment. The proportion has changed considerably with the passage of time, but my patients are still preponderantly Jewish.

How powerful an influence did my numerous contacts with Jews, beginning at age eleven, have on me? Do such contacts, ones that occur after early childhood, help form our Self—our identity—or is it already, in childhood, definitively stamped by genetic and ethnic influences and by our nuclear and extended families? Did I internalize my later Jewish models? To what extent? Was my experience typical or was it specific to my particular background?

I suppose the first question I must pose is, how Jewish am I? You recall that when I once asked a patient whether she thought I was Jewish or Italian, she replied laughingly, "Oh, you're Jewish!" About ten years ago, I was leading a group of ten people. One was a southern WASP who started making subtle anti-Semitic remarks. Naturally the others picked her up on this. They asked her who in the room she thought was Jewish. She looked around and said, "Well, I don't suppose any of you other patients are Jewish. I guess the only one who is Jewish is the doctor." In fact, every one else there was Jewish but me. Her mistake taught her an unforgettable lesson. Recently I had a parallel experience. A patient said that almost all her acquaintances assumed she was Jewish, and figured I would make the same assumption. She was pleased that I would believe her to be Jewish, she told me, for since *I* was Jewish I would take better care of her! After confessing that she was not Jewish, she asked if I was. I said no, and wondered how she had drawn that conclusion in view of my obviously Italian name. She replied that she had thought I was an Italian Jew. After laughing at the misunderstanding, my patient felt she was "in good hands" again since now we shared our non-Jewishness!

This anecdote illustrates why the question of how "Jewish" I am is extremely important to people's experience of me—though it is important to bear in mind, of course, the pervasive notion that *all* psychiatrists are Jewish. But more important than the views of others toward me is the degree to which my "Jewishness" influences my perception of myself. I truly believe that until recently I perceived myself to be more Jewish than Italian. What does that mean subjectively? My task is to work beyond the accepted stereotypes and toward a realization of the ethnic differences between Jews and Italians as they pertain to myself.

Let me reiterate that I am being *subjective*, not factual or realistic. The entire psychoanalytic way of experiencing and thinking about life is, in my *subjective* view, Jewish. After all, Freud and most of his follwers were Jewish. The idea of commitment to one's personal emotional growth is, in my experience, Jewish. Not many Italians I have known believe in this ideal. I remember seeing a television interview with Federico Fellini. He said, "I don't understand these people who spend their whole lives trying to figure out who they really are. After they find out, so what?" Many of his movies, especially the introspective "8½," are attempts to understand himself, but he does not acknowledge this; he calls them "artistic expressions." Now *that* is typically Italian! Not many run-of-the-mill Italians, or at least Italo-Americans, would write a book trying to figure out who they are, where they came from, or how they got to be what they are. So, in my

105

personal experience, the quest for self-knowledge has proven to be a characteristically Jewish approach to life. It was Jewish friends in high school who introduced me to psychoanalysis—a gift that I could never begin to repay. My life has been a never-ending search for self-understanding and personal emotional growth, a value I certainly did not internalize from anyone in my nuclear or extended families. Michelangelo was committed to knowledge and success, but certainly not to self-knowledge. Nor were Domenico, Attilio, Jerry, Beniamino, Robert, or Aldo. None of the men or women in my family had any stake in personal emotional growth or any notion of its existence. None ever went to an analyst. My search for the truth about myself, and my commitment and insistence on my growth as a person, have carried me through some very rough periods. Whenever I have left a relatively secure emotional plateau to plunge into some unknown place that has left me frightened, shattered, and insecure, I have always told myself that I am committed to change and that change cannot take place without panic. I have always reassured myself that out of my present chaos and disorganization would come an organization on a higher level of maturity, with more possibility of experiencing life. To me, life is an adventure, with certain periods of security and consolidation interrupting a continual and steady movement to some higher level of involvement and intimacy. After I feel I have plumbed the depths of a person, a psychoanalytic theory, or even a place, I feel a push to move on to something new and different. That is one reason why I have left so many women, and so many psychoanalytic positions. All of this movement toward growth and change I must attribute to the Jews in my life.

Why is it that Jews constitute such a great proportion of analytic patients? It is not because they are sicker than most. It is because for some reason—genetic, historical, or cultural—that I do not feel qualified to discuss—the Jews, at least the ones whom I have met, are committed to dealing with their emotional problems by trying to explore them, understand them, and grow through the experience. Other ethnic groups do not seem to have this way of dealing with their problems.

My father, grandfather, and two of my uncles were Italian doctors in New York. If any of them had had psychiatric referrals to make they would have made them to me. The network of their friends among other Italian doctors in New York was vast. Many of them would have referred their psychiatric patients to me. Why did I practically never get an Italian patient from them or from anyone else? The reason is that many Italian doctors rarely recognize a psychiatric problem unless it is a psychosis. When they do suspect a psychiatric problem, they are loath to diagnose it as such because their patient will not understand and may feel insulted. And when an Italian patient is told he or she has a psychiatric problem, medication will probably be the treatment rather than self-exploration. Yes, there is no doubt that my greatest legacy from the Jews is their way of dealing with their feelings through self-exploration rather than medication or denial. As if my work and my own analysis as a patient were not enough, I constantly expose myself as an "equal patient" in five therapy groups a week. And then, as I have mentioned, in my free time I am a member of a group of all-male therapists dedicated to exploring male-to-male relationships and men's difficulties in achieving intimacy with one another. My life is a constant search for self-knowledge and growth. Some might agree with Fellini that after you find yourself, so what? I can understand that point of view. I don't believe my way of life is necessarily the best way for everyone. But I do know it is a very exciting way for me to live. It unifies my existence, giving it a meaning beyond immediate pleasure and pain, beyond comfort and security, beyond anything material. It is *my* spirit, *my* philosophy, *my* religion, and I know there is no way I could have discovered it without the help of the Jews in various schools; without my Jewish teachers, friends, colleagues, and analysts. So, while my genetic and biological heritage is Italian, my spiritual heritage is clearly and unmistakably New York Jewish.

What else have Jews given me? One thing that comes to mind is a sense of humor. Like Henny Youngman, I am king of the one-liners. My humor is usually appreciated, and most people enjoy my endless store of jokes. I said earlier that in college I could practically go round the clock without repeating a joke. My analyst friends tell me that my jokes, like most comedians' humor, are a hypomanic defense against despair and depression. In plain English that means I have to keep laughing because if I don't, I'll break into tears. An accurate formulation up to a point. I utilize my sense of humor a great deal in my therapy, and even when lecturing before a psychoanalytic society. I would love to be a stand-up comic who really wows them. The last heart-pounding anxiety attacks I had were ten years ago while I was telling jokes—I suppose I was putting myself on the line then and risking humiliation. Today I still tell a lot of jokes, but I no longer suffer those anxiety attacks. My sense of humor is Jewish, not Italian; at least I didn't pick it up from anyone in my family. My comic heroes are Henny Youngman, Milton Berle, and Don Rickles—all Jewish. Next to my commitment to self-knowledge and growth, perhaps the legacy of humor I received from my Jewish friends is most important to me, and in many ways, but clearly not all, I have experienced myself as much more Jewish than Italian—much more like my peers, teachers, and colleagues than like the members of my nuclear and extended family. If I were pushed to identify myself by one word, it would be "psychoanalyst," not "lover," "tennis player," or "author." "Psychoanalyst" is certainly connected much more with my later identifications.

I must also explore the absence of cultural impact and influence on professional choice from my nuclear and extended families. Why was there such a vacuum in this area that I was an open vessel ready to be filled by new ideas from age eleven on? How did my upbringing encourage, or at least permit, these later introjections to form such a substantial part of my Self? First of all, it is clear that no one in my nuclear or extended family, with the exception of my sister, Betty, had a very great emotional connection to me. My father and Michelangelo indoctrinated me to the work ethic and to the pursuit of knowledge, but alongside of this there was a dearth of ideas. The Catholic church offered ritual and mysticism, but the carriers of its ideas were nuns and priests who stimulated me neither with their wisdom nor with their intellectuality. Perhaps at that point if I had fallen into the hands of an intellectual Jesuit things would have been different. But I didn't.

So when I arrived at grammar school, then at high school, I was aching to apply my dedication to learning and hard work to *ideas* that could excite me. My peers were talking about communism, socialism, atheism, and psychoanalysis. They were brilliant, intellectual Jewish boys and my teachers were brilliant, intellectual Jewish men. A high school teacher was the first to fire my interest in reading. I read day and night— everything I could get my hands on. I had found something to fill the void—new ideas to which I could apply my intelligence and dedication.

My particular Italian background, in addition to providing little in the way of ideas, was lacking in roots, ethnic pride, and a sense of cultural heritage. This was true of both sides of my family. My rich Italian heritage in art, literature, music, and architecture was almost totally neglected, and I didn't discover Italy until I went there in my early thirties like any other American tourist. I then fell so in love with the country that I went back for ten consecutive years. But until then practically everything Italian was disparaged by almost all the members of my family. My father looked up to every non-Italian as being better than he was. On the contrary, the Jews I met, though some had mixed feelings, were inevitably proud of their heritage as God's chosen people. They were fortunate in having Jewish-Americans like Einstein and Felix Frankfurter to hold up as examples. There were very few prominent Italo-Americans in the twenties and thirties with whom I could identify. I must have deeply envied my Jewish friends and must in some ways have become an honorary Jew—a term I have frequently used in describing myself—to fill another gaping hole in my identity.

What I can glean from my own experience is that identifications that occur later in life can play a tremendously important part in the development of one's identity. In many ways this is

109

cause for optimism, for it means we can constantly make positive accretions to our sense of Self and to our feelings of self-esteem right up until death, since we can continue to internalize parts of people whom we have previously admired and idealized. In doing so, we will then admire those parts in our Self. It is clear too that the more one internalizes positive qualities from one's own nuclear and extended family, and the more one values one's ethnic heritage, the less need there will be to turn away from one's background in order to internalize other figures such as peers and teachers. I think this is the reason why people who have enjoyed positive childhood experiences tend to perpetuate their cultural heritage, whereas those whose childhood experiences have been negative are more apt to disavow their parents' cultural and religious values. I was an extreme example of someone who set aside many if not most of my ethnic and cultural influences—though clearly not all of them—and adopted a philosophy and a way of being that was quite different from those of my parents. Fortunately for me, the persons I had around me during my formative years from eleven to eighteen—years which are especially important for internalizing role models—were Jewish intellectuals. I am grateful that I could internalize these people who had such a strong sense of ethics and integrity, and who held learning, self-knowledge, and emotional growth in such high esteem.

# 7

# My Self

It is funny and also significant that when I thought about what the next chapter would be, I forgot that I was supposed to write a chapter about my Self, not just my family and friends. This isn't false modesty, but a genuine symptom—a rather gross one—of a part of me that is self-effacing. I used to think this modest; at times it is. But to those who really know me and care about me it is more of an annoyance and a burden. As I begin the chapter, I still do not understand why I don't recognize how important I am to some people; how grateful they are to me; how much they really care about me. In a rare moment of intimacy one of my patients told me how I had changed her life and how much she loved me as a person, not just as a skillful therapist. She said she somehow knew that I could never get it through my head that people really liked me for what I am, not just because of what I did for them. In the main she was right. But it wasn't until I was thirty-eight, had divorced two wives, and enjoyed the love of many women that a lover told me how much she liked me and for once I actually believed it. I jumped up, smiled, and exclaimed,

111

"Hey—you really *do* like me!" It was a revelation, a new experience. I can now occasionally believe that someone actually loves me, but I find it hard to retain the idea. I need to have it repeated over and over again, and in a short while I often will be speaking of this person as if he or she were really only grateful for services performed. I did not necessarily mean to start this chapter on my Self—my identity—with this theme, but perhaps this incomprehension, this blind spot, is the most unresolved part of my Self. The situation is very different now than when I was a child and felt unloved—probably correctly—or even five or ten years ago, when I felt unloved—probably incorrectly. Today I know intellectually that I am loved, and I sometimes *feel* loved, but the feeling is still very tenuous and fleeting and requires reinforcement. I must explore this difficulty—taking in love. My last book, *Your Own True Love*, addressed this problem, but it is still not resolved for me personally.

I just thought back to my earliest memory. (As an analyst, after all, I put a great deal of stock in people's earliest memories.) I was two. My mother was in the hospital having my sister. I was sent off to a house in the country with an aunt and some teenage cousins. They were all sitting around the kitchen table eating and laughing. I was under the table, where it was quite dark. I felt very lonely, as though no one cared for me or thought about me. I was probably right, for I was undoubtedly a burden who interfered with their pleasures. They were all happy and I was sad and full of self-pity. But why not? After all, I had been separated not only from my mother, but from my grandfather, my grandmother, my father, and my home. I am sure I was never given any explanation of what was going on, merely parked with a group of self-absorbed youngsters. When I went home after about a week, I found my crib had been preempted by my baby sister and I had been put out of my parents' room and into an alcove off my grandparents' room. There I stayed until I went to high school at age twelve and was given a room of my own on a different floor. Feeling unwanted and displaced was hardly inappropriate under the circumstances.

My mother sent me off to her sisters or to my father's wealthy relatives most weekends, holidays, and summers. As a little boy, I did receive a certain amount of attention from girl cousins. One of the few pleasant memories of my childhood was one of them reading me a bedtime story and tucking me in. That never happened at home, and only two or three times with her. I always felt like and in fact was an interloper in these relatives' homes. They put up with me to do my mother a favor, but they rarely wanted me around. At my mother's not-so-rich relatives, I was mostly an afterthought or a plaything.

I was also an outsider at Friends Seminary, not one of the WASP elite. I got points for being bright and was even elected class president, but I never felt I belonged. And even in the rest of my school experiences I was the different one—the rare non-Jew. By the time I reached analytic school, I felt more like an "honorary Jew" and a member of the group, but I was still essentially different. Being Italian still meant occupying the lowest rung of the ladder, just as my grandfather Michelangelo and my father had experienced it. Do I still feel like an outsider? I wonder. I am very intimate with many people; some say I am too indiscriminate in this way. Yet I maintain a very strong sense of being my own person. I am responsible only to myself; I do not entrust responsibility for my life to anyone else; yet I am totally available, without reservation, at any time, not only to my patients but to my friends as well. I feel that *I* am sure *I* am there for many people, but I never in my heart fully feel that anyone will ultimately be there for me when the chips are down. On the contrary, in my mind I *know* there are many people who stand by me. I, like Tom Sawyer, can imagine my funeral. I realize that there would be hundreds of people who would sincerely weep for me and who would feel genuine loss at my death. Yet alongside of this knowledge the feeling from time to time creeps in that I don't really count. I suppose once I really *didn't* count much, and even all my years of analysis and group therapy haven't totally corrected or reversed that idea.

Perhaps there was a small part of me that did matter back

113

then—the part that was connected to my sexuality. Inherited from the Candelas, it was not entirely obliterated by the Robertiellos—by Michelangelo and Attilio. It overtly asserted its existence when I was fifteen and watched the strippers in Minsky's burlesque house on Irving Place in New York. It lived on in my weekly visits to the famous Old Howard in Boston's Scollay Square during my years at Harvard. That buried part of me kept me alive through my marriages when I went to the strip joints in Greenwich Village and midtown Manhattan. I even crossed the river to sit in the burlesque house in Union City, New Jersey—God, what a dump that was! But I was an addict. I needed my fix of selfness or selfhood and that was the only sure way I could obtain it. My sexuality—or at least the bad boy part of it—was reserved for me. Of course I made love to my wives, and sometimes other women, but there was always an element of fusing my Self with them, of pleasing them, of merging with them in the sex act. My voyeurism was strictly my own; I didn't even want to share it with the stripper. Though I have gone to a few, not many, prostitutes in my time, none of them were strippers. I was invited by some strippers in nightclubs to sleep with them at prices I could afford, and once I was even invited to sleep with one because she liked me. But I never permitted even the stripper to invade this bastion of my Self, my identity, for by doing so I would have had to share with her an experience that was precious to me precisely because it was my own. I have wondered until this moment why I have never slept with a stripper; why I never made any sort of pass at one. Why didn't I ever fondle a well-shaped breast, kiss one of these women, or even touch her hand? Many of the women were extraordinarily beautiful, so it wasn't a question of looks. The reason was that anything except visual contact would have destroyed the excitement and the magic for me, for the stimulation the strippers provided had to do with reinforcing the boundaries of my Self; even caressing a hand would have represented a sharing that would have reduced the experience to nil. My Self had been assaulted furiously by Michelangelo and Attilio, and even in relationships to women I had sacrificed a part of it to

114

them. After all, I had had Michelangelo, the best animal trainer since Frank Buck, to teach me how to give my Self up to him and subsequently to every other person I was ever close to. However, my relationship to him had helped me accomplish the most difficult and important separation of all—from my mother. I guarded jealously my one last citadel of selfhood; the lone survivor of the systematic destruction of my Self. I went to great lengths to hide my burlesque-house experiences from my wives, terrified that if they found out about them they would take them away from me. In that way I was being more "Jewish" than "Italian," with perhaps one difference from most Jewish males. I feared my wives not because they were women but because they happened to be the persons I was attached to—after all, I grew up in a strongly patriarchal home, not a matriarchal one as many Jewish-American ones are.

One of my wives was very suspicious about other women and constantly accused me of having affairs with my female patients and colleagues whereas in fact I was totally, perhaps unfortunately, faithful to her for the twelve years of our marriage. Because of her suspiciousness, she noticed some minor time discrepancies which I had tried to conceal. Where had I had been in the few minutes between the time I left my office and when I arrived home? Whom was I making love to? I was caught redhanded and had to confess I had stopped at a strip-tease club on 52nd Street. Perhaps because she was so relieved it wasn't (directly, anyway) another woman, and possibly because she somehow intuited the innocence and the necessity for my one act of separateness, she seemed to understand me and forgive me. I think that moment was the only one in my twelve years with her in which I experienced a deep feeling of what I called love for my wife. I suppose it was the only time I felt accepted for myself and not as an extension of what she wanted me to be. (However, this feeling may very well have been illusory.) She may have loved me; she certainly expressed it frequently and in many ways. But I think that she, like every other person I have attached myself to, had become an extension of Michelangelo, enemy of my Self and my soul, a person whom I had to please and be perfect for, one who would accept me only if I fulfilled a fantasy of what I should be. *My* only fantasy, my only secret Self that was not for anyone else—not even for a stripper—consisted in my watching a woman take off her clothes on a stage.

Someday I will have to open my deepest areas of vulnerability to a person who can really make me feel that I count. It may be a man or it may be a woman—my gender or theirs will have nothing to do with it. My sexuality has too long borne the burden of making me feel whole. I make love, therefore I am. Or even: I get turned on in a burlesque house, therefore I am. There has to be some other way of knowing I matter. It can't be through sex or writing books or being a good analyst. It has to be some rock-bottom naked me that I expose without any edges, defenses, or performances, that I feel is accepted by another person just for what it is. Is that possible? I think so. *I* have had that kind of feeling about a few—not many—people. I have experienced delight just being in the same room with them. They were not necessarily women, and they were not necessarily physically beautiful, but there was something about their face or their being that brought out in me the sort of adoration that the Magi felt for the Christ child. I have felt that about others; has anyone ever directed similar feelings toward me? I am sure they have and they do, but I have difficulty experiencing those feelings— letting them in. Perhaps someday I will open myself up and find a person who will have the gleam of recognition in his or her eye that neither my mother nor anyone else in my childhood aside from my sister had for me. Perhaps my first wife had that feeling. Yes, I think she did. But I was so puzzled or frightened by it then that I couldn't let it in. Perhaps now that I understand it better I may be able to. Then I would less frequently feel so lonely and unloved despite being so close to so many people whom I know—in my head—really do love me.

I see that when I started to tell you about my Self, I quickly got down to my real Self, which doesn't consist of my curriculum vitae. It is how I now subjectively experience my Self—as a lonely, unwanted child who still feels he doesn't

116

matter. That is a part of who I really am. The rest of me is there too—the person who is an analyst, a husband, a father, a writer, a lover. But where I really live more than I would like to is with that unhappy little boy nicknamed "Mopey Dick." Even when my face is smiling, my voice still comes from Mopey Dick. I am not always fifty-six—sometimes I am still two years old, huddling under the table. No, I am not feeling sorry for myself; I have *compassion* for myself, which is much different from self-pity. And I desperately need to find someone who has a gleam of recognition in his or her eye for that two-year-old. I hope I will find that person before I die. I think that I will. In any event, I will not give up hoping and looking.

In the old days, whenever I did anything involving social contacts—attending school, visiting a patient, going to a party—I almost inevitably felt like that two-year-old. Gradually I attuned myself to my professional part. When I was an intern I felt like a little boy who was playing doctor, and I experienced the same thing as a novice analyst. It was only when I was further into my career that I began to feel the analyst was a real part of my Self; that I was not playing, or pretending, or defending against infantile vulnerability. But almost everywhere else—at a party, as a father, in bed—I was either the little boy or denying the fact with a supertough macho façade. In more recent years I have felt like my Self while with my patients, teaching classes, giving speeches, even on national TV. In situations that involve my professional identity, I feel I am my Self—confident that I am not only adequate but excellent. I also have experienced my Self in those social gatherings where my expertise is known. However, a patient recently came to me for consultation. She told me the thing that would terrify her the most would be going into an East Side singles bar. I replied it would scare me, too. I would be completely anonymous, with no credentials to fall back on. I would feel like that miserable little boy, afraid of rejection and even humiliation. Each time I have begun a romance, even if the woman has known and respected my

117

credentials, I have reacted in the same way. This never stopped me from pursuing women; in fact I have always been counterphobic about it, compulsively doing what I feared the most. But no matter how often and how successfully I pursued women, my fear never diminished very much until recently. When I was sixteen, a freshman at Harvard, I went out almost every night, trying to pick up girls along the Charles River—girls we affectionately called the "river rats." I was always scared to death, but because of my counterphobic compulsion, was successful more often than my classmates. I was nicknamed "the Dong," and I would regale my housemates at Thayer Hall and later at Leverett House with descriptions—at times embellished—of my triumphs. This macho defense against the fear of being a vulnerable baby who is essentially unlovable and will be rejected by women has unfortunately persisted to some extent as part of my character. Women, especially the ones who have been involved with me, have found it sometimes attractive and sensual but also very annoying. The ones who have loved me deeply have put up with it but wished it would go away. It is difficult for me to let go of it because it brings me so many secondary gains. Men almost invariably like it. I boast in a tongue-in-cheek way that apparently does not threaten them or put them down. By making fun of myself as the baby trying to be the Great Lover, the men I talk to identify with me more than they compete with me. Some feminist women find it both repulsive and infuriating. Some men and women find it amusing. In any event, for me it is a problem, for I am not playing for laughs. I may start a relationship on a fairly equal basis, receiving as much affection as I am giving. My pattern has been to begin to fear that I will be rejected and humiliated. As a defense against this threat, my mind, trained in analysis, quickly and very much without my conscious awareness unearths her most intimate needs and weaknesses, and she, instead of me, is thus often reduced to the position of the dependent and vulnerable child. But in this process of eliminating my own terror, I end up with another child—one that *I* must take care of and sometimes one that is angry with me and exploits me—

118

rather than the mother whose love and support I had originally sought and sometimes obtained. I win the battle and lose the war. Women have fallen in love with me easily because they divined that I understood them and that I would sustain them. Which I have almost always done. Almost all the women I have ultimately left have, after they have expressed their rage at me, given me some credit and expressed a certain amount of gratitude for all that I gave to them in every way—emotionally, intellectually, sexually, and even materially. But in each case my hypomanic macho parent defense against my own vulnerable little boy did us both in. By playing the parent to them I often unwittingly aided their regression, so they became less able to take care of themselves. I would often unknowingly—while at the same time consciously encouraging it—hinder their potential for independent growth. Some of them regressed and lost their autonomy. Some of them used me and exploited me as well, but could only restore their Selves after I had departed. And as they regressed further and further, they gave less and less to me. I frequently had merely added another patient to ,my heavy schedule. One of the women I subsequently married had been in consultation with me several years previously. I did not take her as a patient, for I did not believe she had the potential for growth that I seek in them. Yet later on I married her. My clinical evaluation was correct: She did not make any great strides in therapy with competent therapists.

I never accept a patient who is schizophrenic, because of their usually limited potential for growth or change. Yet two of my long-term primary love relationships—though not marriages—have been with schizophrenics. I certainly have gone a long way in defending myself against my dread of my own vulnerability. I have often attached myself to women who are clearly much more vulnerable than I am. More recently, though I have been able to see through my defensive maneuvers and have tried to ally myself with stronger women, I have still managed at times to ferret out their Achilles' heel and make them dependent on me. I am not boasting as I write these words. I am not proud of my ability to get an edge over women—which, incidentally, I do *not* achieve by turning them into household drudges. In fact, I have always encouraged their professional growth. I feel sad for them and sadder for myself. Recently I have been trying to lessen the tendency by presenting more and more of my needy, helpless child to them. This has helped to a great degree and has reduced the inequality of power in the relationships. But I and they must be constantly vigilant against my inclination to take over, and in so doing, making both of us the loser. I do not receive the nurture I initially received from them that the needy child is crying for. The women are nurtured, but they can easily be lulled into letting go of their Selves. Eventually I have tired of having to give so much and receive so little and have become dissatisfied and left. Initially they are usually crushed and then furious with me, but then they recover and feel better at having lost their addiction to me and sometimes even stronger than before they met me because of what I have given them.

So those are two important parts of my Self—the vulnerable baby and the strong, controlling parent who defends himself against this baby. Those of you who are familiar with Eric Berne's book *Games People Play* and with the theory of transactional analysis will recognize the child and the parent in me. Berne defines both of them as being pathological. For me they certainly are. I am not ashamed of them, and I understand their origins in my particular history. But I certainly do not condone them either. I want to diminish them and increase the third part of Berne's triad, the adult.

What about the adult in me? I know intellectually he is there. But I have been so concerned with the experiencing of myself as the vulnerable child and with defending this child from injury that the adult part of me has frequently gotten lost—at least in the subjective view of my Self. I have not paid enough attention to my adult; I have not experienced him enough as part of my real Self. As I have said before, this split between real Self and false Self is largely romantic—the persona I show to the world is as real and unique a part of me as the vulnerable baby or the controlling parent. I have to think about who this adult is, what *his* unique qualities are.

After all, most of the people I have touched or been touched by have related to this part of me; they know me as this adult. Even my lovers, who have seen both my baby and my parent, have for the most part experienced me as my adult. Everyone in the world knows him well except me. I must literally force myself to approach him intellectually—with my cognition—rather than with my feelings.

So be it. I must still, in whatever way, try to meet this person whom everyone else in the world identifies as me. I experience a reluctance. For one thing, I suspect that I will brag like my father, Attilio, did. Perhaps that is why I am so self-effacing that I refuse to recognize this adult. I know I have a problem here. I recently wrote a book called *Your Own True Love*, in which I described the dynamics of self-effacement as being connected with a fear of grandiosity. (I almost always write books about problems I have not yet solved for myself.) My best and closest friends are invariably annoyed by my self-effacement. Sometimes when people first meet me they find it endearing and attribute it to genuine humility, but when they know me better they realize genuine humility is not its origin. My self-effacement distorts my perceptions of myself and others' reactions to me and it puts a burden on them that they could well do without. I am still stalling . . . I am still resisting facing my adult Self. However, at least now I know that one of the reasons for my evasion is that I am afraid I will appear to be a braggart. It is interesting that when I boast *defensively* about topics such as sex or power over women, I am not afraid. That is because somewhere I know it is defensive boasting and does not really add to my stature. What I fear is acknowledging my *real* strengths and my *real* assets.

I must deal with my adult Self and not postpone it anymore. My fear is of being hated or being made fun of because I think I am so great. I am afraid to be found an intolerable egotist like my father. But in any event I will have to come to grips with this part of my Self. When I have been forced to do so in therapy marathons or even in personal nontherapeutic encounters, the other person has invariably neither humiliated nor belittled me.

But now I see another part of it. Every time I brought a real accomplishment to my father's attention—my Harvard scholarships at age sixteen, my passing the psychiatry boards, my professional papers, my books—he always put me down. That son-of-a-bitch is still running around in my head! He is still running my life, even from his grave. Of course. Of course that is why I am afraid to acknowledge my adult achievements. Attilio, with his rivalry toward me, my brother, my son, his brother, and his colleagues, would ridicule and destroy me. I hardly ever heard him say a good word about any of his colleagues, whom he ran down as thieves and incompetents. I suppose I cannot acknowledge my genuine accomplishments because I still fear vicious attacks from my internalized father. *For the relationship that exists between our Self and the internalized persons who inhabit our minds is often more important than that between our Self and the real people in our lives.* The real people in my real life are almost invariably happy to learn of my triumphs. They are rarely competitive or envious, are almost always supportive, appreciative, and congratulatory. But I—and almost all of us—inhabit an internal world, not the real, external world, and at moments my internalized father can carry more weight than the sum of all the external figures in my life. Even the exacting Michelangelo would give me occasional approval for my accomplishments, though perfection was his goal. My mother never really cared, even though she pretended to. But she is not the problem here. Her lack of interest was a disappointment but not a threat. No, Attilio is definitely the culprit. I have not gotten him out of my head, and I still fear his scathing attacks. The only time he ever smiled—a cruel smile—was when he was in the process of destroying a rival. I worked on my Oedipus complex for years and years in analysis. When I began, it was the only thing analysts knew how to deal with, so I went over and over my dreams and anxieties that Attilio would castrate me if I competed with him. But now I suddenly understand. It is not castration I fear, it is humiliation and mortification. Until recently most of us analysts really knew little about these emotions. Though I went to excellent analysts, no well-formulated psychology of the Self existed then; there was no deep comprehension of the pain of humiliation or of wounds to the Self; of the necessity for the preservation of self-esteem. My father did not castrate me for my accomplishments; he humiliated me. That is what I fear and that is what was never analyzed, and that is why I am so drawn to the psychology of the Self.

I do not know if I can succeed in banishing Attilio from my mind, but I can surely try to block his attempts to prevent me from describing my adult Self and my achievements. I will no longer succumb to his taunts—at least not at this moment.

Where shall I begin? The logical place is with my intellect. The tests I took at age five clearly placed me in the upper range. I attended schools for gifted children, and when I put my mind to it I usually came out at the top of my class. That was so at Hunter Model School and Townsend Harris High School; it was not the case at Harvard or at Columbia Medical School, because in those schools I was either not that interested in what I was studying or I was coping with social or sexual problems. (And, to be sure, there were other students brighter than I!) I certainly do not claim to be the most brilliant person I have ever met. But I do have a first-rate mind, especially in the field of psychology. I have a knack for taking a complex mass of material about a person and conceptualizing and synthesizing it. That is why I am a good therapist, teacher, and supervisor, and I can. almost accept this talent as a part of my real adult Self. Also, I can turn out an enormous amount of work efficiently and without tiring. People are always amazed at how productive I can be with seemingly little effort or effect on my mind and body. This is a gift that I can really appreciate, and I am sure it is connected with my grandfather's training. I usually get up at six, start working at eight, and finish about seven in the evening. I don't work much in the evenings on weekdays, but I spend many hours of my weekends reading and writing. This is my eighth book. For me, writing is a hobby, an avocation not a vocation. I can hear some of my writer friends saying at this point, "Yes, and sometimes the way you write shows it!" But even though I am not a professional writer, my books are filled with ideas. And perhaps that criticizing voice comes not only from my literary friends, but also from Attilio and even Michelangelo. OK, I'm not Hemingway, but eight books and forty professional papers are not inconsequential. (This need for self-justification shows that Attilio is getting at me again, but I will try to push him away.) One quality that even Attilio cannot take away from me, since I have already given him credit for it by letting him serve as a role model, is my commitment, my dedication to my work and to my patients. I know I am in a high percentile in that department.

As I write, I suddenly feel sad. Tears come to my eyes. I am that poor vulnerable little boy again. What happened? I can only imagine that Attilio did his usual hatchet job on me again without my even realizing it, for I dared to tell a bit about my adult Self and suddenly internally was reduced to a child again. I am overwhelmed with despair. I feel as if I can never put it together again. Yet my real life is rich in self-fulfill-ment—more than it has ever been. What happened? What else? Attilio is doing his usual number on me. Damn him! I must go on. I can't let him stop me. If only life weren't always such a struggle against one's internal ghosts! The people who inhabit my real life are so much more loving than those from my childhood who populate my mind. I need comfort, support, and mothering to counter Attilio's destructive at-tacks. Perhaps I'll take a break, try to find that support, and then go on. I almost cannot do it alone. Or perhaps if I had to, I could be my own good parent. But if my wife is around, I will try first to get a little comfort externally.

When I spoke with her at lunch and told her of my anguish while I was writing, she commented on how hard it is for us to get over the wounds of our childhood. I have had about as much psychoanalysis by as many good analysts of different persuasions as anyone I know. I have been in my groups as an "equal patient" five times a week for the past ten or fifteen years as well as in several group therapy marathons (group sessions that are prolonged for many hours) as patient and analyst, and I am now in my leaderless group of all-male

124

analysts. I also spent several years in a leaderless group of male and female analysts. And yet my father comes up and hits me over the head while I'm in the midst of listing my accomplishments.

Am I discouraged about psychoanalysis and what it can accomplish? Not really, because I can recognize more of what it *has* done for me than what it has failed to do. For openers, it has kept me alive. There is no way in the world that I wouldn't have killed myself without analysis. Of course I did make two serious attempts at nineteen and twenty-three, but it was only after the second try that my real analysis started. I had been to see a few analysts on a short-term basis before that, starting at age sixteen, but they were part of a referral service from college and medical school. Two of the analysts were quite famous and undoubtedly skilled, but I wasn't in therapy with either of them for an extended period. After my analysis began, though I have thought of suicide many times, I have never gone to the point of making a determined attempt.

Being alive is no longer a burden now. Though I may feel momentarily anxious, depressed, or insecure, these periods are short-lived. Most of the time I feel comfortable, and I frequently experience joy, hope, and satisfaction. When I entered my first real analysis, every moment of my existence was filled with dread. My triumphs meant little to me and my failures were excuses for self-flagellation. Michelangelo, inside of me, ruled me, criticized me, demanded perfection of me, and beat me mercilessly as he had in reality when I dropped below perfection, such as getting 99 instead of 100 percent on a test or giving myself less than a perfect grade for my handling of a patient in the office or a woman in bed. Michelangelo is still there, but I can cope with him much better than I used to. Only a half-hour has passed since I began writing about it, but I have been able to ward off Attilio's onslaught. For years and years I was the victim of both their mental representations. I was given no peace from either of them. So, when my wife asks me if I am skeptical about what analysis has accomplished, I say I am not. Considering the number of assaults on my Self during my early years, I must view the number of my successes in life, together with the general improvement in my subjective feelings about myself, as a minor miracle. Despite all of my problems, anxieties, and insecurities, I am basically very happy in my work and in my love life. Not many people I know can honestly say this.

Also, I am much more impressed by my patients' progress than by my own. Many of them have suffered as bad or worse childhood trauma than I. Probably one reason they have healed faster and more completely (though never *very* fast or *very* completely) than I did is that they have had a much better analyst in me than any analyst I ever had, owing to an impressive evolution of psychoanalytic theory and technique in the past fifteen or twenty years. Another reason is that though I have had many fine analysts, none was as committed or as emotionally involved with me as I am with my patients. I have been the parent with the gleam of appreciation in his eye, who really cares deeply about his patients to a degree that is quite different from any response I ever enjoyed from any analyst but one I saw as a patient. By that I do not mean that they were *un*caring or not serious about their work, but their training often inhibited them from either feeling or expressing their feelings to me. Of course, *my* original training did that too. Why I was able to transcend that—even with my first private patient—I don't know. Perhaps it was so clear to me that *I* needed involvement from my therapists that I was able to put aside the rules against emotional contact that had been drummed into me. (I just noticed I dodged a blow from Attilio.)

I have just said that I believe I am a first-rate analyst, not only because of intellectual but also because of personal qualities. And it is owing to these same qualities of caring, and my being able to express that caring, that despite the numbers I have done on them I have been able to give a good many women a great deal of love. The number of women I have loved—often simultaneously as well as serially—has undoubtedly been stimulated by my fear of rejection or abandonment by any one of them, and by my macho defenses against my vulnerability. Nevertheless, with many of them, I was very

126

caring and affectionate. Our relationships often lasted a long time—sometimes with interruptions. Most of my lovers have told me that I gave them a great deal emotionally even if our relationship was temporarily suspended or ended unhappily. I used to think of sex as one of the most important ways of giving to a woman. It certainly is *one* way, but I know now that even in my most exciting and fulfilling sexual relationships, this was not what either of us treasured the most. Mutual loving, caring, affection, understanding, and support meant more. I must remind myself, as I counter one of Attilio's sudden objections, that my relationships with women were not only my acting the role of the needy child or the giving parent. An adult-to-adult, person-to-person intimacy was at the core of many if not most of them. Attilio is after me again! I realize that I will have to try very hard to impress on my memory what I have just written, otherwise he will degrade and humiliate me. He will say I have been a mere lecher and a male chauvinist pig, that I have used women and then discarded them. Once, when I informed him of a forthcoming marriage, he asked, "Who's the next victim?" This was the real Attilio, in the flesh, not the one running around in my head. If the criterion for determining how much you give a woman is whether you stay with her forever, then I have indeed failed, even though most of my relationships have had an impressive longevity. But being as objective as I can, I am convinced I have given them a great deal more than I have taken from them. Part of this was defensive, because I needed to play Daddy, but part of it was that I honestly like to give to people.

Where did this quality originate? Was I always like this? I don't think so. Though during my adolescence I was always madly in love with some woman or another, I think I was much more interested in the glory of conquest than I was in giving her affection. I was married when I was twenty. Despite all the problems that mainly I, in my immaturity, introduced into the marriage, I have never doubted for a moment that my wife and I deeply loved each other. When our marriage broke up five years later, largely because of my emotional difficulties, I woke up in the middle of every night with a tremendous

127

sense of a void and an unbearably painful loss. I don't doubt that my ex-wife went through the same suffering. I started my first real analysis in the middle of that marriage, after my suicide attempt.

Perhaps my ability to be concerned about another person was an internalization of the caring attitude of my many analysts toward me. Even if they couldn't show it overtly, even if they were being paid for their services, here were men and women who sat alone in a room with me and listened to what I said, who cared about what I said, who were trying hard to understand me and to help me. Even if their efforts were at times misguided or ineffectual, they filled a need that had never been met in my childhood except briefly by my sister.

Even if analysis does not work as it is supposed to, by interpretation and insight, it functions in another way that may be even more important. Heinz Kohut and his followers (of which I am one) point out that for many people the most curative aspect of psychoanalysis lies in the fact that there is someone who cares. This person is then internalized by the patient, who in turn among other benefits is able to care for another person. That is why nonanalytic relationships with astrologers, gurus, family physicians, and clergymen can often have immense and unexpected therapeutic value. A caring relationship or, as Winnicott puts it, a "holding environment," may well be a most essential part of the improvement through therapy.

I believe almost all the analysts I have known as supervisors, patients, colleagues, supervisees, or in their professional capacity, have been basically dedicated and caring men and women. They of course have varied greatly in intelligence and talent, but I could name only a handful of out-and-out exploitative scoundrels among the hundreds I have met. That speaks quite highly of my profession and compares very favorably with my experience of the medical profession as a whole.

Why have I had twelve analysts? (It may be close to a world's record!) As I have mentioned, in my teens and early twenties some of them were part of the medical services offered by schools I attended. I saw these people briefly, and more on the basis of crisis intervention than prolonged analysis. When I entered analytic school, I was compelled to exchange my first important long-term private analyst for one on their staff. Later, when I felt a need to return to analysis because of emotional pain or a crisis in my life, some of my former analysts had died. I agree with Freud that an analyst should return for additional analysis at periods throughout his or her life when confronted with problems that have not been present or pertinent to him or her previously. Life is, or should be for an analyst, continued flux and growth, which brings new areas of study and new issues into focus. These have to be worked out and understood by an analyst so he or she will not be blind to them when they appear in patients.

This brings up the other obvious and frequently asked question: How can a man who has suffered so much psychic pain, and is even now so subject to self-doubts, be able to help another person? The classic reply is: "You don't have to be crazy to be a psychiatrist, but it helps!" Now, when I say "crazy," I don't mean it literally. My emotional problems have never greatly interfered with my professional performance. Even if I have been contemplating suicide that day, it never keeps me from giving almost undivided attention to the patient. I like to compare myself to Judy Garland, who would put on a terrific performance and then try to kill herself. Sometimes, suffering intensely as a patient entered my office, I would say to myself, "Dick, you, like Judy Garland, are a pro. You're going to put aside your own problems for this patient and give it your best!" If I had felt I couldn't do this, I would have been professional enough to cancel the session. But I have never canceled a session because of my own emotional suffering, nor have I been unavailable to help a patient with at least 80 if not 100 percent of my Self despite whatever personal crisis I may have been going through.

Almost everyone who becomes an analyst or a psychotherapist has been guided in that direction because of his or her personal internal suffering. Many of my patients have been psychotherapists. Some of them have become psychotherapists after their treatment. The fact of having experienced a great deal of pain and of having attained some degree of understanding of it in analysis makes a person much more able to empathize with a fellow sufferer. So it not only *helps* to have been "crazy," it is essential! Clearly, if the "craziness" is of the sort that leads him or her to be irresponsible with patients, to abuse them, or to be unable to empathize with them, this is a different matter. There are some analysts and therapists whose problems in fact render them dangerous or ineffective. We try to weed them out by insisting on standards of personal analysis, intensive supervision, and continual self-examination and examination by peers. These safeguards cannot work all the time. Yet, as I have said, those in my field who are downright scoundrels, who do not care about their patients, or who are basically harmful are few. There may be relatively few superb analysts and therapists, but how many are superb in any area of endeavor?

One might ask, how can I write such a self-revealing book and think that it will not cause me to lose patients? I reply that I never pretend to myself or to my patients that I am emotionally healthier than they are. They do not come to me because I am Mr. Mental Health; they come because, partly as a result of my own psychic pain, I will be able to empathize with and help relieve their suffering. I offer them authenticity, self-honesty, and years of training and experience. I do not pretend to be better or stronger than they are, or to have transcended my own problems through my own good fortune or analytic help. An analyst who presents him or herself as a pillar of mental health, or even necessarily as superior to the patient, is by definition a fraud.

So I am a good analyst and a relatively good, though hardly perfect, lover. What else constitutes the adult me? I am very sensual; I enjoy eating, smelling, kissing, touching, seeing, and hearing to a much greater degree than most people I have encountered. This aspect of me probably comes from the genes transmitted from Domenico. I am very much interested in expanding my knowledge and very curious. That probably comes from Michelangelo, Attilio, and Robert. I have a good body which has resisted serious physical illness, allows me to play a decent game of tennis, and gives me more endurance than many people my age and younger. That's probably partly genetic and comes from both sides of the family. I have a calling, a dedication to personal growth, and a good sense of humor, things I attribute primarily to my Jewish internalizations.

I suppose those are at least the most important parts of my adult Self. So I did evade Attilio's blows; an adult is present whom I can be proud of and include in the chapter on my Self. I am more than a vulnerable child and a defensively controlling parent. So there, Attilio! I know you will rise up every once in a while and shatter me. I will go to pieces, not hysterically, but in my own quiet way, as though I had no cohesive Self to hold me together. I will feel as though the parts of my Self that were held together by my analysts and other helpful internalizations have suddenly become unglued. But I have learned to control my panic when this occurs, for I have somehow acquired enough "inner glue" for a temporary repair job. I have developed—at least partially—an inner structure that assures me everything will be all right, a comforting inner parent who can sustain me through these crises when everything else is disintegrating, as well as a network of people to whom I can turn for comfort and support. They will be there when I need them, and I am prepared to help them when called upon. Even more importantly, I have developed the ability to reveal myself totally to these people, show them the helpless, needy child. Too many people—including myself until quite recently—have not developed the capacity to bare their weakest and most vulnerable part, and to put it into the hands of someone they trust. I have compassion for them, for I couldn't have survived had I been unable to do that. Gradually, the soothing function thus offered us is internalized as a part of us, even if we did not receive it from our mother. That certainly has happened to me. Today I don't run as often or as desperately to others as I used to. But when something or

131

someone I had depended upon lets me down—even if it is only my car—I can experience it as a loss of a part of my Self, and I may need an external source of consolation if my internal ones are not sufficient. I am not ashamed of this. I feel fortunate that I have been able, probably largely through my relationship to my analysts and close friends, to develop a means to save my Self when it is crumbling. So I possess more of a Self than before, and the means to rescue it if and when necessary.

# 8

# My Brother, Charlie

I hesitated before writing a chapter on my brother, Charlie. He is about ten years younger than I, so he was not a role model during my childhood. He is now a successful journalist who has lived in Rome for the past twenty-five years. And, since I left home to go to college when I was sixteen, I lived in the same house with him for only about six years. Charlie kidded me about suing for slander if I reveal anything too personal about him, but even aside from this, I want to respect his privacy. Actually, what I will reveal will be things that are personal about *me*, and my feelings about him. After all, he is a male in my nuclear family, and perhaps my feelings about him were in part transferred to my feelings about my son.

My earliest memories of Charlie are of his lying in a crib. I recall gazing at him with love. Today, as an analyst, I do not know if this emotion was real or whether it was what we call a reaction formation (denial by reversal) of feelings of hostility and rivalry. I like to think and I do think the emotion was genuine. On the one hand I believe I was old enough to experience him as my *child* rather than my competitor, but in addition I have some vague memories of watching my mother nurse him at her rather good-sized breasts and being angry and jealous. I also remember an incident that followed shortly after his birth. There was an argument in the house, and I threatened to run away. Instead I hid in one of the hall closets. Soon everyone became concerned about my absence. They scurried about and finally called the police to report I was missing. Throughout this scene I was enjoying myself immensely, since this proved to me that they really cared about me (more than about my brother?). I finally came out of my hiding place, but not until I had received my satisfaction.

When Charlie was small, I played with him a great deal. One of our games was football. He would try to run by me and I would stop him. I am sure I enjoyed winning, but I was probably old enough and sufficiently diplomatic to let him win occasionally. Once he came crashing, head lowered, past me. He was about four and I was fourteen. I neatly stepped to the side and he cracked his head against a door, splitting the skin and causing a good deal of blood to flow. I am sure my motive was hostility and competitiveness. This was one of the only incidents involving him that I can remember before I left for college. After that we lost contact. I went off to college and graduated from medical school when I was twenty-two. When Charlie was twenty-one or twenty-two, he enrolled in medical school in Rome, since he was not accepted by an American school. For ten years he was in Rome, supported by my father, ostensibly studying medicine, but in fact never even getting through the first semester. I recall being very envious that he was being supported and rewarded for *not* working, while I, who had done all that was required of me, received no praise, reward, or money. Finally, out of a combination of envy and concern, probably both, I prevailed upon my father to stop this farce and force Charlie to come to grips with adult life. After ten years it worked.

I am sure I feel glad that I have competed successfully with my brother athletically, professionally, and financially. I cast a jaundiced eye upon some of his financial investments without really understanding them, and am not convinced I am totally in favor of his succeeding. I know I am jealous and angry that my mother seems to favor him over me. I always feel that I shoulder the duties and responsibilities for my mother while he is thousands of miles away in Rome, while he receives her affection and I do not. It may be childish to feel these things, but I know I do. Nonetheless, Charlie and I get on together well, and I enjoy his company. When he and his family come to America, they stay at my home, and I am delighted to have them with me.

I frequently confuse my brother's name, Charlie, with my son's name, Bobby. Bobby and Charlie are obviously close to one and the same in my unconscious. Just as Michelangelo was jealous of his older brother—or was it his sister and his sons?—and Attilio was jealous of Beniamino, and of Charlie and me, I am also obviously jealous of Charlie and of my son, Bobby.

But here, out of deference to Charlie's desire for privacy, I will end this chapter.

# 9

# My Son, Bobby

Again I hesitate. I do not want to write this chapter. I have not been and am not now the father to my son I would like to be. Let's start from the beginning. Bobby was very likely conceived on my wedding night. It never occurred to me that I had the choice *not* to have a child. In those days, in the early fifties, a Robertiello grew up, became a doctor, married, and had a family. I deviated slightly from the pattern, for I had had a five-year childless marriage before I married Bobby's mother. Why I didn't fertilize my first wife I really don't know. In any event, my first marriage was explained away by my family as youthful folly. After all, I had married her when I was twenty, during my first year of medical school. The second marriage was "serious." I was now a doctor and ready to wed the "right girl," settle down, and have children. My wife, apart from the fact that she was divorced and had a child by her previous marriage, was otherwise the "right girl." She was Italian (from Italy, not Italo-American), beautiful, cultured, polished, intelligent, an excellent cook and homemaker, a consummate hostess—in short, the perfect wife for me. She also, which

137

pleased my family, had not allowed any intimacies before marriage. So when we married, she immediately stopped using her diaphragm (that was before the Pill) and proceeded to get pregnant on her wedding night. That was fine with me, for I had proven my masculinity—in those days I think I really felt that way. I also felt *this* marriage was forever, was delighted my wife was pregnant, and confidently and eagerly awaited the birth of my son. Of course it was going to be a son—my wife's other child was a daughter, then four and a half, whom I adored, and now she would present me with a son! If I remember correctly, I wasn't present for all of the labor or for the birth because I was occupied with patients, but that was excusable since the labor was brief. I experienced all the pride a father is supposed to feel at having produced a son. In retrospect I cannot really understand why, since the act of conception was a matter of chance as was the sex of the child. I went to see the baby at the hospital several times. He did not look particularly attractive to me—more like a scrunched-up, hairy prune—but that was all right too, since most of the other babies looked the same way.

Then my memory grows a little hazy. As I mentioned, I used to gaze at Charlie in his crib and feel intense love for him. I am quite certain I had the exact same experience with Bobby, who after a few days or weeks began to look absolutely gorgeous to me, and I began the Adoration of the Magi number with him just as I had with Charlie. Then there is a blur in my memory. Then, after a little while, all I can recall is Bobby's screaming all night and keeping me awake and my being aware, though I would joke about it, of an intense hostility toward him. The little bastard was ruining my life! Those were the days when I was working as a full-time resident in psychiatry. I had a considerable private practice in the evening, was in personal analysis three or four times a week, was going to analytic school three nights a week, and was in addition studying for my boards in psychiatry and neurology. I needed like a hole in the head to be kept awake every night for two years. I tried earplugs. I tried sleeping on another floor. Nothing worked. My subjective memory is that I didn't sleep for two years because of Bobby, and this was during an extraordinarily stressful period of my life. I hated him for keeping me awake, and it overrode my pride, my wanting to have a chip off the old block, and everything else.

In his early years Bobby was a very difficult child. He was active, demanding, and rather regularly indulged by his mother as well as by me. I was knee-deep in the psychoanalytic idea of the time that children's problems are caused by insufficient love by their parents and by too rigid restrictions. Spock had just written his book on a more permissive child-rearing. From my own experience as a child, I could certainly accept the idea that I had had too many prohibitions and not enough love, permissiveness, and indulgence. In short, I believed myself to be an excellent example of a person whose life had been affected very negatively by poor parenting. Bobby was going to have an upbringing totally different from mine. I held him and hugged him. I bought toys for him. I took him to amusement parks, zoos, movies, and baseball games. We ate out together frequently. I played a great deal with him. We had a lot of physical contact. When he was four, we would wrestle in such a way that it appeared to be a fair contest but I would let him win. He was not going to suffer from the fear of competing with his father, as I had. I tried playing at boxing with him and let him hit me as hard as he could, but that ended when one day when he was four, and he gave me an uppercut that nearly floored me! So we stayed with wrestling, which dealt with the same issue in a safer way for me. I took him to the circus five or six times, and became so bored with it that now I can never go to the circus again. As I write this, I am somewhat surprised. I feel guilty about my relationship to Bobby. I did not describe the things I did for him out of the need to justify myself; I had honestly forgotten about them. I had myself stereotyped as a prototypical bad father who had not cared enough for his son. I had internalized Attilio again, the father who had disowned and disregarded me. In fact, though I could have been more of a father, I now am in some strange way giving myself credit rather than blame, a happy and totally unexpected develop-

139

ment. I wrote this chapter to criticize myself, not to praise myself. It will probably still come out that way, but I have to acknowledge—probably to perfectionistic Michelangelo in my head—that I was not an entirely bad father. I tried to be everything Attilio was not. I took Bobby to Europe, Florida, and the Caribbean. I held him and adored him, roughhoused with him, and listened to him.

Once, when Bobby was four, he said to me very innocently, "Daddy, when I rub my penis, wonderful marvelous things happen to me. I see stars and fairies and beautiful lights and the whole world is beautiful." I told him "You keep rubbing your penis as often as you want to. Let yourself enjoy all those beautiful feelings and never stop doing it." That was certainly something Attilio, Michelangelo, or even my mother would never have said to me. I don't think Bobby has suffered from any serious sexual inhibitions. He has no inhibitions about using his hands, whereas I had terrible masturbatory guilt and can now hardly screw in a light bulb. Bobby can take a watch or a TV set or an air conditioner apart and then put them together in a way that always makes me marvel.

Did I do all those good things for Bobby mechanically, because I was trying to be a Spock parent? I think not, for I recollect experiencing intense joy and love toward him during his early years. Of course Spock influenced me, but I have always been too authentic to do anything for long that is contrary to my actual emotions. The hatred I felt when Bobby kept me awake did not preclude genuine love for, and pride in, him.

What happened to spoil this bliss? One thing was that when Bobby entered his Oedipal stage around age five and fell madly in love with his mother, she fell madly in love with him too, and on a certain level I was no longer the apple of her eye. Like Michelangelo and Attilio, I had been displaced by my son—or so I experienced it. That was too much for me. I recall a rage directed at Bobby when he was five or six. It was not accompanied by a word or an action, but I knew he understood. I was furious with him and with his mother because I had once again been displaced—as I had been by my sister and then by my brother. That is clearly why I confuse Charlie's and Bobby's names. After he was five I tended to be irritable with Bobby, and though I continued to play with him, travel with him, and give him gifts, my heart wasn't really in it anymore. And, after my divorce from his mother when he was eleven, I didn't really enjoy my weekly or biweekly visits with Bobby, and I often paid more attention to my former wife than to him. So there was a dry spell in my communication with him when he was between ages eleven and sixteen.

When he was sixteen I remarried, and Bobby, my new wife, and I found a compatible triad. She liked him a great deal and got quite close to him, and to me this time that was a plus, for I never felt she favored him over me. That clearly was the key issue—I honestly rejoiced in her closeness to him as long as he did not replace me. During that marriage, which lasted five or six years, he was again the apple of my eye and a chip off the old block, not a rival but an extension. I was proud of his good looks, his social graces, his enjoyment of life. Since he was in college, majoring in psychology, he was going to be just like Dad. I visited him there and even lectured to his psychology class on one of my special interests—female homosexuality. I was proud to be there and Bobby was proud of me. He and I were friendly and intimate. I knew all about his love life and before I remarried—when it was a little more varied and interesting—he knew all about mine. We were buddies.

But then came a split, one that in retrospect was brought about more by him than by me. Bobby decided to change his major from psychology to music. He wanted to become an opera singer, and I passionately hate opera. I said to him, "Why couldn't you become a pimp or a junkie or a bank robber? You really know how to hurt a guy." But I swear I was kidding, honestly, and Bobby knew it. I strongly supported his changing his major. We remained buddies, and we talked for hours about his decision.

But for Bobby that was symbolic of a much bigger separation from me. Shortly thereafter he started pulling away. When he came to New York he phoned me dutifully, the way one phones a distant and not-very-favorite relative. The tone was obvious. I became very angry, told him I didn't want to be patronized; he shouldn't do me any favors. He was now twenty and had to push away from me to establish his identity. I can see that now; I certainly didn't then. I was furious and reciprocated. One day, at my office, he said to me, "You know, you really don't even like me." "You're right," I answered. "I really don't."

Bobby then went into **a** tailspin. He had to get away from me, but he needed my support. I didn't realize what was going on. I just felt hurt and angry that he had cut me out of his life, just as the other men in my family had done to me. He became depressed and unsure of himself. He returned, but crawling, looking for help from me, not just as a father but as a psychoanalyst. We spent hours and hours talking. I tried, but I suppose I wasn't very helpful or sympathetic. Bobby's desperation and depression increased. I had made my major suicide attempt at twenty-three; he was now twenty-one. He started to feel hopeless, to think about suicide. I couldn't deal with the situation either as a father or as a therapist so I sent him to the best therapist I knew. Within six months he was well enough to stop treatment. It had taken me about thirty-five years, so that was a bit of an improvement. However, we were still a little edgy with each other for a while. I suppose it is almost as difficult for a father to let go of a son as it is for a mother to let go of a daughter, and I still felt some resentment toward him for leaving me.

We have been much closer during the last five years, and discuss the events and feelings that are important to us. Then there was the trip to Chicago. We spent twenty-four hours together and were on the Donahue show. We talked a lot and basically both let it all hang out. I could be close, but I couldn't really be totally *with* him or completely affectionate. But it's pretty good now, not perfect but not bad. When you have Attilio as your father, it's a little tough to be like Robert Young in *Father Knows Best*; I didn't exactly have the best role model.

I thought I'd finish this chapter, and the book, depressed and guilty about the damage I have done to Bobby. Actually, I am pleasantly surprised. I haven't been perfect, Michelangelo, but under the circumstances I guess I really didn't do too badly. And I tried. That's all I can hold myself responsible for. I can't help how I *feel*, I can only be responsible for how I act. I haven't been that bad. I had internalized Attilio as a bad father, and then I had hated myself for being him vis-à-vis Bobby. I haven't been perfect, but even so I haven't been him.

Bobby, in my opinion, has turned out pretty well. How much of me and of others *he* has internalized is for him to determine. He is still pursuing his operatic career, teaching and studying musicology, and seems basically happy about his life and his relationships. I must respect his need for privacy and not delve too deeply into his life. He still wants more from me than I can give him, but at least I try to communicate honest feelings, both positive and negative. There is still distance between us, and I still find it difficult to be affectionate either verbally or physically. We both know this. I cannot and will not pretend otherwise.

Part of the reason I began to write this book was to try to understand how I developed into the man I am and how it affected my relationship with Bobby. In retrospect I can now see that I started out pretty well with him. I was verbally and physically affectionate in his early years despite my anger with him for disturbing my sleep. However, when his mother favored him over me, it was an intolerable blow, one that too closely paralleled my displacement in my mother's affections first by my sister and later by my brother. On another level it replayed for me the loss of my sister, since I had attached at least some of my love to Bobby's mother and I felt Bobby (like the angel of death with Betty) had taken her away from me. So, for quite a while Bobby became a rival and a depriver in my eyes. I was no longer able to love him, and I simply went through the motions of being a father. I wonder how frequently this pattern or a variation of it occurs in other fathers—not necessarily with my exact history. From Bobby's point of view, he started out with a relatively loving father, and then suddenly and certainly inexplicably lost him *emotionally* from age five to about sixteen. I, for him, went from being an ally to

143

being an enemy. It must have been very difficult for him to take this loss. The analysts I went to then were very Freudian, and focused on interpsychic issues rather than current real ones, so they were of no help to me. Though Bobby did not or could not formulate it and express it to me then, he certainly must have felt it deeply. He recognizes it and can talk about it to me now. In addition to abandoning him emotionally, I left him physically when I divorced his mother when Bobby was eleven. From eleven to sixteen he saw me briefly, and we had one of those typical divorced father-son relationships, distant and *pro forma*. I often see fathers taking their sons out to dinner on their weekly visit and am struck by the lack of any emotional connection between them.

When Bobby was twenty-one, he must have felt he was getting too close to me, losing his own identity and individuality and becoming too much of a carbon copy of his father. The healthy forces of separation-individuation arose in him. He correctly changed his major from psychology to music, not just as a gesture of not becoming me, but because he was clearly much more excited by music than by psychology. He was not just rebelling, he was actualizing his real Self, and the process of emotional separation from me was a necessary step in his growth toward becoming an autonomous individual. However, as with most such separations from a parent, the move was accompanied on his part by some hostility toward me, of which he had accumulated an ample reservoir from ages five to sixteen. The separation was necessarily rather violent and disruptive—necessarily for *him*. I, however, experienced his move as a personal rejection and as a loss of my narcissistic extension. Bobby had to some extent become for me from ages sixteen to twenty what I had been for Michelangelo in my early years. His pulling away from me represented another loss of an idealized loved one, even though much of my projection of magic onto him was that of the "magical" part of myself, and included in it were my hopes of achieving immortality through him. Erik Erikson writes about how parents attempt to perpetuate themselves through their children, and I certainly had that attitude about Bobby

144

when he was sixteen to twenty. It was intolerable when my illusion of a blissful emotional rapport was yet again shattered, as it had been by Betty's birth, Jerry's suicide, Betty's death, and then by my loss of both Bobby and his mother when he became her favorite. This is where I really failed Bobby. Instead of backing him in this separation from me and assuring him of my continuing love even if he did have to reject me for a while, I became angry and felt abandoned. Though I paid lip service to his desire for independence, I was not there for him emotionally. I am not proud of this; I wish I had been able to understand and respond positively. However, I did not. This is what I basically want Bobby to comprehend and forgive in me. Perhaps he realizes what failures in *my* life prevented my being able to be there for him then, and to some degree now. As I mentioned, he went into a tailspin of sorts at age twenty-one, one that revolved around his conflicting need to break free from me as a man; yet he needed my support and reassurance during this process. When I let him down, he fell into a period of self-doubt and despair at about the same age that I had. Just as my father failed to give me support, I failed Bobby. We talked together for hours and hours during that period, and he expressed his need for me openly and dramatically. I was powerless. He became more despairing. At that point I had had to turn to my first important analyst as a man who would support me in place of a parent. In this parallel crisis I had to send Bobby to an analyst who served the same function for him.

The angry child in me has still not forgiven him for taking his mother, and then himself, away from me. I hope this book will help me "forgive" him for "sins" he certainly did not in any conscious way commit, and that he will be able to understand and forgive me for the transgressions I unwittingly committed against him.

One of the reasons I wrote *A Man in the Making* was to explain to Bobby where I came from and why I haven't always been what I wanted to be for him. The book has been an attempt to bridge a gap between us. I hope it has succeeded; that he will be able to be a better father to his sons than

Michelangelo's father was to my grandfather, than Michelangelo was to Attilio and Beniamino, than Domenico was to Jerry, than Attilio was to me, and than I have been to Bobby.

# 10

# The Formation of Male Identity

## I. The Psychology of the Self

How does a man get to know who he is, attain a subjective feeling of his Self? What is a Self? What distinguishes a male Self from a female one? Before we discuss the question of what constitutes identity, we must define the word Self. Oddly, until recently most psychoanalysts, both American and non-American, have avoided utilizing the term in dealing with their patients, thinking it too vague, too ill-defined. Freud believed the mind consists of three parts: the id, which is the instinctual, biological part; the superego, which is the conscience incorporated from parental and societal values; and the ego, which is the "executive" part that mediates the demands of the instincts, the conscience, and the outside world. Some existential writers, though not denying the usefulness of Freud's constructs, felt they left out a very essential issue—the way a person subjectively experiences him or herself and his or her relationship to the world. (This differs from the ego, which primarily serves an executive function.) We all see ourselves as

147

the center of the universe. Even though we may also experience ourselves as little cogs in a big wheel, much of the time our focus on ourselves reflects our sensitivity to our bodily sensations and our feelings as the primary aspect of our perception of the world, though we do not simultaneously exclude (unless we are grossly psychotic) a perception of the outside world, of external reality. So let us begin by defining the word Self as the subjective feeling and cognition of our being at the center of our attention and of our psychological universe. This definition of Self is not a pathological one, as occurs in some forms of narcissistic disturbances in which there is an excessive focus on the Self and a withdrawal of interest in the outside world. Rather, it is a universal human subjective experience involving the entire person rather than a fragmentation of different parts of his or her mental apparatus. It defines how we experience ourselves rather than how we behave or function. We can get by very well in the world while simultaneously having a very poor sense of Self; my own history is testimony to that. However, a behavioral psychologist would not find much that is or was pathological in me. I have coped extraordinarily well with the world—scholastically, socially, economically, sexually, and professionally. I fit in relatively well with my society, my culture, and my specific subculture. I have had intense, intimate, and long-lasting relationships with men and women. I never seriously transgressed the laws of my society. I have acted in ways that would qualify me to be a good sibling, son, friend, lover, and even perhaps husband and father. From the point of view of behavioral psychology, in many respects my *functioning* and my *behavior* would score well above average. And yet, throughout my life, despite all these successes and stamps of approval, my subjective experience has been that I am a sad, lonely little boy; not really bright or sophisticated, not lovable, and frequently on the verge of an inner sense of fragmentation so painful that it twice led me to suicide attempts.

The psychology of the Self is a relatively recent concept in psychoanalytic circles, and the first international conference on the topic was the one I attended in Chicago in 1978. So, though obviously people do experience themselves as the center of their universe, and are aware of a subjective view of themselves—of how they perceive themselves rather than the face they put on for the world or how others experience them—psychoanalytical interest has lagged far behind. One reason of course is that the human Self is far less accessible to scientific investigation than overt human behavior. Psychology has been so afraid of losing its status as a precise science that it has simply ignored what is perhaps *the most important psychological view of man*—the way he experiences himself. That is why, even though over the past four decades I went to the best psychoanalysts available, not one of them had a really basic sense of what my "problem" was. They defined it as fear of succeeding in my work, as sexual inhibitions, as fear of abandonment by a woman, as the urge to control others—all of which were certainly correct. But solving these problems was like putting a Band-Aid on a cancer. Even though I told all my analysts literally thousands of times about my panic, my fear of disintegration and fragmentation, the terrible fluctuations in my self-esteem, they could not understand that my basic problem was my relationship to my own being. What I lacked was an inner structure of Self that would allow me to go through life with a modicum of inner tranquility and security, and an ability to experience joy—that profound feeling of satisfaction involving the entire being, in contrast to pleasure, which is a satisfaction of a part, such as eating when one is hungry.

I think one of the reasons (apart from convenience and exhibitionistic display) that I selected myself as the subject to explain the formation of male identity and the concept of the Self is that in my life there was such a clear and startling disparity between the outside view of my Self—as well as my own objective view—and *my inner, subjective view.* "How could you have any problems?" many people asked and still do ask me. "You are wealthy and successful professionally. You're loved by many people and respected and admired by many more. If I had the things you do or your ability to get what you want, I'd have it made." Most people don't understand that

149

"having it made" on the outside has little to do with one's internal state. I have had countless patients who thought that if they could just acquire an MD or a PhD, marry, have a child, or become wealthy, happiness would ensue. My cousin Robert said all he needed was a million dollars and a beautiful blonde. He got his million as well as a gorgeous blonde who was so devoted to him she followed him in death. Yet Robert's years with her were miserable. He was constantly tense, constantly driven. External circumstances had changed for him, but his inner experience of himself as the child who had been deserted by his parents and turned over to his callous and cruel grandfather, Michelangelo, had not.

I saw a man in his early forties recently. He had climbed from poverty to financial success; married a beautiful, sensual woman; had an enormous house in a fashionable suburb; two marvelous children without the usual adolescent problems; and his share of mistresses. But he felt totally empty. Until recently he had been so busy doing the "right" things that are supposed to bring one happiness that he had been cut off from his feelings about himself. He derived no joy from his work, from his family, or from lovemaking. He described his life as an emotional desert. He had no contact with his Self.

So, by using myself, patients, friends, and colleagues as examples, it behooves me to search for the origins of the feeling of Self, and for the experiences in our lives that either help give this Self a structure and a solidity or help destroy it.

## II. Identity and Self-Esteem

We must distinguish between identity and self-esteem. Identity consists of the clear sense of the boundaries of the Self and the feeling of its being a person separate from other persons. Self-esteem simply means the degree to which we value (or fail to value) ourselves. They issue from different sources and different experiences. One can have a very clear sense of being a separate, unique individual and at the same time suffer from low self-esteem. I believe I am an example of this and shall try to explain why. The converse can also be true—one can have a poor sense of identity and a relatively high level of self-esteem. Our society has taught us how to turn out well-functioning individuals who are productive and who fit in. If we are destroying a more important aspect of these persons—their subjective sense of themselves and their ability to experience joy—then we must understand the process by which this takes place so we will be able to prevent a repetition of it in future generations. Two of the most important problems at this point in history are alienation and lack of identity. In the past ten years, much that is valuable has been written about this process in women; here I want to focus my attention on the development of the Self in men. Sometimes the evolution of men and women in terms of the Self coincide, sometimes they do not.

The most crucial period in the life of any human being, the period that influences his or her self-esteem, though not necessarily the feeling of identity, is the first year. Starting literally from day one, the infant is extremely responsive to admiring looks, tones of voice, smells, tastes, and tactile nuances in the muscles and skin of the mother. Through all of the senses the baby can differentiate between a warm, loving, adoring response and a hostile, indifferent, or anxious one, and will either feel loved, admired, and soothed by the perceptions of his or her mother or will feel rejected or experienced as a burden. For instance, my mother must have been frightened to death of the responsibility of caring for me, her first child, during the initial year of my life and thereafter. She was never hostile, destructive, or even excessively intrusive with me, which is sometimes even more harmful than indifference or anxiety. But my Mother's background had not provided her with any confidence that she could handle her responsibility, and in fact she delegated it as soon as she could to Michelangelo or to anyone else who volunteered. She probably panicked, as she did all her life and still does when faced with responsibility. Her muscles and skin must have been taut. Her perspiration must have had the characteristic odor that infants associate with anxiety. For just as a dog can detect a frightened person from his or her smell, so can an

151

infant, especially during the first year. I cannot say that I remember my mother's milk, but it is a fact that the quality of the milk is influenced by the presence or absence of anxiety, by the preponderance of love and acceptance and joy at having a child, or of terror, fear of responsibility, and perhaps even hostility toward it. Mother probably did not have much of a delighted gleam in her eye when she looked down at me in my crib; she did not worship me as a new Christ child. There may have been a few incidental Magi around in the form of aunts and cousins bearing gifts from afar (like from New Jersey!), but no one in my nuclear family—my mother, my father, my grandmother Bettina—were the type of person to have that look of joyous admiration, or the cooing voice, tender touch, or cradling, relaxed muscles that go to make up a "holding environment." So my self-esteem—my feeling that I was a wonderful person to be with, one who could elicit love, adoration, or even just basic liking and acceptance in others by his mere presence, not by having to *do* anything—was clearly missing. Several years ago, when a patient had worked through a particular problem and was feeling good and resting on his laurels for a session, I suddenly felt anxious. Why would my patient want to remain in the same room with me? At that moment he did not need me to perform my analytic tasks for him, and I saw myself as completely worthless. My "logic" was that, just as when I was an infant, who obviously couldn't (a) be of any practical use to anyone and (b) was unable to evoke any positive, loving response from those around me, why shouldn't the patient walk out on me? Of course, my intellect realized that the patient was grateful for my help in having worked through the problem, and admired me even though I was of no practical use to him that session. But my feelings were based on people's original response to my mere presence, not on my intellectual awareness. Also, I have been very, very uneasy any time I have felt useless to a woman; I could not understand that she could like me or love me for myself. That is the explanation for the profound joy I had that day at age thirty-eight when my girlfriend, who in truth both loved me and liked me dearly, told me how much she liked me. For the first time in my life I experienced the wonderful feeling that I was liked for myself. Whenever I have been impotent, I have felt devastated and worthless; I literally have felt I am only as good as my last performance. For example, after five years of an excellent sexual and romantic relationship with this same woman, one day I was impotent. I felt sure that she would leave me immediately, that I was no longer of any value to her. My happy and successful history with her counted for naught.

I am sure Michelangelo had a pleased gleam in his eye when I arrived on the scene, but it was not one that mirrored my presence as a heaven-sent gift who was beautiful and wonderful just in his being. For he jumped at the opportunity to train a baby to become what he had wanted to be. I was a narcissistic extension, a person he would use to fulfill his own failed ambitions. I did not exist for him as a person in my own right, and approval came only if I met his requirements of becoming a perfectionistic, superintellectual, smoothly functioning person who produced, received acclaim, and never made a mistake. In grammar school, especially, I projected my internal representation of Michelangelo onto every teacher. I was absolutely terrified every single day of school right through high school, fearing that if I made one mistake I would get the strap or at least a severe tongue-lashing. So conditioned was I to associating school with fear that I once even had an anxiety attack on Parents' Day when visiting my son's school and his teachers. I still feel very uncomfortable in schools—especially elementary schools—and try my best to avoid them. I did get approval from Michelangelo for my stellar performances, and until very recently, and even now to some degree, I feel I must live up to his expectations. In my professional role—as a therapist, supervisor, lecturer, and even as a media performer invited to appear as an expert—I have by now such a backlog of good performances so as not to feel such anxiety. Michelangelo trained me so rigorously and so well that I rarely fail to come through. However, when I first began practice, taught my first classes, or gave my first speeches, I experienced the same terror that I always had with him or in school. During my first two years of professional life there was little money in my bank account of self-esteem.

We have seen that the original determinant of a person's self-esteem is the loving, positive response a baby is given merely for his being, exclusive of factors of usefulness or compliance with the wishes of others. Although a positive response is valuable and even necessary to the infant, sometimes its absence effectively, albeit prematurely, forces the infant to develop a cohesive sense of identity (in contrast to self-esteem). *Identity and self-esteem are not mutually exclusive.* A child reaches a high level of self-esteem by being admired, then attains a strong sense of identity by being permitted to be as independent as is appropriate to his or her age. The painful realization of the total lack of response to his or her real Self can push the child to reinforce its sense of boundaries, for no one else can be counted upon. "Remember," Lily Tomlin says, "we're all in this alone." I knew this from the beginning. There was no one besides Betty who would recognize or relate to my real Self, only to my accomplishments, and only Michelangelo even to those. I was thus forced to develop a consciousness of my ability to survive, without any response to my real inner Self. And though I certainly did not in any way like this inner core of me, I had to learn to live in the world with it. I had to adopt a way of being that kept me in touch with this inner Self, unappreciated and perhaps defective though it may have been. Even though I had to conceal it from everyone in the world, even my most intimate friends, *I* had to maintain a sense of a me that was not just the façade I presented to the world, not just the hardworking, compliant person who reaped approval from his usefulness.

The part of me that I felt was most individualistic, idiosyncratic, and uncompromising, was my sexuality. This part was, until I started getting involved with women at age fifteen, all and only for me. I do not remember anything about my sexuality until I was four or five. Then I recall fantasizing about, then trying to peek up my sister's skirts, those of other little girls in my class, and undoubtedly those of adult women around me such as my mother, and especially my Aunt Peggy. I fantasized at that age being a king or an emperor and having my henchmen go through the country and bring me the most beautiful women in the kingdom. I would then strip them and have them put in irons in a dungeon, so they were available to be looked at and also (and this is vaguer) to be tortured at my will. I did not at that point know of anything else one could do with women. I wanted them completely under my domination and I wanted to look at their bodies, for I think that I adored them then, and have continued to adore their bodies in a way I wanted my own body to be adored when I was a baby. My voyeurism, among its other determinants, was a way of supplying myself with love and adulation I had never received. The women who filled my five-year-old's fantasies did not have to perform, all they had to do was to be there, naked for me to worship. But in addition to the psychodynamics of my fantasies (ones that included not just adoration for *being*, but also the less clearly defined sadistic parts stemming from my fury that most of the women in my life *failed* to adore me), the mere fact that I possessed an imaginative world that existed to please me and no one else proved to me that I had a Self distinct from my façade. So, even after I was married and my sexuality became an attempt to obtain my wife's approval by striving for superlative performances, I had to retain a part of me that was only for myself. And that part was looking at *Playboy* spreads or watching a stripper. It was to reinforce the sense of my Self as a separate person; it did not add to my self-esteem. In fact it lowered it because, until I was thirty-five I often felt that I was dirty—immoral and perverted—for having to leer at naked ladies.

The distinctions between real Self and false Self, and between self-esteem and sense of identity, are to my way of thinking very important elements in arriving at an understanding of our development as human beings, and I believe there has been and still is a tremendous amount of confusion among these concepts, even in sophisticated psychological and psychoanalytic circles. My criticism of behavior therapy, sexual therapy, and family or couple therapy is that there is excessive focus on external behavior. The therapist attempts to cure a specific complaint, make the patient perform better in bed, or relate better to those around him or her. Behaviorists deal almost exclusively with the so-called "false Self" in us, our façade, with the way we deal with other people. They seem to have lost the conception of one's internal world, of the way one relates to him or herself, and to the introjects, the persons in his or her past who have become a part of this inner world. My grandfather Michelangelo, though his influence is greatly diminished, remains a more important part of my subjective experience of myself and of the world than are many of the actual, living people in it. He is constantly criticizing me, judging me, and expecting more and more from me. And those moments when he seems to leave me, I often project him into a mate, a patient, a friend, or a lover. Guiding my conduct vis-à-vis the real people in the real world might help me, but it might also tend to obscure the core issues that trouble me. I have already mentioned that a sharp division between the real Self and the false Self may be somewhat oversimplified and romantic. Just as we are more than the person whose behavior in the world and with people can be observed, we are also more than the person who lives only in his or her inner world. Our "false Self" is also unique and idiosyncratic and derives from our specific genetic and environmental past, so "false" is perhaps a misnomer.

In delineating what gives us our sense of Self, our self-esteem, and our identity, I notice I have fallen into the common psychoanalytic custom of neglecting genetic background. For I am in fact a strong believer in the genetic root of many psychiatric illnesses, including schizophrenia and manic-depressive psychosis. In my opinion, with genes that head one in these directions, neither love and approval nor internalizing idealized figures may be enough to halt the process. Though this conclusion, like practically all conclusions in my field, can be disputed, I am convinced that the twin studies of Dr. F. J. Kallmann, made in 1946, are definitive. Dr. Kallmann studied 691 families that contained twins, at least one of whom was schizophrenic. He found that among fraternal (two-egg) twins, if one was schizophrenic, the chance of the other one being so was 14.5 percent, which was essentially similar to the expectancy among siblings (14.2 percent). Among identical (one-egg) twins, if one twin was schizophrenic, the chance of the other being so was 86.2 percent. Dramatic? Yes. But genes do not influence only the major psychoses, they also influence certain tendencies to be compulsive, depressed, or emotionally unstable. While I am relatively content with my genetic heritage, one could also, for example, make a pretty good case for a genetic as well as an environmental cause behind my preoccupation with suicide. In a more general way, our ability to develop strong sense of self-esteem, as well as a feeling of identity, will contain genetic factors.

I had little acceptance of my real Self and very little adoration. But, in intellectual areas, I received a great deal of approval for certain accomplishments and disapproval for failures. And from this I traversed my early years with a very low sense of self-esteem but also with a rather strong sense of identity. Michelangelo reinforced the idea that though I wasn't lovable, I was a unique person who had talents that set him apart from others. I was a leader, and entitled to special treatment. It must have taken a strongwilled little boy to convince his principal to let him go into the first grade at age five and to convince her at the same time to allow his mother to sit in the classroom with him for two weeks! Here again we run into the contrast between my low self-esteem and my highly developed sense of uniqueness and identity. I am thus a good example how the strengths of these two different aspects of the concept of Self can be mutually exclusive. Of course, with parents who admire their child, but also let it go and encourage independence at an age-appropriate time, they both can be present.

My sense of being a special person, despite low self-esteem, also allowed me to be elected president of my class in grammar school and president of several secret clubs. And, of course, I was usually the scholastic leader. Nonetheless, there coexisted with these triumphs the reality of being the despised Italian

157

kid in the elegant WASP school. These opposing views have never left me. Behavior therapy, which might offer me a better way to relate to my wife or to cope with a specific problem in life, could never break through to the origins of my negative inner view of myself. (This is not true for everyone, however. Some are helped by being shown how to deal with a particular issue in their lives and thereby increase their self-esteem.) Although I am a person with a strong sense of identity and a low feeling of self-worth, I can easily imagine the reverse. A child with doting parents who tend to restrict his or her independence may grow up with a poor sense of identity, but with higher self-esteem than I enjoyed.

The ideal situation is one in which there is a very strong bond of affection and mutual adoration between mother and child, especially during the first year of life. If the child is really fortunate, there will be a similar bond between him or her and the father, and there will be shared child-rearing. This connection with the father will help the child, from the latter part of the first year on, in the process of separating emotionally from the mother and gradually achieving a sense of identity and autonomy as a separate person. The child's intimate relationship with loving parents will make him or her feel wonderful about him or herself as a person who is a treasure and a delight. The child will learn from the parents the day-by-day human ways of relating to other people in a thoughtful, affectionate manner, as well as deriving from the parents the capacity to experience joy in a relationship with another person. Then, as the child matures, the parents will not try to bind him or her but will encourage independent activity at a suitable age. They will encourage the child to walk at one year, will toilet-train at about three, will send the child to nursery school at three or four, and to sleep-away camp at nine or ten, thus simultaneously conveying an optimal amount of self-esteem through their adoration and inculcating a strong sense of identity by encouraging independence. The parents will also be available for refueling and reassurance if some efforts at independence are aborted or unsuccessful—falling off a bicycle, for example. Oh, that we all had had such ideal parents!

But then I wouldn't have many patients, would I?

That earliest memory of mine of being under the table at age two in a foreign place while my sister was being born, of feeling lonely and unwanted, is the same feeling I have sometimes today even though I am not alone and am loved by many people close to me. The way a child is dealt with when a sibling arrives can have an important impact on self-esteem. Characteristically, my parents handled my sister's arrival with their usual genius for being as destructive to my Self as possible. They could have prepared me for the event, for instance, by playing out the arrival by placing a doll in a new crib and assuring me I would not lose any of their affection. But they didn't even make me aware of the meaning of my mother's pregnant belly, and sent me away from home to be with relative strangers rather than having me at least maintain a continuity of the physical environment around me. This established the pattern for me of connecting the coming of a rival with abandonment and exile. How could a two-year-old feel any security under those circumstances? And then, when I was brought home, I was displaced from the parental bedroom and from my crib and put into my grandparents' room. I have wondered at my seeming lack of jealousy and been suspicious of it. Only lately have I begun to be in touch with the fact that it must be so enormous and overwhelming that I have had to build a strong wall of denial over it lest it break out into its primitive fury. The few times I have experienced this jealous rage, even briefly, have been all but unbearable. So the lonely, rejected, unwanted child continues to live alongside the leader and achiever, and the fact that the child was displaced so abruptly and so callously made him feel even more unwanted. If the birth of a sibling is handled correctly and with compassion and empathy, damage to the self-esteem does not have to be major or long-lasting.

There is a set of factors that tends to contribute to the sense of identity in a male—being able to experience himself as a unique individual; as someone possessing clear boundaries between himself and the wishes of the persons surrounding him; as having the right to be himself even when it means making mistakes; of being able to do things his way without excessive concern about fitting in or obtaining outside approval; of having the courage to be different or perhaps creative. Here again I will use myself as an example, one supported by my having verified my own pattern against that of other men who appear to have some of the aforementioned qualities as well as similar childhood configurations. Of course, as before, we don't want to underestimate the importance of a favorable genetic background. But beyond this, it appears to me that the type of mother who is likely to produce a man with a strong sense of his identity is one who is there in the sense of being available for ministration, loving contact, and required personal care, but who does not merge with the child, does not live her life through him or try to bind him to herself. She must be involved with herself or her husband so that her whole life does not, at least after the first year, revolve around the child. She does not intrude or try to get into the child's mind or try to take him over so she will have a companion to keep her from being lonely. She is not so heavily invested in his achievements, and in what he will do to enhance her existence, that she becomes domineering and exacting. Though my grandfather was this way, my mother was not. Since the crucial separation in the struggle to establish separateness and a sense of identity is from the mother, attachments—even strong ones—to other persons such as the father, the grandmother, the grandfather, or siblings—tend to aid the process of the formation of a sense of separateness rather than diminish it. This is a strong argument in favor of shared child-rearing. The men I know who have a strong sense of themselves are more apt to have had mothers like mine who were present but relatively disinterested and noninterfering. Most of my male friends, and certainly most of my male patients, are Jewish, and have had "Jewish mothers," literally and figuratively. One obviously does not have to be Jewish to have a "Jewish mother"—one who is overly entangled and involved with her son emotionally. She may be very loving, affectionate, generous, and empathetic. She is

160

often overprotective. She is frequently possessive, and often binds her son to her through guilt-producing threats. She tends to be somewhat seductive with her son, and tries to separate him from his father and his siblings, sometimes by running them down in his eyes and forming an alliance against them. These attitudes add up to an overinvolved mother from whom it is difficult for a son—and, God knows, even more difficult for a daughter—to separate. My mother's relative lack of involvement with me, coupled with my grandfather's intense if narcissistic concern, helped me make the split and become an individual—albeit one who was afraid of being abandoned by his mother. So, while self-assertive enough at age five to demand to be put in the first grade instead of kindergarten, I also needed my mother's presence in the classroom and was strong enough to insist on this condition. Though I am always fearful of being abandoned by women, I never compromise my ideals in order to please them. And because of this strong sense of identity, I really don't care much what people think. That is one reason I am able to write this book. I am very little concerned about revealing myself or of being disapproved of because I have done so. It is odd that despite having had such a judgmental and disapproving grandfather, I am relatively oblivious to other people's opinion of me. I believe this is because of the great difference between having had a disapproving grandparent as opposed to an overinvolved mother who may also be disapproving. For, once separation from the mother can be successfully effected, no one else can constitute a major threat to one's sense of identity or ability to do things his or her own way.

Men certainly have a much easier time separating from their mothers than women do. For one thing, because they are of a different gender, there is less chance for merging—for becoming one with the other person. For another, our society encourages independence in men while it often rewards the lack of it in women. Women are encouraged to remain extensions of their mothers and of their men rather than human beings in their own right. Of course, the feminist movement has made a start at changing this, but it is only a beginning, and it will most likely take several generations before women are truly free.

So, we have seen that in the relationship with the mother, what is needed for a sense of identity to develop in a man is continuous physical presence and availability for services—not necessarily for love, affection, or interest, although they are highly desirable. Men who have lost their mothers at birth, or in the early years, or whose mothers have deserted them or gone off to work in their first year may not have enough of the constant presence of a maternal figure to be secure enough to begin the process of individuation. They may have a poor sense of identity and lead very chaotic lives socially and emotionally.

### III. Toilet Training

The toilet-training period is crucial to the development of both the sense of identity and the feeling of self-worth, and I believe Freud and other analysts were correct in focusing a great deal of attention on this period. From the point of view of the formation of identity, toilet training represents the first major clash of wills between mother and child. The mother wants the child to control its bladder and bowels; the child wants in the main to continue to have the freedom to urinate and defecate at will. A "good enough" mother will not begin the process until the child is over two, won't be concerned if the process of training is not completed until after the third birthday. She will persist, but she will do it gently—by giving rewards rather than punishments—and by allowing her child to express a great deal of opposition and rebellion against her during this time without responding in a punitive, disparaging, or humiliating manner. One of the cornerstones of the establishment of a sense of identity is the ability to say no. The more a young child is confident of its ability to say no, the less willing it will be to yield autonomy to any person or group. When a child is trained before age two or three, it does not possess adequate physiological and neurological controls to permit training without force, and thus a surrender of a tremendous part of his or her autonomy. The child's toilet training at such an early age can be accomplished only by a process of domination and intimidation. It must by necessity be enforced by punishment, not just by rewards. It must be accomplished by an invasion of the child's autonomy and his or her sense of Self and identity. I do not know when my toilet training was accomplished or by whom or in what manner. If it was done by my mother, which it must have been at least in part, then I can assume that she was not intrusive or punitive and that my sense of identity was reinforced in the process. As I have mentioned, my mother is never, nor has she ever been, authoritarian or punitive. It is very easy to say no to her. She never enforces her will on me or on anyone else. I am sure Michelangelo was involved in training me and that he was cruel, punitive and domineering. But since he was not after all my mother, my major process of separation, and my development of a sense of identity and autonomy, may very well have already been established before he took over his training of me. He was interested in me as an intellectual extension, so he probably left early feeding and toilet training to my mother. After all, even today, and certainly a half-century ago, those functions were not considered to be part of a man's role—and my grandfather was very much a man in that sense. So it is very likely that with all the damage that was done to my self-esteem by my mother's relative rejection and indifference, my sense of identity was reinforced by her personality. Otherwise I couldn't properly explain my ability to stand up for myself even at age five or ever since. I have always had a tremendously strong belief in my convictions, even recognizing that I often change them yearly. I give myself the right to be wrong, and I don't care excessively about what people think of my unconventional beliefs or behavior either in my practice as an analyst or in the way I choose to lead my life.

The other very important aspect of the toilet-training period is the negative effect it can have on a child's self-esteem. A mother who is compulsively neat and clean and/or who toilet trains a child too soon because she is repelled by excrement gives her child the feeling that he or she is dirty, smelly, has weak self-control, and is an undesirable person. And no matter how successful, bright, and handsome we are, if we experience ourselves as dirty or smelly we will believe ourselves unacceptable to others. There is logic in this assumption, given the mother's original distortion. Someone who is bad-smelling is, in fact, not nice to be near regardless of his or her other qualities. Some of my male patients have an unconscious emotional view of themselves as being "caked with shit" despite their intellectual, cognitive, awareness to the contrary. They feel inferior, undesirable, and unacceptable no matter how many successes they have in reality. Women in general have this problem to an even greater degree. Girls are taught to be fastidious and sweet-smelling whereas boys are encouraged to be scruffy and to get dirty in their play. Nevertheless, men can react very negatively to domineering or punitive mishandling during their toilet training and to subsequent condemnation of disorderliness or dirtiness. I remember at age ten I had played baseball and was covered with dirt from having slid into second base several times. I took a bath but neglected to wash out the tub. The maid scolded me soundly—not for having forgotten to wash out the tub, criticism that would have been merited, but for getting myself so dirty, which was perfectly natural under the circumstances. I felt humiliated for having been found out to be such a dirty boy. However, since my mother very likely did not deal with me in a similar way, I was able within a relatively short time to recover my self-esteem. But other men I know who have had overly compulsive mothers, or mothers who were obsessed with cleanliness and order, have grown up not only feeling that they smell bad and are "dirtier" than other people and therefore undesirable, but also that they lack sufficient inner controls and have something organically or characterologically wrong with them. In order to counter this, they sometimes become overly controlled people who incorporate their mothers' negative image of themselves and are constantly self-critical and punitive despite their attempts to be good, clean, and orderly. These men are often "nice guys" who lack a certain healthy aggressiveness and are so apt to be submissive to women in a deep sense that women find them uninteresting sexually. Then there are men who have such critical, punitive, and denigrating mothers that they live out the role of the bad boy that they have been cast in by their mothers. They are offensive in their manners, their dress, and their speech. They are often disorganized in the way they handle their professional life, money, eating and drinking, and toilet habits. They still retain the critical mother in their inner world, but instead of yielding to her they rebel against her. Women may be more sexually responsive to these men than to their submissive counterparts because these rebels are more adventurous and aggressive, but being involved with one of them leads to a chaotic sort of existence that lacks the stability, care, and sense of comfort that are essential ingredients of a satisfying relationship. These men may have a somewhat stronger sense of their identity than the ones who submit totally to their mothers' wishes, but they are certainly not autonomous, mature adults. Rather, they are perpetual adolescents who must always prove they are not excessively merged with their mothers. In terms of self-esteem, they often have a very low sense of their value, constantly mess up (*double entendre* intended) their personal and professional lives, get bad feedback for it, and realize that it is in fact their own lack of organization that complicates existence and elicits the put-downs they get from others. They may enjoy a greater sense of gender identity as males than the mama's boys who are extensions of maternal wishes, but they have to pay a price for this in the discomfort they feel about themselves and in the serious problems they create in their lives.

In any event, it is by now quite evident that to men a tremendously important source of both a sense of identity and of self-esteem reverts to the kind of mother they had, especially in their first few years. This is hardly a surprise to a psychoanalyst, but to laymen its significance is frequently overlooked. The degree to which your mother beamed happily at you during your first years of life has a powerful effect on whether or not you feel wonderful and desirable and have a high level of self-esteem. How much your mother permitted you to be an independent person, was able to let you go in your second and third years, as well as later on, has a tremendous impact on your sense of identity and autonomy, and even on your sense of being male—different in gender from your mother. The more your mother tried to invade you, possess you, and entangle you in her web, the more she used guilt as a way of manipulating you, the less freely you will experience yourself as someone who has the right to seek your way of dealing with life. I emphasize this, not just because I am such a good example of it myself, but also because it focuses so sharply on the paradox that one can have very low self-esteem from having received very little in the way of loving glances from one's mother or others and at the same time have a very strong sense of identity and of one's masculinity by having a mother who is not binding, possessive, interfering, or intrusive. Fortunate are those persons whose mother loved them and adored them during their first year of life, but then was gradually able to relinquish them and to support their efforts to become adventurous, individualistic, and even rebellious.

## IV. Relationships to Men in the Family

And, of course, to have a father, grandfather, or sibling who was emotionally, not just physically, in the picture, as an ally in the enormously difficult battle to break from Mother, is a tremendous help in achieving a sense of identity. Though Michelangelo was a negative influence in so many ways, he was still a transitional figure in my journey from being merged with Mother to my becoming an autonomous adult. Though he lowered my self-esteem by being critical and perfectionistic, he also raised it by thinking of me as a budding young genius. The reason my father or other men almost invariably appear later in the process of maturation is certainly not because I, for one, would like it to be that way—it is simply because in our American society, and in almost every other society in the world, fathers are not much involved in the process of child-

166

rearing during the first few years of life. Feminist writers and some social psychologists deplore this, and I have read some writers, notably Dorothy Dinnerstein in *The Mermaid and the Minotaur*, who even go so far as to say that almost all of the world's troubles would be eliminated by shared child-rearing. I am essentially in agreement with this opinion. Having the father involved from birth or in feeding, changing diapers, and holding the baby would provide an added opportunity for positive mirroring response and would certainly aid the process of separation from the mother. As I have emphasized, my own grandfather, Michelangelo, was an enormous help to me on both these accounts despite his brutality, narcissism, and destructiveness. Imagine how much more of an aid he would have been if he had been kind and loving! An important part of his impact on me was his being constantly at home. He did not work. How many fathers are there in our society who spend much time with their children during the first years of life? First of all, very few of them are at home often during the child's waking hours. Secondly, the cultural norm (being gradually changed by the impact of feminism) is for them not to be very much involved in the day-to-day care of the child—feeding, diapering, and holding. All too often the father spends virtually no time being close to his son during the first two years; perhaps slightly more time with him from four to five. So for most boys, Dad doesn't get into the picture much until the boy is quite active, mobile, and articulate. Most American fathers seem to become interested in their sons at about four if they take any interest in them at all. At that age, perhaps a little later, a dual process begins in the father-son relationship. The two main issues are *competition* and *identification*. In the usual situation the son competes with the father for the attention—especially the sexual attention—of the mother. This is the well-known Oedipus complex. Four-, five-, and six-year-old boys are extraordinarily sexual. Earlier I described how when I was in first grade both boys and girls were constantly preoccupied with sex, how we talked about it all the time and exposed ourselves. A parallel process occurs at home. The boy is very interested in and attracted to his

167

mother's body, and wants her to be interested in his. He expects—not unnaturally—that his father will disapprove of his interest and will compete with him for his mother's attention. He tends to experience a fear of castration, since his sexual sensations are genital ones and he expects his father to punish him for desiring his mother by removing the "source" of his sexual interest in her. If the father is relatively secure in his own sexuality and happy in his relationship with his wife, he will notice his son's rivalry and interest in his wife, but he will not be threatened by it. Instead he will be slightly amused and also somewhat proud of his son's budding sexuality, and will have mock fights with him like my wrestling matches with Bobby. His wife will also enjoy and accept her son's sexual interest, but she will not be provocative or seductive in response to him. The son's fears of his father's anger and castration will be alleviated by the father's acceptance, without rancor, of his son's sexuality. The son will see that as much as he might hope to separate his parents and run off with his mother, she really prefers his father to him and he will not be able to fulfill his wish. Finally, out of an awareness of reality and a recognition that his mother is not available to him as a sexual partner, he will turn his erotic interests to some little girl and will have resolved the Oedipal dilemma with a minimum of trauma.

In my family things were hardly so idyllic. All of the men in it, unfortunately including myself, were very jealous of and competitive with their sons—even when the sons were children of four, five, and six, and thereafter. Domenico was jealous of his son, Jerry. Rather than being supportive of him during his adolescence and in his first sexual encounters with women, Domenico was disapproving, punitive, and angry. We cannot know exactly what went on in Jerry's mind, but he certainly did not have a solid relationship with his father, but a hostile and competitive one, and this was without a doubt a factor in Jerry's youthful suicide. We do not know much about Michelangelo's relationship to his father other than his description of it as very negative, for he blamed his father for thwarting his ambitions. I clearly recall how hostile, negative,

168

and competitive Michelangelo was with my father, for Michelangelo in turn tried to thwart Attilio's career and never contributed a cent to his medical education. Michelangelo also disparaged Beniamino, which contributed to my uncle's suicide. Attilio, of course, continued this pattern with me and my brother, Charlie. He was always angry and competitive with me from my earliest childhood and furiously resented any affection my mother gave me. All through my life, to the day of his death, he minimized my achievements rather than experiencing them as accretions to his self-esteem. I was a hated rival for my mother; later a professional rival. The result was that I never felt I had any support of any kind from my father; he was an enemy rather than a friend. Luckily for me I had the strength to accept the challenge and decided my salvation lay in outdoing him. However, this choice resulted in years and years of almost unbearable anxiety, from which I suffered almost without respite until the completion of my first analysis at age twenty-seven. My dreams during that analysis were filled with symbolic and overt references to my castration. Many times I considered giving up altogether. On the two occasions when I attempted suicide I *did* give up. Though my self-esteem was at rock bottom then, my strong sense of identity allowed me to follow my option to die. After these attempts failed, and with the support of my analyst, I began to be able to put together the pieces of my shattered self-esteem. Significantly, the more determined of the two suicide attempts occurred after I had graduated from medical school and was forced to live with my father, since an intern's salary in those days was a wretched $40 per month. I am sure Attilio was especially destructive toward me then because he saw me as a professional rival who was already faring well in his, Attilio's, chosen field of medicine. Though the suicide attempt was triggered by a rejection by a student nurse, I remember in the hours I spent pondering death before I took the pills that many of my thoughts turned to Attilio; to the terrible times I had passed with him. So I chose to destroy myself to avoid the pain of his destruction of me. Later on, in analysis, I elected instead on the alternative of destroying *him* by outdoing him. But each step of that process was filled with intolerable anxiety. Having a father who matches your rivalry rather than accepting it with grace and humor can have marked detrimental effects on your ability to see yourself as a man capable of being assertive. My brother basically yielded to my father's will and was a serious underachiever until he was thirty. And I, of course, regrettably carried on the family tradition by competing with my own son for the attention of his mother. I feel that Bobby, too, has not attained his full potential, and I recognize that I am at least partially responsible.

The major effect of having a competitive rather than a supportive father is that it tends to interfere with the other, noncompetitive, part of the process that should go on smoothly between fathers and sons—the process of identification. One of the most important ways of building self-esteem, after that initial loving gleam from the mother's eye which provides us with a positive mirroring of ourselves, is through the idealization of traits of people around us, notably but not exclusively our father, followed by the internalization of these traits as parts of ourselves. If we thought highly of Dad's sense of humor and made it part of ourselves, we will take pride in resembling that admired part of him. This process, called "transmuting internalization" in the analytic literature, is the principal way we form accretions to our self-esteem after our first years of life. It is a process that continues until death, for we never cease to find teachers, doctors, priests, colleagues, or friends whose traits we idealize and make our own. For a man, of course, the primary focus is the father. In order for the process to work optimally, we should have a father who in some way or another is admirable. He should also enjoy our adulation of him; that we want to be a chip off the old block should delight him. My father in many ways was very admirable, especially in his professional dedication. He wanted to be respected for his achievements, and spoke of them constantly—ad nauseum in fact. Despite our appalling relationship, I internalized many of his admirable traits. But he did not especially enjoy my emulating him, experiencing it as a threat. Nonetheless, probably because of their genuine value, I

170

went ahead and internalized some of his good qualities anyway.

In addition to internalizing positive traits, another process that occurs between parents and children is *incorporation*. This is unconscious and means that we take in parts of our parents that we do *not* like. This is done in order to maintain the illusion of a bond between parent and child, and to avoid open confrontation and a split. The child hates this added part of the Self, but avoids hating it openly in the parent. It is significant that I never had an open battle with my father. My classical confrontation with him occurred when he was eighty-four and I was fifty-three. It was very low-keyed; there were no angry recriminations, and we continued to maintain the façade of a peaceful relationship until he died. I expressed my anger with him indirectly throughout my life—by withdrawing emotionally in his presence, by complaining to my mother or others about him, by trying to outdo him. I never really took him on; instead I unfortunately took him *in*. For what I took in, less consciously than by identifying with his professional commitment, was his self-effacement, his complaining, his need to control, his rivalry with his son, and his impatience. These unpleasant traits, rather than adding to my self-esteem through idealization, were despised by me in him and in myself.

By contrast, my relationship with my two grandfathers was characterized mostly by the internalization of positive qualities. Michelangelo certainly wanted me to be a chip off the old block, and I admired his intellectual curiosity, his persistence, and his perfectionism, so I took many of these qualities into myself. Because of his physical abuse of me I had more open confrontations with him than I did with my father. (Thank goodness brutality was one of his qualities I did *not* incorporate!) I took from Domenico his interest in food, sports, and sex, and his ability to enjoy life's sensuous pleasures. All of these internalizations and incorporations either added to or detracted from my self-esteem.

After the Oedipal period and the wish for total, even sexual, involvement with the mother, and the boy's subsequent failure to supplant his father, he usually goes into a period of renouncing women from about ages eight to twelve. He shores up his relationships with other boys, and ultimately to himself, as a man separate from a woman. He has very close relationships that sometimes include sex—frequently mutual masturbation—with the other boys. These do not usually lead to a homosexual life-style. Rather, they reinforce his feeling that if he must, he can live without Mother or contact with other women. I remember my close friendships during this period with two or three of the boys on my block. We played stickball, marbles, and Monopoly. But we also talked for hours about what the world was all about; we discussed philosophies as well as batting averages.

How much of a role hormones play in gender identity, or what the effects of hormones or other influences on a fetus are, is still an open question. Until very recently, friends of mine who are experts in the field of transsexuals claimed that there was no detectable organic, biochemical, or even hormonal difference between transsexuals and other human beings; transsexual men are ones who from early childhood have experienced close identification with women, feel they *are* women and eventually through surgery have had their male genitals removed and have had false vaginas and breast implants made. There has been little proof that the cause of this unusual situation was other than psychological. Recently, however, there has been some work suggesting that there may be biochemical and hormonal changes occurring *in utero* that cause this dramatic shift in gender identity. Whatever its origins, the problem obviously cannot be corrected in any major way after adulthood, so if a boy child shows a strong propensity to act in a feminine manner, it might be advisable to consult an endocrinologist as well as a psychiatrist or psychologist.

Returning to my own sense of identity—especially gender identity, my security about my masculinity—I was quite fortunate in that respect. Almost all the men in my family—Michelangelo, Domenico, Attilio, Jerry, Aldo, and Robert—were very certain of their maleness. Only Beniamino perhaps was not. Part of my sense of maleness very likely originated in my genetic endowment. Part of it also perhaps came from my patriarchal ethnic background, though certainly not all men with this background have strong gender identities. And part of it came from my role models. As I have pointed out, the fact of my mother's *not* merging with me, her allowing me to separate from her, helped immeasurably.


## V. Relationships to Other Men

I have always been involved in sports, both as participant and observer. I played association football and stickball on the streets of New York, and attended baseball and football games from early childhood. I heard a great deal of "jock-talk." These peer relationships with friends, teachers, and colleagues helped me and help other men firm up their identity, especially their gender identity.

After having passed through what used to be and still is referred to by some writers as the latency period—the time from about eight to twelve when a boy establishes his connections to other boys, partly as a result of his failure to win his mother sexually—the entire process of establishing his identity as a separate male person is jolted by the onset of puberty. Physiological factors increase sexual feelings; the young boy again experiences a tremendous drive toward women. In early adolescence, boys and girls clearly are sexually attracted toward each other, but in this society they generally try to resist their sexual drives, compromising by name-calling, fighting, and roughhousing in which they sometimes touch each other, but do not actually join, for this would threaten identity and separateness. Boys are still very much involved in their male-male relationships. They engage in sports, games, or intellectual discussions with other boys, while experiencing an almost overpowering need for girls. I attended an all-boys' high school from twelve to fifteen. I was drawn to girls but was at the same time frightened to death of them and pictured them as alien, unfathomable beings. I had

173

no sisters at home or girl cousins my age; I saw no women at school; thus girls were not people to me but sexually alluring temptresses whom I longed for in a manner I could not define. Today I am opposed to all-male schools and regret having attended one, for it gave me a distorted idea of women.

During those years I studied hard and read practically everything I could get my hands on. I had no contact with girls and only a few with boys, and even the few close associations of my latency period tapered off. I was on a big push to become the intellectual my grandfather wanted. The boys in my class were mostly middle-class Jewish liberals, and they quickly converted me from Catholicism to atheism; politically they influenced me in the direction of socialism. They had a tremendous impact on my intellect and on my psychoanalytic view of the world, but I did not get close to any of them emotionally, as I had to my friends in my latency period or as I would later in my adolescence and adult life. I saw none of my high school classmates until the twenty-fifth class reunion, which was fun, and interesting to see how they had turned out, but was also proof that I had never been emotionally close to any of them. Although my experience may have been atypical, many boys in fact go through a period during the later latency years in which there is a loosening of emotional ties with other boys and a greater concentration on work, sports, or hobbies. This period can represent a time of reinforcement of the Self and of the establishment of an identity separate from both other men and from women. Prior to this break, boys frequently become vaguely aware of homosexual feelings; of merging with other boys. They respond to these feelings either by becoming overtly involved in homosexual activity, which could lead to a homosexual lifestyle, or, more frequently, by reducing the degree of intimacy with their male friends. During this part of the latency period, aside from my intellectual pursuits, I became very compulsive about memorizing batting averages. This was another fixation on maleness, but it was an essentially solitary one, not one necessarily shared with other males. And, later in my life, following periods during which I had enjoyed a very intimate relationship with a woman, I would sometimes withdraw and bury myself in work. I generally succeeded in preventing the siren song of some attractive woman from luring me away from my Self. Both sexes, of course, engage in all sorts of tactics to defend their identities, but women have rather the worse of the bargain, since they are not given as many tools for establishing a separate identity as men are, and they often succumb to the lure of being taken over and becoming extensions of men. Nonetheless, men suffer from this problem too. For example, many men surrender their identity to play the role of the monogamous, breadwinning husband and father in a home that in their subjective view is dominated by their wife. (She may experience it in quite the opposite way.) These unfortunates speak of themselves derisively as being "henpecked," but what they really mean is that they have been unable to resist the easy and pleasant temptation to hand over their sense of Self, their autonomy, their identity, to a woman, who in fact may be far from pleased by this sacrifice.

## VI. Adolescence

Adolescence brings to the fore, in a most dramatic and intensive manner, the conflict between the desire to merge with another person and the need to establish a sense of Self. A young man has not yet established a firm sense of his identity or his boundaries, yet at this time he must cope with tremendously powerful sexual forces. A young man is reputed to reach his sexual peak at seventeen. That is the time when he has his greatest need for sexual contact with women, but it is also a period when he in most cases has a very poor sense of identity. In our society, a seventeen-year-old male usually hasn't decided what he will be when he grows up. He doesn't have a firm idea of his gender identity. He hasn't internalized stable role models, and is in the process of rebelling against and competing with the very father or other adult males with whom he wishes to identify. He is drifting, and frequently seeks a woman, or women, to serve as an anchor.

175

Adolescence was a desperate, anxiety-filled period of my life. It is, I believe, for most men and women a time that tests their ability to survive the worst psychological stresses. It produced in me the urgent, constant, and almost insatiable need for close contact with one or more women. Once I had gone out on my first date at age fifteen, I immediately fell madly in love and stayed that way throughout most of my adolescence. When I failed to receive a call or a letter from the woman I had designated as the provider of the love I sought, I became depressed and often thought of suicide. Though I had developed some sense of identity, my emotional needs were so great that the basis of my self-esteem lay largely outside of myself. I felt I literally could not survive without her love, that she was irreplaceable. Between fifteen and twenty I was either desperately in love and in fear of rejection or else compulsively searching for my next love. Though I had sufficient sense of my identity to recognize and pursue my need, I simultaneously had such a low sense of my self-worth that I was convinced I would be rejected and humiliated by the women I approached. My gender identity and sexual preference were stabilized, but I was very insecure about my acceptability as a man to women. Mother had in many ways rejected me, and Aunt Peggy had seduced and then humiliated me. I had my role-model identifications with Domenico, Jerry, and Aldo, so I was always a very macho, very sexual male. As I have said, adolescence is a period in which role models can be easily introjected and exert a decisive influence on the formation of identity. I am sure I introjected parts of some of my teachers and of my Jewish peers as well during this period, which had an effect on many of my intellectual and artistic interests. Sexually, I was frequently the one who served as a role model for the others. In reality (though not in my subjective view) I was quite successful with women. However, I longed for an affectionate, permanent attachment to a woman who would love me deeply.

# VII. Adult Life

I met my first wife at age eighteen. I really felt loved by her. When she threatened to go out with another man unless I made a commitment to her, I quickly agreed to marry her, and did so as soon as I could, without my parents' consent, at twenty. She was three and a half years older than I and she gave me the kind of unconditional love and acceptance I needed so desperately. But my need for her and for her maternal qualities threatened my identity and autonomy as a man, so I had to reinforce my sense of Self by being difficult and oppositional. Though I loved her deeply and needed her urgently, I finally chose my identity and integrity of Self. She was a marvelous, loving, sensual woman. If I had had a greater sense of my Self then, our marriage would have worked. After I left her, I woke up every night with a sense of emptiness and loss. I could hardly survive not having her love, but because of my childhood, which had emphasized autonomy over the need for love, I was forced to leave her.

The separation was followed by a period when I attempted to reinforce my identity and my ability to survive without a loving, feminine connection. I strengthened my relationships with men and decided for a time to forgo emotional liaisons with women, and to have my sexual needs met by prostitutes so as to avoid any possible repetition of a close involvement, followed by fear of loss of Self, followed by a painful separation. I indulged my interests in sports, both as participant and spectator, and plunged into my work. This period of drawing back into my Self was necessary for survival. Naturally it did not last very long. Once I had "convinced" my Self that I could indeed survive without a woman, after some months I found another one. My adult life, like that of many other persons, has been spent in the eternal struggle between the need for a secure tie with another person, at the price of the soul, and the urge for autonomy, creativity, and self-expression. In my experience, people who simultaneously enjoy an intimate, loving connection and who at the same time do not lose some of their individuality and creativity are quite rare. There have been periods of my life when superficially I appeared to have both. But frequently my relationship was either with a woman who in reality lacked my intellectual or emotional resources or with one whom I subjectively devalued. Thus, I was on top and was in less danger of losing my Self to her. The other way that I—and I believe many others— cope with this dilemma is to have periods of intense intimacy alternating with periods of emotional separation from their mate. This of course can lead to somewhat rocky relationships or even, as in my case, to serial relationships. Many people meet the problem by renouncing their individuality, sexual adventure, and the zest for life once they become connected with another person. For too many, marriage is not only the deathbed of sex, but also of real living. It doesn't have to be, but it often is. These unfortunate people are generally those who were enmeshed by their mothers and consequently tend more toward merger and loss of Self than toward personal autonomy and assertion of identity. They lead comfortable, secure, but unexciting lives, and are subject to depressions especially about age forty (midlife crisis) or later on, at the menopause or male climacteric when they realize much of their life has slipped by without joy, excitement, or adventure. Those like myself, who are more prone to choose autonomy over security, must face periods of intense anxiety when they are changing partners or pushing off in their own direction while retaining a mere structural connection with the same partner, who no longer gratifies their need for an intense relationship. Choosing independence places a severe strain on the relationship, often evoking anxiety and/or rage from the mate, which disturbs any sense of calm and security.

Throughout a man's adult life, he has many opportunities to choose between satisfaction and security. Though his choice is affected by the kind of parenting he experienced, he still has a certain amount of free will. I have always—granted because of my background—found that I never regretted the "heroic" choice of eschewing security. The only regrets I have about my life involve those really very few situations in which I played it safe. When asked about my greatest regret, I can think of only one specific event. I was at a concert with a woman with whom I enjoyed a close, long-term relationship. She was intensely jealous and possessive. She was sitting on my right. On my left was a lovely young woman I had never seen before. For whatever reason, there arose a tremendous mutual attraction between myself and the beautiful stranger. I was torn between trying to communicate with her in some way and either get her phone number or give her mine and realistic fear of my companion's appropriately jealous rage. I excused myself to go to the men's room during intermission, hoping I would meet her. Unfortunately, though she too had left her seat, we never met. When we returned to our seats, I realized that the only way I would ever see her would be to leave my card with her. I carefully took out my card and put it into my jacket pocket. The next move was to have been to slip it out and place it in her hand without my lady friend on my right noticing it. I was all set to do so, but at the last moment my courage fled. I had no guarantee that the unknown woman would be the love of my life, or even that she would ever phone me. What upset me was that I was disappointed in *myself*. I chose the cowardly rather than the bold and heroic move. We are faced with decisions—some trivial and some major—fairly frequently in our lives, and within the limits of our childhood experience we have some options, some free will. Some of us may have been so entangled with our mothers that the height of our ability to be heroic is sending a poorly cooked dish back to the restaurant kitchen. Nevertheless, even that act can represent choosing selfhood over merging with the "other"—in this case the waiter. When we take the daring path, we reinforce our sense of Self and our autonomy. When we choose the timid, safe option, we lose some of them. Additions to and detractions from our identity are governed by these options.

The opportunity to exercise options involving the Self occurs in practically every aspect of life, but in my opinion it is in our sex life that we can best choose to be in touch with our real Self (or not to be in touch with it). Involvement with the Self can be achieved with the minimum of undesirable social con-

179

sequences when sex is the touchstone. For example, my holding fast to my pleasure in a harmless form of voyeurism—burlesque shows—was crucial to the healthy maintenance of my sense of Self. One reason for my general opposition to sexual therapy is that it may tend to standardize erotic functioning, though I am told that a really skilled sexual therapist would not do so. For one of the few places in the world that is, or should be, completely private and outside of any "moral" judgment or intrusion by individuals or society is the bedroom. There, one can, if desired, indulge in erotic fantasies that exclude one's partner or mate, or, as I have, enjoy partnerless sexual activity of a masturbatory, voyeuristic, or fetishistic nature. If a partner is involved, and your special pleasures are approached vis-à-vis your partner with discretion and sensitivity, he or she may not only go along with them but eventually come to enjoy them. Thus, sexual idiosyncracies are an area of opportunity that we can utilize throughout our life to reinforce the identity, for if we are sufficiently liberated to acknowledge them—even if only to ourselves—they can represent the most unique, inviolate part of our nature. Getting in touch with our desires is a reinforcing experience in itself; being able to discuss them, or, better, participate in them with another person, when appropriate, can be even more strengthening.

"Midlife crisis" is perhaps an over-used cliché, but even so I believe the concept possesses a great deal of validity. I have helped countless patients of both sexes, but especially men who, around forty, suddenly begin to feel their lives are meaningless. They have struggled for professional and economic success, to rear their children, and to "work on" their marriages. They have done all the right things; most have reached the plateau they aspired to. Yet they feel they have been seduced by false promises of happiness. What has actually happened to them is that they have been so involved in fulfilling their parents' or society's blueprint for how one should live that they have lost touch with their own unique wishes and desires. Drifting, they come to therapy with little

180

sense of themselves, no goals that excite them, no sense of adventure, no ambition and no ideals, no creative or not even many strong sexual impulses. They have perhaps one final chance to put their lives on a course that is closer to their uniqueness. After middle age it is more difficult, though not impossible, to make the shift from security and conformity to self-actualization. If one has made heroic choices before forty, midlife crisis may never appear. If one can correct previous stagnation by changing to a more identity-reinforcing position around forty, one may be able to live the rest of one's life, even through very old age, without losing the sense of Self or experiencing feelings of meaninglessness. So the way a man handles midlife crisis can be decisive for the rest of his life. Those who fear death excessively are often those who realize that they have never really lived, never been themselves. Those who have lived full, satisfying lives do not wish to die, but generally meet their end with more equanimity.

So the way we handle our options, and even more importantly, the realization that we *have* options during our adult life, can either reinforce our identity or diminish it. "How can I leave my wife?" a patient once asked me. "We're getting new wallpaper for our bathroom this Friday." Here was a trivial excuse to avoid making a decision central to the patient's very being. For people must be aware of their freedom—that they have the option to leave their mate, change their job or residence, and vary their sexual patterns or partner or even the gender of their sexual partner. They may with very good reason *not* choose any of these options, but they should never lose sight of them. Marriage vows in a certain sense should be repeated *by choice* every day. No relationship should continue merely because it exists. If a person does not enjoy his work, it should at least be recognized that one can resign. One must be fully aware of the consequences entailed by change, but if it is decided not to change, the advantages of staying put should clearly outweigh the disadvantages. The important thing is that a man's* mate, job, and life-style grow out of and reflect

*I deliberately restrict the discussion here to adult males.

his own uniqueness. He should never see himself as a mindless cog fitting into a wheel from which he has no option to disengage himself. If he decides to stay put, it should be *his* choice.

Another important way of reinforcing one's identity in middle and later life is through one's role as parent and/or grandparent. A man can strengthen his feeling of being a mature, integrated person in his relationship to *all* his children and grandchildren, male and female. However, there is a special kind of identity reinforcement (corresponding to Erik Erikson's "generative stage" in *Childhood and Society*) that occurs in a man's relationship to his sons, for a son can provide the mirror of the father, the idealization and hero-worship that the father needs at an age at which some of these positive reflections may be diminishing from other quarters. The son's idealization of, then identification with, the father can increase the father's self-esteem in a way that no other experience can. Of course, the father must be ready to relinquish this pleasure for a while at least while his son goes through the necessary period of separation and establishment of identity. As I mentioned, this was perhaps the most important time I failed Bobby. I did, however, enjoy basking in his admiration, as well as admiring him as an extension of myself. Mutual admiration existing between fathers and sons, or between grandfathers and grandsons, contains positive elements for old and young alike. Michelangelo derived a great deal of satisfaction from my looking up to him as well as from my role as *alter ego*. Unfortunately, my father neither gave nor received much admiration, and this situation repeated itself between Bobby and me when he was five to sixteen, and still exists, though to a diminished degree. This book is, among other things, an invitation to both of us to regain some of the vanished closeness, affection, and mutual admiration that existed during the first five years of his life, when he was sixteen to twenty-one, and that we recently have, somewhat tentatively, begun to re-experience. I think it will be a serious blow to both of us if we fail to recapture that rapport.

As the end of life approaches, and one realizes emotionally that death is inevitable, not just an abstraction, one's male and female children, especially sons and grandsons, can help ease the pain of this awareness. A man can thus feel perpetuated by them if he has not had the good fortune to believe that his work has immortalized him. This self-perpetuation is perhaps the most important aspect of the reinforcement of both identity and self-esteem during the final years. Old people who do not have a loving connection with their children are bereft and pathetic. I have witnessed painful and touching scenes in nursing homes, in which old people who have been unable to make a continuing, binding, emotional connection with their children have been deserted. When these connections are present, or in societies (unfortunately not our own) that value them highly, old age does not have to be a period of alienation and despair, but can be a gradual, satisfying relinquishment of life.

*     *     *

We have examined the formation of male identity from the cradle to the grave. This identity need not stop growing or being reinforced until the actual moment of death. Some of the things that reinforce or diminish it are environmental, genetic, or possibly prenatal, but its enhancement or diminution are, within limits, the result of options that rest with us.

183

# Epilogue

After Bobby read this book, I asked him what he thought of it. He liked it and believed it was helpful in his understanding of our relationship, but I felt he was a bit less than effusive in his praise. I also pointed out to him that he seemed put off at the places in which I praised myself, preferring the passages in which I tended to be self-effacing.

"Self-effacing? *I* didn't think you were so self-effacing!" he said.

"Now, you couldn't be acting a bit competitive with me, could you?"

"Of course not," he replied with a smile. "I'm being completely objective."